Destiny's Call

Book II of The Quietus of Fate

By Brian C. Kershner

Acknowledgements

The Quietus of Fate Series has become a labor of love over the last twenty-five or so years. But it has also been born out of stress, frustration, and troubled times. The emotions that the characters in these novels go through on some level come from a real place, either from the mind of the author, or from the experiences of people who have come in and out of my life over the course of writing these novels. To me, each and every one of these characters is a living, breathing person with their own motivations, drives, goals, and feelings. And while at times they may be somewhat loosely inspired by people I have known, they are largely amalgams of a great many people, showing facets of the great and diverse culture of people in this world.

From the classic artistic standpoint, the old adage of suffering for one's art is true. Anyone who spends so many years working on any one project becomes invested in a way that cannot be divorced from the passions and the demands of life. Through every triumph, every loss, every joy, every bitterness, and every defeat, the emotions will be reflected in the art; for better or for worse.

Great characters stay with us. They teach us something about the primal drives of the soul. I can only hope that in following the journeys of my characters that some of the lessons they learn and teach stay with you to light your way through a dark time as they have so often done for me.

B.K.

Table of Contents

Appendicies

The Dragon shall wade deep into mystery,
Doubt and suspicion his only armor,
Threats shall challenge his Soul and his very Essence,
And a lingering Shadow shall dog his every step.

Turmoil shall arise in the ranks of the Fallen,
A Raven shall raise his claws against his flock,
A Wolf shall stalk confident prey,
And the Viper shall strike at the hearts that beat slow.

And the Hand of the Divine,
Will once again touch the face of the world.

The future is not yet written,
The past never truly dead,
The present favors the driven,
Time is how legends are bred.

-   Aralias Imstra
Prophecies of the Coromor

Prologue

The First Battle

Of all the things that Pike had done in his life, being captured was not one of his favorites. Despite all of Gwydeon's reiterations of his beliefs about the man called Hawk, Pike's feelings were not eased. There was something that was not right about the whole situation. It was something more terrifying than the thought of being captured. They had all been captured before, and they had managed to work their way out of that with no one dying. This uncertainty about their future was nothing new, but the same feeling of fear that had gripped him before the fated battle with Hawk's forces still clung to him. They had been allowed to talk and move together as they walked toward Sador, and they had taken full measure of this allowance.

"This isn't good, Gwydeon," Eldar said as the city of Sador loomed closer on the horizon.

Their pace toward the town had been steady, and they had been walking for almost an hour.

"There's no telling what's actually going to happen to us once we get to Sador," she continued, her fists balling in anger. "Even money Hawk goes back on his word and kills us all."

"That won't happen, Eldar," Gwydeon said, doing his best to reassure both Eldar and himself. "I'm certain that this Hawk fellow is on our side, or at least on his own side. It may not seem that way now, but I saw something in his eyes when he spoke about his lord, and I'm pretty sure that he and some of the members of his army are just waiting for an opportunity to revolt."

"Revolt?" Talon said, trying to keep his voice low but still conveying the shock he felt.

"Yes, a revolt. For all we know, there are allies to be found here. When the time comes though, we'll need someone to take the lead," Gwydeon continued.

Pike looked back a Gwydeon and suddenly realized that every one of his friends was looking at him.

"No," Pike said quickly, "don't go volunteering me for a crazy stunt like this. I'm not a leader, Gwydeon, you all know that."

"Look how you pulled us through in Sarmeel, Pike," Eldar said confidently, "it takes a true leader to overcome those kinds of odds."

"Besides," Midarin added, "it seems that you have been Logan's second ever since the day I joined you. Look at the faith he placed in you at Rama."

"That was different, Midarin. I was trying to protect my friend, and keep him from doing something that would get us all killed. Sarmeel was something different entirely. I was just lucky that I had my powers, or we wouldn't be having this little conversation."

"You're too hard on yourself, Pike," Eldar said reaching out and clutching his hand. "The way you handled Hawk back there was one of the bravest acts I've ever seen."

Pike looked at Eldar for a moment and then shook his head.

"It really wasn't that big of a deal. Talon or Gwydeon would have done the same thing, I was just a bit closer, and I reacted when I saw he threatened you."

"Oh please," Talon mumbled.

At that moment it seemed that Eldar remembered herself and pulled her hand away from Pike's. The tenderness was gone a moment later.

"No matter what we all think about Pike's ability, or lack thereof, we still need to come to a decision as to Gwydeon's plan," Lane interjected.

"Fine," Pike countered, "Why don't you lead, Gwydeon? You did a great job against them an hour ago, so as far as I'm concerned, you can keep on doing what you're doing."

"Which is nothing," the harsh voice rang out from behind them.

Gwydeon looked back over his shoulder at the man on horseback who had ridden up behind them. He was of average height, but he had a very broad chest, and his arms were muscle-laden. He was easily as big as Pike through the shoulders, but even Talon's arms were not as big as this man's. He had a short black beard that was trimmed very neatly, and his mustache was also very well trimmed. His long black hair was slicked back on his head, giving it a smooth, glistening appearance in the sunlight. He wore a haughty smile on his face, not unlike the ones that the Jeresei always seemed to have on their faces. Something inside of Gwydeon wanted to hate this man with all of the strength that he possessed, but another part of him respected this man as a soldier, and wanted him for an ally.

"Hawk," Pike growled, "do you often make a habit of spying?"

"Only when it amuses me, Rhuiden. You really must learn to keep your voices down if you intend to keep anything secret around here, especially from those with a practiced ear. I'm sorry to say that people here just don't have the common decency that you Aradonian people do. Knowledge here in Sador is power. The more you know about the people in power, the higher you will climb in the hierarchy. It's just a matter of how sensitive the information is, and how much the people want to keep it a secret."

"You bastard," Midarin replied angrily, "you're nothing but a mercenary for hire, looking for some dishonest way to get to the top of the ladder."

"And am I supposed to be insulted by that? Is it any different in Brea, Princess Rice," Hawk taunted. "Don't look so shocked that I know who you are. In fact, I am very good friends with a very important person in your life."

"He can't be that important if you know him," Midarin said brushing off the comment.

"Oh, but he is. Does the name Arin Domae ring a bell, princess?"

Midarin hesitated for a moment and then looked up at Hawk with wrath in her eyes.

"Never say that filthy bastard's name in front of me again, or I'll see that you burn in hell on the Great Dark One's spit."

"Come now princess," Hawk prodded, "don't tell me that you still hold a grudge against my dearest friend."

"Your 'dearest friend' cost me everything. If he wouldn't have been nosing around my room in the dead of the night, I would still be in Brea, and I would probably be sitting on the throne by now."

"It is hardly all of his doing, Midarin. Excuse that I don't address you formally any longer, it bores me. It is your lust that got you thrown out of the kingdom, not Arin Domae. And what's more, he was doing his duty, unlike the spoiled little brat he was charged to protect. Now look at you. Dressed in rags, tagging along with these commoners. You have no home, you have no future, and you will end up a bitter broken old maid with nothing to look back upon but your own failures."

At his response, Midarin did the one thing that Gwydeon never thought he would see; she began to cry. Gwydeon took her in his arms reflexively, and he felt the weight go out of her body. They couldn't stop, so Gwydeon picked her up and carried her as she clung to his shoulder, the tears beginning to soak through his shirt.

"Never speak to her that way again, Hawk," Talon growled.

"I will if I choose to, Aielin. You Aradonians are so easy to manipulate. You speak too much with your heart and emotions and not enough with your head."

"How do you know so much about us, Hawk?" Lane asked.

"You should have been listening to me, Lane. I told you that knowledge here is power, and there is also a price for any such information."

"Would you like to tell me how we are expected to pay for this information?" Talon scoffed.

"Why with information, of course," Hawk responded, not missing a beat, "there are a lot of holes in the information that I have been provided with, and you could fill some of them for me."

"Very well," Gwydeon said still cradling Midarin in his arms, "but I don't wish to talk to you while you are riding, there are too many people who could hear this information. Besides, my neck is getting tired looking up at you all the time."

Hawk laughed at the response and answered.

"Maybe you Aradonian people do use your brains once in a while after all."

As Hawk began to dismount and walk up to them, Midarin tugged on Gwydeon's sleeve and told him that she wanted to walk. Gwydeon stopped for a moment to let her gather her feet under her and then still held most of her weight with his strong arms as she walked. She eventually pushed him away gently and smiled in his direction as they walked. Hawk approached and then began volleying questions.

"Why does my master want you so much?"

"An answer for an answer," Pike said roughly, "that's the deal."

"Yes, of course," Hawk answered, "an answer for an answer."

"The reason that your lord wants us is because we are in league with the new *Coromor*," Pike said.

"The new *Coromor*? How is it..."

"Now Hawk, remember the rules," Pike said a hint of comedy in his voice, "an answer for an answer."

Hawk sighed and cursed a little under his breath. He then nodded, conceding that he had let himself be duped into this little game.

"How is it you know so much about who we are and where we come from?" Gwydeon asked quickly.

"Most of my information comes from Lord Zarsi. He has alluded to the fact that he gets his information through spies all over the world. However, my information about Miss Rice and Miss Merin come from sources in Brea. Now, it's my turn. How is it that you have found yourself in league with the *Coromor*? Is it because of your powers?"

"That's two questions, Hawk," Talon replied, "but one will answer the other. Pike and I are members of the *Erieal*."

"Incredible. No wonder my master is so interested in you. I have but one more question to ask, and I am afraid that I cannot now, for our little journey is at an end."

Pike hadn't noticed that they had walked under the huge arch made out of bent trees, nor had he noticed the procession of soldiers they had walked through. It also seemed strange that they were so free with information around this man Hawk. They had told him things that they never should have aired to anyone, especially a prospective foe, no matter how well-informed he seemed to be.

"Hopefully you will live long enough after the meeting with Lord Zarsi for us to continue our conversation, but I wouldn't count on it."

No one could answer. It was not one of the most pleasant pieces of news that they had gotten since this quest started, but they had almost become accustomed to being threatened with death, if one can become accustomed to that. The doors to the ivory tower parted, and the soldiers stopped. Pike and the rest of his friends continued into the tower, not knowing what the next few minutes would bring them. The doors closed, and Hawk was left standing outside, his head filled with ideas.

"Those are brave people Hawk," a familiar voice said from behind him.

"They are indeed Jasef. For that we must do something."

"The men stand ready at you orders, Lord Hawk."

"You know the orders Jasef, almost as well as I do. May fate have mercy on the foolish."

At that moment Hawk wasn't sure if he was talking about himself or his prisoners.

* * * * * * * * * * *

Pike could not help but to look at the two guards who led them through the palace. There were two behind them and two in front. Just as this Lord Zarsi had appeared to underestimate them in the field, he had also underestimated them here in his own palace.

"We can take these guys out and escape, Gwydeon," Pike whispered as they walked.

"And how many more will jump us from the shadows if we do? Take a look around Pike; these aren't the only men who are guarding us."

Pike looked around and then he noticed the thing Gwydeon had known all along. In recessed crevices in the walls, men with long sheathed blades stood like silent sentries. They made no move, and no sound. Pike doubted that anyone could hear them breathe if the hall was totally silent. The silent guards could have been statues for all they knew, but apparently, Gwydeon had seen a flash of movement out of the corner of his eye as they walked, and he was very sure that it came from one of these men. Maybe Zarsi had not underestimated them after all.

The guards continued walking down this long passageway until they came to a staircase that appeared to be in the back wall of the chamber.

They walked up the staircase and then turned a corner to another passage. This passage was quite a bit shorter, and in a matter of moments, they stood facing a huge set of wooden doors. The guards opened the doors, and then Pike and company were ushered through.

Just as with the walls of the palace, the walls of this new room were completely white. On the far end of the room, there was a large throne. On the throne sat a man who was easy to distinguish from anyone else that Pike had ever seen. He appeared to be an older man, his dark hair filled with streaks of gray. On one side of his face was a huge scar that could have only been made by the blade of a sword. The scar was too erratic to have been made by a dagger, but an axe was too clumsy a weapon for the task. Only a sword, a very sharp sword, could have inflicted this wound.

"Leave us," his voice rang through the throne room.

The guards bowed, turned, and then left the room, closing the large wooden doors behind them.

"Approach," the voice rang out again.

Pike hesitated for a moment and then walked forward, quickly followed by Gwydeon and the others. They walked up to the foot of the throne and stood, waiting for another word from their illustrious captor.

"Which of you is Gwydeon Sandar?" the man asked.

Gwydeon took a step forward and stared straight into the eyes of the man on the throne.

"I am Gwydeon Sandar."

The man on the throne stood and approached Gwydeon.

"It is a pleasure to finally meet you Gwydeon. I must say that I did not expect you to be with your friends Pike and Talon."

"And where did you expect me to be?"

"With my brother of course," Zarsi replied.

Pike stepped forward and pushed Gwydeon away.

"I don't know who you think you're dealing with here Zarsi, but..."

"Lord Zarsi!" he thundered. "I can deal with a bit of impertinence, but never address me as simply Zarsi. I know exactly who I'm dealing with weakling. I'm dealing with a petty band of boys who think they are serving the *Coromor* but they are actually following a fake."

"We'll see," Pike said smiling. "Now!"

Suddenly a gale force wind slammed through the windows in the throne room and hit Zarsi by surprise. Pike's hands thrust toward Zarsi, and soon he was enveloped in ice. Pike backed away, and the wind died down. Zarsi still stood in that same shocked position, frozen by the strong crystalline prison.

"Another victory for the forces of the Dragon!" Talon cheered.

"Well done gentlemen," Midarin said. "I must admit that I didn't expect you to ambush him like that."

"Neither did I," Gwydeon said, disappointment thick in his voice, "and unfortunately we're no closer to solving the mystery of why we're here."

Before Pike had a chance to answer Gwydeon's concern, the ice that surrounded Zarsi shattered. Everyone was caught flat-footed by Zarsi's freedom, and no one was able to prevent what happened next. Zarsi cried out in anger and then struck Gwydeon with his fist. Gwydeon took the full force of the super-human assault and went tumbling to the ground. Pike was the first to recover his senses and water began to spew from his fingers again. Zarsi lifted up his hand and the water turned back and Pike became the victim of his own attack. Before he could move, the water froze, leaving him encased in ice. Talon was beginning to use his powers, but the wind died before it could do any damage and Talon found himself trapped in a formless bubble-like prison. Lane mumbled incantations, and a stream of fire burst from his hands and sped toward Zarsi. Zarsi raised his other hand and a stream of green flame leapt from his palm and collided with the oncoming attack. The flames battled for the advantage, and then Zarsi's green flame began to gain the upper hand. It pushed further toward Lane and eventually the green flames enveloped him. Lane's robe began to burn, and he cast it off, leaving a burning heap on the floor of the throne room.

"You pitiful fools," Zarsi laughed, "did you really believe that your puny powers would be enough to topple Lord Zarsi, son of the mighty Shauling."

"You're a phase?" Gwydeon stammered in disbelief.

"As if there was ever any doubt, Gwydeon Sandar. I expected more out of you though, I haven't even seen your powers, but with the fuss my brothers are making over you, you must be powerful. I hope you are more of a challenge than these pitiful *Erieal* and that pathetic spell caster."

"I am not the *Coromor* if that is what you think, Zarsi. I have no powers to battle you with except my sword."

"Fool! Of course you are not the *Coromor*, but what do you mean you have no powers? I was told that you killed Antrobus and that you were most likely on your way to destroy one of the phasia. I never dreamed that Saurn would have sent you against me, but I was glad my spies followed you."

"I didn't kill Antrobus! I don't know anyone named Saurn! What do you think I am?"

"You are the *Chosen One*, of course."

Zarsi's haughty smile faded a moment later.

"Wait. You have never met my brother Saurn? Give me your hand."

Without a word, Gwydeon lifted his hand to Zarsi. He examined the palm for a moment, and then looked at the other one.

"His mark is not here."

"You see, I was telling the truth."

"That is not good for you, Gwydeon Sandar. Before, you were a curiosity that I could have put to use. Now you are simply an irritant in league with my enemies. You have become expendable."

"Give me a sword, and let me die like a warrior then," Gwydeon said, his voice filled with hatred and anguish.

"You are not afraid to die?" Zarsi asked, as sly smile coming to his lips.

"Not in the least. If you are a phase, then I am no match for you, but I would gladly sacrifice my life to save the rest of my friends."

"There is no saving them, Sandar. They are pawns of the *Coromor* and the prophecies. They will never leave this place, and neither will you."

"Well then," Gwydeon responded, "it looks like there is no need to be frightened at all."

"What? You and your friends are about to die, and you are not afraid? What kind of man are you Sandar?"

"A strong one. I know I will die with honor, so I die with no fear in my heart."

Zarsi let his gaze fall past Gwydeon, until it rested on Eldar.

"Are you afraid, young one?"

Eldar and Midarin had been standing there together the whole time, afraid to say a single word. Midarin was trying to do her best to free Talon from his predicament, while Eldar was trying to help Lane free Pike. When Zarsi spoke to her, she turned toward him and shook her head.

"I am afraid of nothing."

"Then you are a liar as well as a fool. I have seen inside your mind, Eldar Merin, and I know that there is fear inside your heart, as well as in the hearts of the rest of your friends. Perhaps after I kill you and your friends, this Sandar will finally start to be afraid. Come here young one. It's time for you to die."

What happened next could merely be explained as sheer willpower. An explosion rocked through the throne room as the ice around Pike exploded and shards flew across the room and ripped through Zarsi's skin. With his concentration broken, Talon found himself freed, and he immediately encased Zarsi in a whirlwind that lifted him off of the ground before he could recover from Pike's attack. Zarsi may have been neutralized at that moment, but Pike was not content with neutral. He wanted Zarsi dead. Pike ran toward the throne and grabbed Zarsi by the leg. As soon as Pike made contact, Zarsi screamed in agony. The screams became louder, but a moment later Zarsi disappeared. Pike shook his head and looked around, momentarily confused by the phase's disappearance. He regained his composure and moved quickly to Eldar's side.

"Are you all right Eldar?" Pike asked.

"I'm fine Pike."

"Is everybody else all right?" Pike asked.

"I'm fine, so is Lane," Talon answered.

"Gwydeon's not!" Midarin yelled.

Pike raced over to where Gwydeon lay. Apparently one of the fragments of ice had struck Gwydeon when Pike exploded from his prison. Gwydeon lay on his side, impaled on a shard of ice. The shard entered the middle of his back and shot though his lung and out the right side of his chest. The force of the blast had sent him half way across the room. Blood poured everywhere, and Gwydeon was unconscious.

"No!" Pike screamed.

If the earlier display out of Pike had been out of sheer willpower, this next display could only be described as love. Pike grabbed the shard and closed his eyes. He placed his other hand on the pool of blood and concentrated. The shard began to turn dark red, the same color as the blood on the floor. However, the redder the shard became, the lighter the blood on the floor became.

"I can't do it," Pike whispered.

His voice was strained and raspy. This exertion of power was more than he had ever attempted, and what he had just done to Zarsi had drained him enough. Talon was standing near, and he quickly put both of his hands on Pike's shoulders. As Midarin watched, still holding Gwydeon's head in her lap, she saw a spark of light come from Talon when he touched Pike. As she looked closer, she could what looked like tendrils of mist twisting down Talon's arms and entering Pike. The shard of ice that impaled Gwydeon began to disappear, and he slowly began breathing again. His breathing was labored at first, but eventually it became easier. Their deed done, Pike and Talon fell to the floor, exhausted. Eldar and Lane hovered over their exhausted comrades, but before anyone had a chance to recover, the doors to the throne room burst open, and Hawk entered the throne room follower by another man. Pike slowly rose to his feet with help from Eldar.

"What do you want Hawk? Your lord is dead, and I've had a very bad day. If you want to tangle with me now, you better have an army behind you."

Hawk smiled and turned back toward his companion. The man turned back toward the door and whistled. Two other soldiers stepped into the room and laid a package on the floor in front of Pike.

"I came to bring your weapons back to you Rhuiden. I also came to thank you for ridding my kingdom of that demon."

"Your kingdom?" Talon questioned.

"Yes," the man standing beside Hawk said, "Hawk was the lord of Sador before Zarsi came, but after our army was defeated, we had no choice but to follow him until we had enough strength to take over. Thanks to you, we were able to destroy Zarsi's army with ease."

"Thanks to us?" Talon asked, still puzzled.

"Yes," Hawk answered, "all of the men you killed were members of Zarsi's private force. I ensured that they were on the front lines, as I do in any battle that I command. The unit that captured you was completely made up of my men. When we got back here to camp, we took over and killed the faction that remained loyal. I'm only glad to see that you are still alive to see the real Sador."

Pike smiled for a moment and then picked up his axe.

"And give me one reason why I shouldn't gut you here and now."

"I'll give you three. I didn't kill you when we captured you. Two, I'm not going to kill you now. Three, I want to help you."

"Those are good reasons Pike," Eldar chimed in.

"Yes, they are," Pike agreed lowering his axe.

"What can I do to help?" Hawk asked.

"First of all you can give us some food and water, maybe a change of clothes if you can spare them. If you still have our horses, we would like them back, but if not, we need some."

Hawk motioned to the soldier who stood behind him. They bowed and hurriedly left the room.

"Done. I suppose that you will be leaving soon then."

"Yes, we will," Pike answered.

"What about Gwydeon? He's still hurt and we should give him time to heal." Midarin said frustrated.

Pike turned around and looked at his friend and then up at Midarin.

"Do you think he can ride?"

"I don't know Pike. I've never seen anyone healed that way before, so I don't know what the shock of riding a horse would do to him."

"I can ride," Gwydeon said softly.

He sat up with some help from Midarin, eventually making it to his feet.

"Good. I hope this battle didn't take too much out of you," Pike said without thinking.

"Poor pun, Pike," Gwydeon said, holding the site of the wound.

Pike turned back to Hawk and smiled.

"Is there a safe town between here and Falke?"

"There is a little town called Dalx about a day's ride from here."

"Can you tell me how to get there?" Pike asked quickly.

"I'll do better than that," Hawk answered, "I'll show you."

"What?" Lane asked. "Why would you do that when you have just regained your kingdom?"

"I owe you people a lot, and if you really are in league with the *Coromor* then I owe it to you to do all I can to help."

"But Hawk," the man beside him stammered, "what about your kingdom?"

"It will wait Jasef. Besides," he said patting his friend on the back, "I'm leaving Sador in good hands."

"Well Hawk," Eldar said walking up to stand beside Pike, "it looks like we'll have time to hear that last question of yours after all."

Chapter X

The Realm of the Wolf

Korrd shook his head violently as he lay there on the floor. The knot in the back of his head throbbed more and more as he tried to sit up. He didn't realize at the time that he had hit his head so hard on the floor. The broken door handle still lay there in his hand, and the door was still shut tight. His saddlebags still lay where he dropped them before his thwarted attempt at opening the door. Besides the constant throbbing pain, there was a kind of serenity that filled his mind. Suddenly he realized that the phantom voices in his head were silent. No more memories of another life flashed in his mind, and there were no more dead pasts waiting to be remembered. There was however a new purpose that filled him. New phantom images appeared, a throne room, and a man named Aerith. All of these were linked somehow. There was a place called the Blight, and a strange man named Saurn.

"Illimar," he said to himself.

It was then that everything began to come back to him. He began to remember a mission and who he was supposed to kill. Then there was the explanation of exactly what he was. All of it engulfed him. Once again he had a purpose in his life. Only this time, he had power to match the purpose. He picked up the saddlebags that lay on the floor beside the door, and then kicked the door open. Somewhere in his mind, there was a new sense of urgency. There was something about this mission that would not wait. If he did not complete it soon, there would be no success. Korrd hurried down the hallway and made his way toward the stables. As he walked toward the stables, he noticed the female servant that had shown him to his eventual on-sided duel with Captain Antrobus. She had with her a stallion, and it appeared to be loaded with the provisions that Korrd had requested.

"Ah," Korrd said upon seeing the young girl with the horse, "you have done very well."

"Thank you sir," she responded.

"Your lord Antrobus will be very pleased. He has asked for you to go to him after I am finished with you. So, you may go."

She nodded quickly and then made her way toward the palace. Korrd could not believe how easily he was about to make his escape. He had entered Rama, killed the commander of the Army of the Dragon, and then made his getaway without anyone ever knowing he was there. It was amazing how much he could do without it becoming common knowledge; such a thing would never have been possible in the small communities like the one he was raised in. Though in the back of his mind, he couldn't help but think that some of his success had to be attributed to his mysterious benefactor, the phase, Lord Saurn. He turned back to his horse, and then placed his saddlebags on the horse and then mounted. He looked around for a moment and then dug his heels into the side of the horse. His steed bolted toward the palace gates, bowing effortlessly to the will of its new master. Within a matter of minutes, Korrd was safe in the forest.

The morning was extremely dark, and when the cold hard rain began pouring down, all Korrd could think about was how fitting the weather was for this mission. The weather had been the same when he traveled to Rama. He had been out for the day on some frivolous errand, and when he returned to the house, he found the letter that would prove to change his life forever. Saurn had now become one of the focal points in his life, and now his life had taken a new twist. He was the *Chosen One* of the prophecies. Though he had never been told the stories about the *Chosen One* when he was younger, he did know what it was. That was one of the advantages of having the memories of at least five lifetimes in his head. But that too had changed when he met Lord Saurn. Somehow the phase had silenced the voices in Korrd's head. At first Korrd was grateful that the constant distraction was gone, but now, when he was all alone in the forest, he wished that the voices were still there to keep him company.

Within a matter of hours, he had passed through the Crossroads of Sarmeel, and continued down the road to Old Illimar. This road was named the River Road because it wound along beside the Illimar River. In reality, the road to Old Illimar was little more than the raised shoreline of the Illimar River. Eventually the Illimar River would branch off in two directions. It would fork off toward Aradon about a mile outside of Illimar, and then just at the foot of the town itself, it would fork off toward the Great Sea. Thus, when Illimar was built, so was the Great Bridge. Korrd traveled for most of the day, keeping to the winding path of the Illimar River. As the sun began to set, Korrd slowed his pace, and eventually came to a stop near a forest that lay to the east of the Illimar River. He dismounted his horse, and tied it to a tree that stood near a small clearing. He then took the saddlebags off his horse and sat with his back to a tree near the fire he had built. The fire crackled loudly as he sat back and ate his evening meal. Korrd looked up at the stars through a break in the limb canopy and relaxed in the cool night breeze.

At least it stopped raining, Korrd thought to himself. *The way that water was pouring down, I thought I would drown. I couldn't have gotten any wetter if I would have swum down the length of the Illimar River. Granted that my chosen path is not the quickest way there, but it is the safest. No one ever uses the Old Illimar Road anymore, not even the peddlers.*

It's nice to be by a fire again. I didn't even have time to build one while I was in Rama. Things were so out of control there. I suppose that if I would have built a fire, I could have attracted attention to myself, but then again, I could just be getting paranoid.

Korrd didn't take the time to think about the mission or what he was any more that night. He knew what he was, at least in part, and there was nothing he could do to change that now. There was one little voice that still remained in the back of his mind somewhere; that little voice that we all have in one form or another. This little voice is the one that tells us when we do something wrong, and eats away at our confidence and morale. While he relaxed, leaning up against that tall, strong tree, that little voice in the back of his mind continued talking. It droned on for hours it seemed, each time digging deeper, finding minute holes in the reasoning that Korrd had used for many years. Then the voice began to question why he had left his family, and why he wanted his brother dead. Now that the other voices in his head had been silenced, this little voice was all that he heard, and even as he slept it kept right on talking.

Korrd faded off to sleep, and he prayed before he drifted off that he wouldn't dream. For the last few years, terrible nightmares had plagued his mind, and that night would prove to be no different. He had nightmares when he was a child too, but these were not about monsters and ghosts. No, these nightmares were about power. Not until he met Lord Saurn did he begin to realize exactly what the nightmares meant, or where inside his mind they came from. At that moment, that place between sleep and awake where we all remember dreaming, he found his answers. He saw a man who shared his face slaughtering innocent people without a shred of remorse. He waded into them using horrible powers, leaving not one standing. In the end, there was nothing anyone could do to stop him. Then the picture changed. The same man was standing in the middle of what appeared to be a town. But the walls of the buildings were cracked and fallen. Others burned like silent torches in an endless night. And that man stood, alone in the middle of the wreckage, surveying his apparent handiwork, and for the first time he looked at what he had really done. He looked at all of the broken, bleeding bodies of the faceless, nameless masses. He saw the swords and flags, some which were his and many that were from other powers. He saw the price that had been paid for his little war. Then that little voice rang out again.

How many were his friends? How many died to try and protect his life? Does he care? Does he know exactly what the price is? Does he care? Does life mean anything to this man? Has he finally become what he had feared as a child? Has he become a monster . . . . have you?

As Korrd slept, unfelt tears began to run down his face. He hadn't cried since the death of his mother and now, whether he realized it or not, he was crying for the death of her son.

* * * * * * * * * * * *

CHAPTER 10

Korrd awoke early the next morning, and upon yawning and doing his normal morning stretch, he snuffed out the last remaining embers of his fire and prepared to leave the serenity of the forest. He untied the horse from the nearby tree and placed the saddlebags back on the horses back. He turned his horse and began at a trot toward Illimar. It was sometime after midday of the second day when he began to see the spires of Illimar rising above the horizon. Within an hour, he saw the Great Bridge and the gate that led to the town of Illimar. Something was decidedly wrong. The two guards that usually stood watch on either side of the Great Bridge were not at their posts. Korrd could also see black smoke rising from somewhere inside town, and the sounds of battle quickly became evident. Korrd got down off of his horse and turned back toward the way he had just traveled. After rubbing the horse for a moment, he slapped it hard on the back and sent it galloping back toward its home.

As Korrd turned back toward Illimar, the sounds of battle became louder and louder. Now instead of the normal clashing swords and occasional shouts of rage, there were battle cries being shouted and war whoops. These sounds were not emanating from Illimar though. Somewhere over a hill to Korrd's west was where the sounds appeared to be from. Then suddenly, he saw something coming over the hill that he never expected to see in Illimar. Coming over the hill, Korrd saw a force of about two hundred Jeresei running toward Illimar. Then a few seconds later, Korrd could see the banners of the Army of the Dragon proudly displayed, and then a moment later the foot soldiers rushed after the Jeresei. Korrd smiled to himself as a plan began forming, and then as soon as he realized that he could possibly be spotted, he ducked behind the raised bank of the Illimar River. Within a few minutes, both the squad of Jeresei and the Army of the Dragon were both out of sight and entering the battle inside the town limits of Illimar. As soon as he was sure he wouldn't be spotted, he arose slowly from his hiding place, and moved toward the Great Bridge.

He drew his sword slowly, and began to edge his way toward the gate. Korrd saw the signs of battle all around, but until he got to the gate, no warriors were in plain sight. As he looked into town, he began to make out four distinct forces of men and Jeresei locked in a battle in which no clear favorite seemed to be emerging. There were three flags visible in various places around the battlefield. The first flag that Korrd saw was the huge white banner of the Army of the Dragon flowing from at least three places. The other familiar banner was the silver Lion on the flag of the Army of the Dragon. The third flag was the one that Korrd had never seen before. It was a huge green flag with a black wolf running through it. It was quickly apparent to Korrd who this army belonged to, and the rumors floated through his head.

This must be Caris' army. I wonder how long she has been pulling men out of the Army of Illimar into her private little strike force. I knew there were rumors of a civil war brewing here in Illimar, but apparently my sources have been holding out on me. This isn't going to be as easy as Saurn thought.

Korrd surveyed the scene and found exactly what he was looking for. The standard battle plan of the Jeresei was that part of the force would strike with a brutal frontal assault while the other half split and went around behind the foe. This strategy confused the opponent and misled them as to the size of their attacker. No matter the size of the force, this strategy stayed constant. Another part of the strategy that stayed constant was the fact that the commander of the Jeresei force, usually their clan leader, stayed in the middle of the attacking force, staying in constant communication with the sweeping force through his battle cries. These battle cries were not only on the audible level, but also on a mental level that was specifically tuned to the patterns of a Jeresei brain. It was a devious, cunning tactic. It also was highly effective.

He found the clan leader of the Jeresei without much effort. He closed his eyes and raised his hand toward the Jeresei and tried hard to remember a trick that Saurn taught him. Behind his closed eyelids, Korrd could see the position he was standing in as well as the position the Jeresei was in. In his mind, he folded the space between himself and the Jeresei, and mentally pulled the Jeresei though. In real time, Korrd closed his eyes, and suddenly the Jeresei disappeared from where he was standing and suddenly appeared beside Korrd. It was the same process as using a portal, except that the portal opened and closed so quickly that it almost escaped the eye's notice. The Jeresei looked around confused for a moment, and then sank back into a crouch. That was often the Jeresei's favorite position to attack from. Korrd opened his eyes and stared at the Jeresei. The Jeresei looked up at

Korrd's eyes and then stood. Quickly the Jeresei retracted his claws and bowed.

"Very good lowborn," Korrd said in a powerful voice, "do you understand now who I am?"

"Yes, sire," the Jeresei spat.

"What are you and your brethren doing here?"

"We are under orders from Lord Zarsi to bait the Army of the Dragon, and lead them here in an effort to wipe them out."

"Interesting. Foolish and probably pointless, but interesting. I will now give you new orders lowborn. You and your force will confine your attacks to the Army of Illimar. You outnumber them, and should easily be able to destroy the lot of them. Let Caris' army worry about the Army of the Dragon. Now, go. Inform your army," Korrd said proudly.

"Yes, my lord."

Korrd nodded his head and the Jeresei disappeared. Korrd didn't bother to look where the Jeresei reappeared, but he quickly made his way into the battle. Immediately, he met with resistance. A man wearing green armor and the symbol of the Wolf on his chest ran toward Korrd with his sword drawn.

"Are you with us or against us commoner?"

Korrd flashed a smile and then thrust his sword directly at the man's heart. The soldier jumped back away from the sudden attack and then looked up at Korrd shocked.

"Does that answer your question, my friend?" Korrd asked facetiously.

The soldier slashed at Korrd with great ferocity and power, and then followed up with a back slash of his sword blade. Korrd seemed to move ten times faster than the soldier, sidestepping both of the attacks and then launching one of his own. He took the flat of his blade in his hand, and as the soldier moved in to attack, Korrd struck him in the face with the hilt of his sword. The soldier staggered back, blood flowing from his mouth and nose, tears blinding his vision. As soon as he was within striking distance, Korrd released the blade and severed the soldier's head from the rest of his body. It fell to the ground and rolled to a stop. The body fell backward and began to spill blood into a growing pool. No one appeared to take notice as Korrd continued toward the palace of Illimar and his new fate.

Korrd thought many times that he would have to fight his way there, but every challenge that presented itself was soon either diffused or eradicated by a member of the Jeresei strike force. The carnage seemed endless as he moved quickly toward the royal palace. The shouts and death-screams of the men and Jeresei around him filled his ears, but as he continued to walked, he suddenly heard something shouted from somewhere inside the ranks of the Army of the Dragon.

"Korrd! You bastard! I'll kill you!"

It was a woman's voice, one that Korrd had never heard before. He turned sharply toward where the voice seemed to come from, and as he watched, the ranks broke under the constant assaults of Caris' army. Korrd then saw someone running toward him. As the person approached, he began to be able to see the features of the person. The woman running towards him was stunning to say the least. She was very slim and elegant, even in the armor that she wore. Her shimmering brown hair was cut short, about the same length as the men in the army. If she had been wearing a helmet, it would have been almost impossible to tell her from the rest of the men. A few steps from Korrd, she raised her sword and leapt at him. The blow crashed down with more force than Korrd had anticipated, and he went sprawling to the ground. He landed roughly on the ground, and as he righted himself, he wiped a drop of blood from the corner of his mouth and then looked up at his attacker, stammered this time not by her beauty, but by her prowess in battle.

"You bastard!" she screamed. "You killed my friend and my commander! The girl was able to give me your description and name, and I am just glad that I was the one to find you first."

Korrd could only smile and laugh. He gathered his feet under him slowly and then stood up. He kept his eye on his lovely adversary the whole time, just to make sure that her rage did not override her honor.

"Captain Antrobus was your friend, right?" Korrd asked playfully. "Let me guess, you were one of his favorite little soldiers. I'm sure that the rest of your army is not so broken up about Antrobus' death. In fact, I suppose they should be thanking me for what I did. I'm sure there isn't another army in the world where you can take it all day from your commander, and then give some of it back to her at night."

The woman's face went red with anger.

"That certainly gives a whole new meaning to serving under your commander now doesn't it, Leane?"

Leane's eyes opened wide, and she slashed wildly at Korrd. Korrd jumped back away from the attack and laughed again.

"Come come, Leane, we mustn't get angry. Fighters do not fight intelligently when they are angry. Remember what I did to poor Antrobus? He fought very poorly because he was angry."

"Shut up! You have not earned the right to call me by my first name only. If you must address me in the time you have left, preferably to beg for mercy, you may only address me as Commander Leane Torne."

Leane screamed in rage and leapt at Korrd again. Korrd, in a split-second drew his sword and blocked the oncoming strike. He knew somewhere in the back of his mind that what he had just done should have been impossible, but he had little time to think about it at that time and place. He had prepared for the strike better this time around, and Leane's rage was only able to force Korrd to his knees. Korrd screamed and forced his way to his feet. As the two combatants locked swords again, Korrd stepped forward and kicked Leane's right leg out from under her. She sprawled to the ground, and landed firmly on her back. Before she could regain her senses or her sword, Korrd struck and buried the tip of his blade into her stomach. She immediately reacted to the pain, and she rolled onto her side, clutching the wound. The battle won, he spit at his adversary, cleaned the tip of his blade, and then continued on toward the palace, leaving Leane there to die.

* * * * * * * * * * * *

The battle had been raging for over an hour. Dead men and Jeresei alike lay together in huge piles of broken bodies and others in pools of blood. For the first time since the battle started, Korrd stopped to survey the destruction. Houses and churches were burned to the ground. Young innocent children lay weeping beside the fallen bodies of their parents, still wondering why their mother or father wouldn't answer them. Wounded soldiers lay everywhere calling out, hoping that someone would hear their cries. The battle still raged on, but it had been pushed outside the wreckage once known as Illimar. The Army of Illimar had suffered much the same fate as the city. Only a few survivors still fought, the rest lay with the dead and mortally wounded. The Jeresei had done their job well. Caris' army was doing their job as well. They were still engaged with the Army of the Dragon, but they had managed to push the now leaderless army out near the Illimar River. The Jeresei were reforming their ranks, ready to assist in the Army of the Dragon's destruction.

"We will pursue the Dragon's forces, my lord," the Jeresei leader said to Korrd. "With our help Caris' army could crush them once and for all."

"No, Caris' army will serve that purpose well enough. Your Jeresei will help me get through the remaining members of Caris' army left here in the palace. You will lead me to the throne room."

"You are attacking Caris? Why?"

Korrd raised his hand and clenched his fist. The Jeresei's hands leapt to his throat, and in a matter of seconds, it had dropped to its knees and was gasping for air.

"Your function in this life is not to question, lowborn. You and your brethren would follow me to the gates of hell if I commanded it. Now, you will form your men and charge the palace."

Korrd released his fist, and the Jeresei instantly released his throat. It took just a second to make sure that it could really breathe again, and then it called out to his brethren in his native tongue. They responded with similar calls, and when they began to move toward the palace, the leader turned back to Korrd.

"We will begin the siege at your command, lord," the Jeresei managed to force out.

"At your leisure, commander," Korrd responded, a weak smile coming to his lips.

The Jeresei let the wide smile leap back onto his face, and then he turned toward his men. The hellish call that bellowed from the Jeresei commander made Korrd's ears ring. The echoed battle cry rose from the rest of the Jeresei army, and they tore toward the palace at blinding speed. Within seconds, the palace doors shattered, and Korrd could hear sounds of battle and the screams of dying men.

Korrd was not in a rush to enter the battle. He knew that once the Jeresei reached the throne room, Caris would obliterate them. To her they were nothing more than annoying insects. As he walked through the palace more and more bodies lined the halls, and Korrd began to sidestep or leap over dying forms, broken bodies, and streams of blood that ran freely across the smooth stone floor. Suddenly a brilliant flash of white light erupted from a chamber just ahead of Korrd.

Ah, it appears as though my army has encountered Lady Caris.

Korrd picked his way to the chamber that appeared to be the source of the bright light. As he walked in, he saw the charred remains of his army scattered around the floor, and a very powerful yet beautiful woman standing in front of the throne. She wore a long green robe that hid the contours of her body, and she held a long sword in her hand that had a jewel-encrusted hilt.

"Another challenge?" the woman questioned with a beautiful flowing voice. "Do you really believe you have a chance against me boy?"

"I am merely a messenger Lady Caris," Korrd responded humbly.

"Is that so? And do men in your line of work often travel with a traitorous band of Jeresei? No matter. Who, pray tell, is sending me this message?" Caris asked whimsically.

"I come from Lord Saurn."

"Saurn!" Caris said shocked. "So, my brother has finally decided to come back and enter the war."

"In a manner of speaking," Korrd mumbled.

"Now, tell me, what is this message?"

"Lord Saurn respectfully requests that you die a horrible painful death!"

A ball of darkness sprang from Korrd's outstretched fingers as the final words came out of his mouth. The ball engulfed Caris. She struggled against the constricting ball, and within a matter of seconds, the ball shattered. Caris stood up gracefully and beamed at Korrd.

"So, my brother has found the *Chosen One* after all. You are Korrd I assume."

"The one and only," he replied bowing facetiously.

"Well Korrd," Caris said slowly, "my brother should have warned you that it takes more than his darkness globe to vanquish me."

Caris stretched out her hands, and daggers of lightning raced toward Korrd. Seeing the attack, Korrd dropped to the ground and rolled away. He came up on one knee, and before he realized what he was doing, he stretched out his hand, and a stream of fire exploded from his outstretched fingertips. The flame crossed the gap between Korrd and Caris more rapidly than Caris could have anticipated, and the flames began to burn the robe she wore. She stripped off the robe and stood facing Korrd in a very tight set of man's clothes.

"Very good, Korrd, you're starting to harness your elemental powers. I wonder if the *Coromor* is learning as quickly as you are. No matter, you will be dead shortly."

This time Caris pointed her hands toward the ground, and pieces of the floor tile ripped up from where they were anchored and hurtled toward Korrd. As soon as he saw the projectiles coming toward him, Korrd closed his eyes and stretched his hands out from his sides. When he opened his eyes again, he was surrounded by a shield of ice. He could hear the projectiles strike the ice shell, but not one penetrated. As soon as he was sure the danger was gone, the shield of ice shattered and fragments sped toward Caris. One piece of the glass-like ice ripped through the flesh in her arm, causing her to drop her sword. Blood flowed freely down her right arm, and she screamed in agony. The first effective attack of the battle had been launched, but it had not been hers. Korrd was standing again, approaching her slowly.

"Now you see that I am no weakling, Caris. That matters little now though. I must now finish the task of my master."

Caris approached Korrd slowly, holding her injured arm.

"Why me? You and I could rule together Korrd. You could easily kill the rest of the phasia and then we could kill Shau-ling."

"Why should I listen to you, Caris? Saurn has offered me the same thing. Who's to say that when I have the other phasia in this same position, that they won't offer me the same thing as well?"

"That doesn't matter, Korrd. Could Saurn or the other phasia keep you warm at night?" Caris asked drawing closer to Korrd. "Could any of them be your lover and your confidant? Would they rule beside you instead of over you? Together we could rule the world as husband and wife. Our children would be like gods Korrd, their powers would be unbelievable."

As she approached him, her clothes shifted from a man's shirt and breeches to a very low cut emerald gown.

"Could Saurn give you all of this?"

Korrd took Caris by the arm and pulled her close to him. She looked up at him and then they locked in a passionate kiss. After a few seconds, Caris stepped away and laughed. Korrd didn't react, he just stood there.

"Fool. Saurn apparently failed to warn you about the feminine wiles that have brought a death to beggars and kings alike. Now, let us see what you know dear, sweet, little boy."

Caris approached him again and laid her hand on his forehead. She closed her eyes and relaxed her mind. Slowly, his memories began to cross over to her. She saw Korrd battle the man that was in her army, and then she saw the battle with Leane Torne.

Interesting girl, Caris thought to herself, *she could come in handy.*

Then she backtracked further in his memory, past the battle with Antrobus, and the meeting with Saurn. Suddenly, she hit a mental wall.

One of Saurn's little markers, she thought, *I wonder what he doesn't want me to see.*

She pushed against the block in his mind, trying to break through so that she could see what was on the other side. Within a matter of moments she had the information she wanted. The plan that formed was one of the most diabolical that she had ever come up with. While still inside his mind, she planted the image of her own death, and then used her powers to render him unconscious. She laid him gently on the ground, his sword still in his hand. She shifted her clothes back to the man's shirt and breeches and then reclaimed the sword that she had dropped earlier. She then took the black cloak that lay beside the throne and wrapped it around herself. As she made her way out of the throne room, she pulled the hood of the cloak over her head and smiled.

I know who and what you are now, Korrd Ranthall, she thought to herself, *but more importantly, now I know how to get to your brother.*

Justice

Logan's anger had not abated when he woke up the next morning. He had not wanted to stay the night in Trelon, and more than anything he wanted to be on his way to hunt down Prince Allan. Aryx thought that the group needed time to recover and to prepare for what lay ahead. Prince Allan had been smart and underhanded enough to attempt his coup, and had it not been for the intervention of Logan and the others, he would have left Trelon with only one heir, himself. It would have been more difficult to take vengeance upon him then. However, with Cairyn still alive, Allan was a fugitive. But the prince was smart enough to have come up with a contingency should his plan to kill both his mother and sister fail. Elwyne, instead of retiring with Logan to their room in the inn chose instead to stay with the ailing Cairyn to ensure that she was properly tended to. It was possible that Allan could have had agents still within the royal court, and it would take time for Cairyn's agents to ferret out all who were disloyal. It was strange that Elwyne and Cairyn had become close; however tragedy can change anyone's opinion and remove unfounded and blind prejudices.

Logan pulled himself to a sitting position and then hung his feet over the edge of the bed and sat up properly. His clothes lay crumpled on the floor, and he didn't feel like putting them on. That pair of breeches had been on him since he left Rama, and they were beginning to look that way. Logan's first inclination would have been to get rid of them, but as rough as the quest had been on clothing, the luxury of disposing of them was not available, at least not yet. As Logan sat looking at his clothes on the floor, his thoughts were cast backwards. It was hard to believe that they had only been traveling for a week, because so much had happened. So far, Logan's best childhood friend David had been killed, he had to save all of his friends in Dreamscape, they had fought the Army of Illimar, rediscovered the Snags in Sarmeel, found a princess or two, saved a kingdom, fought about three hundred Jeresei, six Shadowwalkers, had a couple of bar brawls, and were all nearly killed about a dozen times.

Frowning, Logan reached down and picked up the pants off the ground and pulled them on. When he finally stood, he grabbed the black shirt from where it had been discarded over the back of the nearby chair and pulled it on. The sword belt followed unconsciously, and a few moments later Logan found himself in the hallway walking toward the larger room at the end of the hall where Cairyn Binosear was resting. Elwyne was sitting in a chair at Cairyn's bedside, and it looked as though the new queen did not have an easy night. She was pale, and as she breathed, Logan could hear the air being dragged in and out with a loud wheeze. Elwyne had just finished dabbing the queen's head with a cold rag when Logan entered, and both women smiled, though Cairyn's was weak at best.

"I must say, Lord Logan, your Elwyne is a kind-hearted woman, though she is more stubborn than any nursemaid I had when I was a child. She would not let me out of this bed for a moment unless she was lording over me like a mother hen."

Logan forced a weak smile, but was saved a moment later as an older man came quietly into the room.

"My queen," the older man said, "the innkeeper has generously cleared the rest of the inn and would be honored if you were to use this place as your seat of power until such time as repairs are made to the palace."

Cairyn smiled and nodded.

"Express my gratitude to the innkeeper and his entire staff. Ensure that they are well compensated for their loss in revenue. Have my physician brought to me. Lady Elwyne will be leaving and I'm sure she wants to make sure I am in good hands before she does so."

The old man bowed and left the room. Cairyn turned her attention back to Elwyne, who smiled as she stood and smoothed her dress to get out the wrinkles from the long night.

"I'm sure your doctors will not be nearly as hard on you," Elwyne smiled. "And thank you for the courtesy, Cairyn, but you know I'm not really a lady. Even with Logan's title, until we're married, I am what I was born, a simple town mayor's daughter."

Elwyne nodded to Cairyn and gave a small curtsey before moving toward Logan and the door. Cairyn reached out and took hold of Elwyne's arm.

"Whatever you are or aren't, Elwyne, you cannot change your soul. In your soul you are a Lady, and perhaps more of one than I have ever been. I will never forget what you have done for me and for my family. You will forever be a hero of Trelon."

Elwyne didn't react for a moment, but finally smiled and gave her best deep curtsey showing deference to the Queen of Trelon. She then crossed the room, took Logan by the arm, and the two left quickly. The older man was waiting for them once they exited the room, and he informed them that the new queen had ensured that they would have everything that they needed, as well as passage on the fastest boat stationed at the docks of Lesin. The royal family had several vessels berthed there, and one would be at their disposal. As the two made their way to the stables connected to the inn, Elwyne informed Logan that Gideon and Aryx had taken Alexander and Talos ahead to Lesin to scout the way and ensure everything was ready when they arrived. Elwyne had wanted to stay with Cairyn, and Aryx thought it best to let Logan sleep while he could. At first Logan was annoyed at being handled in such a way, but Cairyn had been right, Elwyne was equal parts kind-hearted and stubborn, and when the welfare of her loved ones was in question, there was nothing that would shake her resolve. In the end, all Logan could do was shake his head. Elwyne could be as arrogant and self-assured as any man Logan had ever known, but in her mind it was the proper reaction to the situation, whatever that situation may have been. In a matter of minutes, they were on their horses and moving quickly down the path toward Lesin. As much as Logan wanted silence to focus on the task ahead, Elwyne had other plans.

"Do you miss home, Logan?" Elwyne asked as they rode swiftly toward Lesin.

"Not really, Elwyne. Everything I had in Aradon I have here with me. There is nothing else in this world that I could want except to have you and the rest of my friends with me."

"If things were different Logan . . ." she started.

"We wouldn't be having this conversation, and you and I probably wouldn't be together. Your father will not be happy when you return to Aradon with me."

"So you do intend to go back."

"Yes," Logan said finally, not shifting his attention from the road, "if we are going to get married, I want to do it the old way."

"You mean that you want to take the vows with me?"

"No Elwyne," I responded tenderly, "the vows are not for us. I want to make the life pledge."

"Logan," Elwyne said shocked, "no one has taken the life pledge for years."

"That was how my mother and father were married Elwyne, and I want to be married the same way."

She didn't respond, and Logan immediately knew why. In Aradon, most people married by going through the vows ceremony. They would go to the old church, trade vows, and consummate the marriage there in the church before going back to the village and telling everyone that they had taken the vows. But that was not the way it had always been done. Back in the years when the wars raged everywhere in the world, Aradon had split into two separate societies. The first society was a warrior society, and the other was the religious society. The vows came from the religious society. In the warrior society, they had no time for that kind of ritual, and most of the marriages came after a battle. The couple that wished to be wed would be enclosed in a circle of warriors and they would pledge to protect each other until one would die. If that were to happen in battle, the one who survived would pledge to revenge the death at all costs. If the death were of natural causes however, the other would pledge never to marry again and live out his or her life married to a memory. Logan's father and mother had taken that pledge and they were happy together for the rest of their lives. The part of the ceremony that was disturbing, and thus brought on the silence of Elwyne, was the fact that the couple during the ceremony would use the others blade to open a wound on their palms, and they would clasp those hands together and become one in battle, because of the use of the other's blade, and one in blood, because of the blood exchange from wound to wound. The ceremony wasn't as beautiful or as haunting as some of the others Logan had heard of, but it was a Ranthall family tradition, one Logan intended to uphold. But many in Aradon were like Elwyne and looked down upon the warrior's ceremony. That was why so many pushed for Arin to undergo the cleansing so that he could have a new life. Perhaps Logan's desire was selfish, but in the end, he wanted to honor the memory of those who came before him.

"We may not get that choice," Elwyne finished. "You are the Lord Dragon after all, and I don't think that Lord Cedric or Cairyn would understand us not having a ceremony befitting your stature."

It took only a sideways glance for Logan to know that Elwyne was mocking him. However, in some ways she was right. So much had already been taken out of their hands already. How much more of their lives would be completely out of their control?

Without pressing their horses too hard, they made very good time on their journey, and were at the docks of Lesin before nightfall. The rest of the group had reached Lesin less than two hours prior and had sought refuge in one of the inns just inside of town, and had already arranged for lodging with the help of orders from the Queen of Trelon. The group was waiting in the inn's common room, and there were very few patrons who shared the room so it made for prime opportunity for Logan to get some questions answered.

"I'm curious about something, Aryx," Logan said after taking a long drink of ale, "you made some comments about the phasia, and later while I was thinking about it, I realized that I don't really know that much about them."

Aryx's eyes were dark at the subject. But finally he nodded softly.

"To tell the truth, Logan, I know little more than you do, other than the fact that I have fought against one or two of them. What I can tell you is that there are ten of them. Each varies in size and appearance, but without exertion of their powers, they start each lifetime as a human, at least in appearance. To my knowledge, there are nine men and one woman."

"What about powers?" Gideon asked.

"Equal to yours or mine, Gideon, and don't ask me why. Logan should be able to overmatch all of them, except maybe Jeroch."

"And why not him?" Talos asked.

"Jeroch is the first born of the phasia, and so he is supposedly the most powerful. Jeroch fought Cedric to a standstill and had it not been for a stroke of luck, we may not have made it to the palace, or Shau-ling. The only other advantage that the phasia would have is their lifetimes of experience with their powers."

"Do the others have names?" Logan asked.

"Yes, but I only know the names of three or four others. There is one called Zarsi, he has a scar on his face that looks like it was made with a very sharp sword. There is one called Farax, he had a high-pitched raspy voice. Another is named Taron, he looks like a walking mountain with arms. And then there's Jeroch."

"That leaves six as a mystery. I don't like those numbers," Talos replied.

"I agree. Have you and the others made arrangements for a ship to the Isle of Thardus tomorrow?" Logan asked.

"As a matter of fact," Aryx answered, "As per Queen Cairyn's instructions, I have. We are to meet on the deck of the Monster of the Deep tomorrow morning at first light. It shouldn't be more than two hours to the island."

"Well then, I will leave you all for the evening," Logan said quickly, "and I will see you all again on the deck of the Monster of the Deep at first light."

Elwyne rose with Logan, and the two made their way to their room on the second floor of the inn. Logan grasped her hand as they walked, but with every step he could feel all of the energy being drawn out of his body, seemingly through the soles of his feet. Logan sat down on the edge of the bed, and with some effort pulled the shirt over his head and let it drop to the floor. By the time he looked up, Elwyne was kneeling before him. When she took his head in her hands, he suddenly felt safe, secure, and at peace. She pressed her lips to his, and they tasted of the ale she had at in the common room, and it mixed deliciously with the normally sweet taste of her kisses. It was a truly intoxicating mixture. She bit at his lower lip now and then, teasing him into going further. She pressed closer to him and Logan could feel her silky skin pressing against his chest. He kissed her again, this time with more force. She melted into his arms, and gave herself completely over to the man that she loved. He pulled her closer to him, and together they fell back onto the bed, still locked in a passionate kiss. When she pulled away from him once more, and smiled down at him with a seductive smile, her form was hazy. He blinked his eyes hard, but had no time to understand what had confused his vision before her lips were on his again. Her hands began to run up and down his naked sides, and it sent chills through him, but as he expected them to light some fire inside of him, instead he was brutally cold. His fingers began to go numb, and when he tried to roll Elwyne off of him, he found he had no strength. A moment later, he couldn't breathe and the consciousness that he so desperately wanted to stay in began to slip from his grasp. The last thing he saw before he lost consciousness was Elwyne pull away from him, the smile in her eyes so bright one moment and then fading into unrelenting and complete terror the next.

* * * * * * * * * * *

"Logan!"

From somewhere in the blackness, Logan was barely aware of the voice saying his name. His ears rang and his sight was only filled with shadows. After several long moments he began to be able to make out shapes and forms above him, but he was unable to properly discern anything. Even the voice was muffled and it wasn't clear whether the voice was coming from a man or a woman.

"Logan!"

It was Elwyne's voice this time. Logan could tell because of her tone, but because he could feel her hand take his. It was then that Logan's vision slowly began to clear, and as it did, he became aware of Aryx and Gideon standing over him with Elwyne kneeling beside the bed holding his hand. It took some effort and some assistance from Gideon, but Logan was finally able to get into an upright position. He became suddenly aware that he was drenched with sweat and that his throat was dry. When he tried to speak the words came out as croaks and a raspy mumble.

"Wa . . ." Logan started to say, the rasp filling his voice and his throat aching with fire.

"Get him a glass of water," Elwyne said quickly.

Gideon handed Logan a glass of water but it did littler to quench the fiery pains in his throat.

"Thank you, Gideon," he managed to croak out before taking another gulp of the cold water. "What the hell happened?"

"Allan was here in Lesin this morning. He gave that pretty barmaid your description and she poisoned you. She didn't give you enough of a dose to kill you, but it did render you unconscious for a number of hours," Aryx answered.

"What time is it?"

"Just about dawn me lord," Gideon answered.

"Get you things together and start toward the docks. Elwyne and I will meet you there in a few minutes."

"Ye should rest, Logan," Gideon answered. "Let me go ta Thardus an keep an eye on dat bastard Allan. Get yer strength back an den we can deal wit' him."

Logan tried to push his way back to his feet, but his legs would not carry his weight and he slumped back to the bed.

"I'm not going to rest until Allan is dead. I'll recover onboard the ship. Just put me in front of him and I'll make him pay for what he did."

Elwyne continued to hold Logan's hand, and Aryx and Gideon both left the room, though Gideon lingered for a moment until being waived away by Elwyne. She ran her hand across Logan's shoulder and then kissed his cheek softly. After some effort, Elwyne helped Logan to his feet and then to get dressed. By the time they left the room, Logan could feel his strength beginning to return, and he hoped that by the time they were on the Isle of Thardus that he would be back into fighting shape. Though either Aryx or Gideon would have been happy to deal with Allan, Logan would not be satisfied unless it was his blade that pierced the former prince's heart.

The Monster of the Deep was not as huge as the Raging Storm was, but it was obvious that the vessel was designed for speed. At Aryx's and Elwyne's insistence, Logan spent the entire trip down in the crew quarters sleeping. When Elwyne woke Logan, he still felt groggy and weak, but he was able to stand on his own without difficulty. He tested his balance and then drew his sword. The blade felt heavier than it should have, but he could hold it and wield it with skill. He felt it would be enough. Talos and Aryx were already on shore by the time Logan made it to the deck, and Gideon waited with Alexander as an honor guard of sorts. The captain had agreed to stay until they returned, and even promised passage to Falke, citing orders from the queen. Alexander, Gideon, Elwyne, and Logan joined Aryx and Talos on shore and began walking toward a clearing in the middle of the desert.

The entire Isle of Thardus was a rocky desert, but because of the sea air, it never got too hot on the island. There was one single clearing on the island, and that was in the exact center. The clearing was nothing but a large glade, and it only took up about a third of the island. A well-appointed palace stood in the center of the glade, but it didn't seem as though the palace had seen much use for several years. This was the hideaway that Allan had picked for his escape. It was a surprisingly uneventful walk to the palace, and it slightly unnerved Logan that no soldiers or any of the black clad figures were waiting for them. Perhaps the prince had overestimated his machinations in Lesin, or simply had all of his forces waiting in the palace. Either way, his arrogant presumptions would be his downfall, as they had in Trelon. As soon as the group had reached the palace however, Logan felt a knot grow in the pit of his stomach, warning him that something was very wrong. There were no soldiers anywhere, and that little voice in the back of Logan's head was screaming that it was a trap. As soon as they opened the large doors to the palace, they found a person waiting for them at the end of a hallway. As the figure approached, Aryx and Gideon drew their weapons, and Logan felt his hand fall to the hilt of his sword. But he waited. As soon as the prince was in view, Aryx pointed the tip of his blade at the man.

"Surrender, Allan," Aryx said strongly, "I place you under arrest now in the name of Lord Cedric Binosear of Marcwell and Queen Cairyn Binosear of Trelon."

"So," he said his voice proud and strong, "the little girl Cairyn survived the blaze. It is such a pity that I wasn't able to kill her as easily as I killed Anne Binosear. It would have been such an accomplishment to kill them both, take the throne, kill the *Coromor*, and burn down the royal palace all in one day, but it seems as if my poison missed its mark."

"That it did Allan, and now I'm here to pay you a little of it back. Unlike Aryx, I'm not so quick to hand you over to the authorities. I fully intend to run you through."

Finally Logan drew his sword.

"By all means," Allan taunted. "Run me through, if you can."

All of the rage and disgust that Logan had been barely containing exploded. Logan raised his blade and charged the next moment. Allan wasn't armed, but Logan was unconcerned with the consequences of cutting down an unarmed man. In a flash, Logan had crossed the distance between the two men and he struck hard at his opponent. The blade sped toward the smaller man's exposed throat, and should have cleanly severed the head from his body, but the blade passed right through him. It was as if he were a ghost. Logan stood there in front of Allan, confused by the occurrence. No believing what had occurred, Logan attacked again, but each time the blade passed through the prince's body without drawing blood or leaving a scratch. The whole time Allan stood there laughing.

"This foolishness has gone on long enough, Dragon. If you are too dense to figure it out yourself, then I have to spell it out for you. The reason you can't hit me is because I have the power to become intangible. Do you know what that means?"

"It means that he becomes like a ghost and anything and everything will pass though him as if he weren't there." Talos answered.

"Very good, wizard. I am impressed with your knowledge. You could serve my master well," Allan answered.

"You aren't Prince Allan are you?" Logan said quickly.

"You catch on quick, Logan, I'll give you that. And no, I'm not the Prince Allan who was born of Anne Binosear. My name is Aldridge and I was born of Shau-ling."

"A phase," Aryx mumbled.

Aldridge bowed and smiled.

"That is correct, White Lightning. And now, without further discussion, I will make Logan's head a prize for my master."

That next second, a stream of flame erupted from his hand and extended into the form of a sword. Logan barely had time to raise his blade to parry, but when the coherent stream of fire stuck Logan's sword, the metal began to burn. Heat burst through the blade down into the hilt, forcing Logan to drop his sword. A bolt of lightning shot between them, forcing Aldridge to leap back several feet from his prey.

"Do not interfere, White Lightning," Aldridge scolded, his voice never shifting from playful yet cold tone, "you know that I could cut off your powers with a thought."

Aryx made eye contact with Logan, and in that instant, Logan somehow knew what he was thinking. The bolt of lightning arched out again, but this time Aldridge was ready for it. He threw the blade of fire at Logan's companions, and before they knew what was happening, they were encased in a cage of fire.

"Don't try to use your powers White Lightning, nor you wizard. Every time any type of magic tries to penetrate the cage, it will shrink. I wouldn't want you getting hurt because of your own foolishness, would you? I want you all to be in perfect condition from when I kill you one by one."

While he was busy prodding and playing with the anger of Logan's friends, Aldridge missed what happened next. The lightning bolt was not in fact aimed at Aldridge, but at Logan. He caught the force of the lightning in his hands, and without even thinking, fashioned it into a sword. When Aldridge turned around, he was again faced with an armed adversary, this time a more formidable one.

"Ah, I see that I have underestimated the powers of the *Coromor*. That should last the rest of the two seconds you will live."

He swung his blade of fire at Logan quickly but recklessly, and Logan met it with an equally strong sword of lightning. There was a huge flash of light, and Aldridge backed off. The sword of fire was gone, and smoke rose from the palms of his hands. The light had caused him to lose his concentration and the fire of his own blade burned him.

"Enough fun and games, Logan," he said, the comedy gone from his voice and the frustration pushed to the forefront. His game had taken an unexpected turn, and he was not happy about it.

He raised his right hand and a dagger of ice sped toward Logan. Logan released the blade of lightning on the whim of a reflex and caught the dagger. He had no control of his body anymore, whatever the *Coromor* that was inside of him wanted to do, it did. The dagger of ice lay in his hands, and Logan crushed it as if it were nothing. When he looked back at his open palm, he saw that it was filled with hundreds of tiny ice daggers, identical to the huge one that had just been thrown at him. Logan smiled back at Aldridge and threw them at him. As Logan half-expected, the phase became intangible again and the daggers passed right through him.

"Please Logan," he said the comedy returning to his voice, "quit wasting my time with these petty parlor tricks and give me your head. I promise that you won't feel a thing."

"No chance Aldridge. Only a coward would hide behind his powers like you. What happened to honor in battle."

The sword of fire sprung back into his hands and he advanced.

"A coward am I?" he screamed.

He thrust his fire sword at Logan's heart, and before Logan knew what was happening, the young warrior caught the blade in his right hand. It took only a moment before Logan could feel the flesh beginning to liquefy in the palm of his hand, but he couldn't afford to give in to the pain. Aldridge was shocked at Logan's tactics and was distracted enough that he did not see the blade of lightning that had extended from Logan's other palm. He looked up when Logan smiled and caught the tip of the lightning dagger in his right eye. Blood spewed from the empty socket, and Aldridge staggered back screaming in pain. Logan only had a split second to hit him before he recovered enough of his wits to become intangible. Dropping both of the blades, Logan extended both of his hands toward the wounded phase. Bolts of red lightning erupted from Logan's fingertips and surrounded Aldridge. He screamed louder and louder as the lightning crackled around him, but the attack had not struck, it merely imprisoned him. Aldridge was far craftier than Logan had anticipated. The blade of fire lay behind Logan and when Aldridge raised his hand, it leapt off the ground and sped toward Logan's back. Somehow Logan knew it was there. He turned and caught the blade in his hands again, only this time instead of burning his palms, the blade froze in his hands. Logan turned, and threw the frozen blade like a javelin and impaled Aldridge upon it. He screamed more and more, yet he would not die. The sword of ice had pierced him through the side, where it would be painful but not fatal. Logan's fury finally won out. Aldridge raised an open hand and seemed to wish to beg for mercy. Logan didn't hear a word that Aldridge said. Logan raised a hand of his own quickly, and then clenched his fist, forcing the rings of lightning around Aldridge to contract. They moved slowly at first, and then suddenly, they shrank to nothingness.

Aldridge stood still and silent for a moment, his blank stare looking right through Logan. His head lolled to one side, and then rolled completely off his shoulders. Then another segment of his body fell off, and then another and another. In a matter of moments, pieces of Aldridge lay strewn around the area. While Logan felt a feeling of finality with the kill, there was no satisfaction. Logan turned back to where his companions had been held captive, only to find that Aldridge's death had freed them from their prison of fire. Suddenly Logan felt weak. He fell to my knees and cried out in pain. Flames burst up all around him and began to circle like a vortex. The flames then changed to streams of water, and then to boulders of rock. The rocks then disappeared, and Logan could see the thin ribbons of air and wind circling around him. Suddenly there was an explosion of light and Logan fell forward onto his face, totally exhausted. When he finally regained his senses, once again Logan found himself surrounded by the concerned faces of his comrades. When Logan had managed to get back to his feet, Elwyne reached out to hold him. She came towards him arms extended, but when she tried to grab hold, she passed right through.

"Logan?" she said puzzled.

"What's happening, Aryx?" Logan asked fearfully.

"You've absorbed Aldridge's special talent. I can't explain in detail, but when the *Coromor* kills a member of the phasia, you absorb that phase's special power."

"That's fine and all," Logan said as Elwyne tried to hold him again but failed, "but how do I turn it off?"

"Reach into your mind and simply turn it off in your head."

Logan nodded and then closed his eyes. He could see the power in his mind, and he imagined a lever that would turn the intangibility power on and off. He switched it off and then when Logan felt Elwyne's arms around him, he knew that it worked. Exhaustion overtook him again, and Logan nearly collapsed into her arms.

"Let's get back to the ship," Elwyne said, mostly supporting Logan's weight. "You need some rest."

CHAPTER 10

Upon returning to the Monster of the Deep, the captain was true to his word and set sail for the port of Falke. Elwyne got Logan into one of the small beds in the crew quarters and sat beside him as he drifted off into sleep. His last thought before sleep took him was that he hoped Pike and the others were already there. It was time for the quest to start again in earnest, and Logan's first order of business was to finally wring all of the secrets out of their illustrious guide, Sir Aryx Terian.

Dalx

Gwydeon left the throne room in a haze of bewilderment. Events swirled in his mind, and he tried hard to decipher what had actually happened. He remembered looking up at the man who had called himself the phase Zarsi, and from that point on his memory faded. Pike's haste to leave had diminished somewhat after Hawk's voluntary defection to the side of the Dragon. Though he had been an unwilling servant to Zarsi, his change of heart and quick rebellion seemed too convenient for Gwydeon. But wasn't it he who insisted on Hawk being an ally? Maybe Gwydeon had guessed wrong. Regardless of Hawk's possible hidden intentions, if there were any, he was nothing if not gracious. Rooms and hot bath water had been provided for the six of them, and their horses had been returned with all of the belongings intact. Their weapons had also been returned, and even before he rose to his feet, Gwydeon insisted that his sword be brought to him. There were not many things about this quest that Gwydeon had found appealing, but a bath was one of the best things that he could think of at the time.

Gwydeon was quite weak after the strange encounter with Zarsi, but he refused to be helped to his chamber. Both Eldar and Midarin had tried, but he would not hear of it. He had been thrust into the role of the leader once again, and he still had not figured out how that happened. One minute Pike was so headstrong and ready to fight the forces of heaven and hell in the name of the Dragon, and now he had reduced himself to just a minor role in the growing epic that they called their lives. Strange as it seemed to Gwydeon, he found himself being thrust ever forward in the grand scheme of things. Inwardly he wondered if Logan ever felt that way.

After the slow and somewhat painful walk down to the end of one of the many palace hallways, Gwydeon stood in front of the door that led to the room prepared for him. Just like the rest of the palace, the hallway was totally white, with not one splash of color anywhere in the chamber. Even the doors and door handles were white. It was an eerie monotony, and Gwydeon could not help but shiver as thoughts of Dreamscape rolled into his mind. But he and his friends together had faced the demons there, and they had faced them in Sador. Their number remained at six, but Gwydeon could not help but wonder how long it would be before one of their number fell to the wayside. Pike had saved them again this time, but a time could come where Pike would not be there to save them, and all could fall if one were ever to be removed. That last thought of utter defeat made Gwydeon shiver violently as he opened the door to the chamber.

Hawk had kept his promise, the chamber was appointed well, and a white wash basin stood in the center of the pristine white room. Just as everywhere else in the palace, this room was also pure white. The sheets, pillows, mattress, curtains, and even the rugs on the floor were white. The lack of color was more disturbing in the room than it had been in the hallway, and for a moment Gwydeon had to remind himself that he was still alive. The feeling of solitude washed over Gwydeon, and he stood there in the doorway, almost unable to move.

"Eerie," a voice said from behind him, "isn't it?"

The voice was familiar. It was the voice of the woman who had the most to prove during this quest. It was the voice of Princess Midarin Rice. She had joined the party under less than perfect circumstances, but she had proved to be an invaluable addition to the forces of the Dragon. Her past still haunted her, but that could have been said for everyone in the party, especially Gwydeon. He started to dwell on the past, but he snapped himself back into the frames of reality when Midarin's soft hand rested on his heavily muscled, yet puzzlingly sore shoulder.

"Are you all right Gwydeon?" she asked her voice so soft and warm.

She could be so cold, and she had been on the battlefield, her cold stare down the shaft of an arrow intent on taking a life, but now her voice changed from the strong, hard tones to a more serene and lady-like quality. This flexibility made Gwydeon stop doubting that Midarin could have ever been a lady in a court. With all she had been through, she, more than any of the others, was probably prepared for the trials that waited.

"I'm fine, Midarin," he replied, not turning toward her, "I was just a little shocked at the color."

He was never a good liar.

"Or lack thereof," she commented.

She released Gwydeon's shoulder and walked past him into the chamber. She ran her fingers through the warm bath water as she passed by and then sat down on the bed. She straightened the black dress that she had apparently just changed into and looked up at Gwydeon.

"Do you like this dress?" she said fidgeting a little.

Gwydeon looked at her and swallowed hard. To say the dress was tight would be like saying that Talon was well-adjusted with a small ego. The charcoal colored almost black dress clung to her slim waist and her bust. The slit in the side of the dress showed her beautiful tan legs, and as he looked at them, she raised her right leg slowly and crossed it over her left. He looked up quickly, immediately sensing the game and rested his eyes on her bright face. Her lips were curled not in a smile, but into a sly grin. Her eyes hid her true intentions well, and she actually looked as if she were concerned as to his opinion. He knew in his heart what he wanted to say, but he didn't think he had the courage to.

"It's nice. I have to say though; I like you better in a shirt and breeches."

"I guess I should have expected you to say that. I had rather gotten used to them too," she commented, shifting slowly on the bed. "However, Hawk insisted that since I was really a princess, I should dress like one."

"A princess that needed a prince to help her regain her kingdom. I suppose that he asked you to come by his chambers so that he could see how you looked in that dress?"

"And out of it," she said, her full luscious lips beginning to curl into a smile. "You read my mind, Gwydeon."

"So why did you come here? I can't be so interesting as to keep you from our wonderful friend Hawk."

"Anything is interesting enough to keep me away from Hawk. But in answer to your question, I wanted to thank you for helping me on the road. I have been feeling like no one wants me here lately. You're all so close-knit since you grew up together, and it's hard to not feel like the outsider. But you saved me in Sarmeel, and then again you protected me here in Sador. You've always seemed as though you cared about my well-being. So, I wanted to say thank you. I also wanted to talk, if you were up to it."

Gwydeon turned and closed the door. He smiled in spite of himself as he turned to the door, and as he turned back to face Midarin, the smile vanished.

"All right. But would you mind if I take a bath while we talk? I know it sounds a bit odd but . . ."

"No, Gwydeon," Midarin chimed in quickly, "I understand."

"So would you mind turning around until I get in the water?"

She tried to suppress a smile when she realized he was blushing. She never would have pegged him for the modest type, not after hearing what she had about his training regimen in Rama. It was almost cute.

"Not at all."

Midarin stood and turned to face the back wall of the chamber. Gwydeon watched as she turned, studying her every move. The dress was as tight in the back as it was in the front, and he stole a few quick looks before walking over and drawing the curtains before returning to the side of the wash basin. His back was turned to Midarin, and as she looked up only on thought came to her mind.

What a wonderful place for a mirror. I'll have to remind myself to thank Hawk for this opportunity.

"You can turn around now," he said softly.

Midarin turned around, trying to hide the inner pleasure of her stolen glances. She sat back on the end of the bed and looked at Gwydeon. He began to soak his arms with the water, and then his chest. Midarin could not help but stare as the beads of water rolled off of the strong hard muscles in his chest. But as impressive as his musculature was, there were hideous scars that marred so much of him. It was amazing that someone so young had been so disfigured and still drew breath.

"So," Gwydeon said, his attention focused elsewhere, "what would you like to talk about?"

"How much do you remember about the fight?"

"Funny, I was going you ask you about that. Would there have been anything in that confrontation that would account for the fact that I don't remember how we won? Or that would account for these new scars?"

"Yes Gwydeon, there was. After Zarsi revealed himself as a phase and attacked us, he had a conversation with you."

"Yes, I remember that. He was ranting about something called the *Chosen One*. I suppose I'll have to talk to Aryx about that when I get the chance."

"Yes," Midarin said uneasily, "but that was not the end of the confrontation. Pike broke loose from the ice at one point, and when he did he sent shards flying toward Zarsi. You got in the way of one of the shards, and you were impaled upon it. I thought you were dead when I first saw you, but Pike and Talon managed to use their powers to save your life. I guess they healed all of your wounds, and pretty much brought you back from the dead."

"So I owe Pike my life one more time on top of the rest. I guess that I'll have to start paying him back one of these days."

"I hope it doesn't come to that Gwydeon. Can I get your back for you?"

Gwydeon looked up at her for a moment and nodded. She rose rather quickly and walked toward the basin. It wasn't until she was walking toward him that he realized what it was that she asked him, or that he had so quickly agreed. She tried not to be too obvious as she looked at his completely naked body through the clear water. She walked around behind the basin, and as he leaned forward, she started to wash his back. The sensation was strange, and for a moment, the two sat in silence, discomfort passing between them. Finally Midarin broke the silence.

"So," Midarin said, her voice wavering, "why did you come along with Logan? I know he's your friend, but there had to be more than that."

Gwydeon smiled, and it came through in his voice.

"Loyalty to friends is a very big deal in Aradon. I would have given my life for Logan before, but the fact that he is the *Coromor* just redoubled my beliefs. Besides, I had to get out of Aradon."

"Why, if you don't mind my asking?"

"No, not at all. You see, every year we have a festival in Aradon. One of the competitions at the festival is a sword fighting tournament. Believe it or not, I have never won that tournament."

"What?" Midarin said shocked, "you are the best I have ever seen with a sword, and after what Leane told me about your training exercises in Rama, I was sorry I missed it."

"You know Leane?" Gwydeon stammered.

"Yes," Midarin replied calmly, "she was my personal guard back in Brea when I was a princess. We practically grew up together, and after the fiasco, her family was disgraced, and she and several others who had once served me went to Rama. Now, go on with your story. Who was it who beat you?"

"Eldar was always better than I was. She beat me every year that I entered. No one else could beat me but her. Last year though she didn't enter."

"Why?"

"At the time, she and Pike were still very caught up in their romance. She and Pike had planned to trade vows in the old church during the festival, so she didn't enter."

"How did they break it off?"

"That's the funny thing Midarin," Gwydeon commented, "no one was supposed to know that they were going to trade vows. I was the only one who knew, and that was only because Pike let it slip once. Not even Talon or Elwyne know, and they are closer to Pike and Eldar than I am. Anyway, Pike and Eldar did trade vows, but afterward they had a horrific argument and they vowed that they would never be able to live with each other. So, the vows were never consummated, nor was anyone ever told."

"What about the preacher and the witnesses?" Midarin asked.

"We do things much differently in Aradon, Midarin. A preacher does not marry people in Aradon. When people want to get married, they go up to the old abandoned church on the hill and they trade the ancient vows that are written in a holy book that is forever encased in glass in the church. After the vows are traded, the couple consummates their marriage there on the floor of the church and then returns to the village proper. At that point they go to the church inside the wall and ring the large bell in the tower. When people in town hear that, they all come running and the couple will tell the village that they have been married. It is at that point that the marriage becomes official, and then the preacher can hold a 'proper' ceremony."

"So, the wedding ceremony is secondary to the actual marriage in Aradon."

"Exactly," Gwydeon replied looking back at her over his shoulder. Midarin walked beside the basin and then dropped to her knees beside it and rested her arms on the edge.

"So in effect," she said trying to understand, "Pike and Eldar aren't really married."

"Right, but they have traded the vows. If they were to consummate the vows and tell someone from Aradon, even in passing, they would be considered married."

"Strange. However, it is probably better than the way it's done in Brea. The ceremony in Brea is everything. After the ceremony, there is no way to end the marriage, even after death. If a person's spouse dies, the person is forbidden to find another. In your society, you could take the vows with a person and then change your mind."

"No," Gwydeon said laying his hand on hers, "you don't understand. If you were to take the vows with a person, you are not allowed to take the vows again, unless the person you took them with first is dead. At that point, you would be taken to the church, stripped naked, thrown into the holy stream that runs through the church, and properly purified. At that point it is as you were never married. It is said that even the memories of the lost love are washed away in the water, but no one has ever been able to find out for sure. You see, anyone who goes through the purification is forbidden to talk about the past or the purification itself. It is just something that is not spoken of. There were many after Logan's mother died who tried to convince Arin to undergo the purification rite, but he always said that his memories of his wife were too important to him. He would rather die than give her up, and he would rather live alone for the rest of his life. Which he did."

Midarin's expression was pensive.

"Like I said," Gwydeon continued. "Loyalty."

That brought a small smile to Midarin's lips. She rested her chin on their joined hands, her eyes never leaving his.

"So what could be done about Eldar and Pike? Since no one knows they have taken the vows, what would stop them from taking them with someone else? They seem to act free enough as it is."

"They know, and so do I. Though it would not be my place to speak of it, I do have that knowledge. However, even if I didn't know, their sacred obligation is to each other, and they cannot defile that. They would not. I can't explain all of the reasons; I can say that it is something that is just not done."

"I understand, as you said, loyalty is important in Aradon. Now, what was this about the tournament?"

Here a grim pall fell over Gwydeon's features. It was clear that this was not a story he told, as the discomfort was clear.

"As I said, Eldar had not entered the tournament, so I was the favorite to win. I easily made it to the final match, and as we fought, my mind wandered for some reason. When fighting in a tournament, we fight with practice swords. They are very thin, and are made out of a certain type of reed. The reed is strong, thin, and flexible. The ends are lopped off and filed, so there are no sharp points. We don't fight to the death, we fight for strikes. The first person to strike the opponent three times in vital areas, except the head, wins the battle. I was up two strikes to none. My opponent made a mistake, and I dropped to one knee to push the tip of the sword into his armor. It was supposed to be a sword strike to the heart. When I struck, the end of the reed snapped, and the sword continued upward, and with a new sharp point, it plunged into his throat. It was a painless death, and I was cleared of all of the charges, but I never forgave myself. His family did, but I couldn't. From that time on, I was just looking for a way out of Aradon, and this quest was a blessing."

Midarin took his hand and held it tightly. She dropped her head down onto it and rubbed her cheek across the back of his hand. She then kissed it softly and looked up at him. He looked into her eyes and moved toward her, until his lips were mere inches from hers. He could feel her hot breath on his face, and her skin smelled of lavender. Then their lips touched. The tentative kiss gave way to a more passionate one, her hands pulling away from his and moving to his head where her fingers twined in his hair. Gwydeon pulled back slightly, and he saw the desire in her eyes. He managed to get to his feet, and pulled her up with him, and he awkwardly pulled her into his arms, and the kiss continued. When we tried to step out of the basin, he stumbled slightly, and Midarin had to catch him. Their kiss

CHAPTER 10

was broken barely and together they laughed. Once back on his feet, Gwydeon was finally able to pull her body close to his, and she surrendered to his strength, letting her head fall back slightly so that the taller man could let his gentle kiss fade into something more primal and longing. He pulled the straps of the dress off of her shoulders and then felt her naked skin against his as the dress dropped to the ground silently. He broke the kiss for an instant as he took her into his arms as he had on the road to Sador, and as she looked up at him with the fires of passion in her eyes they began the kiss anew. He then turned away from the basin and carried her to the bed.

* * * * * * * * * * *

Pike was uneasy as the six companions and their newest addition, a man named Hawk, rode through the gates of Sador down the tree lined road that had once not long ago been turned into a battlefield. Hawk had not been too talkative since the battle with Zarsi, and Pike could feel that something was desperately wrong with the entire situation.

"What can you tell me about this man Logan?" Hawk asked.

The break in the silence almost unnerved Pike. He had been talking about the *Coromor* ever since he found out Pike and Talon were members of the *Erieal*. This was the question that Pike had been waiting for. He had better be a good judge of Hawk's intentions, because if he wasn't he could let something slip that would get them all killed.

"Logan's a great man," Talon replied. "I've never met anyone quite like him."

Good answer Talon, Pike thought, *you didn't say anything bad. Just the kind of useless answer I was hoping for.*

"He's a great warrior, and a caring friend," Gwydeon added.

Good.

"What do you think Midarin?" Hawk asked.

Please don't say anything else, Pike pleaded.

"There's not much else to say. That's exactly how I would have described him."

Whew! That was a close one.

"Now," Midarin said turning her attention from Gwydeon, "what about you Hawk?"

Good, Pike thought, *turn it back on him.*

"There's not much to tell really. I was born to a noble lord, a king in reality. He was a great man, and he commanded great respect. I chose a different route when I was supposed to take over his throne, so I made my own fortunes in Sador."

"Those fortunes nearly got you killed," Lane commented.

"Such is life I'm afraid," Hawk responded whimsically.

Damn! I thought we had him. But, we are no closer now than we were five hours ago.

"So," Eldar said trying to break the tension, "what is this place called Dalx like?"

"Oh," Hawk responded, "it is a wonderful place. We should be there in a few hours."

With that he rode farther ahead. Pike looked around, and the only response he received was a puzzled shrug from Talon. The next three hours were slow and long. Midarin and Gwydeon were wrapped in some sort of conversation. Pike could not understand how two people could go from so frigid to each other to this new relationship so quickly. Eldar rode close to Pike, almost too close to be considered casual. Maybe the fact that he saved her life was beginning to get to her. Talon rode on the other side of Pike with Lane beside him. For once, Talon did not have a joke or a story, or if he did, he was not in a mood to tell them. After hours of riding, Hawk stopped his horse short of a town and then turned to the rest of the group.

"Welcome to Dalx my friends. There is a small inn on the far end of town, and I think it will be suitable enough for us tonight. Tomorrow we can ride for Falke if you like."

"That will be acceptable," Pike said, his voice remaining even and cold.

Hawk turned back toward the village and began to ride. The town was not very special, at least, not in comparison to Sador or Illimar. It was just a simple village out in the middle of nowhere. Hawk continued to ride forward, and as he passed a few buildings, he stopped and turned back toward the rest of the party. Pike pulled up on the reins as did the rest of the party.

"What is it, Hawk?" Eldar asked.

Hawk chuckled to himself and then pointed skyward. Pike looked up and immediately saw that the roofs of the surrounding buildings were filled with armed men.

"Ambush!" Pike screamed.

At that moment the men leaped. Most of the party was dragged from their horses, and as Pike struggled back to his feet, he jerked the axe out of the loop in his belt and stood fast. Another of the men leapt at him, and without moving, Pike swung his axe, and he caught the man in the side, mid-jump. Blood flowed everywhere as force of Pike's blow propelled the man into the wall of one of the nearby buildings. He turned quickly and watched as Eldar buried the blade of her sword into another of the savages. She motioned to him that she was all right. That moment four or five more rushed in on them. There was a flash of light, and several of them burst into flames. Lane had done his job well.

Gwydeon had gotten to his feet, and collected Midarin behind him. Several of them came on him at once. The first took a quick slash to the neck. Blood poured as he fell in defeat, but another had stepped up to take a cut a Gwydeon. Gwydeon slashed again, but his strike had over extended his defense. The third attacker would have easily buried his sword in Gwydeon's ribs had it not been for the fact that he hadn't counted on Midarin's short sword being aimed toward his. More and more of them fell to the combined attacks of the two new-found lovers, and it looked as if they would make it out of this battle alive.

Talon stood his ground, his sword lowered in front of him. He had gotten close to Lane, and Talon did his best to cut down those who rushed at him while Lane made the others into walking fireballs. One of the armed savages ran through the flaming remains and slashed wildly at Talon. His slash was off the mark, but Talon's was not. The broad stroke of Talon's blade severed the head of the attacker and the arm of another. Men fell left and right, and all the time, Hawk sat in his saddle at the far end of the building, his arms folded, and his eyes trained intently on the battle. They had been effectively set up.

The battle was over minutes after it had begun. All of the attackers had been properly dealt with, with brutal and lethal efficiency. All six of the friends still stood, no blood had been drawn by the attackers this day. It was becoming sad that battle had become second nature to the six of them, but it was a cross they had to bear. Talon dropped his sword and ran toward Hawk. Hawk merely flicked his hand toward Talon, and he was thrown to the ground. Pike stared up at Hawk and clenched his fists. Suddenly, it began to grow colder. Pike's clenched fists had become encased with ice. He raised his hands toward Hawk, but before anything could happen, Hawk raised his finger to his throat, and as he slid it across his neck, the ice around Pike's clenched fists shattered, and then was gone.

"What the hell is going on here?" Gwydeon screamed approaching Hawk.

"You are pathetic, Sandar. Do you really think that you are powerful enough to trifle with me?"

"We bested Zarsi together, and I think we can take you out too," Midarin replied angrily as she approached.

"Zarsi was a weak blind fool. Had he known what you were capable of, he never would have let you get that close. He was arrogant and vain. He could have robbed you of your powers more easily than I have."

"So," Pike said, his anger rising uncontrollably, "you are a phase too. I should have known."

"You know nothing, Rhuiden. The phasia are weak and corrupt. They quarrel amongst themselves, and do not care about real power. One of them has vision, and he should have destroyed Shau-ling himself and taken the throne. If that would have happened, the prophecies would have not been a factor and the even the mighty *Coromor* wouldn't have been able to save the world. My father would have shaken the world."

"Let me guess," Pike prodded, "then you and he would have split the world right down the middle. Get a life, Hawk, your father is a pathetic weakling, and if he had any power or courage at all he would stop hiding behind a pathetic whelp like you and come down here to face us himself."

Hawk's fury began to build. His hands came up and bolt of lightning crashed into Pike's chest. Pike fell to the ground, the front of his shirt blackened and smoking.

"Do not trifle with me! I am the son of the great Lord Jeroch. Jeroch the Shadow, the First-Born of the Phasia. His power is my power, and I will kill you all. You *Erieal* are nothing without your powers. Zarsi was a short-sighted fool, and I am all-powerful."

"You are an all-powerful fool," Lane replied quickly, "I'm not an *Erieal*. Your powers are meaningless to me."

There was no time for Hawk to react. The stream of flame emerged from Lane's hand even before he finished speaking, and as Hawk and his horse burned, Hawk's final curses could be heard. Pike rose to his feet slowly, still feeling the blast from the lightning in his chest. Talon was also on his feet, rubbing his head slightly. The fires ceased, and as Talon's hand rose, the winds picked up and scattered the ashes into oblivion. The six of them recovered their horses, and without a word turned their sights and their steeds toward Falke, toward Logan, and toward their futures.

Crusades and Crusaders

The Pen stirred with electricity as the beasts felt the power of a portal forming above their heads. Suddenly, a person fell through the portal and landed in an open space. The beasts had cleared the area around the portal for fear of what might happen. The man rolled over on his stomach, and the portal above him closed. Several Jeresei shoved their way through the crowd, surrounding the visitor. When one of them got a good look at his face, he approached and tried to help the man to his feet.

"Lord Zarsi!" he exclaimed grabbing the man by the arm.

Zarsi pulled away from the Jeresei, rolled onto his side and thrust his hands toward the impetuous creature. A stream of fire pulsed through his fingertips and engulfed the shocked Jeresei. The death was slow and painful as it burned there in front of the rest of his brethren and clan members. The skin finished burning, and as Zarsi rose, he swatted at the burnt husk of what used to be a Jeresei and watched as it fell to the ground in a pile of ash.

"If any of you Valtamine ever lay your hands on me again," Zarsi yelled through the crowd, "I will kill you all."

None of the beasts answered the threat.

"Do you all understand me!" he shouted.

"Yes, my Lord Zarsi," everyone in the Pen answered.

"Zarsi!" a voice called over the growing din of exaltations.

The crowd parted, and a huge man proceeded through the crowd. He was short of stature, but he was one of the most physically powerful of all of the phasia. It was thought that his strength could even match that of a Stone. Zarsi had been allies with the man many times, but he had also been his enemy. He could honestly say that he knew this man from both sides of the equation. His friend, his brother, Warron.

"What in the name of the shadows happened to you, Zarsi? I felt the portal forming, and I rushed here to see what was the matter."

"No time," Zarsi said, his breathing just beginning to calm, "I must see Shau-ling right away."

"He has just returned from the Council, and he is currently meeting with Taron."

"Taron? What is that overgrown behemoth meeting with master about?"

"I don't know, Zarsi, but whatever it is it must have been pretty important to meet with him privately and not wait for the Council to reconvene when Basille returns."

"Have you heard from Basille, Warron?" Zarsi asked concern thick in his voice.

"No, I have not. In fact, the last I knew, he left here just after we went back to our kingdoms. I traced the path of his portal back to his kingdom of Scalla, but after that, the line of power became untraceable. It was as if he layered ten different portals with ten different destinations on top of each other."

"Apparently," Zarsi replied, "our brother's special power in this line makes him virtually untraceable when he wants to be. It would appear that he has known how to find our friend Saurn all along and he did not want us to discover that information. I believe that we have been deceived my dear brother and that our plans are now at the mercy of that lunatic Saurn."

"I believe that you are right," Warron added, "but we cannot let it hinder our plans. Caris is still alive and there is a chance that we could convince Farax, Taron, and Erdric to help us."

"You fool, do you think we would actually stand a chance, just the six of us. Besides, the chances of you and I convincing Erdric to join us are about as good as if we were trying to convince Jeroch."

"Caris could convince him," Warron interjected.

"True," Zarsi said as he fixed his hair, "but that still leaves us one short of the seven we need. What about Aldridge?"

"You haven't heard?" Warron asked.

"Heard what?" Zarsi asked turning back toward his friend.

"Aldridge had an unfortunate engagement with the forces of the *Coromor*."

"Unfortunate, but we all knew it would happen. Tell me the details on the way to the Hall."

Zarsi turned and began to walk toward the Hall of Terrors. Warron walked behind him and began to tell him of what happened.

"As Aldridge had planned, he got the *Coromor* out of Trelon long enough to set fire to the palace and kill the Queen. His attack missed though when the *Coromor* and his companions returned in time to rescue the princess. Eventually, Aldridge was tracked down, and trapped on the Island of Thardus. After that, there is very little to tell. The *Coromor* and his allies destroyed him. The last I heard, they were on their way to Falke."

"Did the *Coromor* know enough to banish him?" Zarsi asked.

"No. I do believe that Shau-ling has been in contact with him on the Other Side."

"That could be an advantage for us," Zarsi continued. "If Aldridge is on the Other Side, he could be able to stop Erika Binosear from interfering in our lives. Her phantom soldiers have cut too many of our Jeresei and Stone armies down in the last few weeks. Her attacks are getting bolder and we need to stop that from happening. Aldridge may have been stupid in his actions, but his stupidity may prove to be what stops this menace."

"Agreed," Warron responded.

The two of them continued on down the passageway with little other conversation and soon found themselves in the entryway to the Hall of Terrors. It was never pleasant when they had to visit the master, but this time it was of their own semi-free will, so it was different. As they walked through the Hall, the beasts in their cages were surprisingly quiet. It was as if for the first time in their long miserable existences that they had finally found some respect for the members of the phasia. Both Warron and Zarsi knew that wasn't much of a possibility, but stranger things had happened in the past. They continued walking down the Hall, and within a minute or two were standing in front of the doors that led to the Throne Room. The Flame appeared mere seconds after it felt their presence.

"Lord Cobra, Lord Boar, the mighty Shau-ling is currently in with your brother Lord Taron. He does not wish to be disturbed, but if you would like me to announce you after he leaves, I will do so and then you will be summoned."

"We do not have the time to wait, Flame. If you would announce us now, it would save us a lot of time," Zarsi replied strongly.

"I would not interrupt one of Shau-ling's audiences if the Great Dark One were standing here asking to see him. You will just have to wait."

Suddenly a portal opened before the Flame. Zarsi was about to step through, but the Flame cut him off and destroyed the portal.

"By orders of Shau-ling himself, there are to be no portals opened, or any powers of any kind used without his express permission. Anyone who would willingly break this rule could be punished by banishment."

Suddenly the door behind the Flame opened, and the Flame disappeared. Then, Shau-ling's voice rang out inside Warron's and Zarsi's heads. The voice was so powerful that it forced them to their knees. The pain was almost unbearable, and it would have killed any normal man or beast. It had been known to even kill Jeresei.

"YOU ARE TO FOLLOW MY ORDERS TO THE LETTER IN ALL TIMES AND LIFETIMES," the voice thundered. "YOU ARE MEMBERS OF MY PHASIA AND IF YOU WILL NOT FOLLOW ME THAN NO ONE WILL. IF YOU THINK YOU HAVE THE POWER TO CHALLENGE MY AUTHORITY, THEN I WELCOME THE CHALLENGE. OTHERWISE, YOU WILL OBEY, WITHOUT QUESTION. DO YOU UNDERSTAND?"

"Yes my lord," they both answered in agony.

"NOW. ENTER MY PRESENCE!"

Zarsi and Warron both struggled to their feet and walked slowly into the Throne Room. Being summoned by the Voice was never a pleasant thing, and no matter where a phase was in the world, he could hear that voice at the same intensity. It was not done much anymore. The Voice was only used if Shau-ling was very angry, or a dire emergency had arisen. The last time Zarsi could remember the Voice being used was when Cedric Binosear had made his way to Lakestone and was about to enter the palace.

They continued into the Throne Room and fell to one knee in the center of the black dragon that was etched in the center of the floor. They both waited for some sign as to their master's intentions, but they just knelt there. It was a long time before anything happened. Jeroch stepped forward from the back of the room and stood above his brothers, laughing down at them.

"You two are pitiful," Jeroch said quickly, "get on your feet and act like phasia. The master wants to see you in his private chambers."

The thought of going to Shau-ling's private chambers made Warron shudder deep in his core. While the private chambers of most lord and kings were pleasant, and filled with things of beauty and great worth, Shau-ling's private chambers were an elaborate torture chamber filled with unique devices best utilized for inflicting pain. Warron and Zarsi rose and followed Jeroch as he led them up the small flight of stairs, past the throne, and to a tapestry that hung on the back wall of the Throne Room. Jeroch lifted the tapestry to reveal a spinning white portal. This portal led back to the well-hidden private chamber. The reason this chamber was white was because Shau-ling and the phasia had all used their powers to make it a permanent one. Any one of the phasia could make any portal permanent, but the power used to keep the portal open constantly would steal so much power that the phase would be almost like a normal human. However, since all of the phasia and Shau-ling himself had added their powers to this portal, the power drain was minimal.

The three phasia walked through the portal and instantly appeared in Shau-ling's private chambers. In the very center of the room was a huge fountain that shot blood red water high into the air. The perimeter of the room was surrounded with gleaming white pillars, and in between each of the pillars was one of the torture machines that Shau-ling had collected over the years. The three of them moved around the fountain and then knelt in front of the reptilian looking man who sat on the golden throne in the back of the room.

"Rise and report," Shau-ling hissed.

The three stood to their feet and Zarsi stepped forward quickly.

"My lord Shau-ling. I have just returned from my kingdom in Sador..."

"Don't you mean your former kingdom?" Shau-ling taunted.

"What?"

"Shortly after I saw your line of power emerge from Sador, I had my spies watch as members of your own army stole control of your kingdom out from under you."

"No matter," Zarsi said angrily, "I can take it back any time. What is truly important is why I left Sador in the first place."

"And why is that?" Shau-ling asked.

"My spies found out about a small force making their way from Rama toward Falke. I then received information that this same force would swing by Sador, and possibly stop. Originally, this force had tweaked my interest when they were linked to the band being led by Aryx Terian."

"You mean the force that supposedly contained the second *Coromor*?" Jeroch asked.

"The same. When I also heard that our agent Antrobus was killed while in Rama and brother Saurn's sign was being flashed around heavily, I did some digging of my own."

"I trust that you suspected a connection with the *Chosen One* as it was mentioned by Basille," Shau-ling commented.

"I did my lord. I assumed that this *Chosen One* may have been traveling with the band led by Terian, and then after the altercation with Antrobus, he and a few members of the original party split off."

"Did your assumption turn out to be true?" Shau-ling asked.

"Not exactly sire, but I will come to that. I deployed my army to stop the six member force just outside of Sador. After a volley, that small group had killed over six hundred men after a use of *Erieal*-like powers. A secondary force was able to capture all six alive with no losses on their side. The man named Hawk that Jeroch told me to watch was the commander of that force."

"And also the leader of the rebels who stole your kingdom, if my sources are correct," Shau-ling added.

"Be that as it may, Hawk brought those people to me and we had an altercation. When I revealed myself as a member of the phasia, the two members of the *Erieal* and another petty spell caster used their powers and encased me in ice. I was rather impressed at the time with their powers, but they were too cocky and I had to teach them a lesson. I was able to generate enough body heat to break the ice, and when they saw I was free, they attacked again. Since I had seen the attacks before, I was able to turn their own attacks against them. I froze the Water Brother in his own stream of water. The Air Brother was easily trapped in an envelope of wind created out of the maelstrom he was making. The spell caster tried to use a burst of flame, but the Blaze was strong enough to push it back."

"You used my green flame, my Blaze, against a spell caster?" Shau-ling growled. "You drew on my powers to stifle a puny magician?"

"It was merely a reaction sire, and it seemed the right one at a time. I apologize for drawing upon the power of the Blaze, but the power used was minimal, and there could have been no danger to you or any of the other phasia," Zarsi said the fear creeping into his voice.

"You best be sure that there was no danger, Cobra," Shau-ling threatened, "or you will answer for what you have done. For now however I will not mention or hold this little abuse of power against you."

"Thank you, my lord."

"Now, continue with your report."

"By your word. After I had neutralized the threat, I began to examine the man by the name of Gwydeon Sandar in order to determine whether or not he actually was the *Chosen One*. After talking with him for a moment, I realized that he was not the one of the prophecies, and then I was about to exterminate them. I am afraid to report that I had underestimated the powers of the one named Pike Rhuiden, the Water Brother, but what he did would have been difficult for a phase to even accomplish. Using his abilities to control water, he shattered the prison of ice that held him and directed the shards toward me. While some of them were able to inflict injuries to my person, one of the larger shards claimed this Gwydeon fellow. The attack caused me to lose my concentration thereby freeing the Air Brother from the predicament he was in. This man, Talon Aielin, then used his control over the winds to surround me with winds and lift me up off the ground, neutralizing me. Apparently sensing the kill at hand, the Water Brother took hold of my leg. He had figured out that he could draw the water out of my blood, and by doing so, he was actually pulling my life away from me."

"Interesting," Shau-ling said, "I have never heard of any of the *Erieal* ever using their powers in such a delightfully lethal way. I must say that I like these *Erieal* much better than I like White Lightning and his positively boring and predictable compatriots."

"My lord," Jeroch said stepping forward, "forgive me, but do you think taking these men so lightly is wise."

Shau-ling hissed at Jeroch and spoke.

"Shau-ling takes nothing lightly, Shadow. I am merely amused at their original tactics."

"By your word," Jeroch responded backing off.

"What have you to report, Warron?"

"Nothing new, my lord. My attempts to ascertain the whereabouts of brother Basille came up empty. Most of my reason for returning was the news about Aldridge."

"Yes," Shau-ling hissed, "that was an interesting little piece of news. I have to say that I very nearly forgot about your friend Aldridge."

Shau-ling waived his hand out in front of him and sat back as a form appeared. As soon as the person finished forming, he was easy to recognize. The same cold hard face, the evil eyes, the stone cold smile. It was the man called Aldridge.

"How are you adjusting to your new home, Aldridge?" Shau-ling laughed.

"Very well, lord. Do you have any orders to pass on to your legions here?" Aldridge asked.

"As a matter of fact I do, Aldridge. Send out you scouts to find the palace of Miss Erika Binosear, and once they do, you will utilize all of your forces and you will attack. Under no circumstances are you to withdraw. I want you to banish everyone and everything that stands in their palace. Once that is done you will report back to me. If you do well enough Aldridge, I may see if I can reanimate you somehow."

"Thank you my lord."

Shau-ling waived his hand again and the form of Aldridge disappeared. Shau-ling then set his cold hard stare on Jeroch.

"Now for your report, Shadow."

"As we feared, Saurn has used his control over the real *Chosen One* to attack a member of the phasia."

"Who was his target?" Zarsi asked.

"Our sister, Caris."

"What was the outcome?" Shau-ling asked.

"I am afraid to say that it has turned out for the worst. After the heavy civil war ended in Illimar, it was discovered that the Queen, Caris, had been murdered. Since she has not appeared on the Other Side, I think it only safe to assume that the *Chosen One* has learned how to banish other members of the phasia. This could be a great step back in our plans," Jeroch responded.

"Do you think Saurn would actually tell the *Chosen One* how to banish members of the phasia?" Zarsi asked.

"Saurn would give the *Chosen One* any advantage he needed over the rest of the phasia," Warron growled, "he wants us all dead so that he can try and take command of our empires."

"He wants more than that, Boar," Shau-ling interjected, "he wants my throne, and he needs the *Chosen One* to get it."

"That will never happen my lord," Jeroch said quickly, "but in the meantime, what is to be done about sister Caris?"

"Absolutely nothing. If she has been banished, there is nothing I can do to save her now."

The gravity of the situation created an uneasy silence that could only be broken one way.

"What are our orders?" Warron asked.

"I have recently learned from your brother Taron that certain members of my phasia have been plotting against me here in my own palace. I have devised a plan that will flush these traitorous phasia out into the open. The whole reason that I sent Basille out to find Saurn was because I had earlier found that he and Saurn had been plotting against me. When Basille returns, he will no doubt try to convince me to reconvene the Council so Saurn will return. When he does, I will flush both he and Saurn out into the open."

"So, we are to report to the Council."

"That you are. I will not send out any calls until Basille returns. Until that time you will wait."

Shau-ling turned from his phasia, his next words filled with malice and disgust.

"I will have my revenge."

* * * * * * * * * * * *

"This is not good of us. If we do what Shau-ling is ordering us to do, there is no way that we can truly survive," Warron said gruffly.

It had been an hour since they had entered the Council. Since then, Farax, Erdric and Jeroch had joined him and Zarsi. The silence in the chamber had been horrible, and Warron could no longer stand it. He had so much anger inside himself that he had to get out.

"What do you mean, Warron?" Zarsi asked.

"You know damn well what I mean, Zarsi. If Shau-ling goes through with the plan as is, we'll all end up being easy targets."

"Warron is right," Farax said in his high-pitched raspy voice, "by doing this, Shau-ling is condemning us as well as himself to death. We have never before had the war of power on when the *Coromor* has raised his ugly head."

"You're right," Jeroch added, "Shau-ling is too worried about spreading his power all over the world to care too much about us or the war for power."

"That is true, Jeroch," Warron responded, "but I never thought that I would hear you say it."

"Why wouldn't I? My neck is on the block just as much as all of yours now. If the war does start anew, we're all at risk."

"We don't have to be," Erdric interjected.

"What are you babbling on about, Erdric," Jeroch asked with a hint of anger in his voice.

"In years past when the war for power was on, there had been times where some of the phasia joined in treaties and pacts where there would be no hostility between them."

"Yes and all were promptly broken after the target kingdom was seized," Warron commented.

"Yes, but, the only other time that a pact of that kind was made was when the first *Coromor* came into being."

"That is true," Zarsi agreed, "but in that time we didn't have that maniac Saurn out there hunting us down with his pet monster. The *Chosen One* wasn't a factor then, and he never had the brunt of our attention."

"Ah," Erdric said quickly, "you have made my point for me, brother Zarsi. If we are divided and killing each other, we make ourselves easier for the *Coromor* and the rest of his breed to pick off. If we were to band together and vow that there be no hostilities between us, then there would be nothing to fear, and we would become more difficult targets to hit."

"Your point?" Jeroch urged.

"I propose a treaty, an alliance if you will. We will all vow that there will be no hostilities between the five of us gathered here, and the Great Dark One help us if we break that trust. Now, who is with me?"

One by one all of the phasia there added their voices to the treaty of peace. It was then that the lights flickered in the Council Chambers.

"It appears that brother Basille has returned from his mission to find Saurn," Jeroch commented.

"Yes," Farax added, "we should take our positions."

"Remember everyone," Erdric said as they moved to their places, "we have vowed not to attack any member of the phasia unless they stand against our lord Shau-ling."

"We have so vowed," the other four said in unison.

The bloody hell I will, Warron thought to himself, *if any of you come between me and ultimate power, I'll gut you before you can say a word.*

Reunion

Looking back at how everything started, the last thing Logan wanted to do was to start a fight. All he wanted was answers and he thought that he was certainly entitled to them. However, what was clear was that things had gone much farther than Logan had ever intended, and the situation had degenerated. Perhaps Logan shouldn't have entered Aryx's cabin armed. Aryx had kicked the chair away from the small table and already drawn his sword. Logan drew his own blade in response, and as the two stared across the table at one another Logan tried hard to remember what had gotten him to that point. What had he said that had taken Aryx down the road of armed conflict with the second Coromor of the prophecies? Would Aryx truly draw Logan's blood?

* * * * * * * * * * * *

The battle with Aldridge had left Logan more than exhausted, and the moment his head hit the pillow on the small bed in the crew quarters of the Monster of the Deep, he faded away into sleep. Because of the glowing and apparently threatening letter of passage from the Queen of Trelon, whatever superstitions about a woman's presence on a ship at sea being bad luck had been quashed quickly, and the captain of the vessel had surrendered his own personal quarters for the duration of the voyage. However, in deference to the beliefs of the men, Elwyne promised that she would only venture onto the deck in a state of emergency. She was certainly gracious and understanding even though in her heart she felt the superstition was nothing more than nonsense. Elwyne understood that the small crew of dedicated men were career sailors, and they were not going to put their lives or their vessel on the line, even for the fiancé of the *Coromor*. Elwyne couldn't begrudge them their beliefs. The group had all been through different things in their lives, and Elwyne understood that myths and legends were the only things that the sailors had left to go on while they were at sea, and who was she to go against their beliefs?

Logan awoke in the middle of the night. For a long time he lay there, trying to get back to sleep, but his mind would not relent. He kept running over the events of the past few days in his mind, and while at times it all seemed like one continuous nightmare, he could not shake the realization that everything had truly come to pass as he had experienced it. But there was another layer, one that existed beyond the memory, or perhaps just below it. There was still the phantom confrontation with Shau-ling, and the cryptic words the beast had spat at him. Forces were driving Logan to a confrontation with Shau-ling, and now it seemed not only Shau-ling but with the phasia as well. Aldridge had been just the first, and it was clear he wouldn't be the last. In his sleeping mind, there were shadows that always waited for him. The figures were malicious, foreboding, and terrifying. It was the remnants of those dreams, visions really, the forced Logan to sit up in bed. He put his feet on the floor and felt the gentle motion of the ship below him, and reached for his sword belt. Part of him wanted to leave the weapon behind, but if the past few days had taught him anything, it taught him that those situations that were supposed to be safe were potentially the most dangerous. Logan headed toward the top deck, but stopped by one of the small private cabins that were set aside for dignitaries that were being ferried from one place to another by royal decree. Logan noticed that the lamp in the room was still burning, an indication that the passenger was still awake. Logan raised his hand to knock at the door and hesitated. Finally, Logan knocked twice quickly on the door, prepared to move on if there was no answer. The door opened a moment later, and Logan barely saw Aryx before he pushed his way past the knight into the small room. Logan sat at on one of the chairs at the small table in the room, and waited for Aryx to join him.

"Good evening, my lord Dragon," he said a little put off by Logan's roughness, "to what do I owe the pleasure of this visit?"

"I'm not in the mood for that mindless court drivel that you have been pushing since day one," Logan replied angrily, "I'm here for some answers."

Aryx closed the door and then moved across the room to the table before cautiously sitting down across from Logan. There was a look in the man's eyes that Logan had never seen before. He looked as if he were puzzled, which would have been understandable, but there was also a twinge of fear in his eyes.

"What would you like to know?"

"Why have you been withholding information? You knew all along about the powers of the phasia, as well as other information about them, and I'm guessing that you know more than you've told us. Also, you've known about my powers ever since before you joined on with us, and you never mentioned them except in half-truths and riddles."

"What are you implying?" he said shocked at Logan's rough tone.

"I'm not implying anything, Aryx. I'm saying that you are not being truthful with me or with my friends, and in this position that could be hazardous to my life, as well as the lives of my friends."

"You do not know what you are talking about," he said coldly.

"Don't I? You knew all along that Allan was really one of the phasia, and you let me walk into the battle blind."

He turned back with fury in his eyes.

"I'm right, aren't I, traitor."

He pushed away from the table and stood, kicking the chair away so that it wouldn't impede him. It took only a moment before Aryx's sword was in his hands, and he had dropped into a defensive stance. Logan quickly stood and drew his own sword. The situation was spinning out of control quickly, but the subject was too important to let go. If it came to blows, that is what had to happen, and Logan was going to get his answers, no matter the cost. Perhaps Logan's first inclination was truer than he knew.

"How dare you call me a traitor," he thundered. "I was serving the forces of light before you were even born, and you have the audacity to call me a traitor?"

"What else would you call it, Aryx?" Logan replied gruffly. "What right do you have to draw your weapon on the *Coromon*? What right do you have to decide what information I need to know and what information I don't? You are supposed to answer my questions and follow my orders without question."

"I do not follow the orders of a headstrong boy who had no knowledge of what he is up against."

That made Logan even madder than he was before. It was clear that Aryx was holding something back, and Logan couldn't figure out what or why.

"The only reason I don't know what I'm up against is because you've been lying to me!"

The standoff continued for another minute before Gideon kicked the door open and stepped in front of Logan, blocking Aryx's path.

"What the hell are ye doin' Aryx?"

Aryx didn't answer. He dropped his sword onto the bed and turned away. Gideon pushed Logan out of the room and slammed the door behind them. He didn't say a word, and he led Logan to the captain's private cabin. Gideon knocked on the door, and Elwyne answered a minute later.

"What is it Gideon?" she said with concern heavy in her voice.

"Somethin's goin' on on dis boat, and dere's no way it's gonna keep goin' on. Someone'll answer for dis. Keep Logan 'ere."

Logan passed out before he even got into the room. Something was wrong with him and there was no answer for it. At least not one that was logical. Everything seemed to be turning wrong side out ever since the group had left Rama. Elwyne tucked Logan under the covers and lay down beside him, holding him as he slept. She was worried, but beyond that she was scared. There were times when Logan was breathing normally, and other times that he was breathing so shallowly that it seemed his breathing could stop at any moment. He was restless for the rest of the journey, but he did not leave the bed until the Monster of the Deep reached Falke. For three days Logan did not regain consciousness, and Elwyne did not leave his side. Talos and Gideon were the only visitors, but they did not remain longer than to bring meals and chat briefly before returning to whatever work Gideon had devoted his time to. Once arriving at the docks of Falke, Elwyne helped to rouse Logan, and though he was groggy and weak, he was able to make it off of the ship under his own power. Aryx was conspicuous by his absence, but once they reached the *Falke Inn*, Aryx was there waiting. Elwyne and Talos arranged for the rooms, and the rest stayed in the common room waiting. All of the tension and exhaustion that racked Logan's muscles was gone the second he entered the common room, and Gideon said that something similar had happened to him when he sat down at the table with Logan and the others. A few minutes into their respite, there were sounds coming from the other side of the door to the inn, and it was clear a moment later that something was very wrong.

* * * * * * * * * * *

The high reaching masts of the boats docked at Falke made Pike relax a little. The incident with Zarsi and Hawk two days earlier made everyone in the group a little jumpy, and they had all caught themselves looking over their shoulders at least once. Gwydeon and Midarin seemed to become more and more romantic during the trip to Falke, and in one of the towns they stopped in, Midarin shared a room with Gwydeon. Pike had romantic problems of his own to deal with. Eldar had been getting closer to him ever since he saved her life back in Sador. Technically they were already married, and they could not choose another, but Pike never thought that Eldar would ever want him back. Their past was too sordid to make any sense, and he could never point out the one argument or fight that had led to the break up. Then again, women had never made much sense to Pike.

Talon had also been surprisingly quiet the last couple of days. He was usually always ready with a song or a story if he thought that the group was becoming too serious for their own good, but now his mind seemed to be elsewhere. Pike began to think that Talon's experience with his powers and the battle with Zarsi had something to do with it, but he tried to ignore the painful memory of Gwydeon's injury. He shouldn't have survived, and Pike found himself grateful to his powers for saving yet another life.

Lane was the strange one of the group. He was never very talkative, but he had this way of knowing what others were thinking when he had to. He had proved invaluable in Sador and then again in Dalx, and Pike was counting his blessings that his friend had stayed with them from the beginning of the quest. He was not the most dynamic person, nor the one with the take-charge personality, but when he set his mind and his powers to something, it usually got done. Sometimes it was hard to even know he was there, but his magic had saved their lives twice. Pike would never again look past Lane about anything.

They hitched their horses at the public stables at the edge of town and decided to get some rooms at the local inn so they could wait for Logan. Pike saw several signs for a place called the *Falke Inn*, and they followed the arrows and were standing outside of the massive structure within minutes. This huge inn would have easily dwarfed the one they had frequented in Aradon, and Pike found himself wondering how many people could have stayed in such a mammoth building. Pike started to walk through the door, but Talon grabbed him on the shoulder and spun him around. Pike turned and looked on as Talon pointed out a man down the alley.

"Isn't that Aryx?"

Pike looked harder at the form in front of them. He could almost make out the face and the clothing, but suddenly the man turned toward them, and the flash of gold on the man's hand told the story well enough.

"Aryx!" Gwydeon said quickly.

Suddenly a bolt of lightning erupted from the Aryx's gauntlet and sent the six of them diving for cover. The lightning bolt splattered against a building behind them leaving a dark smudge on the wall. Midarin jumped to her feet and fired an arrow down the alley before Pike even knew that she had nocked one. The girl was fast, probably faster than even Aryx. The arrow sailed down the alley and stuck Aryx in the arm. There was another flash of lightning and several arrows of light flew the length of the alley in a second and struck. Midarin did not expect the counter attack, and had it not been for Gwydeon diving through the air and dragging her to the ground, she surely would have been killed. Mammoth claps of thunder raged everywhere, and Aryx turned toward the six of them and started toward them. Pike was on his feet again, and he was looking at Lane. Lane nodded, sensed the plan, and after a flash of recognition from Talon, the now familiar shattered ice trick began to take shape. Aryx had attacked a member of their party without provocation, and for that, the kid-gloves came off. Before they could do anything, another bolt of lightning raced toward them. Pike didn't see it until it was far too late.

* * * * * * * * * * * *

Logan was on his feet and out the door with Gideon barely a step behind him. As soon as he jerked the door open he only had a moment to react as the blast of lightning burst by the door. Gideon dragged Logan to the ground as the bolt passed over them, and by the time the two men got back to their feet, Logan saw the target of the strike and was shocked and confused. Pike and the rest of his group entered Logan's field of vision, but a moment later another bolt of lightning crossed the distance, aimed directly at Pike's chest. Logan knew that he had to act. Instantly, Logan's hand darted out in front of his face and caught the bolt of lightning before it could strike. When Pike turned and saw his friend's somewhat bewildered face, he was more puzzled than ever. Pike wanted to say something, but more lightning was racing toward them. Logan grabbed Pike and pulled him out of harm's way. Gideon helped the rest of the group dive for cover as more and more lightning pulsed from Aryx's hands out of the alley.

"What the hell's going on, Logan!" Pike yelled over the crashing thunder.

"I don't know Pike, but I think we have to take Aryx down before he can do any serious damage." Logan answered.

"We've already got a plan, Logan," Pike assured me, "but we need a couple seconds to pull it off."

"I'll try to buy you some time."

"Logan."

"What is it Pike?"

"Do you want him contained or killed?"

Pike's face was dead serious. This was the question that Logan hadn't expected. Pike and Talon had apparently harnessed their powers to a lethal intensity. Pike was ready to kill Aryx, and now Logan knew it.

"Did he attack first?"

"Yes."

"Take him down, but don't kill him. I have to know why he's doing this."

The attacks of lightning had not slowed down, and Pike looked back more than a little worried.

"What if we can't contain him?"

"Then kill him, but only at my order."

"I'll do my best."

He turned and motioned to Talon. Talon nodded back and put up three fingers. Pike nodded and motioned for Gideon who was just emerging from the open door of the inn.

"What da hell is goin' on?"

"That's what we'd all like to know, Gideon," Pike answered. "Aryx has started this little war, and we're going to finish it."

"What ya need me ta do?"

"You think you can manage a little rock wall behind him?"

"Give me three seconds and ye'll 'ave it."

Pike nodded and waived back at Talon. Talon pointed to Lane and nodded. Logan was trying to follow the unspoken strategy, but didn't have the faintest idea what they were planning. Whatever it was, it was going to have to be impressive to take down someone as powerful as Aryx.

"We're ready Logan," Pike said. "I could use that diversion now."

Logan nodded, and it felt strange that Logan was needed for something like a diversion when his powers were supposed to be greater than theirs. The attacks of lightning and fire had lessened for the moment, so Logan rolled out into the alley and stood up. Aryx stopped in his tracks when he saw Logan, but that lack of motion didn't last long. Blue and white streaks of lightning erupted from his outstretched hands. Logan extended his hand and caught the onslaught. The fires began to burn the skin on his hand, but he did his best to block out the pain. The force Aryx exerted through his attacks was amazing, and it was all Logan could do to hold his ground.

"Now!" Pike screamed.

Out of the corner of Logan's eye, he saw Pike and Talon emerge from their hiding places. Gideon rolled out behind Logan, and though the sparks of light, he saw a wall of rock rise behind Aryx. Aryx's attention did not turn away from Logan, and the intensity of his onslaught increased. With his free hand, Logan reached out and grabbed Gideon by the arm, and suddenly Logan could feel a jolt of power race through him. Gideon stood and thrust his other hand into the bolts of lightning. Talon motioned to Pike again and ran up to Logan. He put his right hand on Logan's shoulder and thrust his left into the light. Logan could feel the power rushing though him. It felt as though heart would burst as the sweet sensations of power flooded through him. A green wave of light extended from their hands and pushed back the lightning. The three joined were pushing back Aryx's powers. In less than a minute the wave of power had pushed back the lightning to Aryx's hands. He was struggling to maintain control, but after one last surge of brilliant green energy, his concentration broke and the green light overtook him.

"Now Pike!" Talon screamed.

Water flooded from Pike's fingers. Aryx had no time to recover before he was soaked with water.

"Lane!"

Even before his name was yelled by Pike, Lane's staff sailed through the air and struck Aryx in the face. The aim apparently was a little much, but it did its job well. The water froze on the impact of the staff, and Aryx was encased in a prison of ice. Logan started to approach, but Talon held him back.

"We've seen people break out of that before Logan, I would be careful if I were you."

"Thanks for the warning Talon, and I have to say that I am more than impressed. I think we make a pretty good team the five of us."

"Just think what would've happened if Pike had joined da link," Gideon added.

Pike smiled and followed Talon and Logan down the alley. As Logan approached the prison of ice, he could see every feature of Aryx perfectly preserved in the ice. Lane recovered his staff and slightly brushed up against the living statue. The ice sculpture that used to be a living person fell backwards and shattered. Lane stammered for an excuse, but when Pike threw up his hand, all remained silent.

"Aryx wasn't frozen," was all he said.

"How can that be Pike?" Talon asked quickly. "We all saw him covered in the water, and we all saw the staff hit him."

"Remember when we fought the army in Dalx?" Pike asked.

"Yes."

That was certainly a story Logan couldn't wait to hear.

"Remember when you shattered them?"

"Sure."

Now Logan was sure. This was definitely a story he wanted to hear.

"There were red shards, shards that looked like blood. Look. There is only the clear crystal, and there is certainly not enough of it here to have been from Aryx."

"So what are ye sayin'?" Gideon asked.

"Aryx isn't here. He wasn't frozen, and I don't think he was the one attacking us," Pike answered.

"Good theory, at least from what I've heard," Logan answered. "But it leaves the obvious question. Who was attacking us, and where did they go?"

Lane patted Logan on the shoulder and pointed to the wall on their right. A look over in that direction revealed what Lane had indicated, a glowing green arrow pointing down at a grate near the ground. The grate looked like the passage behind it was large enough to crawl through, and it was perhaps the escape route for the mysterious attacker.

"That looks like an open invitation to me," Talon said quickly.

"Everything looks like an open invitation to you, Talon," Pike answered sarcastically.

"We should go in," Gideon interjected.

"Agreed," Logan added.

"Should I get the others?" Lane asked.

"No. You go back into the inn and keep everyone else there. I told them to stay put, but you saw how well Gideon took my orders, and it's a safe bet that the others will be along shortly. Besides, I think the four of us can handle this one."

Lane nodded and grabbed Midarin and Eldar as he walked back toward the inn. Gideon pulled loose the grate and motioned for Logan to go in first. After a nod, he wedged himself into the opening. At best, Logan had expected a small tight tunnel, but when he fell into the wide spacious cellar that was apparently below the *Falke Inn*, he was more than pleasantly surprised. The others fell in behind shortly after, and they stood up and started looking around.

"Well," Talon said surveying the area, "it could have been worse. It could have been a sewer."

Gideon tapped Logan on the shoulder and pointed to the ground. Another one of the green arrows was painted on the ground, and it pointed down toward the north end of the cellar. Racks of wine bottles lined the walls, and several racks sat out in the middle of the room marking something like crooked aisles. They followed the green arrows down several aisles, and then eventually came to the northwest corner of the cellar. There in the floor was a rickety old ladder. Each climbed down the ladder in turn, with Logan going last. When his feet hit the water below, he turned to Talon.

"You were saying?"

Talon nodded in defeat, and then pointed down the passage. There was a pulsating green light coming from the far end of the chamber, and the group started in that direction. The water came up to their ankles, and the water was cold, colder than it probably should have been. Within a minute, they had crossed through the flooded chamber into a one with a higher elevation and a dry floor. It wasn't a large chamber, but it was spacious enough that the four men could stand side by side with almost an arm's length between them. In the center of the chamber was a pedestal, and on the pedestal was the source of the green light.

Imagine that you could freeze a flame. Cut off a portion at the top of the flame and then color the icy flame black. After you've done that, place diamonds, sapphires, emeralds, and azure stones all over it. That picture would best describe the item that lay on the pedestal. Logan started to approach it, but a figure stepped out of the shadows and barred the path to the object. The form looked very much like Aryx, but it was clear from the bright green light that radiated from the man's eyes that it was not.

"Welcome to the Chamber of the Flame gentlemen. I am Asperon Thorne. You are the *Coromor* of the prophecies, yes, I know. The three men with you are Gideon Viruci, Talon Aielin, and Pike Rhuiden, members of the *Erieal.* I am the Guardian of the Flame."

"Why do ye look like Aryx?" Gideon asked.

"I took his body to test you to see if you were worthy to take possession of the Jeweled Dragon's Flame. Thanks to your combined powers, you were able to defeat me, and thus you may lay claim to the sacred Flame."

"What about Aryx?" Talon asked.

"Once you take possession of the Flame, I will disappear, and Aryx will return to you unharmed. He will not remember any of the last day, and you are not to tell him anything of this ordeal. He will be made aware of enough when he sees that the Flame is in your possession."

"Master Thorne," Pike said quickly, "what do we do now?"

"That is truly up to you. I do believe that it would be in your best interests to consult this man Aryx Terian. He is truly a powerful ally, and his heart is good."

"That is all well and good," Logan replied annoyed, "but I find it hard to trust a man who keeps secrets from us, secrets that could get us all killed in the end."

"All men have secrets, Logan," he answered, "even you. Do not fault a man who makes choices in his life if you will not fault yourself. Men's motivations come from many sources, and until you understand the source, you can never understand the man. Sometimes a man cannot understand the motivations behind his own actions because he does not know himself."

Thorne paused for a moment.

"Or perhaps he cannot remember himself."

Shaking himself from his own internal dialogue the guardian fixed his eyes back on Logan.

"Take possession of the Jeweled Dragon's Flame and follow the green arrows back to the *Falke Inn*. Remember that you are not to speak of me or anything that you have seen here. Now, go."

Aryx's body slumped to the ground. Logan picked up the Jeweled Dragon's Flame and placed it in a bag that hung from the side of the pedestal. Pike and Talon picked up Aryx's limp body and the five made their way back to the cellar. The ladder had been replaced with a staircase, and they followed the green arrows through the cellar to another set of stairs. Emerging from the doorway, they found themselves back in the common room of the inn. By this time Aryx had recovered, they all were sitting around a huge table and enjoying a drink and catching up on the events of the past few days.

"Well," Pike said taking a sip of ale, "we have the Jeweled Dragon's Flame. What do we do now?"

"The Monster of the Deep will take us to Marcwell by way of the town of Taren," Aryx answered. "There is one other thing that we must do in Taren before we can meet Lord Cedric in Marcwell. Now, if you will excuse me. I will see you all tomorrow morning on the deck of the Monster of the Deep."

With that he got up and walked away.

"Not exactly the friendly type now of days is he?" Elwyne said as he walked up the stairs. "He's been that way ever since Aldridge died."

"And who exactly is Aldridge?" Eldar asked.

"A very mean boy, lass," Gideon answered. "One of da phasia. Logan took him down after he revealed dat he was da one who killed Lady Anne Binosear."

"Lord Cedric's sister?" Gwydeon asked a little shocked.

"It's a long story, my young friend," Talos interjected.

"Now," Logan asked leaning further over the table, "what have you been up to the last couple of days?"

"Well," Pike answered, "we also had a run in with one of the phasia, and I'm happy to report that we killed him."

"As if that weren't enough," Midarin chimed in, "we also had to deal with a child of one of the other phasia."

"Some of the phasia have children?" Elwyne asked shocked.

"I was as surprised to hear about it as you were Elwyne," Pike replied. "Thanks to Lane though, we were able to take care of him."

"And I thought we were busy," Logan said scratching the burn on his shoulder. "But we didn't go up against any armies, let alone two. All we had to do was run through a burning building and save a princess."

"You get all the easy jobs," Pike said trying to hold back the laughter.

Chapter XI

The Puppetmaster Calls

Korrd rolled his head slowly from side to side as he awoke. He sat up and looked around quickly. His sword still lay there beside him, and as he looked at the blade, he noticed that it was covered in blood. He grabbed a partially burned rag off of the ground near him and then cleaned his blade slowly. As he polished his blade, he looked up and saw Caris' dead body lying at the foot of the throne. He rose to his feet slowly, trying to shake out the remaining remnants of sleep that still fogged his mind. He stood for a moment trying to regain his composure, and then he walked out toward the palace gates. His head still swam from the earlier battle with Caris, and only had fragmented memories of the battle itself. As he entered the hallway that led to the palace gates, he tripped over the body of a fallen Jeresei, and that's when he began to snap back into the reality of the situation. The haze that clouded his mind dissipated, and he began to realize more and more of what had happened mere minutes earlier. The Jeresei had proven effective against the men in the armies that they battled, but once they were faced with Caris, they had been utterly defeated. The same fate had been encountered by the army of Illimar when they came face to face with superior numbers of Jeresei. Despite the apparent victory though, there was still an incredible cost. Two armies of innocents had been trapped into this little war, and he knew somewhere in the back of his mind that the fight was far from over. As he walked through the palace gates and into the streets of Illimar, he noticed that the streets were empty and that no one could be seen from the widows of the houses. As he wandered further into the town, he began to notice that the fallen bodies of men in all of the armies no longer had their swords and shields in their dead hands.

Before long, Korrd made his way out to the Great Bridge that served as the only safe way in and out of Illimar. He walked out slowly onto the bridge, clutching his sword in one hand and a mysteriously aching rib in the other. Whatever had rendered him unconscious after the battle with Caris had certainly taken its toll on him physically. When he looked out onto the glade; Korrd saw what had become of the civil war that had erupted in Illimar. The Army of Illimar had been completely wiped out except for a few stragglers that still hung onto the banners and flags as they joined one of the other armies in the fray. The other contender in the fray was Caris' army which was denoted by the black wolf that was on their banners and the breastplates of their armor. They looked as if they still had a large amount of their force remaining, and were battling hard to complete the takeover of their town. The third force should have never been there in the first place. The Army of the Dragon had been baited into the fray by a warped scheme of one of the phasia.

There was a new army entering the fray now though. This army was not marked by flags or even by shiny armor with emblem covered breastplates. These were not high-born knight with money or power, most of them could not even furnish enough money to have a good hot meal every night. These were the common men and women of Illimar. When the battle for control of their town had broken out in the streets below their windows, they were not going to be shut out by another dictator. They decided, when they saw that an army of total strangers was fighting for them, that they would no longer sit by and let others make the decisions for them. They would now have a hand in their own destiny.

Korrd watched as the commoner army waded into the fight with reckless abandon. Now it would be very little time before one of the groups had enough strength in number to vanquish the other and take over the town. Korrd knew that whichever army won the battle, he would be in great danger. If Caris' army won, they would want him dead for killing their queen. If the Army of the Dragon won, they would want him dead not only for killing Antrobus, but also for killing Leane Torne. The only way that he would be safe would be if the group of commoners was to destroy both Caris' army and the Army of the Dragon. Korrd knew all too well though that wasn't very likely to happen.

After watching the battle for mere seconds, he turned around and hurried back toward the palace gates. He knew that if he was spotted, he was dead anyway. If no one knew he was there until he wanted them to, he had a chance to make it out of Illimar alive. There were only a few options left open to him that didn't include his death at the end of them. He entered the palace minutes later, and then began to pull off his shirt as he ran toward the throne room. As he threw his shirt to the ground, he unfastened his light chain mail, and then threw it into a pile of discarded weapons. By the time that he made it back into the throne room, and looked out into the courtyard below, it was obvious that the battle was finally over. He took a deep breath and then ran out onto the foyer trying his best to look panicked. Almost immediately, he was spotted by the group of commoners and army men.

"Come quick!" Korrd shouted his voice intentionally wavering. "Someone has murdered the queen!"

Within minutes, the throne room was filled with people. The crowd filtered in quickly, trying to get a glimpse of what had happened. Several people made statements concerning the dead men in the room, while still others pointed out that they were not men at all, but monstrous Jeresei. The examination of the queen and the forms around her went on for some time. No one seemed to care as Korrd walked out of the room. As he walked down the crowded passage that led out to the courtyard, many people noticed him and asked him what the throne room looked like, and if the queen was really dead. He tried his best to look disturbed and worried, which wasn't very hard considering he was the murderer that everyone was looking for, and he answered their questions. When he finally made it out of the palace, he collected his sword from the place he had hidden it, and then he walked toward the Great Bridge.

As he walked through town, he noticed that a saddled horse had been left hitched to a post near a small alley. No one appeared to be watching the horse, so he walked over and stood for a moment. As he stood there beside the horse, he took a morsel of food out of his pocket and fed it to the horse. After another minute of standing there, he untied the horse from the post and led it toward the Great Bridge. As casual as possible, he walked out of the town limits of Illimar and started back toward Rama. He mounted the horse and began to ride back down the Old River Road. The sun was shining on this trip, and Korrd was happy that the rain was gone for now. Some of the storm clouds still lingered in the skies above him, but they would prove not to be a threat for the rest of the day. The only lead that he had was to go back to Rama and hope that another letter from Lord Saurn was there waiting on him. It would take him a day or a day and a half for him to reach Rama, but there was still no guarantee that Saurn would be there waiting for him. He could always try his folding space trick that he had used with the Jeresei, but something told him that it was not safe. Until Saurn taught him to use the phasia portals, he would have to travel by foot and by horse. He rode on for a good while longer, and then it happened.

It was like time slowed down for a few seconds, and Korrd found himself moving like he was under water. The dark clouds rolled in thicker than he had ever seen them. There was a flash of lightning and then a huge clap of thunder. Korrd's horse spooked at the sound and then bolted out from under him. He was jolted from the saddle, and he began to fall to the ground. That same instant, the lightning flashed again, and Korrd found himself floating again in the nothingness of the Blight. The shock of not hitting the ground stifled him for a moment, and when he realized that he was in the Blight, his fears and discomforts were not soothed. There was a part of him that never did want to serve the Shau, and being here where all of that evil started made that voice scream out in terror. There was still a sort of strange familiarity with the Blight that stayed with Korrd. Even though the flames had not appeared, he was still able to reorient himself. After a few minutes, the stone floor appeared, and he was standing again waiting for his mysterious benefactor, Lord Saurn. He wandered around for a minute, trying his best to keep patient and wait for his master, but he failed miserably. Suddenly, two huge flames burst into existence not three feet in front of him. Seconds later, Lord Saurn stepped out of the center of the flames.

"My lord," Korrd said quickly.

CHAPTER 11

"You have done very well young one. Killing a phase is not an easy task, even for a man such as yourself. Killing one with more experience in the ways of their powers must have proven to be a difficult task."

"Indeed it was Lord Saurn. I must say that your sister is a very power fighter, and that I was lucky in defeating her."

"That may be true Korrd, but you did defeat her. All of my siblings are powerful fighters, and I must say that Caris was physically the weakest of the ten. You appear to have escaped the fray unscathed, young one."

"Her attacks were easily avoided, my lord. My powers proved to overmatch hers as you had anticipated. It appears as if my powers heighten my reactions and instincts in battle."

"Really? That might prove to be an interesting side-effect to your powers. How did you handle the absorption?"

Korrd looked at Saurn puzzled for a moment, and then did his best to respond to the question.

"Absorption?"

"Yes, young one. Every time the *Coromor*, the *Chosen One*, or one of the *Erieal* kills one of the phasia, he absorbs that phase's special talent. However, because none of the other phasia know who has what power, it is impossible to tell who killed who."

Korrd just stared at Saurn.

"What I mean is when the phasia battle and kill each other we would absorb the other's power much like you would. The only downfall is that we do not retain these powers from one lifetime to the next. The other part is that a single phase will never possess the same exact power twice. My power in this lifetime is the ability to instantaneously teleport to anywhere without the use of a portal. Because of that, my movements are untraceable by the other phasia."

"I can do that," Korrd said quickly.

Saurn was more than a bit shocked at Korrd's bold and seemingly rash statement. He looked straight at Korrd for a moment and then took a step toward him.

"What?"

"When you were explaining to me about my powers, you were telling me that it was possible for me to speed up my attacks by using my powers to fold the space between me and my opponent, so the flame, or whatever I was using at the time, would travel from point A to point B without crossing the intervening space. Well, as I was trying out my new powers, and thinking about what I could do with them, I thought about what you said. I thought that maybe there was more than just flame and energy that I could push through that fold in space. I thought that maybe I could push a person or maybe myself through. So, when I was in Illimar, I decided to try that out.

"I was standing on the Great Bridge watching the battle. The Jeresei force was struggling against the Army of the Dragon, and as I was looking around the battlefield, I saw the leader of the Jeresei force. Without even thinking, I just folded the space between him and me, and mentally pulled him through."

"That is a very dangerous trick young one. Original, but still very dangerous. I wouldn't recommend that you try that yourself," Saurn cautioned.

"Why?"

"There is a chance that you could end up dead. Imagine that you step through the portal and something causes you to lose concentration for just a second or two. I think that's about all it would take for the space that you had folded to unfold and scatter the pieces of you all along that stretch of space."

"Ouch," Korrd said quietly.

"Exactly. If you intend on trying that little stunt, or any of your other powers for that matter, you are probably going to need this."

Saurn reached into the pocket of his cloak and pulled out a coin. The coin was big enough to fit into the palm of a man's hand. It was made out of a sort of black metal, but when the light caught it, none of the light reflected. The surface of the coin still remained dull. On one side of the coin, there was the same viper symbol from the letters standing out from the rest of the surface of the smooth quarter-inch thick coin.

"Think of this as a key. Place it in the palm of your hand which carries my mark, and then close your fist. The next time you use your powers, you will notice that you are able to do things much faster, and with greater accuracy. Also, the strength of your powers will be magnified."

Korrd took the coin from Saurn and looked at it for a few seconds before placing it in the pocket of his breeches.

"Now, I put the question to you again. How did you handle the absorption?"

"I don't really remember too much about the aftermath of the battle my lord. I remember a little about the battle itself, and some of the things that I did with my powers, but as to specifics and times, my memory is still a little hazy. All I really remember is waking up with my sword in my hand and seeing her lying dead at the foot of her throne."

"The magical feedback of the power transfer must have rendered you unconscious young one. No matter. Do you feel the power that you absorbed? It will stand out from the rest of them."

Korrd put his hand in his pocket without thinking and clutched the coin. He began to feel strange, like he had just woken up from a long, deep sleep. He closed his eyes and looked deep into his own mind. Memories flooded in to meet him, but he had no time to be sorting through them, trying to figure out which were his and which belonged to another set of lifetimes. He stood there for a long few moments, and nothing appeared to be happening. Then, his face and body began to change. First his face and body shifted to that of Caris. Then it changed to Saurn, and then his appearance would shift randomly between the people in his memories. When he opened his eyes, his body had returned to its normal shape and appearance, he was Korrd again.

"Amazing," Saurn remarked, "Caris had the power to change the appearance of her face as well as her body. I am going to assume that she also had the power to disguise her voice as well. It was a very fitting power for her personality. No wonder she was able to take over her kingdom so quickly in this lifetime. I should have suspected that from her. No matter."

"What is my next target lord?" Korrd chimed in.

"Are you ready for another chore already young one? You have not been here more than ten minutes after you killed my sister, and already you want to take on another of my siblings. I like your enthusiasm. I have a bit more of a challenge for you this time though young one. Make your way toward Kandor any way that you please, but I would refrain from teleporting anywhere in the vicinity of any of the major kingdoms. There is no telling where my brothers have entrenched themselves. If the flag of the Vulture still flies over Kandor, you will find my brother Farax sitting on the throne there. Kill him."

"Yes, Lord Saurn."

* * * * * * * * * * * *

Illimar. The clouds began to roll in as the commoners and the members of the Army of the Dragon alike began to bury the dead from the massive battle that had just occurred there. This war was the worst kind imaginable, a senseless one. There was no reason for all of those people to be dead, common or high-born, they were still people. However, one of the people among them was not a commoner, nor was she a member of the might Army of the Dragon. She wasn't even supposed to be alive. She walked unnoticed through the crowd like a ghost, and if certain parties inside and outside of Illimar would have had their way, she would have been a ghost. The so-called queen of Illimar was still very much alive though, and she was far from human. She was in fact the only daughter of Shau-ling, and she was also the most devious of all of the phasia. She was Caris, the Wolf.

She really shouldn't have survived. Saurn had caught her completely off guard when he threw the *Chosen One* at her. Her powers had barely been enough to keep her alive and she knew it. Any fool who would go one-on-one with the *Chosen One* deserved to die a painful death. Basille had learned that lesson first when he took it upon himself to tangle with Aerith Seth. No one but Saurn had dared to try and get close since then, for good reason.

There was a part of the prophecies that were still hazy in the minds of not only the phasia, but also the wise ones and Shau-ling. The *Chosen One* was supposed to be far more powerful than the *Coromor* was ever supposed to be. What was also very rarely known was that if one of the phasia were to ever join either the *Coromor* or the *Chosen One*, that they would be able to vanquish all of the other phasia as well as Shau-ling. It was not a pleasant thought that Saurn was actually acting on the prophecy.

This plan had better work. I've given up too much for this plan to fail. I've given up my kingdom, my ties to the rest of the phasia, my ability to draw an army from Shau-ling, and to top it all off, I had to give up my changeling powers. It had to be done though. I had to convince Saurn that I was dead, and I knew that the first thing that he would check would be if Korrd had been able to absorb my power. If he wouldn't have been convinced, I would have never been able to proceed with my plan. All of them will pay for this treachery though. Saurn may have control of the Chosen One, *but that will matter very little once I have total control of the* Coromor.

Caris walked through the crowd slowly, trying to keep her identity a secret. Everyone may think that Queen Saris is dead, but it would be very hard to explain how she seeming looked exactly like her. Her pace was almost methodical, too slow and aimless to be the gait of anyone important. Her ruse turned out to be more effective than she had ever planned. But her gait had never been part of the disguise. She was merely walking the way that she felt at the time. Her thoughts were turned inward, and the voices and vivid images that she had pulled from Korrd's mind had begun to haunt her. The voices screamed curses, wondering where they were, and why they had been robbed of their home. She still retained control though, and her mind proved to be less susceptible to the voices' interventions than Korrd's. The voices eventually died out, and Caris' mind was again free to think.

Saurn thought he was so clever. That mental wall he created might have been able to hold out some of my brothers and their feeble mental abilities, but against me, it was little more than a wall of wet parchment. None of the other phasia are as gifted in the telepathic aspect as I am, not even Saurn. Perhaps that was why I was his target.

Saurn proved to be more clever than I had anticipated. He knew that I would break through the wall in Korrd's mind, so then if I survived, I would be plagued, or at least distracted by the voices and images until Korrd recovered to kill me. Too bad that such a brilliant plan would have to fail. To think that once long ago, Saurn and I were willing allies. No matter, now that I have seen inside Korrd Ranthall's mind, I know that he is nowhere near worth worrying over. His role in this is small, the fact that he is the Chosen One *notwithstanding. Now that I know that his brother Logan is the* Coromor, *I have an edge over my ambitious brothers. Logan Ranthall will soon be mine, not Elwyne Tamerlane's.*

She laughed quietly to herself and then continued to walk through the streets of Illimar. She walked until she came to a place that she remembered seeing in Korrd's mind. She remembered the duel and the girl Leane falling to the ground, mortally wounded. As she looked around, she found the girl. On the ground near a growing pile of dead bodies lay a short-haired girl clutching her sword in one hand, and a gaping wound in the other. She had done a very good job of stopping the bleeding, but she had long since passed out, and soon she would be dead. Caris could tell that the girl was still breathing and that she still had some time left. She took the girl up in her arms and carried her into a nearby secluded alley.

A pleasure to meet you Miss Torne. You are going to be my accomplice in this little plan that I've cooked up. You are going to help me get to a man named Gwydeon Sandar, a friend of yours I believe. Then, through him we will get to Logan Ranthall. If what Korrd remembers about you is true, we could take control of the Coromor *and alienate the* Erieal *in one fell swoop.*

Caris looked down at the girl for a moment and then noticed that she was beginning to regain consciousness.

"W...who are y..y..you?"

"Simply a friend my dear sweet girl. Soon though, you and I will be close friends, inseparable in fact."

Caris put her hand on Leane's forehead and then closed her eyes. She felt a twinge of pain run through her body as she made the connection with Leane. Caris moved her hand down to Leane's stomach, and relaxed her mind. Within seconds, the wound began to close, and then it was completely healed. Caris kept her hand firmly planted on Leane's forehead and concentrated.

This would have been much easier had I not had to give up my shifting powers. I could have just let this girl die, dispose of the body, and then just become her. I have never physically melded with a person before, and to actually think about it frightens me. Other members of the phasia have done it before, but not me. I never thought I would have to, but I guess I was wrong. I hope we both survive.

Caris twitched a little and then bared back down to her task. Within a matter of seconds, Caris began to disappear. After a minute, she was completely gone. At that very moment, Leane's eyes snapped open, and she sat up. Quickly she examined herself, and then the closed wound in her stomach.

Strange, the thoughts said inside Leane's mind. *I can feel through Leane's body. Her consciousness is still here, but it is subdued. Now it is time for the real test.*

"Hello? Hello?"

Leane's voice. This is more than I could have hoped for. Excellent, there is a chance that . . .

"Commander! Commander Torne!" a man yelled.

She turned her head and looked at the man who was rapidly approaching her. Caris knew that she had never met this man before in her life, but Leane had. This was one of Leane's best friends. So through Leane, Caris knew this man well. Every thought, every memory, they shared. Inwardly Caris wondered if the street traveled both ways.

"I'm here Sol."

"Are you all right commander? We saw you going after that man you called Korrd, and when you didn't emerge, we thought that bastard had killed you."

"It wasn't much Sol, merely a flesh wound. Now, what is the situation here in Illimar, I haven't seen much of the battle. He must have knocked me out."

"Queen Saris has been murdered."

"Are there any leads as to who is responsible?" Leane asked.

"No, Commander. I know that you believed that Antrobus' murderer would come here, and perhaps you were right and that individual is responsible for Queen Saris' death as well. If you would share the identity of this villain, it would help our search greatly."

Caris considered for a moment.

"I only had the vaguest description from the girl who found Antrobus' body. I'll make sure it is distributed to all the men."

Of course Caris had no interest in having the Army of the Dragon hunting down Korrd. She would have her own revenge in time, so any description she was to give would lead as far away from Korrd as possible.

"Who has taken command of the army Sol? What is the status? How many of us survived the fray?"

"We lost three hundred during the battle commander. Third battalion was completely destroyed. When you fell, Ebios raised the banner himself and took command of the army."

"Take me to him."

Sol saluted and turned back toward the street. Leane smiled quickly to herself and then rose and started to follow him. Soon, Leane found herself standing in an all too familiar throne room, facing a group of men and women she hardly knew. Most were excited to see her, and when she was finally through all the jubilant followers and lieutenants, she was led to the acting commander, Ebios. Ebios was slightly taller than Leane, and though he was more muscular than Leane, they had roughly the same build. They had been friends for many years, and after they had done their training in the Raman army together, they became even closer. Now they were almost like brother and sister.

This will be the greatest test. Being around all of these familiar people has put a strain on my control over Leane. She is starting to break through my little block, and she is becoming more and more difficult as the minutes pass. If I lose control of her now, I'm lost. If I retain control and am able to fool this Ebios fellow that Leane seems to care for so much, my power will be supreme.

"Leane!" Ebios exclaimed as soon as he saw Leane.

He rushed from where he was standing and grabbed Leane up in his arms. While on the outside of Leane, everything seemed warm, caring, and safe, inside of her, a silent war was beginning.

Where am I? Leane's thoughts called.

Shut up girl! Caris' thoughts screamed back.

Where am I? Who are you? What are you doing in my head? Leane's thoughts demanded.

Quiet!

Leane's thoughts struck back for a moment and then went silent. The battle of wills had ended for now, and Caris still retained control of the body.

"Ebios," Leane said calmly, "how are you old friend?"

"I am fine now that I know that you are safe."

"Thank you for your vigilance and courage in the face of the current adversity. However, I must ask."

"The Army of the Dragon stands ready for your command Commander Torne."

"Thank you Ebios."

Leane walked up the small set of stairs that led to the throne of Illimar and then turned to face her people.

"My friends. You have all fought well to save your lives and the lives of the people who dwell here in Illimar. This petty civil war is now over, but its beginnings still remain a mystery. Though the fog that hangs over us is about to be pulled back. You all came here ready to fight an opponent that was given to us by Shau-ling, but instead of killing Jeresei, we ended up slaughtering our own kind. This battle was not fought in vain however.

"The civil war that was just now beginning was not caused by civil unrest. Nor was it caused by unfair taxes, poor army defense, or even the brutalizing of citizens by member of the Army of Illimar. No, this civil war was nothing more than a plot hatched by Shau-ling and his phasia to destroy not only the town of Illimar and their resistance in the name of the Lion, but also to destroy the Army of the Dragon, his hand and fire in battle."

Everyone in the throne room reacted with disbelieving looks and scattered conversation. None reacted more strongly than the commoners though.

"Please, listen. You have yet to hear the depths to which this deception sunk. The Queen of Illimar, Queen Saris, never should have sat on this throne. She was no more of a human than were the Jeresei whose bodies you see littering this room. Saris was none other than Caris, the one and only daughter of Shau-ling."

The conversation and mumbling stopped, and it seemed as if everyone in the crowd was dumbfounded.

"How is it then, that this mystery man, the one who almost killed you, killed the phase Caris?" Sol asked.

"That's an easy explanation, Sol," Ebios interjected, "this assassin must have been one of the other phasia in disguise. Obviously the War for Power has started again in earnest."

"This is my suspicion as well, Ebios," Caris agreed. "There is a way to find out though. That will require the Army of the Dragon to mobilize again though. Sol, send the order that we will march for Kandor tomorrow at first light. I have reason to believe that this will be the assassin's next target. There have been rumors that the phase Farax has been commanding the kingdom there."

"Yes, commander."

"After you do so, return here."

"Yes commander," Sol said. He saluted to his commander and then turned to leave the room and relay the orders.

"Who is the commander of the commoner army that I have heard assisted my forces in the final battle?"

A young farmer stepped forward and saluted. He raised his sword for a moment in honor to the commander and then bowed his head. Leane returned the salute quickly and then smiled.

"A soldier, eh?" Leane asked.

"No Commander Torne, at least, not any more. We do not have any formal commanders, but I suppose that I serve the closest to that function."

"Very well. What is your name, and where did you serve?"

"I am Jerrard Mystic, formerly of the Lion's Mane."

"Well, how many of your army would be willing to become the Illimar extension of the Army of the Dragon, with you as their leader."

"All of us," Jerrard replied without hesitation.

"Very well, Captain Jerrard. You may send all of your reports to Commander Ebios as he will be ruling Illimar in the Lord Dragon's name."

"Thank you Leane."

"You've earned it Ebios," she replied smiling.

It was at that moment that Sol returned to the throne. He made his way to the foot of the throne and then saluted Leane.

"Your orders have been passed to the men, Commander Torne."

"Very good Sol. Now, gather a force of fifty men and women out of both the new Illimar army and the existing Army of the Dragon, and then return to Rama."

"But commander . . ."

"Not buts, Sol. I have to send someone back to replace Antrobus and send reports to the Lord Dragon, now don't I?"

Sol's face lit up like a young child's, and then he quickly regained his composure and saluted. Leane smiled and then returned the salute.

"As for the rest of us, tomorrow we march for Kandor."

For Every Action

Basille stepped out of the portal and emerged in his own throne room again. He had stayed longer in the Blight than he had ever intended to, but his brother's final words still tugged at him. Saurn had never been the most stable of all the phasia, but the way he had been acting in the past years was bordering on madness. Maybe being away from the Council was starting to have an effect on him. No matter what had detained him in the Blight, he had left quickly enough when he was finally ready. He hadn't taken the time to disguise his departure as he had when he left Scalla. There wasn't really a need. Even if one of the other phasia had decided to wait for him to emerge, there was no way for them to find the origin of the portal. There was a way to track the string of power that a portal used, and every phase knew how. However, the only way the string could be traced was from the origin to the destination, not vice versa. That gave Basille a slight advantage.

He moved quickly from the middle of the throne room and sat on his golden throne. He had taken his kingdom by force many lifetimes ago, and in each lifetime he returned to reclaim it. Never had it been lost to another member of the phasia, and his subjects had enjoyed a five thousand year reign by their immortal king. He picked up and rang a large bell that rested on a table that stood beside the throne. Seconds later, the huge double doors that led into the extravagant throne room opened, and two female servants entered the room. They moved promptly down the length of the audience hall and then knelt at Basille's feet.

"What is it that you require my great and powerful Lord Basille?" they asked in unison.

"I want you to send for Minister Talmon. After he is brought to my presence, then you will have the other servants prepare my evening meal."

"As you wish my lord," they responded.

The two women stood, bowed, and then turned to leave the room. Basille could only smile as he watched his servants go. He had trained them all well, and he took great pride in his accomplishment. But the feat had not been his alone. His people had taken to him from the minute he took command of the kingdom, and there had never once been a revolt or a civil unrest. It wasn't like the kingdoms of the other phasia. Some like Jeroch and Basille's friend Warron ruled their kingdoms with an iron fist, intimidating their subjects, striking fear into the hearts of men. Then there were those like Erdric and Farax who ruled through double-talk and deceit. They were never seen in public, and their emissaries ruled in their names. Then there was Caris who ruled by controlling the minds of her subjects after she seduced her way into the royal bedrooms. Basille's control had always been derived through mutual respect and love. He had watched most of his current servants grow up, and he took a personal interest in their lives. He had learned that from some of the greatest leaders of years past. One of the most important lessons was learned strangely enough from his mortal enemy, probably the greatest king to ever rule a kingdom, Cedric Binosear.

Even though he was supposed to hate everything that Binosear stood for, Basille could not help but marvel at the way he ruled Marcwell. He took great pride and care in the structure and the people of his kingdom. In some of his visits to Marcwell on diplomatic missions, Basille had noticed Binosear walking through Marcwell, stopping and talking to people, sitting in taverns and inns having discussions on their level, not on his. He was a truly caring man, and it was not only in act, but also in demeanor. A secret that he kept from the rest of the phasia was that he had actually met and dealt with Cedric Binosear on many occasions before and even after it was discovered that Binosear was the *Coromor*. Scalla had always been one of Marcwell's greatest allies, and Basille and Binosear had been the best of friends for many years after Binosear's father passed. Binosear's father had also trusted Basille, and when the then eighteen year old Cedric took over the throne, there was only one diplomat that his father dealt with that he knew and trusted. Cedric had once told Basille that he was like a second father to him and his sister Anne, and from that day on, Basille and Cedric had been close friends. If Cedric had only known what he was dealing with at that time.

Within a few moments, the double doors opened again to admit a new member of Basille's underlings. He was a huge man that nearly toped seven feet in height, and to any man but Basille or another member of the phasia, this man would have been the tallest man they had ever seen. But to Basille his height was merely average. Basille's brother Taron easily was taller than this man by more than a foot, and his physical presence was also greater. He was clad in black armor that bore an engraved symbol of a raven in flight on his breastplate, and he carried a large sleek sword at his side. He walked slowly and graciously, seemingly to make all fully aware of his presence. This was a mark of pride that Basille allowed only because this man was his second in command as well as the warlord that commanded all of his armies.

"You wished to see me my Lord Basille?" the man asked as he reached the foot of the throne. His voice was deep and powerful. It reminded Basille very much of Cedric Binosear's voice, only in the way that it bellowed deep in his chest.

"I did indeed Minister Talmon. I was curious as to the status reports of my army."

"Yes my lord. As per your orders, your forces invaded the town of Quea to the east. I am pleased to report that the siege went well, and our forces captured the town with limited casualties to our forces, and almost complete obliteration of the enemy. The Queans put up a very limited fight, and only a splinter force of their army still opposes us. I expect that they shall be subdued in due time."

"Good. Were the mines taken intact?"

"Yes my liege. Some of the men in the army noticed some burn marks on the beams that held the entry to the mines. We have theorized that the Queans had attempted to use explosives and seal the mines before we could take them by force. Their efforts proved to be futile, and our forces arrived before that end could be reasonably achieved. Upon further inspection of the area, the mines were found to be totally intact and are now at your disposal."

"Very good, Talmon. I want you to send two of your best crews into the mines. Near the lower levels of the mines they will find an ancient crypt. Under no circumstance is the crypt to be opened, but I want you to be sure the path there is clear. Once the crypt is found, your crews are to backtrack out of the cave. They will seal every passage down to the crypt behind them, except for the longest and most treacherous. I warn you again that the crypt is to be left undisturbed. Once the paths have been sealed, your men will surround the entrance to the mines, and then you will deploy five garrisons from the main force to guard Quea."

"Five garrisons? My lord, if you send that many of your troops to Quea, there will be no way that the remaining soldiers will be able to adequately guard your palace."

"You needn't worry yourself about that, Talmon. I suspect that I shall not be spending too much time here in Scalla. Besides, it has been over twenty years since a force tried to storm this palace. Now, go. Carry out my orders."

"By your word."

Talmon straightened, saluted with his sword, and then turned and walked away proudly. Basille had to chuckle to himself as he watched Talmon leave. He seemed to remember an arrogant young battalion leader by the name of Talmon many years ago, and it was hard to believe that man was now twenty years older and in charge of the entire army.

A few minutes after Talmon's exit, another woman servant appeared. She was much different than the two that had been in his presence earlier. She had more of a regal appearance to her, if that were possible for a servant. Basille remembered her slightly. She was born of a noble family who had given their daughter to him as a servant in an effort to win Basille's favor. It had been a successful attempt, and now that family was one of the richest in Scalla. The cost had been their only daughter. Basille wondered inwardly if the cost was worth it. The woman moved gracefully toward the throne and knelt at the foot of her master.

"What is it that you desire for your meal my lord?" she asked still looking at the ground.

"Nothing from the kitchen now young one. Perhaps a bit later. However, you may show yourself into my private chambers and wait for me there."

The servant looked up at her lord for the first time since she had entered his presence. Her eyes were filled with a sparkle of half-hidden excitement and anticipation. A smile quickly leapt onto her face. She rose, bowed, and then made her way to an antechamber in the north wall of the throne room. Basille rose from his throne a minute or two later. As he walked toward his private chambers he unfastened the sword belt from around his waist, and then started to pull off his shirt, eagerly anticipating his evening meal.

* * * * * * * * * * * *

Basille emerged from his chambers some hours later, rubbing his neck and shoulders slowly. The beads of sweat that rolled down his naked chest glistened in the moonlight that flooded through the huge panes of glass behind the golden throne. He wiped the beads of sweat off of his forehead and neck as he strolled to his throne. Just as he seated himself, the double doors swung open and into the throne room strode Minister Talmon.

"Lord Basille, a word."

"You presume much Minister Talmon. To enter my throne room without being summoned or at least properly announced is bordering on treason, not to mention madness. This news had better be worth the price you will pay for your impertinence."

"I beg your forgiveness for my blindness in this unfortunate oversight my liege," Talmon said kneeling.

"For now I will consider your apologies enough Talmon. Pray that I do not become lax in my leniency. Now, what is this urgent news?"

"Sir, I have received a report from our spies in Illimar. The civil war there has ended my lord."

"Do tell."

"The Army of the Dragon arrived shortly after the beginning of the fighting, along with an army of Jeresei. The fighting was fierce, but after the intervention of some of the town's commoners, the Army of the Dragon triumphed. The Army of Illimar and the queen's personal guard were totally wiped out as well as the Jeresei."

Basille clenched his fist and brought it down hard onto the armrest of the throne.

"No! What of my sister?"

"Lady Caris, I'm sorry to say, is believed to have been killed by a man named Korrd. While it is uncertain exactly who this Korrd is, it is commonly believed that in reality he is merely the disguise used by another one of the phasia."

"Undoubtedly," Basille said masking his true reaction.

"A man by the name of Ebios has taken the throne of Illimar in the name of the Dragon. The Army of the Dragon however has appeared to split."

Basille looked at Talmon confused for a moment and then responded to the remark.

"Explain."

"One force of the army has appeared to head back toward Rama, while the word traveling throughout the camp is that the large segment of the army will march toward Kandor. The third force, made completely of Illimar commoners, will be remaining under the command of Ebios and another man."

"Does this other man have a name?" Basille asked, quickly losing his patience.

"His name is Jerrard Mystic, sire."

Basille bolted from his throne and grabbed his sword from the scabbard that lay on the table beside him.

"Did you say Jerrard Mystic?" he replied angrily.

"Yes, my liege," Talmon returned tentatively.

At the reply, Basille screamed in rage. He turned quickly around and brought his sword crashing down on the table beside him, shattering it under his heavy blow.

"No! That bastard child can't still be alive! I'll see him dead before my feet if it's the last thing that I ever do! Talmon!"

"Yes, my lord," the man replied fearfully.

"Dispatch my armies to Illimar. Crush the life out of everyone there. Then you personally will bring me Jerrard Mystic."

"But sir, what about Quea?"

"Do not question me!" Basille thundered. "Carry out my orders or face my wrath!"

"Yes, my lord," was the only reply.

Talmon rose quickly and hurried out of the throne room. After he was out of the throne room, Basille turned his attention to the doors themselves. He brought his hands up and slapped them together roughly. The doors shuddered for a moment and then slammed violently. Basille turned again, sheathed his sword and then fastened his sword belt around his waist. As he was pulling his shirt over his head, the servant girl appeared from inside his private chambers.

"Is there anything else that you require my Lord Basille?" she asked almost at a whisper.

"Be not afraid child. No, there is nothing that I need now, except a little peace," Basille replied slowly, his voice beginning to calm. "Inform the rest of the servants and guards that I am leaving now. I do not know when I will return. Until I do, Talmon is in charge, and as usual no one is to be admitted to my throne room until I call."

"Yes my lord."

She bowed to her master and then hurried out of the throne room. Basille sat back on his throne for a moment to reflect. His sister was dead, and none could be blamed but Saurn. The other phasia were plotting against Shau-ling, and the *Coromor* was alive and hunting the phasia down one by one.

Now I have to worry about Mystic again. My own flesh and blood betrayed me and now I have to face him all over again.

The memories swam through Basille's mind as he opened a new portal. A time years past came to his mind. A time when the War for Power had become lax, and his kingdom prospered in a way that it never had before. He had all the time to do what he pleased. For the first time he allowed himself to fall in love, and that love gave birth to a single child. A child that he named Jerrard. No one there in that village knew what Basille really was, his wife didn't even know. He lived with his family in a little village on the borders of his kingdom. There he watched his boy grow and mature. But happiness for Basille could never last.

The war between the phasia began again in earnest, and Basille abandoned his family in an effort to protect them. However, the treacherous Jeroch had already learned of the existence of Basille's wife and child, and they immediately became targets. Basille soon got word that the village had been burned and that his wife and child had been killed. That personal vendetta against Jeroch still had yet to be paid. That was not the end of the story though.

While the massacre had claimed the life of Basille's love, it had not claimed his son. Jerrard had survived. He was rescued by Basille's friend, Lord Cedric Binosear. Jerrard was then given to a noble family in Marcwell who were unable to bear children of their own. He was raised as a member of the court, and after Binosear discovered that he was the *Coromor*, the Lion's Mane, Cedric's elite guard, was formed with Jerrard Mystic a charter member. The irony would not stop there.

In the second battle of Lakestone all of Shau-ling's servants fought together to keep Binosear out of Shau-ling's palace. The attempt would eventually prove unsuccessful, and three phasia ended up dead. Basille would also lose his life in that battle, but not to his friend Binosear. No, Basille's end came when a headstrong section leader of Binosear's army cleaved his heart with a sword strike from behind. As Basille lay there dying, he heard a familiar laugh with a hint of maturity to it. It was a terrible thing to want vengeance on one's own son.

Basille sighed softly to himself and then stepped through the portal. Mere seconds later, he was standing just outside the entrance to the Hall of Terrors. He made his way slowly down the length of the Hall of Terrors, and stopped just outside the door to Shau-ling's throne room. The Flame appeared quickly and stood there looking at Basille.

"Has master returned from the Council?"

"He has indeed Raven. Though I must say that he is not in one of his better moods. Your brother Taron was with him for several hours, and I gathered that the meeting was not at all pleasant."

"You gathered?"

"Taron left rather in a hurry, and when I looked into the throne room, there were the tell-tale signs that Shau-ling had thrown one of his little temper tantrums."

"Indeed. Well, I hope I fare far better than my brother."

With that the Flame disappeared and the door to the throne room opened. Basille walked in quickly, and the door shut behind him. The throne room was dark, darker than Basille had ever seen it before. Suddenly, the familiar ball of green flame erupted from the golden throne in the back of the room, and the reptilian Shau-ling made one of his more theatrical entrances.

"Ah, Raven. You have returned quickly. I hope that you have succeeded in your task," Shau-ling said disgusted.

"What has happened master?"

"I sent yet another force of Jeresei to stop the Dragon and his cohorts. This time their mission was simply to burn down an inn and kill everyone that ran out. They can't even do that right."

"I take it that they failed," Basille commented.

"Of course they failed, you twit!" Shau-ling thundered in response.

Basille flinched a little bit at his master's increasing irritability. However, he pressed onward.

"What of my brother Taron?"

"What of him?" Shau-ling replied slyly.

"I have heard that you met with him for a long period of time after you returned from the Council."

"That is correct Raven. The matter however is little of your concern. Now, report."

Basille sighed and cursed a little under his breath.

"My lord. Per your request, I sought out my brother Saurn..."

"I am well aware of the parameters and goals of your mission Basille, get on with it," Shau-ling growled.

"Yes, lord. However, I would like to request that you reconvene the Council."

Shau-ling rose quickly from his throne and took a few small steps toward Basille.

"You request? You request?" Shau-ling said angrily. "You dare to ask me to reconvene the Council? Not even Jeroch, the first-born, has the courage to ask me to reconvene the Council. I would have thought more sense from you Basille, especially because you are last-born."

"I'm sorry master, but Saurn told me that the only way he would come back was if you reconvene the Council."

"Saurn dares to dictate terms to me?!? He will most assuredly answer for this one Basille, as shall you."

Shau-ling abruptly turned away from Basille and made his way back toward the throne. The familiar blue portal appeared, and Shau-ling stepped through without a word. Basille followed reluctantly, not sure of the fate that awaited him.

As Basille stepped through the portal, and emerged inside the Council chamber, he found that the rest of the phasia were already there, save Caris, Aldridge, and Saurn.

"You have already convened the Council?"

"Yes Raven," Shau-ling answered. "The calls for you and your brother Saurn have yet to be put forth."

"But . . ."

Shau-ling put up his hand and turned his back to Basille. Basille nodded dejectedly and then walked to his Council position. Shau-ling continued walking until he had reached his position in the very center of the Council. At that moment, a ball of blackness and a ball of brilliant violet light shot from underneath Shau-ling and sped skyward. The ball of blackness turned and headed quickly toward Basille while the other continued upward until it was out of sight. Within a matter of moments, a hooded figure had appeared on the violet circle.

"Brother Saurn!" Farax exclaimed in his high-pitched raspy voice. "It is good that you have finally returned."

"That has yet to be seen," Saurn replied, the hood still drawn over his head, hiding his face.

"Why do you face us wearing a shroud brother Saurn?" Jeroch asked more baiting than inquisitive.

"He is hiding his eyes from me Shadow. He does not want me to be able to read his thoughts, so he hides them from me with a piece of cloth," Shau-ling answered.

Saurn laughed quickly and then threw the hood of the cloak back.

"I have nothing to hide from you weakling."

"Weakling!" Shau-ling screamed. "You dare to challenge me here in my own Council?!?"

"As a matter of fact, I do. We phasia have lived under your boot for far too many lifetimes now Shau-ling. You bark, sometimes bite, but you never do anything but sit here in your palace, protected from the rest of the world while other creature do your dirty work. Then, whenever the danger of the *Coromor* is gone, you pit us against each other, hoping that we never realize just how powerful we all are. Hoping that we never realize that we could team up and destroy you like the prophecies say. By the time we do find out though, your hopes are realized and it's too late."

"Quiet traitor," Jeroch boomed. "None of us have ever plotted against Shau-ling."

"And you are a fool as well Jeroch," Taron laughed. "Basille, Warron, Zarsi, and Caris were conspiring with Saurn to overthrow Shau-ling. There were also rumors that brother Saurn has found, and is in league with the *Chosen One.*"

"What!" Shau-ling roared.

Shau-ling turned toward Saurn again and screamed. Before Saurn could react, Shau-ling struck at Saurn, encasing him in an airtight prison of glass.

"You see my friends," Saurn called out from inside the prison, "Shau-ling does not want you to know that the number seven not only applies to the *Coromor* but it also applies to the phasia. If seven of us were to . . ."

"Quiet!" Shau-ling roared again.

Instantly, Saurn disappeared, leaving the prison of glass empty. He reappeared on the other side of the Council chambers near the place where Erdric and Basille stood.

"Listen to me," Saurn pleaded, "anyone who wishes to join me, you are welcome to come. I declare war here and now on any member of the phasia, or anyone else who would willingly stand beside Shau-ling and be trampled under his boot. You all know where to find me if you wish to."

With that last statement, he and Basille disappeared.

The Shattered Mirror

The sun was just beginning to rise over the mountain range to the east of Marcwell. This was the part of the day that Cedric Binosear always found himself dreading. As usual he hadn't slept the night before, and he stood out on the foyer outside his bedroom window as the sky became a fiery torrent of day colliding with the night. Cedric turned as the sun itself rose into the newly lightened sky, and he walked into his bedroom, softly closing the doors behind him. He walked through his room slowly, stopping before his fireplace, staring up at the picture above his mantle. His bride-to-be Erika Belnosian was pictured there, her eyes seemingly staring back at him, still full of the love that was present from the day they met until the day she was taken away from him. Her hair was pulled back, and she was dressed in the same blue gown that she was to be married in. Arathorn and Mailock had nearly convinced him a few years ago to take the picture down and store it away in the basement with the rest of the valuable, yet outdated art. Cedric would have, but something in his heart would not let her go, and so Arathorn lost his argument.

Cedric had never held anything against Arathorn and Mailock for trying. He knew that he had to get on with his life, but it seemed that the memory of his lost love would not let him. It was as if he was still tied to the past, and there was nothing he could do to change that. Lately it seemed though that even the past was giving out on him. He knew deep in his heart that there was not much time left for him, especially if Logan succeeded in vanquishing Shau-ling.

That was the funny thing about the prophecies. Even though Cedric had succeeded in killing Shau-ling, he came back to plague the world in Cedric's lifetime. Shau-ling wanted to make sure Cedric suffered. If Logan did make it to the Throne of Power, and if he were able to kill Shau-ling in this time, Cedric would be as good as dead. So, now the future was in peril, the past had abandoned him, and all he had left was the present. So much for the present.

Cedric turned away from the picture and grabbed the pair of black breeches off of the bed post and slid them on slowly. After that, he took the sword belt and wrapped it around his waist as he headed into the hallway. Several guards stiffened into attention, and then saluted as he passed. The affairs of his vast kingdom had now been delegated to different lords and ladies in an effort to take some strain off of his ailing mind. Erdric Belnosian, the son of the late Mayor of Marcwell, and brother to the late Erika Belnosian all but ruled Marcwell now. Cedric had become what he had always feared he would become, useless. Since his father died on his eighteenth birthday, Cedric had been the strong one. He had to grow up and take responsibility long before his time, but now that he thought about the past as he walked to the receiving room, it all seemed fitting. When he was twenty-three, Shau-ling's forces invaded Lakestone, and in the two years that followed Cedric grew a lot quicker than he ever could have imagined.

The day he was crowned at eighteen, his twin sister, Anne Binosear, left Marcwell to seek her own fortunes as well as to help Cedric. She saw herself as a hindrance to his happiness in that time, but that couldn't have been further from the truth. Anne was one of the few things in his life that Cedric could depend upon. It wasn't as if he was losing his mind back then, but then again maybe he was. He couldn't remember a time, even before Erika was killed, that he slept through the night without nightmares. Maybe that's why he and Anne were so close in those times. She always seemed to have a way to bring him back to reality. Her leaving made him have to deal with the pain, and he was truly alone in that huge palace.

He was always involved with something it seemed; a restlessness that could never be explained or sated. Maybe it was an excuse to get out into the world. He was a reckless adventurer, with no clue as to who he was, or what he was destined to become. But then the world he thought he knew came crashing down around his ears. Marcwell's oldest and truest ally in those times, Lakestone, had fallen under the siege of nameless beasts. Their intentions were not known, but terrorism seemed to be most of their tactics. When Lakestone fell, Cedric wanted to help. He had intended to gather an army together for a siege, but the mayor and the city council had beat him to the punch, and he was already volunteered. He was to leave with very little formal backing, and he was actually told to leave in the dead of the night, so that no one knew what he was up to. He had bowed to the wishes after a tense argument, and then he found his first ally.

He had never in his wildest dreams expected that the little fragile girl that he had grown up with would have endeavored to follow him on his quest. Erika Belnosian was one of the frailest, but most beautiful girls that Cedric had ever seen. When Cedric was getting ready to leave for Lakestone, Erika had come to his palace and told him that she was going with him. It was a humorous sight to see this frail sixteen year old girl arguing with a lord older and more experienced than her. It was more humorous when you finally realized that the lord was backing down and the girl had won. Cedric then had to contend with falling in love.

Love was easy to master for Cedric because he fell into it willingly. Erika was also willing and able to oblige with her reciprocal love. Death was the thing that Cedric always had trouble swallowing. Not three days into the quest, Cedric witnessed the deaths of two of his allies, as well as the deaths of twenty or thirty Jeresei and Kalbraks. For all the death, he made friends. He met Lord Arathorn, the knight who should be king. Arathorn.

Thinking of his old friend, Cedric turned down a hallway adjacent to his bedchamber and wandered down toward Arathorn's study. The door was closed, as usual, but it opened after a few knocks. Arathorn stood inside the doorway in little more than a long shirt; it was still very early in the morning.

"Sorry to wake you old friend. I just wanted to see how things were abroad," Cedric said apologetically.

"It's all right, Cedric, I needed to wake early this morning as it was. As for the world abroad, I know as much as you. My eyes and ears seem to have been lax it their reports, and I have been unable to determine why," Arathorn replied yawning.

"I feared as much. Without Aryx here to find out things, it is difficult. I should have received a reply from Anne as to my last letter by now, Arathorn. I'm really starting to get concerned. It's not like her to stay out of touch this long."

"Don't worry my friend, it's probably nothing. To be sure, I'll send a few riders out toward Trelon today."

"Thank you, my friend."

"Did you sleep last night, Cedric?" Arathorn asked, his voice suddenly changing from thoughtfulness to concern.

"Truth?"

Arathorn sighed, and shook his head.

"Well then, yes, I slept like a baby."

"That's what I thought. Maybe you should ask Mailock if there is anything he can do to help."

"You know better than that, Arathorn," Cedric said, his voice filled with misplaced anger. "I want nothing to do with that conjurer. You know what he did to us in Sador. I still have the scar from where that dragon clawed me."

"That's in the past, Cedric. Mailock is one of the *Erieal*, and he could do nothing to harm you. The sickness is twisting the facts in your mind."

Cedric grabbed Arathorn by the arm and squeezed hard. His other hand shot for the hilt of his sword and began to slip it out of the scabbard.

"I don't care what that traitor claims to be," Cedric thundered, his voice lowered an entire octave. "His actions caused the death of two of my friends and hundreds of my soldiers. No matter what he does, only his death can ever atone for that."

Cedric released Arathorn and then turned sharply back toward his chamber. He then began to try and remember exactly what happened. Then the doubts came. Was Arathorn right? Was the sickness taking more of a toll than he could realize?

That time in the past played out in his mind over and over again. He and his army had to pass through the strange town of Sador on their way to the port of Falke. In the fields of Sador, Cedric and his army met with one of Shau-ling's forces led by a huge red dragon. It wasn't one of the phasia, just one of the beasts Shau-ling had decided to let out of its cage in the Hall of Terrors. The red dragon and the Kalbraks and Shadowwalkers were not the only opposition though. Mailock stood with the forces of the Shadow in that battle. But something was not right. Mailock was supposed to be dead, killed by the blade of the phase Warron. Arathorn and Mailock had been looking for a mythical sword when Warron came upon them and killed Mailock. Arathorn was quick to retaliate and killed the phase, but the damage had been done, and Mailock was dead. Then the battle in Sador happened, and Mailock was back. Cedric had never put that right in his mind, but he had never taken it to this extreme in the past. It must have been the sickness getting to him.

Part of Cedric wanted to go back and apologize to his friend, but the other part of him knew that it would do little good. His friends knew him better than he knew himself, and there was no need to apologize for something he had no control over. Cedric wandered back to his chambers, and only partially noticed that the guards who had been at his door earlier were now gone. He pushed the door open, not even realizing that the door was cracked open a bit already.

As the door opened, it revealed a tall, slender man dressed in all black standing in front of his fireplace. His long black hair stretched down the length of his back, and one of his hands rested on the mantle while the other rested firmly on the hilt of his sleek black sword. Cedric would have known this man even if he were long past insane. This was his longtime friend, Lord Basille of Scalla.

"Basille," Cedric said walking into the room slowly.

Basille turned away from the fireplace and met Cedric halfway across the length of the room. They embraced for a moment, and then Cedric pulled away and walked over to his bed and sat.

"I wasn't told that you were coming old friend. I would have had a feast prepared had I known."

"That is all right, Cedric," Basille replied, "I'm afraid that I can't stay long as it is. I am here merely on business."

Cedric smiled. He knew Basille much better than his friend thought. Basille never came to Marcwell with business on his mind.

"What is it friend?" Cedric asked coyly. "Don't tell me that you have found an old man's diversion here in Marcwell. I must say though that you do not look like a man who had just passed his fiftieth birthday."

"I am a young fifty Cedric, but then again I have felt eighteen as long as I can remember. No, I haven't found a woman here in Marcwell, not that there aren't enough to have here. Truly, this trip is for business only."

Cedric stood and walked over to the mantle to stoke the fire. As he did, he looked instinctively back up at the picture than hung over the mantle.

"I see that you are still torturing yourself, Cedric. It's no wonder that you look my senior at forty. Why can't you let the dead rest? You need some peace in your life, especially now. Why don't you find a woman here in Marcwell and settle down?"

"It's not that easy, Basille. You weren't there when she died." Cedric looked up at his friend with tears welling up in his eyes. "You didn't hold her in your arms there on the floor of the church as she died. You didn't see the look in her eyes when she looked up at me and told me she loved me just before she died. You don't live with the nightmares, you don't see it every night in your mind over and over again," Cedric insisted, his voice filled with anger, frustration, and pain.

"No, I don't," Basille replied strongly. "But you don't live with my pain. You didn't marry a wonderful woman and have a child with her. You didn't have to leave and learn that one of your sworn enemies had burned down the village that she lived in, killing her and your son, only to find out that your son wasn't dead, but that he served your enemy and hated everything you stood for."

Cedric looked at Basille puzzled for a moment and then gripped his shoulder.

"I am sorry my friend, I didn't know."

Basille smiled, the anger swelling somewhere deep inside of him in that secret place that hated Cedric and what he was.

"Of course you didn't, my friend," he said managing a smile, "but now to business."

Cedric smiled and nodded.

"Of course old friend. What did you have in mind?"

Basille reached into the pocket of his cloak and pulled out a parchment. He unrolled the parchment and handed it to Cedric.

"This document gives you control of my kingdom until I return here to reclaim that paper. I am leaving on a long trip with an old ally, and I do not know when we will return."

"But . . ."

"No 'buts' Cedric. Take my kingdom with love, and promise me you will take good care of my subjects until I return."

"I swear, Basille," Cedric answered with little hesitation, "but I wish you would tell me where you were going so I could possibly help you."

"You cannot help me this time old friend," Basille replied, "this is something that I must tend to. You must understand the position."

"That I do."

"I'm afraid that control of my kingdom is not the only reason that I came to see you."

Cedric scanned Basille's eyes for a moment and then sat down on the bed.

"I know that look Basille. That's the same look you had on your face when you told me that my father was dead." Suddenly it hit him. "Has something happened to Anne?"

Basille looked dead at Cedric for a moment and then nodded slowly.

"I'm sorry Cedric, one of the phasia posed as her son and murdered her."

Cedric looked at Basille for a moment, unable to react to the news. A single tear fell from his eye, and his mouth opened a few times, as if he were trying to speak. He couldn't talk. His mouth and throat were dry, and even if they weren't, he wasn't sure there were words enough to express his anguish. It was as if a part of him had died, and now there was only the smallest fragment of him still holding on to sanity. Finally he managed to croak out a response.

"What about Cairyn?"

"She is safe Cedric. A man named Logan Ranthall and his companions managed to save her, but their efforts were not enough to save Anne. Cairyn has taken her mother's place on the throne, and she now rules in your name."

Even as Basille was speaking, Cedric rose. He walked over to the fireplace, and rested both arms on the mantle, staring up at the painting of Erika Belnosian. The tears were now streaming down his face, and he pressed his head onto this crossed arms, his knees buckling under him.

As Basille walked over to comfort his friend, he heard him mumbling under his breath.

"What am I going to do now? What am I going to do?"

Then he raised his head again and looked up at the picture.

"What am I going to do now Erika? What am I supposed to do now that Anne's gone? Help me Erika. Help me."

Suddenly, rage burst somewhere inside of Basille. He grabbed Cedric shoulders from behind and spun him around roughly. He then shook him with all of his might.

"Why do you still hold on to her Cedric? She is not the woman that you thought she was! Didn't you ever wonder why that frail little girl that you fell in love with as a child changed so much in just a matter of days? Didn't it ever bother you that she was a completely different person? By the Light man, you weren't going to marry Erika Belnosian, at least not in the end."

"What are you saying, Basille?" Cedric replied shocked and confused all at the same time.

Basille walked Cedric over to his bed and sat him down. He then backed away from him and went to one knee, looking up at his old friend.

"Erika Belnosian died in a riding accident when she was fifteen. No one knew about it, because a woman who looked like Erika Belnosian came back from that riding trip, and no body was ever found. The woman you thought you loved was not a woman at all Cedric. She was a bloodthirsty, conniving little minx who posed as a human. Erika, at least the Erika you thought you knew, was really Shau-ling's daughter, Caris."

If the shock of his sister's death hadn't left Cedric nearly unresponsive, Cedric would have leapt at his friend and called him a liar. But in his present condition, all he could do was sit there.

"It's true Cedric, but don't ask me how I found out about it."

"But she loved me Basille, she told me she did."

"That wasn't love Cedric. Caris knew all along what you were, and she was trying to rule you. The crossbow dart that you have believed to this day was meant for you on your wedding day, was really truly meant for her. Some of the other phasia found out about Caris' scheme and wanted to destroy her before she had a chance to turn you against them and Shau-ling."

"But I never would have found out about Shau-ling if they hadn't killed her. Dammit Basille, she told me she loved me!"

Basille grabbed Cedric again, this time with more force.

"She didn't love you man, get it through your thick skull. She was just using you to get back at the rest of the phasia. It was not love that she wanted, it was merely power. Caris doesn't have emotions, never will. I tangled with her once, and she is the most cold-hearted witch you would ever have the misfortune to tangle with. Don't feel bad Cedric, she has taken better kings than you to her bed and not one has escaped as well as you have."

Cedric shook his head again.

"Believe it Cedric, it's the truth."

Cedric wanted to argue, but the strength had long since left his body. There was nothing left for him in his life. His sister was dead, and the woman he thought he had loved turned out to be one of his greatest enemies on the planet. If it hadn't been Basille who told him these things, he never would have believed them.

"How do you know all these things about the phasia, Basille?"

"I have dealt with them all once or twice, in one form of another. They are notorious for taking control of a kingdom and then pushing for war with the neighboring kingdoms in order to tighten their grip on the countryside. I also have a lot of spies."

"I thank you for being straight with me Basille," Cedric managed. "With your amount of information, you should help my friend Logan."

"Logan?" Basille asked.

"Logan Ranthall, the man you said saved my niece Cairyn. He is my successor."

Basille looked at Cedric puzzled for a moment, the joy and expectation growing quickly in that secret place in his heart.

"Your successor? You mean this Ranthall is the second *Coromor*?"

"The same," Cedric replied.

Basille's heart felt like it would burst with joy. He tried to hide his pleasure with a thoughtful face, but he knew it would not be contained for long.

"I wish I could help him Cedric, but as I said I have other things to attend to. In fact, I had better be off now."

Basille rose and started toward the door.

"Think about what I said Cedric, but do not dwell on it. For the Light's sake, try and get some sleep tonight, you look like you haven't slept in a month."

Cedric smiled and nodded.

"I thought so," Basille returned. "Farewell."

With that, he was gone. As mysteriously as he arrived, he was gone. Cedric walked over to his wardrobe and took out a blue shirt and a white pair of breeches, and began to change. After he was dressed, he took his saddlebags out of the bottom of the wardrobe and then put a few outfits in. He closed the wardrobe, threw the saddlebags over his shoulder and then headed out the door as he was strapping the sword belt around his waist. He closed the door behind him and then made his way back to Arathorn's study.

Even before Cedric had a chance to knock, the door opened and Arathorn emerged. Arathorn appeared shocked to see him at first and then spoke.

"Cedric," he said quickly, "where are you going?"

"I am going to Taren."

"Taren?" Arathorn asked. "Why on earth are you going to Taren?"

"When Logan and Aryx find the Jeweled Dragon's Flame, Aryx will take Logan and his friends there. I want to be there to meet Aryx and relay his new orders."

"What about . . ."

"Security?" Cedric finished. "Don't worry Arathorn, I sent a garrison there a few days ago in anticipation of Aryx's arrival."

"At least let me go with you."

"No Arathorn," Cedric replied, "I have another assignment for you old friend. I have recently learned that Anne has been murdered and Cairyn has taken the throne."

"Cedric I'm . . ."

"No," Cedric interjected. "Take a garrison to Trelon, secure the area, and then return here and prepare for the Dragon's arrival."

Arathorn weighed whether or not to console his friend, but with a sharp bow, he decided against it. Cedric turned sharply and then strode toward the stables.

* * * * * * * * * * *

Basille closed the door behind him and smiled. He didn't like misleading his friend when it came to his true identity, but then again, he had never exactly lied. Everything he ever told Cedric had been mostly true, but sometimes some of the facts had to be changed to protect himself. Now Basille found that he had the weapon he needed to complete his leverage advantage over the rest of the phasia. He had the identity of the *Coromor.*

While that did prove to be the most elusive piece of the puzzle, now that he had it, there was nothing he could do with it. He couldn't very well go and hunt down this Logan Ranthall, especially with the war on. Also, with Caris dead, there was no way that Logan could be seduced, and that could be both a plus and a minus. Then the two pieces clicked. Logan Ranthall. Korrd Ranthall. The *Coromor,* and the *Chosen One.* The coincidence was too big to be ignored. The chances were good, at least keeping the prophecies in mind that the *Coromor* and the *Chosen One*, could come from the same family. And, it was a possibility that it had happened in this generation. It was an unheard-of occurrence, but with the vague parameters given by the prophecies of Aralias Imstra, anything was possible.

That was the strange thing about the prophecies. They were very vague in times and places, but the one overriding factor was that the *Coromor* was always named specifically. However, to a person who didn't know what they were looking for, the prophecies could appear not to mention a so-called *Chosen One* at all.

Now the phasia had been cut down to eight, and they were divided. There was no way that seven of the phasia could be gathered to destroy Shau-ling. Jeroch would never turn against his master, and it was getting to the point that Erdric was the same way. That destroyed that possibility. There was only one *Coromor* in the time, so he wasn't enough to destroy Shau-ling. The same held true for the *Chosen One*. Cedric proved that the *Coromor* and the four *Erieal* together had not been enough to kill Shau-ling, so that wasn't a possibility, and Basille assumed the same would hold true for the *Chosen One* if he were to unite the *Erieal* under him. Now, the *Chosen One*, the *Coromor*, and the *Erieal* together had never been attempted, but something about that didn't sit right with Basille. Then he figured it out. The number seven was the part of the prophecies that couldn't be altered. Basille knew what he had to do, and his thoughts were troubled all the way back to the Blight.

CHAPTER 11

Chapter XII

Mysterious Figure

Pike rolled out of bed well before dawn. He hadn't slept well since the quest started, but he wasn't surprised that he was able to get an hour's rest since he was reunited with Logan and the rest of the company. His covers were mangled, and he could tell that the hour or two he had spent sleeping had not been very restful. So much had happened, and so much with little to no explanation. If Pike had been dreaming, he didn't remember it. All he knew is that he looked forward to the day that he could put his head on a pillow and just sleep. Of course he could always take Talon's half-hearted advice and start drinking more heavily. Pike grabbed his shirt off the chair beside the bed and started toward the door. It couldn't have been better timing. As he swung open the door, he found Eldar's face staring up at him. She was a bit shocked that he answered before she could even knock, but that didn't last long.

"Aren't you going to invite me in?" she asked.

Despite himself, Pike felt the heat rush to his cheeks and he wondered if Eldar could still tell that he was blushing. He stepped aside and let her in, and caught the quick flash of a coy smile come to her lips. The look on his face told more than he wanted it to, and he was sure that she could read the shock and sudden expectation like a book. She walked past him and sat on the bed. He turned toward the door and shut it silently. He hoped that she could not hear as he softly mumbled a prayer.

"What can I do for you Eldar?" Pike said turning back toward her. "Or can't you sleep either."

"Not a wink. I'm worried, Pike."

"About what?" he said walking over to her.

As he crossed the distance, he first thought about sitting on the chair across from the bed, but seeing where she sat on near the corner of the bed, he knew she wanted him to sit beside her. He sat down beside her on the bed and looked at her. She turned to face him and took his hand in hers.

"I'm worried that we'll never get a chance to have what Logan and Elwyne have. Did you see them today Pike? They looked so in love, and I started wondering if you and I would live long enough to work things out."

Pike shook his head and exhaled hard. He had been dreading this conversation ever since Sador. But that was the way they had always been. They were good in the moment, just not very good at talking about the moment.

"We've been through this before. You and I both agreed when we took the vows that we were too young and too inexperienced to be married. We would just get on each other's nerves and end up hating each other, and I don't want that for us."

"It's different now Pike," Eldar urged. "This quest has changed us. You are much more mature than I ever thought you could have been if you would have remained in Aradon. Even Talon has mellowed in the past few days. And we're a long way from that day. And the day after."

Pike shook his head again and looked back toward the window. He wanted to tell her that she was right. He wanted to tell her that he loved her with all of his heart, but he couldn't find the words. They were out there, ready for him to use, but they were somewhere out of his reach. Eldar put her finger under his chin and turned his face back toward her. She searched his eyes, trying hard to find something that would give her a clue as to what he was thinking. He could only hold her gaze for a moment, and then he looked down at the floor, ashamed that his words had failed him in a battle fought not with swords and shields, but with words and sentiments. In this battle, Pike found that he was greatly overmatched, and he couldn't even lift a simple weapon to defend himself.

"What are you feeling?" Eldar urged.

She couldn't have realized how powerful a question that was. He looked up at her again, trying to put all of his words and thoughts into one look that she might be able to understand. But at this too he failed. She just kept looking him straight in the eye, further defeating him without as much as a word.

"I wish I could tell you what I was thinking. I'm trying to find a way to say it, but it all just sounds so wrong in my head."

Eldar put her hand over his mouth before he could say another word. She closed her eyes for just and instant and then shook her head. When her eyes opened again, they stared straight into his.

"Don't use your brain Pike," she said softly, edging closer to him, "use your mouth."

She pressed her lips to his as her hand dropped to his thigh. He closed his eyes instinctively and pulled her closer to him. They barely made it to the ship by first light.

* * * * * * * * * * *

Logan knew that he was dreaming. The instant the flames appeared around him and the laughter started, Logan knew. Granted knowing didn't help matters any, but at least he knew it was only a dream. This dream had plagued Logan every night for the last three days, and each time it was the same. Waking in a circle of flames, surrounded by ten men and three women. They all laughed at Logan as he rose to his feet. One of the men Logan always recognized. Aldridge always stood to Logan's right, laughing and pointing. He always seemed to enjoy the situation more than anyone else. Beside him stood a staggeringly beautiful woman dressed in green. She slightly resembled Elwyne, but as Logan looked closer at her face, it began to shift into that of another. The harder he looked, he could almost make out the other face, but then it slipped away without truly making a clear appearance.

Other faces in the crowd were blurry, but Logan could make out some more clearly than others. One of the men was tall and broad; he looked more like the side of a mountain than a man. Another was as large in the shoulders as the previous man, but he was short in stature. Beside him stood a man in black who was thin as a reed, and another whose face was clouded with shadows. The other two women were total opposites in appearance, but each appeared as if evil flowed through their veins instead of blood. The first woman was dressed completely in white with a pale complexion and stark white hair, while the other was dressed in red and possessed a deep tan and hair like fire. The others were not as clear, except for one man whose features rang out like the church bells of Aradon during the spring festival.

"Welcome to the Circle of Judgment Logan Ranthall," the man in violet robes said coldly. "You have been brought here to face judgment for your crimes."

"You should be the one on trial, Saurn," Logan said.

It was never his voice, nor was it he who spoke. That same part of Logan that took over in the alley outside of the inn had taken over in the dream, and it seemed as if the *Coromor* was a totally separate entity.

"I did not destroy the lives of hundreds of women and children trying to get revenge for one death."

"No," Logan's voice replied angrily, "but I did not butcher thousands in the quest for perfect followers. You killed for pleasure, and you killed for fun. You are more of a bastard than your brother Jeroch, and no less sadistic."

"I appreciate the kind words Ranthall," Saurn replied going into a facetious bow, "but I'm not sure that Jeroch will favor the comparison."

"To hell with Jeroch. We can finish this now if you like, or I can pick the rest of you off one on one like I did Aldridge."

At that comment Aldridge frowned and tried to charge Logan. Some of the others held him back, but soon he was calm again, laughing and cursing with the rest of Logan's captors.

"No, no, no," Saurn replied laughing. "I have something much better planned for you my dear Logan."

He turned and motioned for another person to approach. The man walked up slowly, his face still hidden by the shadows cast by the shrinking firelight. It was then that his face came into view.

"Korrd," Logan said without thinking, this time the voice his own. "I should have known it was you."

"Yes dear brother, and now I'm going to prove that I was always the strongest."

Logan woke up screaming even before his blade entered Logan's flesh for the first time. Logan had never slept that long, nor had the dream taken that kind of a twist. His brother had been dead for years, and there was no reason that a dead man should have been making appearances in his dreams. Elwyne was quick to calm Logan down. She had a wet rag in her hand and she was wiping his brow. He tried to say something, but nothing would escape his lips but gasps of terror. For some reason this dream was more than a dream. There was a message somewhere that Logan felt he was overlooking, but he couldn't tell what. Elwyne eased his head back down onto the pillow and laid her head on his chest. Logan didn't close his eyes again the rest of the night, and he couldn't wait until morning.

* * * * * * * * * * *

Gwydeon rolled over and exhaled slowly. Midarin rolled onto her side and ran her fingers through his chest hair and smiled. She wiped several beads of sweat from his forehead and then laid her head on his shoulder and chest, draping her body over him again. He stroked her hair softly and then kissed the top of her head.

"I think I'm falling in love with you Gwydeon," she said softly, trying not to sound too soft.

"There's no question here Midarin, I'm sure that I am in love with you. So sure in fact, that I want you to come back to Aradon with me after the war and be my wife."

Midarin raised her head and looked up in his eyes. All she could see was the sincerity that she had been chasing all of her life, but she was never able to find in her father's court. If he truly wanted her as his wife, than all she had to do was say yes, and her fondest dreams she had had as a child would be just one step away.

"That is so sudden," Midarin teased, "what kind of girl do you think I am?"

She started to pull away, but Gwydeon saw through her faux resistance. He wrapped his arms around her and pulled her back to him. She struggled, and before a few moments passed, they were both laughing. After a long kiss, she propped her elbow on his broad chest and let the seriousness of the moment come to her face.

"I will Gwydeon, I will."

In that moment, after they had laid everything on the line for each other, laid bare their souls and touched that place they once feared to let show, they both realized the limitless hope and potential that lay ahead of them. There was the one twinge of potential for tragedy that haunted their thoughts as well, but they had come to accept the risk when they began to forge their romance. As they gazed deeply into each other's eyes, perhaps for the first time, they recognized the faces and emotions that they saw written there and understood the part they were about to play in the other's life.

The human body may only be a shell within which a heart beats during its long journey into the night ahead. But these two lovers had found a small shred of light even in the bitterest darkness that hung like a shroud over the sleeping world. The ever present danger that was Shau-ling could not dim the light of love that filled their hearts, nor could it darken the stars shining in their eyes. They were both simple mortals trapped in the center of a battle between murderous gods. Darkness swirled around them constantly, with flashes of light that were as deadly as they were hopeful. However, if on this travel the heart and soul makes through the darkness, a person should meet another of like mind, like spirit, and like soul, than truly the darkness becomes a little lighter because of it. Whether that connection should be for a single night, or for a lifetime, it is worth the experience of true love. That kind of love would last through even the darkest ages of man, and in truth could even transcend death.

* * * * * * * * * * * *

The entire party met on the deck of the Monster of the Deep at first light. The captain made arrangements for the increased number of important passenger, and once again gave his private cabin to Logan and Elwyne. Additionally, Pike and Eldar, as well and Gwydeon and Midarin were given two of the private cabins. While the pairing caught many in the party by surprise, none more so than Pike and Eldar, there would be time enough for explanations at a later date. The rest chose to take cots in the crew quarters, except for Aryx who was extended the courtesy of taking the last of the private cabins. Aryx still had not spoken to anyone since that night in Falke, and it was a safe bet that they would not hear from him again until they reached Taren, or perhaps Marcwell. The captain said that Aryx had come aboard long before dawn and had gone straight to his cabin and had been there ever since. That in itself wasn't alarming, but when added to his strange behavior from the days past, it made Logan start to wonder.

It hadn't been five minutes before there was a knock at Logan's cabin door. Elwyne answered it, and when Pike, Talon, Gwydeon, and Gideon entered, Logan knew it was going to be interesting.

"What can I do for you fine gentlemen?" Logan asked trying to keep his tone light.

Pike looked at the others for a moment, and when they all sat down at the table, Logan started to get a little worried. Pike and Talon would normally have reacted to the old joke between friends, but this time, there was no comedy or playfulness to be found. The conversation most certainly wasn't going to be pleasant, and if there was a chance of getting out of it gracefully, it went out the window when the first words escaped Pike's lips.

"We've all been talking, and we decided that it would be in the group's best interests if we didn't go on to Marcwell."

That took Logan completely by surprise. The thought had never entered his mind, and he could only see Aryx's recent behavior as any kind of provocation for this step.

"Is there a reason for this?"

Gwydeon stood and walked over to Logan. He reached into his pouch and pulled out a parchment. It took only a second to unroll and then Gwydeon put it on the table in front of Logan.

"Talon found this in the alley after the battle with Aryx."

"Is that true Talon?"

"Yeah, it is. I know I should have returned it to Aryx, but I was curious so I opened it. After I read it, I showed it to Pike and Gideon. We're all glad I kept it."

"What does it say?" Logan asked.

"It is a letter from some unknown party," Pike answered somberly. "In essence it says to go on as planned and all would be taken care of in Taren."

"We all figured dat if da attack would fail in Taren, da next place dey would try ta get ye would be in Marcwell," Gideon added.

Logan thought it over and then glanced down at the letter. It basically said what Pike had stated, and as he had alluded to, the letter was unsigned. The handwriting was not in a style that Logan recognized, but it was certainly not in the flowing script that came from Lord Cedric's hand.

"What does the rest of the group think?" Logan asked.

"No one else knows about this but the six of us," Talon replied.

"I'm sure that no matter what decision you make, the others will follow without question," Gwydeon added.

"That just begs the question then doesn't it," Elwyne chimed in, "what would you do if Logan decides against your plan?"

"Elwyne?" Logan said looking over to her, surprised she would ask the question.

"It has to be asked, Logan. There's been a growing rift in this group since the second set of orders from Cedric came through and you followed them blindly," she answered brutally. "It was that division that nearly killed us all, and we were never even sure that those orders even came from Lord Cedric. After all, we saw how easy it was for Aldridge to lead us astray in Trelon. It could have been the same person who wrote this letter to Aryx. Now, I put it to you all again, what would you do if Logan decided against you?"

"I am loyal to Logan because he's my friend," Gwydeon answered. "If he gives an order, I may not like it, but I will follow if I can."

"As will I," Pike responded.

"And me," Talon added.

"Me too," Gideon put in.

"The way things have been going, I'm not sure I deserve this kind of faith, but I thank you for it," Logan said finally. "Unfortunately, I can't say that I see any other choice but to continue on to Marcwell as planned. No matter what Aryx's motives or intentions may be, I still have to believe that Lord Cedric is everything that he seems to be. No matter what though, we're going to have to keep our eyes open in Taren."

"That's all we can ask Logan," Talon replied.

The conversation changed to something happier, and all took turns grilling Pike and Gwydeon about their burgeoning love lives. Even though the conversation was lighter, there was still a pall that hung over every word; the darkness that could never be completely forgotten. Elwyne got sick of the conversation after a few minutes so she left to talk to Midarin and Eldar to 'get the real story' from them. The group stayed together most of the day, talking about various things, comparing notes about the powers of the phasia and what anyone knew about the others. Logan wanted so much to tell them about the dream he had the night before, but for some reason he couldn't find the words to talk about it. The night passed quickly enough, and so did the following day. By noon on the third day, the Monster of the Deep had docked at the town of Taren.

* * * * * * * * * * * *

Pike and Talon wandered around the town of Taren looking for some trouble to get into. They had disembarked from the Monster of the Deep about an hour earlier, and they were already bored with waiting. Elwyne, Midarin, and Eldar had dragged Logan and Gwydeon out to look for some new clothes, and Lane and Talos seemed too caught up in their talks about magic and history to do much else. They had even gotten little Alexander involved and he was soaking up as much as he could. Gideon was also somewhere in town, and Pike found himself thinking that he was in one of the many taverns that Taren had to offer. Aryx had locked himself in his room in the *Inn of Good Faith* the minute they had arrived, and it was a good bet that they wouldn't see him for a while. So, that left Pike and Talon together, just as they had always been, and they liked it that way. Pike felt a little guilty that he had been spending so much time with Eldar and neglecting his friends, but this was an opportunity to make good. They wandered through the town together, marking places of importance, like the taverns, the marketplace, the training grounds, the women's holy sanctuary - for future reference of course - and the town square. As they were passing by the *Inn of Good Faith*, Talon stopped in front of an alley. He reached out and grabbed Pike's shoulder and pulled him back.

"What is it Talon?"

Talon pointed down the alley and Pike looked. He saw three men armed with swords and daggers running down another alley. As he looked farther up the alley he saw that they were chasing someone.

"What does that look like to you?" Talon asked quickly. "Looks to me like a party."

"And they didn't invite us?" Pike said, trying his best to sound hurt.

"Want to crash it?"

"You know I do."

"Let's do it."

No sooner had Talon said that, Pike had his axe drawn and ready for a fight. Talon drew his sword and sprinted down the alley. Pike followed, and eventually the alley dead-ended, and they found the three men they were looking for. One of the men had a woman in his arms, and one of the other's was tearing off her clothes. The other stood by watching, obviously ready to take his turn.

"Excuse me," Pike said after loudly clearing his throat, "is this a private party, or can anyone play?"

"Get out of here you two," one of the men replied, "find your own toy to play with."

"Wrong answer," Talon said as he buried his blade into his back.

The man who had been ripping the girl's clothes stood and drew his sword. The man who was holding the girl threw her to the ground behind him and also drew a sword. He advanced and quickly fell to Pike's axe crashing down on his head. The other man backed up and grabbed the girl by the arm. He put the blade of his sword to her throat and laughed.

"Don't make another move, or I'll kill her."

"Let's think about this shall we," Talon said in a smart voice. "We move, you kill her, and then we kill you. You let her go, we let you live. You don't let her go, we kill you anyway. It sounds like an easy choice, doesn't it?"

The man looked at Talon for a moment and then released the girl. He dropped his sword and started walking toward Pike. Pike and Talon both stepped away and let the man walk past. He had made a very wise decision. Pike immediately removed his cloak and wrapped it around her. She was beautiful, even more so without proper clothing, though they tried their best not to look. Her blond hair hung loose around her shoulders, and her body was slim. She smiled when she looked up at her saviors and spoke with a soft, deep voice.

"Thank you both for your help. How can I ever repay you?"

"No need," Pike tried to say as gallantly as he could manage.

"At least tell me the names of the men who just saved a poor helpless girl's life."

Pike smiled and nodded.

"I am Pike Rhuiden, and my not-so-modest friend here is Talon Aielin."

Talon bowed slightly at the compliment and smiled. The girl giggled at the show and then she smiled as well.

"Well gentlemen, I am Jasmen Hiedra. I'm sorry I couldn't introduce myself to you properly dressed, but some people just can't take no for an answer. Where are you two from?"

"Aradon. A little farm town in the middle of nowhere, you probably haven't heard of it," Talon answered.

"In that you would be right," she answered. "Could I at least buy you two a drink?"

"If you wish," Pike answered quickly. "Is there somewhere we can walk you to so you can get into some proper clothes?"

"I'm staying at the *Inn of Good Faith*. I'm the entertainment in the common room tonight."

"Do you sing?" Pike asked.

"Yes," she answered.

"Funny, so do we," Talon said smiling.

Pike knew that look. It was the 'oh boy do I have a great idea' look. This was going to be trouble.

* * * * * * * * * * * *

Logan had heard Pike and Talon sing before, but to see them up on stage was probably the funniest thing he had ever seen in his life. At least Logan was happy to hear that they had picked one of the more tame songs that his father had taught them. Though he had never heard it sung better, when the young lady with blond hair who had called them on stage joined in, it sounded even more spectacular. The three of them stayed on the stage for more than two hours, because each time they would try to leave, the crowd would scream for more and they would sing another song or two. It was very impressive to say the least. Later that evening the three entertainers returned to the table with smiles all around.

"Logan," Pike said sitting down across from me, "I'd like you to meet Jasmen Hiedra. She is a minstrel and a bit of an adventurer."

"Really," Elwyne said, not at all surprised.

"Yes," she answered quickly. "Pike and Talon here have told me about your quest, and I would like to offer my services to you and your party."

"And those services would be?" Eldar asked.

"In a kind of quest like yours, spirits can be low at times. I can sing songs and tell stories to liven up the spirits. I can also turn your quest into a story and spread word of your deed around the world."

"It would be nice to be remembered Logan," Talon urged.

"And we can always use another person who can fight," Pike added.

"Will you stop it you two? You don't have to convince me. Miss Hiedra, do you understand the serious nature of your request?"

"Yes, I do," she replied calmly.

"Well then," Logan said smiling, "welcome to the People of the Dragon. Have Pike and Talon introduce you around, and we will give you notice before you leave."

"Thank you, Logan, you won't regret this."

That remained to be seen. There wasn't much opportunity to sit and talk long as the owner of the inn convinced the three of them to do another session of songs and stories. The place was wild and full of laughter and happiness. As Logan was sitting at the table talking to Elwyne and Eldar, he got the sudden feeling that he was being watched. Logan turned and saw a man at the back of the common room. His face was hidden in shadows, just like the man from Logan's recurring dream. Logan started to get up to go over to the strange man, but Elwyne distracted him when she drew his attention back to the story being told on stage. When Logan turned back around, the man was gone. Even though the man was gone, the feeling of being watched would not relent.

Complexities of the Heart

Logan and Elwyne left the common room just after the last story was over. There was something about the atmosphere in the common room that bothered Logan. The man who was shrouded in shadows still tore at his memory and his current thoughts. More than once on this quest Logan's dreams had proved to be accurate markers of what would eventually come to pass. He wasn't sure if that was going to happen as a result of this dream or not, but it was most certainly true that his dream meant something, but what would remain a mystery. Logan could foresee the resolution of the dream coming in a form that he wouldn't recognize until it was too late and there was nothing that he could do about it. It was not a proposition that Logan found himself comfortable being faced with, but every member of the group had been faced with worse during the last week, and this would just be another that would have to be dealt with. As the evening blurred into night, Logan's mind whirled with torrents of thought, worry, imagination, expectation, and fear. Elwyne sensed Logan's troubled mind and squeezed his hand tightly. As he turned to face her, the worry and fear in his face could not be disguised and his thoughts were clear in his eyes.

Logan had been a private person as far back as he could remember. It was never easy to open up to anyone, but at some point there becomes a limit as to how much could be kept inside. Once it was just Logan and his father, though the two were close and never had problems getting along, they were not exactly connected on an emotional level. They would talk, but they spent more time talking around issues than they did talking through them. Sometimes they got to the point where they didn't talk at all, which was often the better and safer option. One thing that isolation never prepared Logan for was dealing with the emotions that would come from falling in love, and it certainly never prepared him for the consequences of who he fell in love with. However, no matter the hardship or the circumstances, there comes a point in everyone's life where they have to open the walls that bind their soul and let someone inside. Logan had no doubt, from the moment that he laid his eyes on her that that person was going to be Elwyne. He looked back into her eyes for a moment and then tried hard to smile. She smiled back meekly and started to say something. Logan shook his head after a moment, not wanting the conversation to start in the middle of the hallway where there was still a possibility of being overheard. There was a barely perceptible nod from Elwyne, and it seemed from the look in her eyes that she understood the gravity of what was swirling in Logan's mind. What concerned Logan the most was that once he started down the path that he intended, he would not be able to stop, and would say too much, and too many of the thoughts would come out only half-formed, and could be easily misunderstood or misinterpreted. There was far too much at stake for that.

For the brief walk down the corridor, they walked hand in hand with very few words until they ascended the small set of steps to their room. The instant they entered the room, Elwyne sat down on the bed and looked up at Logan, her blue eyes filled with a mixture of anticipation and concern. However as she sat there looking at him, all Logan could feel was her gaze piercing him to the soul. That was the one look that had always unnerved Logan. It was a look that made Logan feel at times as though Elwyne knew exactly what he was going to say before he said it himself. It was said that the eyes were the gateway to the soul, and as far as Logan was concerned through all of the experiences of his life, that axiom was an extremely accurate account of reality. When he would look into Elwyne's eyes, he sometimes could tell what she was thinking, but nowhere as clearly as it seemed she could. There were things like love, understanding, fear, pain, hope, and wonder that came out in her eyes so clearly, but those were easy for anyone to see if they knew what to look for. There were times though when the fog of uncertainty and vagueness would be lifted from her azure eyes and Logan could see deeply into her mind. Somehow her thoughts would seem as clear to him as his own. It was a humbling experience to look at a person and be able to tell how they feel and what they think. That was one of the most frightening things about any relationship that advances to that level of familiarity and intimacy. You become so close emotionally and physically that when you look at the other person, it's just like looking into a mirror. Logan saw himself when he looked into her eyes, or at least to parts of her that touched him so deeply that she had become a part of him. It was a kind of love that dwarfed everything else.

But for every level that that familiarity, emotion, and love that was reassuring and uplifting, there were levels that were frightening and could fill you with such unrelenting doubt. Knowing that Elwyne could see to the very depths of him could make Logan feel as though everything he felt was foolish, or imperfect. She made him feel as though she knew so much more than he did about everything, and that all of his misconceptions made him less intelligent. He would wrangle with words for hours, rehearsing everything that he wanted to say to her, and then when she would look in his eyes and a knowing glimmer came to her smile or to her eyes, his heart would sink and he would immediately feel completely inadequate to the moment. He had never been as comfortable with his words as it always seemed that Pike or Gwydeon had, and when Elwyne would look at him the way that she was looking at him sitting on the edge of the bed, his heart would feel empty and every word would feel like a shadow of what it should. That night though, he could not afford to let his doubt and fear override his ability to say what he needed. If he didn't let the words of his heart flow from him at that moment in time, there were too many things that could go wrong between them, especially in light of the events of the past few days. More than that though, with the danger and the changes for tragedy lurking around every corner, he would not be able to live with himself if something happened to either of them and he didn't say what needed to be said.

Logan sat down on the edge of the bed and tested the moisture in his mouth with a simple swallow. He was worried that his throat would dry out and his body would seize up when he attempted to speak. She took his hand, and he could tell by the way that she squeezed his hand that she was feeling the anxiety that had to be rolling off of him in waves. There were little behaviors that he could recognize, no matter what was going on around them, and Elwyne never held his hand like that unless she was worried or scared, and Logan supposed that what she was feeling would have qualified as both. She had never been a fan of the serious and introspective Logan, and once she had told him that he didn't do it very well. It was meant to be a joke, but it was certainly an accurate assessment. There were times that Logan dwelled so much on what was inside that he would draw away from her unintentionally, and she would become scared or annoyed, and think that she was losing him. She never said so, but he knew she was always afraid that one day he would find something in his heart or his mind that would cause him to leave her. Sometimes his mind could convince him that the worst things were the right thing. And there were times that something inside of Logan would tell him that leaving her would be the best thing to do. Not for him of course, but for her. He would never intentionally hurt Elwyne, but some of the things that he would do to protect her eventually came back and hurt her far worse than he could have ever envisioned. Truth is double-edged sword that must be dealt with in its own time and in its own way. She kept staring up at him, trying to read something into the expression on his face. When she finally sighed and got that perfectly defeated look on her face, he knew that it was time to open up.

"What is it Logan?" she said softly. "What are you hiding from me?"

"I'm not hiding anything from you Elwyne, but I do have something that I want to say to you. Believe me that this isn't easy at all to say, and I don't even know where to begin."

"At the beginning, Logan," she replied pulling me closer. "Everything in our relationship had a beginning, and so that is a good place to start for us."

Logan smiled and pushed himself off the edge of the bed. He dropped to his knees in front of her, taking her hands and pulling himself as close to her as he could.

"I've been thinking."

"I could tell," she responded.

"That obvious?"

She just nodded.

"Things have been going further out of control ever since we left Aradon. I can't take much more of this Elwyne, its really starting to weigh on me."

She smiled and rubbed his hands reassuringly.

"I've been wondering how long it would take you to figure that out. You may not realize it, but you have been acting a lot differently ever since Dreamscape and I'm not sure that it hasn't made you a stronger and more loving person. You would have never shown your affection for me as openly as you do now. You wouldn't have argued with Pike or Gwydeon before, nor would you have been so resistant to outside authority. You've done a lot of growing up in the past week Logan, and I think it makes you a better person."

"You don't understand," he said frustration filling him and shaking his head. "It's not as simple as all of that. I've almost been able to come to terms with David's death, but there was something that always tugged at me. It could have just as easily been me as David who is lying in the church yard dead. Shau-ling missed, and for that, we will all suffer. More than that, it could have been Pike, or Gwydeon, or you."

"No," Elwyne said pulling his chin up so that she could look in his eyes. "this is what Shau-ling wanted. Have you listened to Aryx's stories? The Shadowwalkers weren't trying to kill you. They were coming after us. They wanted to kill those close to you. They wanted to take the fight out of you and hurt your heart. It was the same with the Tarnae and with the Jeresei in Sarmeel. It wasn't until Aldridge that they took a direct shot at you. They want you hurt and distracted. This is what they want, you feeling like this."

Logan frowned.

"That's may be true, Elwyne, but of course it doesn't make me feel any better. In fact, I think it makes me feel worse. The truth of the matter is that I don't think I can make it to Shau-ling. The quest is getting harder and I'm starting to wonder how long it's going to be before one of us doesn't make it out of a battle. I nearly lost you once Elwyne, and I'm not willing to let it happen again."

She looked down into his eyes a little bewildered not only by his words, but by the meaning hidden under them. She opened her mouth to speak, and as if she thought better of her words, she closed it again. The silence was uneasy for a moment, and it wasn't until later that Logan realized that his words had more than the meaning than he had intended. The words were meant to convey love and protection, but there was the hidden meaning that Logan would have done anything in his power to protect her, even if it meant sacrificing himself and others to save her. She knew what he meant, and it bothered her more than mere words could express.

"Logan," she said looking away from him down to the sword that was still so painfully strapped around his waist. "Will we ever be able to settle down together and be normal?"

Logan thought hard about the question. He wasn't sure what it meant to be normal any more. It seemed such a far proposition from what he had been living for better than a month. If anyone still had a sense of normalcy left in them, Logan thought it would have been Elwyne, but apparently he had been mistaken. He wanted to allay her fears and let her know that there was a light at the end of the long dark tunnel, but she would have seen the lie in his eyes. Perhaps he wanted more than anything to believe that lie.

"I wish I could say yes Elwyne, but with the prophecies the way they are, I can't see the world ever being normal again until Shau-ling is destroyed once and for all."

Elwyne nodded in defeat.

"Then there has to be a way to do it now and not five generations in the future."

Elwyne was right, but more so than she could have ever imagined. Logan squeezed her hand tightly, knowing that there was nothing he could say. But there was something he could do. Now more than ever there was a need to get all the information possible. Everything needed to come out and be put on the table, because without the truth, it was Logan's vision of the future and not Elwyne's that would come to pass. He stood up slowly and went to the door. He turned back before opening it and smiled his best smile at Elwyne.

"Wait here my love," Logan said as reassuringly as possible, "I'll just be a moment."

She tried her best to smile back as he left the room. Logan wanted so much to be with her as she had always wanted, back in Aradon, married under the stars that shone through the open roof in the old church, and living out the rest of their lives together with few cares other than each other's happiness.

As Logan wandered down the hallway toward the common room thoughts of the past and the future seemed to flood in from out of nowhere. There was still so much that Logan wanted to say to her, but he didn't have the faintest idea of how to put it when he was with her. Now that she was out of his sight though, the words came back to his mind and he tried to coach his way through what he wanted to tell her. There were strong feelings in his heart that Logan didn't even want to acknowledge. Logan knew that if he could choose from every woman that breathes on their world, the face that he would most love, the smile, the touch, the heart, the voice, the laugh, the soul itself, every detail and feature, down to the last strand of hair, they would all be Elwyne's. But he could never tell her that. It just seemed that the feelings were there but the words to express them didn't want to come out. If the heart is a harp variable to the player's hand, than the music she played was out there beyond Logan when he reached, but there and waiting to be found. The music so pure and perfect, that no other song need ever be sung. The common room was empty when he got there. The bar keeper walked up to Logan slowly and yawned.

"What can I do for you my lord?" he asked.

"Nothing really. Will there be any more activity in the common room tonight?"

"No my lord," he responded stifling another yawn. "The entertainment ended twenty minutes ago, and almost everyone was so tired that they went straight home. Your friends were so entertaining that we didn't even have to deal with anyone passed out on the floor."

"I really hate to do this to you my good sir, I can see how obviously tired you are, but I would like to ask you a favor. Is there a way you can set up a large table here in the center of the common room and make sure that no one comes in after a small meeting starts?"

"After the wonderful entertainment tonight and the amount of money that your friends made for me, I'd even let you marry my daughter. The least I can do is give you use of the common room. I can lock the door to the common room after you and your associates start the meeting, but if you would like anything, I can have one of my serving girls set the table with ale and food for your companions."

"So you can do it then?" I asked.

"Of course my lord. Anything for my friends and generous patrons. The table will be set as I have said."

"How soon can you have it ready?"

"It shouldn't be longer than a half of an hour my lord," he responded quickly.

Logan nodded and turned back toward the hallway. As he walked back toward his room, Logan could feel the words and thoughts colliding in his head, trying to make some sense out of his emotions. As he pushed on the door handle and entered the room, Elwyne stood and greeted him with a hug. There were still concern in her eyes, and at the very least, Logan could understand that. As much as he wanted to console her, his thoughts had already shifted away from his failures at communicating his feelings to the greater concerns of the quest.

"What is it Logan?" she said softly as she rested her head on his chest.

"Time."

"What?" she said looking up into his eyes.

CHAPTER 12

Logan knew he should have said something to quell the fears that he had just placed into her, but he had no idea what he could say. Logan's mind was in thirty different places at once, and he didn't know when it could be focused on only her again. For the moment she would have to forgive his single-mindedness.

"I need a favor Elwyne. I need some time to myself, but not long. Could you tell everyone to meet me in the common room in twenty five minutes? That would make it just about midnight. Tell Jasmen to come down too. It's time we get everything out into the open. Like you said, we can't just keep running into these walls blind trusting that we're doing the right thing. There has to be another way, and if we can't think of one, we're not trying hard enough."

"Alright Logan," she said as she pulled away. "But I want us to continue this conversation before we leave Taren."

"I promise."

She smiled at Logan again squeezing him tightly and then left the room. After the door closed behind her, Logan unfastened the belt that held the scabbard and sword that hung from his left hip. He laid the sword on the bed, and then sat down. It felt good to not have it weighting on him, and there was something comforting about the freedom of that moment. Even though he was still on-guard emotionally, and the sword was still within arm's reach, there was a strange peace to the distance. It was as though Elwyne's assurance that there was another way could actually be true. There were so many half-truths and rumors floating around his head, and Logan found it hard to differentiate them from the things he knew to be true. Was he to believe what Cedric had told him through the initial letter, or the stories that Aryx told? Was he to believe Lady Ann and the picture she painted? Or was Logan to believe the words spoken during the phantom confrontation with Shau-ling, or the very real confrontation with Aldridge. How much of it all could really be true? And how much of the stories were just a product of the passage of time.

Time was a strange thing. No matter what happened, no matter what you do, things change. You fight the inevitable as much as you want, but it does no good. Time shapes your life more and more every day of your life until it changes you completely. When that happens, nothing can ever be the same again. That is a scary proposition when you think that your life is at the mercy of the one thing you can never control. Logan was finding more and more of his life at the mercy of elements that were completely out of his control, and the further he traveled down the path that had been chosen for him, the more clear it was that time was not his ally. As time drew on, the control he once had on his life began to slip through his fingers. And as some unconscious metaphor, Logan had lost track of time and didn't even realize that he had been sitting there for more than a few minutes. The next thing he knew, there came a knock at my door and when he answered it, the inn keeper was waiting on the other side.

"Yes?"

"The common room is ready as you requested my lord," he said. "All of you friends have assembled and are waiting for you."

Suddenly the loss of time hit Logan and though he was off-balance and still shaking off the haze of his introspection, Logan thanked the innkeeper for his work and for his tireless dedication. He assured the innkeeper that he would require nothing else from the man, but the innkeeper insisted that if anything at all was needed, Logan needn't hesitate to call. After a quick, yet bleary-eyed smile, the innkeeper bowed slightly, turned, and headed back down to the lower floor. For several long moments, Logan just stood there looking at the slightly open door, wondering what would happen once he walked through it and joined the others. The whole idea had been constructed on a whim, and now that he was moments away from the culmination of it, doubt began to flood through him. Finally, after a long sigh he stepped through the door and as he turned back to shut the door behind him, he caught sight of his scabbard and sword lying on the bed. This time there was no debate. He would not be walking into the coming meeting armed, and so he closed the door. He could hear some murmurs of conversation as he approached the common room, but all of it stopped when Logan came into view.

There were many puzzled faces that looked up at Logan when he entered the room. Neither Elwyne nor Pike looked up at Logan, and he could tell that there was a sense of foreboding that filled both of them. This conversation was a long time coming, and though neither of them was happy about the circumstances, both knew it was necessary. Jasmen and Talon appeared to have been wrapped in conversation, but now their focus was completely on Logan. When he looked around the table, Logan noticed that Gwydeon and Midarin were holding hands. Some thoughts ran through his mind of a situation that happened just after Illimar, but Logan pushed them aside. They were entitled to as much happiness as they could claim from the darkness. Logan continued to scan the faces of his friends. Gideon seemed to be looking up at Logan and keeping an eye on Aryx at the same time. No matter the excuse that his actions were lent by the mysterious Asperon Thorne, it appeared that Gideon and some other members of the party were still a bit concerned. Eldar sat very close to Pike, which seemed a bit odd, considering the fact that they had hated each other for about a year. Lane and Talos seemed to be continuing their seemingly never-ending discussion about magic, and Elwyne had even told Logan that Alexander was beginning to use the art. Finally though, Logan's eyes came back to the dark and somber face of Aryx Terian. Aryx didn't look in Logan's direction, and his eyes just stared off into the distance, wrapped in his own thoughts. After standing for a matter of moments, Logan took a seat at the table beside Elwyne. Gideon looked over to him again and then passed Logan one of the mugs of ale that had been provided by one of the serving girls as the innkeeper indicated. There was an uneasy silence in the room and when Logan finally stood again, he knew that the next few minutes would be far more difficult that even he had envisioned.

"Friends, it's been a while since we have all been together like this so that we could talk. But a lot has happened since the beginning and I'm not quite sure that you are all aware of it. From Illimar to Sarmeel, to Rana and Rama, Trelon and Sador, we have dodged danger and tried to keep our wits about us in ever more insane circumstances. But even through the insanity we have found allies and those willing to put their lives on the line to ensure that we make it to the end, and do what fate as ordained for us to do. To that end, the young lady sitting beside Talon is named Jasmen Hiedra, and she has joined our force. She has done so of her own free will, but if any of you have an objection to her joining us, I will understand and hear you out."

No one spoke for a moment, and then Aryx stood.

"My Lord Dragon?"

"Yes Aryx?"

"We do not know this woman or what her aims are. Remember what we learned in facing Aldridge. Remember that there are enemies around every corner. The larger the force you gather around yourself, the greater the target you prove to be. Until you reach Marcwell, you cannot afford to be taking these reckless chances with your life, and it seems that you have been unbalanced since your encounter in Rama. And certainly since the altercation with Aldridge. I suggest you reconsider your actions and focus on getting to Marcwell and fulfilling your responsibilities to this quest and to this world."

Pike's hands cracked as he balled his fists.

"We're not going to Marcwell, Aryx…"

Broken Faith

Pike's words hung in the air like a thunderhead that threated to explode with uncontrollable fury every moment, and it seemed as though everyone was holding their breath as not to hasten the explosion. All eyes had turned to Pike and for the briefest of moments Logan felt as though Pike was going to falter under the growing pressure, especially as Aryx's eyes burned through him. However, Pike's resolve remained firm, and he took only a short breath before un-balling his fists, placing his hands palm-down on the table and then pushing his way to his feet. He held Aryx's burning gaze for another moment before looking over at Logan and speaking. His voice came out proud and clear, without the barest hint of a waiver.

"With Logan's knowledge and permission, the members of this generation of the prophecies have decided that after all of the obstacles we have encountered and all of the trials we have undertaken that the path to Marcwell is not safe. It is the obvious course, and so it is the one that Shau-ling will plant with the most dangerous traps. So, that considered, we have decided, that we will not be going to Marcwell, but instead will make for Kandor. From there we will plot our next move and chart our own course, as Cedric once did."

Aryx looked a bit shocked, but only for a second. The dark stare returned to his eyes and he spoke with a strong underlying tone.

"Lord Cedric did what he did out of necessity of the circumstances. To deny that he knows far more about the state of the war with the Shadows is to confirm that you are fools. Lord Cedric has offered his help to you, and if you do not accept than you will surely suffer because of it. Lord Cedric is not doing this all just because of you and your friends. He is trying to save the world from Shau-ling's tyranny. If you go to Kandor, you may suffer a fate that will condemn the world to darkness for the rest of eternity."

"You're the fool, Aryx," Talon said standing. "If you think that we are going to trust Cedric after what happened to us in Sador and what happened to Logan in Trelon, you can forget it. Speaking just for myself, I'm tired of being led around by the nose and not having any say in what happens in this quest. These are our lives, and I'm not going to have the Lion sit up in his palace in Marcwell and dictate that to me."

"There are those of us that believe as you do, Aryx," Gwydeon said, still holding Midarin's hand, "but there are too many variables, and we all feel uncomfortable. Try to look at things from our perspective. Zarsi, Aldridge, the Jeresei, the Shadowwalkers, the Tarnae. For all of the information that you and Lord Cedric have to offer us, it just seems as though we continue to run blindly from one crisis and mystery to another. If you would be more upfront with us . . ."

"We might find your insights and orders a little easier to take," Midarin finished.

Aryx sat down and looked back at Logan.

"I have no control over what you do with your lives, and I never have, and perhaps that is as it should be. At some point you were going to have to take ownership of this quest, and of your own fates. I know that Lord Cedric's only thought was attempting to spare you some of the hardships inflicted upon him, but perhaps that is not possible, and perhaps it was a misguided pursuit from the beginning. However, that said, I do still feel that changing course and making for Kandor is folly. Marcwell is still the best choice for destination, and the resources available to you there would dwarf any you would find elsewhere. What could I do to convince you to go to Marcwell?"

"As Gwydeon and Midarin suggested," Lane answered, "you could be totally honest with us and tell us everything we ask you to if it is possible for you to answer at all."

Aryx grimaced.

"Very well," he replied. "It appears that if you are intent on this course, then it would stand to reason that you should have all of the information that I can give you. Where would you like to start?"

"The phasia," Gideon said quickly, "tell us about dem."

Aryx sighed at the question and shook his head. It was obvious that he knew that question in particular was coming, and it also looked as though he was anxious about answering it.

"Despite our experience with the forces of the Shadow, none of us know very much about the phasia, except the fact that they exist and that there are ten of them. We have met two of them since we have been together, and I only know of two others. They all have similar powers, but each of them favors a specific realm of their powers over the others and that is how they attack and focus their energies. All ten of the phasia exist because there must be a balance of power in the world. Just as there is a balance between good and evil in the world, inside each of the two, good and evil, there must be a balance. No one thing in either of the two can have more power than any other. When the four *Erieal* are linked, they are as powerful as the *Coromor*. The same is true when seven of the phasia act as one. When that happens, they are as powerful as Shau-ling himself."

"Why only seven?" Lane asked.

"The truth is in the prophecies of the *Coromor*, Lane," Talos interjected. "Seven generations, seven *Coromors* will unite to defeat Shau-ling. So too must it stand to reason that seven phasia, if they are as powerful as the *Coromor*, would be powerful enough to unseat their dark master."

"So if Logan were to unite six *Erieal* behind him, he would be able to take out Shau-ling?" Talon asked.

"Unfortunately, things are not that simple," Aryx answered. "It seems that from one generation to the next, the powers of the *Erieal* are drawn from the same source. If Pike were to join the link, Mailock would not be able to because they are both from the line of the original Water Brother. And though Talos' logic is sound in his interpretation of prophecies, Shau-ling would not be so foolish as to leave his own fate in the hands of his unruly children. While the phasia have control of powers similar to that of the Coromor and the Erieal, they are also possessed of a polarity of a sort. In the final battle against Shau-ling's forces in Lakestone, we were certain that the phasia would be able to overwhelm our meager force, but it turned out that they either were unable or unwilling to work together against us. Mailock later theorized that their powers were not compatible with one another in the same way that the powers of the Erieal are. I'm afraid to say that even if the phasia wished to, they could not rebel against Shau-ling."

"What about the *Chosen One*?" Gwydeon asked.

Aryx's head jerked toward Gwydeon and he stared for a moment.

"Where did you hear that name?"

Gwydeon faltered for a moment at the roughness of Aryx's voice.

"When we went up against Zarsi, he was under the impression that I was this *Chosen One*," Gwydeon answered. "He said something about his brother Saurn and a mark. When he saw that the mark was not on my palm, he was finally convinced that I wasn't the *Chosen One*."

"So," Aryx said warily, "the *Chosen One*, has fallen into the hands of the phasia. That makes them twice as powerful as they once were. Now it is possible that the phasia could destroy Shau-ling."

"How is that possible?" Logan asked. "You said that the phasia could not link their powers in any way that would allow them to defeat Shau-ling. Who and what is this *Chosen One*?"

Aryx braced himself for a moment and then put both hands on the table and slowly eased himself back into his chair.

"The *Chosen One* in the strictest sense is the equivalent to the *Coromor*. In reality, and purely according to legend, they have the same powers, but what sets them apart from one another is how they derive their powers. One could say that the *Coromor* actually derives the largest measure of his powers from the *Erieal,* and in turn would be able to draw equally from a member of the phasia. However, since the phasia draw their powers from Shau-ling, the *Coromor* would in theory also be drawing power from Shau-ling himself. While nothing in the prophecies specifically speaks about the *Chosen One*, there has been much conjecture about its true nature and purpose. Some say that the *Chosen One* is a kind of cross-breed that was accidentally born. Those that subscribe to this theory believe that something occurred within the circle of phasia that caused the Creator to spin out another equalizing factor. That factor turned out to be the *Chosen One*. It is thought that the *Chosen One* can only draw on the phasia for his powers, making him slightly less powerful than the *Coromor*."

"That is an awful lot of ifs, Aryx," Logan commented.

Aryx shook his head and continued.

"There is one school of wise men who have studied the prophecies that disagree with this claim. They believe that the *Chosen One* is also able to draw on the *Coromor* for power, and through the *Coromor* he is able to draw on Shau-ling. According to the wise men however, this does not work both ways, and the *Coromor* cannot draw on the *Chosen One* for power."

"An over-simplification," Talos added. "The Moridon are the ones who have done the most work and research in an attempt to understand the significance of the *Chosen One*. The most troubling conclusions always center on the possibility that the *Chosen One* is neither a being of light nor darkness and therefor can draw upon all powers equally. However, there is no amount of research that has been able to ascribe motivation or purpose to the *Chosen One*, and that is perhaps the most troubling fact."

"And he is in the possession of the phasia," Jasmen added for the first time in the conversation. Her stories must have touched on some of these subjects before, but now she was in the story. Inwardly Logan wondered how she was adjusting.

The implication hung heavily in the air, until Elwyne's voice cut through it.

"In theory, could the *Chosen One* kill Shau-ling?" Elwyne asked.

"In theory, yes," Aryx answered finally. "However, until now there has only been one recorded *Chosen One*, and he served beside Aralias Imstra long before the *Coromor* was created. So, we know as little about him as we do about the phasia, perhaps less. Most of the records of that time were lost, even to the Moridon."

"Unfortunately, that is true," Talos said, his voice somber. "Little is known other than the man's name. Aerith Seth."

Logan sat still for a moment and then stood.

"I say we put it to another vote. Since all of you know what we are in for, I think that we all deserve a chance to vote. Aryx, if we decide not to continue on to Marcwell, will you travel with us?"

"No. My work with you ends when I deliver you to Lord Cedric. If you decide not to continue on to Marcwell, I must return to convey your wishes to my lord and friend. I doubt that going to Kandor will in any way dissuade Lord Cedric from doing what he can to assist you and thereby assist all those threatened by the tyranny of the Shadows."

Logan turned to the others.

"The vote then," he said as calmly as he could manage.

"Marcwell," Elwyne said softly.

"Marcwell," Eldar added.

"Against my better judgment, Marcwell," Pike said grudgingly.

"Kandor," that came from Midarin, Gwydeon, Talon, and Gideon.

"I will not vote," Jasmen said, "it doesn't seem fair."

"I also refuse to vote," Talos added. "The Moridon have always been followers of the will of the Coromor, so where the *Coromor* goes, so shall I follow."

"Marcwell," Lane said slowly.

"That leaves you and I Alexander," Logan remarked.

"I go where you go, Lord Dragon," he replied like a true soldier.

"Well then, I guess it's up to me. Unfortunately, I see no other option than to go on to Marcwell as planned. From there we will do as we see fit however, and we will take no orders, but we will welcome suggestions from those who are more knowledgeable."

"A very prudent decision, Logan," Aryx replied. "If that is all, I would like to get some rest."

"Yes, that will be all, as far as I can see. All of you get a good night's rest, and we will leave in a few days. We have rushed around enough, and now that we have the Jeweled Dragon's Flame and that race is over, I think we can find some well-deserved respite here. Good night, everyone."

With that Logan turned and left the room with Elwyne close behind. She grabbed his hand as he walked toward their room, and when he stopped to look back at her he smiled and nodded. She smiled back at him and they went back to their room. Logan didn't sleep very well that evening, and for the most part, he lay there holding Elwyne and taking comfort in the fact that she was there with him. It seemed that in those moments when it was only the two of them, the he loved her more than ever. Logan couldn't imagine what life would have been like without her. What he felt when he was with her was more than merely love; it was like a strange mix between wonder and fear. Once he was a whole person, whole but alone. But that part in his life was dim and hard to remember. It felt that now he was only half of a person. She was his other half, and Logan could not honestly see himself without her ever again. If the two of them were ever ripped apart by death, the other who lived would surely not live long. If Logan were to lose Elwyne, he would surely die quickly and miserably. He could almost say the same for her.

Every night the stars take over the evening sky. They rise, burn bright, and then fade away in the morning light. Then the next night the stars come out again, but they are never quite the same from night to night. Humans live their lives like the stars. However, their night can last up to sixty years. But eventually a star must fall, and humans end their lives either in a jubilant torrent of wind and fire like a comet or a shooting star, or they die with a whimper like those stars that fade away into the morning. Sometimes you look up into the sky and you see a star that burns brighter than the rest. Maybe that is not just one star, but two that circle close together in the heavens and give off their light and fire as one. When one fades away, so does the other, and that is how Logan saw Elwyne and himself. They were like those stars who give off their light as one so that you forget they are separate. Perhaps it is true that those stars forget in time too.

The next morning couldn't have come quick enough for Logan. Elwyne decided to drag him around for more shopping that morning and afternoon, and if it wasn't for the fact that Eldar was on the same page and she dragged Pike along, Logan would have been completely bored. Later that evening they got a reprieve as they sat in the common room of the inn and listened to Pike, Talon, and Jasmen as they told yet another set of stories in front of a packed house. The stories were actually told by Pike and Talon, but Jasmen played her harp and lyre behind them, adding different musical phrases to spice up the rather familiar stories. Apparently, Pike and Talon had sat down and turned the fight in Illimar into a song and story. As they sang and talked through the fight, people laughed and talked. Suddenly, a dagger shot from somewhere out of the crowd and barely missed Talon. When Talon grabbed his sword off of the stage and Pike jumped behind him with ax ready, Logan stood and noticed that the rest of the party were ready to fight as well. A small scuffle started near the front of the common room, and it was over almost as quickly as it began. Men in chain mail stood from the front row and quickly separated the two opposing sides and dragged them out into the street. Seconds later, the men reappeared and took their seats at the front of the common room. The circumstance was strange to say the least, but the patrons seemed less concerned than Logan, and one of the serving girls mentioned that it was a common occurrence. Within an hour, the show had ended, and Pike, Talon and Jasmen walked over to the table where Elwyne and Logan sat.

"So, what did you think?" Pike asked.

"I've never heard better Pike," Elwyne answered, "you and Talon were in great voice tonight."

"Jasmen made the show with the music though," Logan added. "For some reason, the story sounded a little too good to be true."

"That's because you were there, Logan," Jasmen answered, "but thanks anyway."

Elwyne laughed. For some reason, neither Pike nor Talon found the remark amusing. They sat talking for another hour, and now and then, other members of the party came to the table and added their voices to the conversation. Pretty soon, the members of the party were the only people in the common room, except for the guards who had stopped the scuffle earlier. When some of the party started to make their way to their rooms, the guards got up and blocked their way. Having seen this, Pike, Talon, and Logan got up and walked over to the guards.

"What is the meaning of this?" Logan asked.

"You will not be allowed to leave this common room until our leader has had a few words with you," one of the guards said coldly.

"We're very tired," Pike urged, "and we need our sleep. Tell your leader that he can talk to us in the morning."

Pike started to walk through the blockade, but he was stopped short when the guards drew their swords and firmed up their position. There were ten of them that blocked the way to the rooms, and there were five more that blocked the door to the outside. Pike took a step back and readied his ax.

"This isn't going to get ugly now, is it gentlemen? I was hoping that we could all get some well-deserved rest here and not have to fight," he said almost sarcastically.

"Either follow the orders that you have been given, or prepare to defend yourselves."

Despite how often it brought him discomfort, it was times like that when Logan was thankful that wearing his sword at all times had become reflex. However, the last thing he wanted to do was get into a fight with the guards. It took some doing to pull Pike away from the rank of guards as it seemed he was just spoiling for a fight, but eventually he stood with the rest near the bar.

"We have to get out of here," Logan said.

"How 'bout dat little trick we used back in Illimar?" Gideon asked.

"There is a grate just behind the bar," Midarin replied.

Everyone's eyes turned to look at Midarin.

"I like to be familiar with all the exits when I sleep in a place other than my own bed, just in case I have to depart quickly in the night without being seen."

Gwydeon was the only one who took that at more than face value. After talking with Pike for another few moments, they had a plan. No one liked the idea of running away from a fight, especially Pike, but Logan was sure nothing was going to be gained by bloodshed.

"Wait a minute," Elwyne said just before Pike was about to unleash the diversion.

"What is it Elwyne?" Logan asked.

"Where's Aryx?"

Logan looked around for a moment and then realized that Aryx had not been in the common room for some time. He had been acting strangely lately, but Logan tried not to rope this coincidence in with the other strange behavior.

"We don't the time or the ability to look for him now, Elwyne," Gwydeon said calmly as he turned away from the guards. "He'll just have to fend for himself."

"Okay," Logan said turning toward Pike, "we could use that diversion whenever you're ready."

Pike looked over to Lane, and when he nodded, Pike walked toward the guards who blocked the way to the rooms. Talon tapped Pike on the shoulder and then turned toward the guards at the door. Pike looked back over his shoulder at Logan, and after giving the nod, a wall of ice sprang up from the floor in front of Pike. Talon shifted his attention back toward the guards in front of him. Winds blasted in from out of nowhere, and slammed against the guards and pinned them to the wall. Everyone could hear the guards behind the wall of ice trying to break through, but it seemed that as Pike backed toward the bar, the wall of ice began to thicken. One by one each member of the party ducked through the opening. Logan tried to keep track of everyone as they exited the passageway, but didn't see Gideon emerge. Pike was the last to escape through the passageway, and after he convinced Logan that he was the last one, they made their way silently and quickly to an inn on the far edge of town. The inn was called *The Golden Dagger*.

* * * * * * * * * * * *

Gideon waited as Talon brushed past where he lay hidden. He had found a small crevice in the passageway and had wedged himself in the hole until everyone had gone. There was something that ate at him. The attack by the guards seemed too much of a coincidence with Aryx's disappearance, and he found it hard to trust a man who had attacked them, no matter what excuses and explanations had been offered. Alone, Gideon crawled back up the passageway and waited just inside the grate. He concentrated all of his powers on his body for that moment, and then stepped through the open grate. As he stood in the center of the room, he noticed that guards Talon had pinned to the wall were already free, and they had all but broken the ice that held their companions. Gideon's plan had worked, and none of the guards had seen him. He had used his powers to render himself invisible, and that could prove to be an affective trick in the future. It took several moments for the guards to free themselves from their confines, and scant moments later, another man appeared from the stairway that led to the rooms. Gideon's blood boiled as soon as he found the man's face, and clutched one of his daggers tightly.

Dat bastard, he thought to himself, *I'll gut dat traitor myself if I have ta.*

Aryx kept his distance from the guards and walked over to a table in the far corner of the room. Gideon saw that another man was sitting at the table, but the shadows prevented him from seeing the man's face.

"The new *Erieal* are very impressive Aryx," the stranger said coldly. "I thought you said my guards could easily contain them."

Aryx frowned and shook his head.

"They are gaining control over their abilities much faster than anyone could have anticipated. They have made some decisions as to their futures and I had not the chance to inform you or your men of the changes."

"You'll have to do better than that, Aryx. You and I have been allies for a long time, and you have never failed me before. You and I both know that I need them. If they go off on their own with the Flame, all will be lost to me and they may actually make it to Shau-ling. We can't allow that to happen. Find them and keep them on the path to Marcwell, no matter what it takes. When they get there, all will be taken care of. Keep on your toes though my friend. There are enemies all around."

Aryx bowed to the man and left the inn. The guards also turned and left. Gideon found himself all alone with the stranger. He moved closer, trying to get a good look at the man's face in spite of the shadows.

"It's no use Alimidarian," the man said just before taking a sip of ale. "The shadows cannot be penetrated by any kind of light, let alone eyesight. If you reveal yourself however, I will be glad to show you my face before I kill you."

Gideon didn't make a sound and started to move back toward the grate.

"Don't bother sneaking away Gideon Viruci," the man said quickly. "You and I both know that you are not at all innocent in this little game. How would your friends take it if they knew exactly who you are? Don't presume to judge Aryx when you do not turn the mirror upon yourself."

Gideon didn't respond to the taunt, and moved as slowly and carefully into the passageway.

"I'll be sure to say hello to your mother for you. I can't imagine how disappointed she is in the way that you have turned out. Too much of your father in you I suppose."

Gideon moved through the tunnel with a heavy heart. The man spoke more truth than Gideon realized, and he could hear the man's laughs echoing through the passageway as he moved to rejoin his companions at *The Golden Dagger*.

Beyond Death

Evil is fought not only in the world of the mortals, but in the world of the dead as well. No one is safe, even in death, until the world is saved from the scourge of Shau-ling. Because Shau-ling's evil lives both in life and death, defying even the Great Dark One's power over eternal night and the death of all that is evil, Shau-ling has made himself the most powerful force in both worlds. However, just as there is a resistance to the power of Shau-ling through the forces of the *Coromor* on the side of the living, there is also a resistance on the Other Side. Not even death can stop the servants of the *Coromor*.

David woke up from his long listless sleep and found himself in a place that he didn't recognize. His dreamless sleep still tugged at him, but he stood and looked around trying hard to recognize anything that would remotely place where he was. However, as he looked around, he saw a sight that made his flesh crawl. He was sitting on a plot of grass beside a large Seluiyn tree. He could smell the rich fruit, and his mouth watered with the anticipation of tasting the delicious fruit. *Logan and Elwyne would be in heaven here,* he thought to himself. The peacefulness of the place was so extreme that not even a single blade of grass moved in the soft breeze. He strolled over the glade and then was shocked. Ten feet from where he was standing, the green of the grass ended in nothingness. David walked over to the edge of this reality and looked down.

It was as if he had turned the sky and the earth upside down. Instead of looking up at the stars during the twilight hours, David looked down at a tapestry of light and motion. Quite taken aback by the shocking sight, he staggered back over to the tree in order to regain his composure. He sat there for a long time before he worked up enough courage to make his way back over to the edge. He crawled on hands and knees back over to the edge and laid flat on his stomach. As he looked down into the void, he caught a glimpse of another island of reality off to his left. There was something moving on the island, but he could not make out what it was. The distance between the islands did not seem that much to him, so he decided to try and jump to the other island. David walked over to the tree, which appeared to be planted in the exact center of the island. He took a piece of fruit from the tree and stuck it in his pocket.

If I make this jump, he said to himself, *I'll have something to eat later. What's the chance on finding another Seluiyn tree with fruit this size?*

David laughed softly to himself and then took several deep breaths. As soon as he felt he was ready, he broke into a spring. He could see the edge getting closer, and at the last possible second he leapt into the void. His momentum carried him almost to the edge of the second island. Then, as if he had a rope tied around his waist connecting him to the tree on the other island, he was snapped back, and he hit hard on the ground of the island he awoke upon.

He lay there for a moment, pain shooting through his arms and legs. He had landed square on the back of his head, and he remembered clearly a few seconds where he was both in sleep and awake. It was the feeling of floating in an infinite sea of dreams and the refreshment of waking. As soon as he was sure that he as alright, David backed up farther and jumped again. As he floated through the air with great speed behind him, he could see his goal coming closer to him. However, just as before he was jerked back by an unseen force, but this time he was farther away from the target island than he was in his previous attempt. The impact from this experience with the forces of this strange world knocked David unconscious. He lay there for a long time, and then shook his head trying to recover.

David rubbed his eyes, and then began to yawn. Mid yawn, he choked and spit something out of his mouth. There in front of him was a small pool of blood. Several drops hit the pool before he realized that he was bleeding from both his mouth and nose. The impact from the attempt to leave his island had jarred him more than he initially realized. Within a few moments the bleeding stopped, and he readied himself for another attempt. He backed up to the far edge of the island and took two deep breaths. Then something came to him.

Wait a minute. The farther back I started, the harder the force pulled me back. If I were to run from there, the impact from this backlash is liable to kill me. Maybe if I were to jump from that edge the force that is holding me here will allow me enough slack to get me over to the next island. If I'm wrong, I'll end up falling to who knows where.

At that final thought, David cringed a little. Thoughts of the terrible stories he had been told over the years ran through his head, despite all of his efforts to stop them. As soon as he had walked to the other side of the island, he had thought about all of the options hundreds of times, and every time the same course of action seemed to be the prudent one. He stood at the very edge, far enough that the toes of his boots hung over the edge. Again he drew his breath, and before he could exhale he was floating in the void, flying toward his intended target. His feet struck ground, and he realized that he was on the other island. He breathed a sigh of relief and took the piece of fruit out of his pocket for a sort of celebration. He raised the fruit to his mouth and was about to take a bite when an arrow snagged it out of his hand and pinned it to a tree, which stood nearby. David spun around and was face to face with a woman of his age.

Her beauty shocked him more than the arrow that could have claimed his life if she'd have wished it. She was nearly even height with David, and she walked proudly as if she had done nothing. Golden hair flowed down the back of her neck and gently caressed her shoulders. David could not help but to stare, and he found her eyes more captivating than her incredible figure. Her eyes were whirling torrents of azure captured by a face whose beauty was incomparable to anything that he had seen in his life. For the brief few seconds that he had seen her, he had almost forgotten about the fact that he was in love with Eldar and that this woman had nearly killed him. He shook himself back to his senses and started speaking.

"What under the Light do you think you're doing?" David screamed.

"Saving your life, you pathetic excuse for a hero," the woman responded.

"What do you mean you were saving my life? And why did you call me a hero? And for that matter who are you?"

"My my my..." the woman said calmly. "You are full of questions and fire. I like that in a man. Well, my name is Christine, Christine Goldenlake. And you are?"

"David Tamerlane," David replied shortly. "Now, how do you call nearly killing me with that arrow saving my life?"

"David. Nice name," she mumbled. "Don't flatter yourself David, and don't belittle my skills. I deliberately aimed for that little piece of fruit there. If I wanted to kill you, I could have easily done it. That little piece of fruit is like an anchor. Once you take a bite, you are leashed to the tree you took it from."

David thought hard for a moment and then nodded in a mixture of thanks and apology.

"Now for your third question," she continued.

"Third question...oh yes. Why did you call me a hero?"

"Everyone who lives...well...stays here is a hero. All who dwell in this place is part of either the army of the *Coromor* or the army of the Shadow. So, how much do you remember?"

David thought hard for a moment, and then he went white as a sheet. Christine walked over to him quickly and took him into her arms and set him down on the ground softly.

"I know. It was hard for me to remember the first time I died."

David looked at her wide-eyed. He saw the picture of a ball of flame engulfing him clearly in his mind, but it was more than a dream or a memory. Every time it ran through his mind, it was as if he were experiencing it again.

"Relax David," Christine said caringly, "it will pass. You get used to seeing your own death after a time. Come on, I want you to meet the others."

David tried to speak, but his mouth was dry and he could not manage to push a sound from his throat. Eventually, he made it to his feet and croaked a response.

"There are others here?"

"Many. Some of them came through after you did."

David looked at her in shock for a moment. Christine sensed his hesitation and then finished her statement.

"Yes," she said, "I have been watching you ever since you arrived. My job was to make sure you got to Lady Binosear alive….bad habit…in once piece. She is the leader of our forces here."

"Lady Binosear? Do you mean Erika Binosear?"

"The same. When she was killed, and she arrived in our land, she took command in the name of Lord Cedric. She told us that our war against the forces of evil was not yet over. As more and more heroes came through we began to learn of Lord Cedric, and the *Coromor*, as well as Shau-ling. Now that you are here, you can tell us what you know of the new *Coromor*. Were you not in his circle of friends?"

"I was. What of the other people who have come through since I have been here?"

"There has been one since you arrived. Anne Binosear, formerly the Queen of Trelon."

David didn't know how to respond, and just asked Christine to lead the way. It was still hard to accept the fact that he was dead. It was also hard to fathom that Shau-ling had the power to control his minions on this side of life. If there was a war raging here as there was in the world of the living, David would still have his piece of the war. Vengeance would finally be his, even in death.

David followed Christine's lead, jumping from island to island. This time, making the jumps was easier. Somehow the fruit was the source of the pull that always seemed to draw him back to the tree. Now, when he jumped into the void, there was no unseen force pulling him back to the island before, and he was almost flying in the nothingness.

Eventually Christine and David landed on a huge island. David looked around eagerly, trying to see if he could trace the edges of this island as he had done with all the others. However, after they had walked away from the edge to the point where he could not see the definite ending of the land, it was just as if he were in the large field back in Aradon. The green glade seemed to extend on forever in all directions. Christine kept walking down what appeared to be a path, but it was more like a rut in the grass than a path. Before long there was a village in sight.

The houses were simple farmhouses much like the one Logan lived in. David could see puffs of smoke rising out of makeshift chimneys on most of the houses. As they walked, David began to see the outline of a larger building. It looked very much like the *Traveling Bard*, but it was larger, and had a front gated instead of a door. As David looked around, he could see no other signs of activity or any sign of another person until they reached the gate of the larger building.

In front of the gate stood two women, both of which had flaxen hair, and wore blue robes. One of the women held an axe, and the other a long spear.

If Pike and Talon were here they would be in love. Just as well, from the look of that axe, Pike would have his hands full. At least these ladies are spared Talon's singing and Pike's jokes. What I wouldn't give to hear one of their songs, David thought.

Christine walked up to the two women and spoke to them softly. She then motioned for David and he walked over quickly.

"David, I would like you to meet the Wind Sisters. This one with the ax is Allahanna, and this is her sister Corin."

They both smiled at him, and David smiled back. They moved out of the doorway and opened the gate. Christine walked into the courtyard, quickly followed by David. The massive courtyard was empty except for a few fully armored guards who stood at the entrances of the doors that led to other parts of the building. In front of them was a large set of double doors that stood wide open. Christine led David through those doors and up a towering flight of stairs. As they reached the top flight, a voice called from one of the hallways.

"Christine!" the man's voice called.

"Here, Galanax!" she replied.

David turned and watched a huge young man walk quickly down the hallway toward them. He was bare-chested, so the size of his muscles showed his obvious physical power. Seconds later he was standing in front of them, eyeing David closely.

"So, is this the one called David?"

"Yes, it is," Christine responded.

"Good. Lady Binosear, well both of them that is, wished to see you as soon as you arrived. They are waiting in the war room. Would you like me to escort you, my lady?" he said with a gleam in his eye.

"No, Galanax, I believe I can manage on my own," she responded with a quick wink.

He smiled and made his way back to whatever he was doing before he spotted them. Christine said nothing else and walked down a hallway that led them to the left. David continued to follow, keeping his eyes open and mentally recording the different passages they took on their way to the place that Galanax had called the war room. Eventually, Christine stopped in front of a set of double doors and entered. She told David to wait outside until she announced him. Seconds later, the doors opened, and he was ushered inside.

As soon as he was in the large room, he was face to face with two men and three women, only one that he recognized. The men eyed him closely; however, the two women in the back of the room seemed to pay him no notice. One of the women raised her head, and David took a step back. The woman in front of him looked so familiar. She was the spitting image of the sister that he had lost. She and Elwyne could have been twins. Christine looked at David, and decided that now was the time to interrupt.

"Lady Binosear, this is the young man who came through before your sister. His name is David Tamerlane, the brother of the one known to be the Lord Dragon's consort."

David was slightly taken aback by the description of his sister, but he let it pass.

I'm sure that they are exaggerating. Father would never allow Logan to marry Elwyne. Besides, I don't think Elwyne could stand to be around him that much.

"Well," Erika Binosear said, "tis a pleasure to welcome you to our little army. Let me introduce you to the rest of us. This is my sister-in-law Lady Anabel Binosear."

The lady standing beside Erika bowed and then went back to what she was doing. She was a bit shorter than Erika, but she seemed to project a power mightier than her stature.

"The man to your left is William Hathaway, and the man to your right is Khisanth Alghri."

Each of the men nodded to David, and then walked back to the table in the middle of the room. Erika motioned for David to walk over to the table. Upon doing so, he saw a map of the entire world on that side of reality.

"David," Erika began, "we have been planning a raid on the forces of the Shadow. Since you were one of the generals that the Dragon appointed, I would like you to lead one of the units."

"Wait a minute. I know very little about Logan's being the Dragon, and even less about being a general. Gwydeon and Pike taught me how to fight, but I am no good to you in a battle. I still have a problem believing that Logan is this *Coromor* that everyone is talking about."

"Careful there David," Anabel commented, "the forces of the Shadow on this side are still able to report back to their lord. If they were to find out the identity of the new *Coromor*, he would be in a much danger as if he were to proclaim himself."

David nodded but continued his argument.

"I would be happy to fight for you, but only as a soldier. Give me a sword, and I will do my best."

"Very well, David," Erika replied. "The forces of the Shadow were massing on an island not far from here according to Christine's latest reconnaissance mission. If we were to strike tonight there would be a chance..."

Before she could finish her sentence, Galanax burst through the door, sword drawn and breathing heavily.

"The forces of the Shau are here! The whole breed of Shadowwalkers has been sent through. They are being led by Allan, your son Lady Anne."

"He is not my son, Galanax, he is one of Shau-ling's children now. He is a phase."

Everyone in the room ran out quickly, all the time barking orders and making plans for defense of the palace. David ran after, trying to keep straight all the names that were connected with his, as well as which unit he was to serve under.

"David, you follow Galanax. You are to be his man in battle."

"Yes, my lady."

Galanax motioned for David to follow, and led him down a corridor away from the rest. He ducked into a room for a moment and then emerged with a sword and scabbard in his free hand.

CHAPTER 12

"Here David," he said throwing him the sword, "make good use of this."

David strapped the scabbard around his waist while running down the hall after Galanax. David finally caught up with him at a towering flight of stairs.

"The army of the Shadow is upon us David; they have already broken through the front gates."

As David looked down the stairs, he saw several men dressed in full armor fighting with several monsters. The only ones that he recognized were the Shadowwalkers. The other beasts were basically human except for their red skin and the fact that they wore no armor in battle. Galanax was already half way down the stairs before David realized what was happening. Without too much more thought, David bolted down the stairs after him.

As he reached the bottom of the stairs, he had lost sight of Galanax, and was face to face with a Shadowwalker. David drew his sword and slashed at his larger adversary in a quick motion. The Shadowwalker was caught off guard by the speed of his opponent, and was unable to defend himself. Pasty blue blood shot from the wound in his chest, and splattered over the clothes that David wore. The Shadowwalker then fell to the ground in agony and slowly disappeared leaving only its screams echoing throughout the halls. All around the room, men and Shadowwalkers fell, adding to the screams of death and terror that seemed to come from everywhere. David spotted Galanax just a few feet ahead of him engaged with one of the human-like monsters. David leapt through the air and severed the head of the monster from its body as he landed. David then began to realize that he had just leapt into a circle of Shadowwalkers, and the only ally in sight was Galanax. The two men stood back to back, trying to fend off the attacks of the monsters. Two of the Shadowwalkers fell to the power of Galanax, and one fell with the slash of David's blade.

"They just keep coming, Galanax!" David yelled. "How are we supposed to hold all of them off?"

"Just hold out for five more minutes, David! Help is on the way."

David nodded and kept striking at the oncoming Shadowwalkers. Suddenly there was a flash of blinding light and lightning began to strike all over the room killing monsters where they stood.

"Make your way to the center of the room David, I will follow!" Galanax yelled over the roar of thunder.

David obeyed, and started moving toward the center of the large chamber. All the time he had to slash at live enemies, and sidestep the dying ones. Eventually, the form of a man standing in the very center of the room became visible. He held his hands skyward, and his eyes were closed tightly. He appeared to be directing the lightning strikes, but David could not be sure. Before he realized what was happening, all of the enemies in the room had disappeared, except for one.

There was a man standing near Galanax, surrounded by members of Lady Binosear's army. He appeared to offer no resistance, but had a large scowl on his face. Galanax pulled on David's arm and led him over to the man who had been controlling the lightning.

"The danger is over now David. I would like you to meet Kahnac. He is a healer, but he learned a few powerful spells from Mailock the wizard during our travels with Lord Cedric."

"Pleasure to meet you," David said slowly. "Thanks for saving our lives."

"No thanks are necessary for doing the work of the Light."

David nodded and was reminded of Lane by the way the man in front of him held himself. Galanax took hold of his arm again and led him over to the prisoner. He was now surrounded by Lady Erika, Lady Anne, Christine, William, Khisanth, and a man that David didn't recognize. They were questioning him, but David was unable to hear the conversation until they were standing about a foot from the prisoner.

"Did Shau-ling give you orders to attack us here, Allan?" Erika asked shortly.

"Address me by my proper name, weakling. I am no longer needed to pose as the son of your pathetic sister. For centuries I have been called Aldridge, and I expect to be known that way for centuries to come. To answer your pitiful questions would be a disgrace upon my name and the name of my master. However, I have been ordered to deliver a message from my lord. He orders you to end your rebellion. Your actions will soon be futile. Before the sun sets in the world on the other side of this reality the Dragon will be dead, and Shau-ling will rule the world if the living for the rest of eternity. You are beaten."

Aldridge laughed for a long time, and then locked his eyes back on Lady Erika with a large scowl painted on his face. His hatred ran deep. It was the normal fare for a servant of Shau-ling to hate all that was good, to the point that hate became the driving force for that being's existence.

"How can we be sure that you are telling the truth?" Anne asked.

"Release my hands from these ropes, and I will show you."

Erika nodded to the guard, and he drew his dagger and released Aldridge's hands. Aldridge closed his eyes and muttered a few words under his breath. He then waved his hands in a circular motion over his head. Above his hands a fog began to appear. The fog began to clear, and all were faced with a hole in the fabric of the Other Side. They could see a force of Shau-ling's monsters massing in the forest outside a small town. The scene then changed to what appeared to be the inside of a bar. David recognized several of the patrons of the bar as his friends.

He could see Logan, Elwyne, Lane, and Gwydeon sitting at one of the tables laughing and talking. Up on the stage sat Talon and Pike singing and telling stories to the full house. David could also see Eldar waiting tables. The scene changed again. Two of the monsters from the forest had made their way into town carrying torches. They were standing at the foot of the in where David's friends were. Again the scene changed, and his friends were there in front of him again. The picture closed in on Logan, and David screamed.

"Logan! They're setting fire to the inn!"

Suddenly, Logan jerked and roused his friends. From out of nowhere a clawed hand came through the rift and grasped Aldridge. The draconian hand crushed him, and dropped his broken body to the ground. The clawed hand pulled back through the rift, and the rift sealed itself. David turned quickly to Kahnac.

"Can you duplicate what Aldridge just did? Can you open a functioning portal that we can travel through?"

Kahnac thought for a quick moment and then nodded.

"Well, do it!"

"Anyone who goes through the portal can stay only one of that time's hours. Anyone who does not return in that time will be lost for eternity. Thought we may not be alive in their way, our weapons can hurt them. However, their weapons will banish us to a place far worse than what the Great Dark One would have in store for us."

"I'm willing to chance it," David said quickly, "who's with me?"

"You saved my life, David," Galanax said proudly, "I'll go."

"My army is with you, David," Lady Erika responded. "Open the portal, Kahnac."

"Yes, my lady."

As Kahnac muttered an incantation under his breath, he waved his hands over his head. David cleaned his blade quickly and took a deep breath. The portal began to take shape in front of them, and David began to see the army of the Shau moving quickly toward the edge of town.

"Hold on Logan," David said to himself. "I said that I was going to help any way that I could. Well, help's on its way."

Chapter XIII

New Old Friends

*T*he *Golden Dagger* was not as large as the *Inn of Good Faith*, but it served the purpose of hiding from the guards and mysterious man well enough for the rest of the night. The innkeeper asked no questions, even though he was awakened in the middle of the night. Jasmen was able to quickly sooth any frayed nerves, and it seemed that she and the innkeeper were well acquainted. The man provided all the remaining rooms that he had, and in payment, he was happy to accept the star attractions from his rival in the persons of Talon, Jasmen, and Pike. Within a matter of minutes, everyone had bedded down for the night, and it wasn't too difficult for Logan to surmise that no one would have a good night sleep that night. Gideon said that there was something that he had to tell everyone, and Logan couldn't help but think that it was about Aryx. Aryx had been missing since the previous afternoon, but with the way that he had been acting the last couple of days, Logan couldn't help but think that was a good thing. Elwyne and Logan got to their room rather quickly, and just after Logan sat on the bed she sat beside him and grasped his hand. The conversation that had started the night before was apparently going to continue much sooner than Logan had envisioned, but putting things off to the last minute was never a good policy, so Logan knew that the conversation had just as well be finished that night rather than leverage the verge of success or failure when everything was on the line.

"Would you go back to Aradon if I send Lane and Alexander with you?"

She seemed more than a bit shocked at the question. That was obviously something that she never expected him to say.

"Why would you ask something like that, Logan? We've already been through this once, and we agreed back in Aradon . . ."

"No," he interjected, "we didn't agree. You agreed that you would come along on this quest so that you could get your revenge for David, but that was long before we knew the depth of what we were stepping into. Now that we have seen the death and the despair that has been caused by Shau-ling and his phasia, I thought you could understand my reasons for my wanting you safe in Aradon."

"And who's to say that I'll be safe there?" she countered. "Do you mean to tell me that since you are out here there is no real threat in Aradon? How long do you think it would take Shau-ling to figure out that someone you really cared for was in Aradon, and just to prick at you a little further, he might launch another assault? If I were there, that would almost destroy you, and you wouldn't be able to fight with a clear head. Look at Cedric. Look at what he has become now. All he cared about was revenge. A fighter who fights only for revenge will never survive a battle, remember?"

The last phrase struck Logan in the chest like a hard punch. Elwyne wasn't fighting fair, and she knew that she was using Logan's own father's words against him. But, what struck Logan the most was that she was utterly and completely right. Though Logan would almost never say it to her face, he knew in his heart that she was far more often right than wrong. With Logan's nod, she knew that he had wisely conceded the argument.

"Why do you have to constantly wear your sword Logan? I know it's a necessity when we travel and all, but we are here in our room together and you still have it strapped to your hip."

Logan shrugged and then started to unfasten the belt. She pulled his hands away softly and then started to unfasten it herself.

"Here, let me do it. You owe me, remember?"

* * * * * * * * * * * *

The knock at the door alarmed Gideon, and his daggers were not far from his hands. He had his privacy in most every place that they had been, and this was the first time that anyone had visited his room. Most of the time they had found him in the common rooms or the taverns to tell him about the meetings, or that they were leaving a certain town. He got up slowly out of the chair and hid the letter that he had been writing in one of his pairs of his breeches. Gideon walked over to the door and pulled it open slowly. Jasmen stood on the other side of the door and she smiled as the door cracked and Gideon came into view.

"What can I do fer ye lass?" he asked quickly.

"I just wanted to talk to you a little Gideon," she responded. "Do you mind if I come in?"

Gideon hesitated for a moment before he stepped out of the way and let her walk past into the room. As she walked by, Gideon could not help but notice her figure. She was not as reed-like as Elwyne or Midarin, and had a stronger and more voluptuous build, but she was still thin. Her blond hair was cut short, but it was still very feminine and it was very flattering to the features of her slim face and high cheekbones. She sat down in the chair and turned back toward him and relaxed. It was as if the chair was made for her the way it wrapped itself around her back and supported her perfectly. Gideon had found the chair amazingly uncomfortable.

"What would ye like ta talk 'bout?"

She smiled warmly and motioned for him to sit on the bed across from her. He did so and then looked up at her, the expression never changing on his face.

"What can you tell me about the members of the group?" she asked flatly.

"That be a very dangerous question lass," Gideon replied. "Ye are new to the group, and some of us don't want too much information 'bout ourselves gettin' out in da beginning. Ye canna be too sure when a person is what dey appear ta be or not."

"I understand a little," she replied.

Gideon could tell that this girl was far from dumb, and there was more of a purpose behind her inquisitiveness than just wanting to know for little other reason.

"Der has ta be more to it den dat. Why do ye really want ta know 'bout me friends?"

She sighed and then smiled.

"I love your accent Gideon. Where are you from?"

"Don't change da subject lass," he scolded. "I put a direct question to ye, and I expect an answer to it."

The smile melted from her face and she sighed. She had not expected Gideon to be this much of a pain, but she should have expected the serious nature of what she was asking.

"All right. I'm going to write all of this adventure into a story that can be sung by the bards from now until the end of time. It will be such a wonderful story, and I didn't think it would be complete without a little background on some of people involved."

"So why did ye start wit' me?"

"Because you are the only one that I can get close to. Pike and Eldar are always together, just like Logan and Elwyne, and Gwydeon and Midarin. I don't think any of the three women like me very much because of the dirty looks I always get from them. Talon isn't answering his door. Lane, Talos, and Alexander won't even look in my direction, and Aryx has come up missing. You are the only other person that I can talk to Gideon. Please. This is a small favor that I'm asking, and if you can help me, I'll be eternally grateful."

"I cannae help ye lass. It would not be right of me ta tell ye things 'bout me friends without their permission, and as fer me, der's nothin' dat ye want to know dat I'm willin' ta tell."

She frowned, a little dejected by the shortness of Gideon's answer. Without any further conversation, she got up and walked out of the room.

Just as Gideon was about to continue writing his letter, there came another knock at the door.

"It's open."

There was a cold chill that rushed through the room. For some reason, Gideon could not help but shiver as the door swung open. The man approached, and as Gideon turned to face him, the memories flooded through his mind, and he stiffened as the fear overtook him.

"It is time."

* * * * * * * * * * *

Pike walked down the hall with Eldar on his arm. Things had been so different between them only a few days earlier, but now he found that they were nearly inseparable. He found it hard to believe that he would ever find a love to rival the one held by Logan and Elwyne, but now he could not distinguish the two.

"What happened to us Eldar?" he asked trying hard to be sincere.

"We encountered some things along the way that made us grow up sooner than we ever expected. I don't really understand all of it myself, but I can't see my life going on without you anymore."

Pike thought hard about that for a moment, and then he started to realize what she meant. He tried to look into his future, but no matter what scenario he envisioned in his mind, he either saw himself dead, or with Eldar. While the former was not a very pleasant end, he was beginning to have his doubts about the later as well.

"I can't help but think that my saving your life in Sador has something to do with all of this. I've never seen you change so rapidly from one extreme to the other in my life."

She just giggled and kissed him lightly on the cheek.

"You're just being silly now."

She kissed him on the lips and then started to pull away from him. He gripped her hand tighter, and when he pulled her back, he could see something strange, yet unrecognizable in her eyes.

"Where are you going?"

"Elwyne and I want to have a little talk away from the rest of you," she responded lightly. "I'll be in later though if that's alright."

"Fine," Pike answered rather shortly.

It appeared as if she paid little heed to his words as she walked down the hallway, and Pike's fears and worries piled on more than ever.

* * * * * * * * * * * *

Gwydeon and Midarin lay in bed talking for almost an hour. Gwydeon could not get over how one-sided their conversation had been, and he felt as if he had been rambling on.

"You know, I'm starting to feel like an idiot just spouting off like this," he said as she snuggled closer to him.

"Don't, Gwydeon. I love to hear you talk, especially when you talk about us. Have you given any thought to marriage?"

Surprise does not even begin to describe what Gwydeon felt at the question.

"I thought that you didn't want to get married, at least that was what you have been saying every time that I brought it up."

"That was the problem Gwydeon," she replied. "You only brought it up once, and I thought you got the impression that I wanted to talk about it some more. Well, since you didn't, I had to bring it up. So, what do you think? Do you want to get married?"

"Yes, I do. I love you Midarin, like no one I have ever loved before, but I need to tell you that under the laws of Aradon, I cannot be married ever again."

Midarin sat up and rested her head on her hand. Her elbow dug deep into the pillow as she sat up to look at him.

"What are you talking about Gwydeon?"

"When I first turned sixteen, I secretly went up to the old church with a girl that I thought I was in love with. I felt so alive when I was with her, and I honestly thought that I wanted to spend the rest of my life with her. We were married and then our marriage was announced to the rest of the town, and we began living together."

"What happened?" she asked rubbing her hand across his naked chest.

"Remember the story I told you about the tournament last year, and the man I killed?"

"Yes."

"That was not exactly true. I did fight in the tournament, and I did kill my opponent in the final match, but it was not a man, it was my wife."

Midarin almost collapsed as she felt the strength flow out of her body. She felt so many emotions swelling inside of her that they collided with each other, robbing the others of their meaning. The sympathy that she felt for him was countered by the unpeaceable feelings of despair and sorrow. Gwydeon continued the account as tears began to swell in his eyes.

"From the day we met, she wanted me to teach her the sword. I did my best, and she was almost as good as I was by the time the tournament rolled around. I begged her not to enter because I had this bad feeling. She did against my will, but I took inner pleasure as she bested everyone. When I killed her, even accidentally, it nullified our marriage in the eyes of the church and the town, but it did not nullify the vows that I took in the old church. Those are to bind me for the rest of my days as a punishment for what I did."

He couldn't hold back any longer. The tears flooded from his eyes, and he buried his face in the pillow trying to hide his weakness. Midarin pulled him to her and tried hard to comfort him. Eventually he fell asleep, and just after he did, she pulled on her dress and slipped silently out of the room.

* * * * * * * * * * * *

Talon sat on his bed, trying hard to relax. He had heard Pike and Gwydeon talk about their nightmares ever since their encounters in Dreamscape, but Talon had never been plagued by those horrible dreams. That was until they reached Falke. Every time he closed his eyes since then, he could not help but see the visions of fire and death behind his closed lids. This night was no different than any other. Every time he tried to lay back and drift off into sleep, the nightmares flooded into his head and woke him rather violently. He would not allow himself to dream long enough to see what plagued his thoughts, but he knew it was never pleasant.

Suddenly there was a knock at the door, and Talon rose from the bed rather sluggishly. His body was drained from the constant fighting of a week, and it seemed as if his wounds screamed out in pain and furry with every single move. It was a horrible feeling. He thought he could feel every bone creak, every muscle burn with life as he moved from one step to the next, and he could feel the fire in his wounds as each one fought to tear open and continue the pain. He got to the door as the person knocked again, and as the door opened, he more than a little shocked at his visitor.

"Well this is an unexpected pleasure," he said softly. "What are you doing here?"

The kiss on his lips more than answered his question.

* * * * * * * * * * * *

Logan rolled over the next morning and found that he was alone in the bed. After a moment he got out of the bed and pulled on his breeches. As Logan pulled open the curtains, the light from the mid-day sun flooded into the room and nearly blinded him. Looking out into the courtyard, he saw that Gwydeon and Midarin were sparring with Pike and Talon watching intently. Logan turned away from the window and grabbed his black shirt off the floor and pulled it on quickly. For some reason, he couldn't find his boots anywhere. As he was looking for them however, the door opened, and Elwyne entered the room carrying a new pair of brightly polished black boots.

"I bought these for you this morning and took your other pair out and put them in your saddlebags."

"Tell Pike and Gwydeon that I want to see them now," Logan said his tone serious. "If you can find Gideon, I want to see him too."

Elwyne just looked at him for a moment and then dropped the boots and left. Something about this whole day seemed wrong. Everyone outside seemed too happy and content with the situation to be real. It seemed as if they had forgotten the incident with the guards the previous night, and they acted as if they were all back in Aradon. A few moments later, the door opened again and Pike, Gwydeon, and Gideon entered the room.

"Ye wanted ta see us Logan?"

"As a matter of fact I did."

Logan turned to face his friends and suddenly he began to get strange looks all around. After a moment Logan approached Pike, but his old friend stepped away as if he had just seen a ghost.

"Logan," Gideon said as calmly as he could, "look down."

Logan looked down and saw that he was standing in the middle of a table. Not to say that he was on top of the table, but if you could cut a person in half and slide the table in between the two halves, that's what Logan would have looked like. He stepped back through the table and sat down on a chair on the far side of the room.

"Sorry about that. If I don't concentrate for a moment or two, it seems that my powers start acting on their own. Please, have a seat, we need to talk."

There were two chairs that were beside Logan, and without thinking he raised my hand and they slid across the floor and came to a stop beside the bed where they stood. Gwydeon was the only one that didn't look shocked as he sat down.

"What's this all this about Logan?" Gwydeon asked.

"We should settle up with the innkeeper tonight so that we can leave in the morning. Aryx is missing, and I can only assume that he has gone ahead to Marcwell to tell Lord Cedric that we will be arriving soon."

Gideon just nodded and relaxed back into his chair.

"It sounds like a good plan ta me, Logan," he replied. "I'll volunteer ta inform everyone of our plans."

"Very well."

Gideon stood quickly and hurried out the door. Logan couldn't help but think that the haste in his departure was caused by Logan's unexpected use of power. The thing that was inside of Logan seemed to be more powerful ever since they had found the Jeweled Dragon's Flame, and he couldn't help but think that the *Coromor* was fighting harder to get out of him. It was as if it wanted to find Shau-ling and everything that served him at that exact moment and end it all in one huge battle that could rage on forever and still not be close to a resolution.

"Gwydeon."

"Yes?"

"Let Lane and Alexander know that they will be accompanying Elwyne back to Aradon in the morning. I'm sorry that we have to lose Lane for the remainder of the quest, but I want Elwyne safe, and I think that he could be of some use to Aradon should the forces of the Shau decide to launch another offensive."

"If that's what you think is best, Logan."

"Dismissed."

Gwydeon rose stiffly and left the room leaving Logan alone with Pike. After a few moments of awkward silence, Logan started to relay his orders to Pike, but he cut Logan off with piercing words of his own that seemed to rip through his oldest friend's heart.

"What the hell is wrong with you Logan? Ever since we met you in Falke, you have been unreasonable, stubborn, pig-headed, and have made a complete ass out of yourself. What right do you have to dictate to Elwyne in the way that you would never dare to order the rest of us? Just because she loves you and wants to marry you is no excuse for the way you treat her. She is scared to death of you now, and I'm not far off."

Logan couldn't speak. He was numb. There was no way that a response would cross his lips. Pike didn't even wait for a response. He rose from the chair and made his way out of the room. He paused at the door for a moment and then looked back at Logan. There were tears welling up in his eyes, and Logan knew that he was dying inside.

"I hope to see you in the common room tonight, my friend. The innkeeper convinced us to tell the story about Rama and the trials of Sarmeel. I hope you can come. If you do, leave your robe and title in your room, because some of us want to see our friend Logan, we miss him."

Logan was left alone with his thoughts.

* * * * * * * * * * * *

The common room was packed that night as it had been in the *Inn of Good Faith* the night before. Even though Pike's words still echoed in Logan's thoughts, he had to hear them that night, and he had to be with my friends. Logan's sword still hung from his hip, a fact that could not be helped given the circumstances. For some reason, Logan felt uneasy about that night, and there was a strange feeling that something was going to go horribly wrong before the night was over. Logan was greeted warmly by some of his friends as he walked across the common room and took a seat with Elwyne. The song was just about to start as he sat down, and as the story began, the crowd fell into a dead silence. Logan noticed out of the corner of his eye that Eldar was not sitting at any of the tables, but she was actually serving drinks at some of the tables. Logan leaned into Elwyne for a moment and whispered into her ear.

"What is Eldar doing?"

"That was another part of the deal that the innkeeper cooked up. He said that if Pike, Talon and Jasmen perform, and Eldar would wait the tables, we could have our room, board and food for free. I think that the inn keeper is a bit sweet on Eldar."

"Well," Logan replied trying to be in good humor, "I can remember Ren's reaction to her back in Illimar, and I can't say as I blame him for his attention to her. She is a lovely woman."

"Married but lovely," she replied innocently.

"Married doesn't mean that a woman loses her beauty Elwyne," Logan answered, "and besides, the innkeeper is married too."

She chuckled and they both turned their attention back to the show. Suddenly a sound pierced through the room like a great crash of thunder. A single thought hit Logan's mind, but for some reason it was not his own. It was as if another person stepped into his head and screamed his name as loudly as he could.

"Logan!"

Logan knew the voice, but he didn't know from where. He jumped from his seat and drew his sword, more in reaction to the voice than to the sound of thunder. The music had stopped on stage, and everyone was doing their best to keep the patrons calm. Lane and Talos started leading the crowd through the back, and when they returned, Logan could see black smoke starting to rush in from under the door. Pike and Talon were already at the door, and as they kicked it open, the orange flames that had been burning the outer walls of the inn leapt into the opening and nearly singed both Pike and Talon. There was very little time to react to the situation, and the twelve members of the group hurried through the open door and found that they had literally stepped from the frying pan into the fire.

A mass of the red-skinned Jeresei flooded all around the inn, and those that weren't surrounding the place were taking great pleasure in harassing the people of the town. When the first twenty or so rushed in, Logan felt as if he were going to be sick. His stomach lurched and his head spun, but the physical discomfort was followed by an incredible rush of power that coursed through his veins. The sickening sweetness threatened to consume and destroy him at the same time. Logan knew that the *Coromor* was fighting to get out and destroy all of his enemies in one fell swoop, and he fought to control it. However, when he turned and saw one of the Jeresei leap at Elwyne, he could not contain the guttural scream that ripped from somewhere deep in his chest.

"No!"

All of the Jeresei around them froze, but so did everyone else. Everything appeared to stop right at that moment in time. Just as quickly as the motion around Logan had stopped, it started again. The Jeresei that had leapt at Elwyne shattered in mid-air and crashed to the ground in a million pieces. More and more Jeresei went down to conventional weapons, but they just kept coming. It seemed as if they would soon be buried by the immeasurable and unending waves of enemies. They were tremendously outnumbered, but they kept fighting. Just when all began to seem hopeless, lightning ripped through the heavens, and a whirling blue doorway appeared out of thin air.

Shadows of the Past

The portal closed quickly as Basille stepped through. Saurn had not been there to meet him when he returned to the Blight, so he had decided to go back home. His mind still reeled from the meeting with Cedric, and his thoughts now seemed to drift from the solidarity of reality to the wonderful cascade of memory. There were still so many things that Cedric did not know; in fact there were far too many things that he had not even guessed at. However, Basille was in no position to tell his friend the absolute and utter truth. At the time there was very little that required his attention, and now that Saurn had declared their intentions to Shau-ling and the rest of the Council, all he could do was watch his own back and hope that one of his brothers did not decide to pay him a visit in Scalla. Basille knew that Scalla was the safest place for him now, and all he could do was sit and reflect, and try to plan out a new strategy until Saurn approached him with the next step in their plan to overthrow Shau-ling.

The events of the past few days had become stranger and stranger. Now, with all of the new information Basille had acquired at the Council and from his old friend Cedric, they seemed stranger still. Basille knew the identity of the new *Coromor* and it would not be long before Shau-ling and the rest of the phasia knew as well. Saurn had taken control of the *Chosen One*, and he also seemed to be sinking further and further into the madness that had held his mind of late.

As Basille walked up to his throne, he noticed that the table he had shattered earlier during the tense moments with Minister Talmon had been replaced. Everything that should have been on the table was there in its proper place, neatly arranged for him. His servants had done their job very well, and he had expected the tabled to have been replaced by the time he returned, and he was not disappointed. Undoubtedly, his servants had replaced the table the second he left, for fear that he would return earlier than expected. Basille smiled to himself and then seated himself on the throne. He reached over to the table and rang the large bell that sat there, summoning his servants. Mere seconds later, the doors at the far end of the chamber opened, and two female servants entered. They moved quickly down the length of the hall and knelt at the foot of the throne. Their eyes were cast down the entire trip into their master's presence, and as they knelt there before him, their eyes remained trained on the ground before them. This was the only true way that they could show that they had dedicated their lives to Basille and that they were totally under his control and were ready and willing to be commanded.

"What is it that you require my great and powerful Lord Basille," they asked in unison.

"Nothing now young ones. I merely wished to inform all that I have returned. Has anyone come here to Scalla and requested to be allowed to enter my presence?"

"Yes my lord," one of the women answered, "Minister Talmon has requested to see you as soon as possible upon your return."

"Yes," Basille replied quickly, "that does sound like the truly impertinent tone that Talmon has been using lately. Have there been any other requests?"

"Yes lord," the other woman answered, "a man named Saurn arrived yesterday and requested an audience. He seemed rather annoyed having to ask to see you though. He said that he would remain here in Scalla until you returned and sent for him."

Basille looked down at his servant, more than a little shocked at her statement. He would have never expected that Saurn would have left the

Blight to seek him out. In fact, he was one of the last people that Basille ever expected to see in Scalla. For Saurn to have left the sanctity and protection of the Blight, one of two things must have happened since his intentions were made known to the Council. It was possible that one of the other phasia had gone looking for Saurn and they had perhaps stumbled on him in the Blight. If that had happened, there was nowhere except Scalla that he could hide. It was very much the same situation that Basille had found himself in, but everyone knew that his kingdom was Scalla, so he found that he was not truly safe anywhere. On the other hand, this excursion could have been made by choice rather than necessity. Saurn could have discovered a new development that was so interesting and powerful that he could not have waited for Basille to return to the Blight. Inwardly, Basille did not know which of the reasons he should have found more frightening. What Basille did next could determine his fate as well as the fate of the future.

"Send for this man Saurn. When he arrives, see that he is taken to the study. Tell him that I have some other business to attend to, but I will meet him as soon as I become available."

"As you wish," the woman responded.

"Now, go and tell Talmon that I will see him now."

"By your word."

The two women rose quickly at their master's dismissal, and hurried out of the room. Basille was left there alone in his throne room, only his memories and his newfound puzzlement to keep him company. Above all else, he had to ponder the significance of his brother's appearance, as well as the new development that Talmon was about to bring him. Basille found that he was not happy with the way the situation was tumbling out of his control, but he had little choice but to accept the way things were turning out.

A minute or two after his servants' departure, the large double doors at the far end of the throne room opened again, and into the room stepped the huge Minister Talmon. His gait was slow, too slow in fact to be comfortable. It appeared as if Talmon was hesitating, unsure of what he had to tell Basille. As he approached the throne of his master, his eyes were trained on the ground before him, another occurrence that led Basille to believe that something was very wrong. When Talmon did raise his eyes to his master, Basille noticed the familiar twinge of fear that he had seen in the faces of many of his adversaries, but never in Talmon's cold hard stare. As he began to speak in that low, powerful voice of his, Talmon kept his head slightly bowed, and his eyes trained on the ground before Basille's feet. There was a waiver in Talmon's voice that had never been there before, and now Basille wondered more than ever what could have happened.

"My liege," Talmon said, his voice wavering more and more, "it is nice to see that you have returned safely from your trip. I hope that your travels were without incident."

"Dispense with the pleasantries, and for the sake of the Light, look at me when you speak. My patience with your continued impertinence is wearing thinner by the minute, and I will not accept much more of this behavior. Now, give me this urgent report, or leave my presence."

Talmon raised his head quickly and looked into the eyes of his master. The fear was still very much evident on his face, but Basille could still not understand why.

"My lord. As you ordered, your men have been moved from guard duty around the palace to the mines of Quea. Also, the raid on Illimar which you seemed very insistent upon has been carried out."

"I have only been away for four days Talmon. How did you manage this feat so quickly?"

"I have friends and a bit of clout in Illimar. I pulled in a few of the favors that are owed to me, and they abducted this man Mystic for me and brought him back."

Basille rose from the throne and approached Talmon.

"Do you mean to tell me that Jerrard Mystic is here in Scalla?"

"Yes my lord. My compatriots brought him to my quarters early this morning. He was taken into custody the minute he arrived by my men, and then he was placed in one of the holding cells below the palace."

"Bring him to me Talmon," Basille said, his voice filled with expectation and doubt, "I wish to see him now."

Talmon bowed and then left the throne room at a slightly faster clip. Now Basille understood the hesitation and fear that had gripped his servant. Talmon had obviously remember the last time he had mentioned Jerrard Mystic's name in front of Basille, and he was afraid that when he brought it up again, it would be his head that was split in half instead of the table. Basille's head spun more now than it had before. He had still not sorted out all of the things Cedric has said to him, nor had he had a chance to dwell on the happenings in the Council earlier. Events around him were becoming more difficult to control, and it seemed as if the world around him was moving faster than he was able to compensate for. Now, Saurn as well as Basille's son Jerrard had been thrown into the mix, and Basille didn't know what he was going to do. He walked toward his private chambers and quickly unfastened the sword belt from around his waist and laid the sword and scabbard on his bed. For all he knew, Jerrard had never seen his face when he murdered his own father in the past lifetime. Basille was hoping that this was true and that Jerrard did not even suspect that Basille was one of the phasia. If that was true, Jerrard has yet to discover what he himself was capable of. As Basille returned to his throne, the doors at the far end of the chamber began to open again. Basille seated himself and watched as Talmon led two very familiar people into the throne room.

The first was a man that Basille wished he knew. He did not appear to be much older than Talmon, and as Basille though back, he recalled that Jerrard and Talmon were roughly the same age. Jerrard was a bit shorter than Talmon, but the air of power still seemed very prominent around him. His jet black hair, obviously inherited from his father, was cut short, and his chin showed the start of a beard. His shoulders were pulled back with pride, and his head was held high, eyes filled with the fires of anger and indignation. He very much reminded Basille of himself when he was younger. Jerrard seemed so eager to fight if he had the chance, and Basille could see in his eyes that he wouldn't let his current confinement break his spirits.

The woman that walked beside him was very beautiful. Her beauty was simple and frail, much like she was, but the beauty was fascinating nonetheless. The white dress that she wore clung tightly to her slim body, and she moved smoothly and effortlessly, much like an angel would on earth. Her auburn hair had a slight curl to it, and it flowed down to the middle of her back. Blue eyes sparkled, filled with care and love, the same soft energy Basille had always seen in her. She and Basille had been together for nearly eight years, and he had raised her as his daughter from the beginning.

Jerrard's eyes glanced from side to side, never quite resting on the face of his illustrious captor. He was obviously weighing the possibilities of escape. For the first time, he looked Basille dead in the face, and when he did, his jaw dropped open and he stopped.

"Father?" he said slowly.

"Guards," Basille said rising, "leave us."

The two lines of guards who had escorted Mystic and the woman into the room stopped. They all bowed in unison, turned, and left the room as quickly as they had entered.

"You are dismissed as well, Talmon. I have important family business to attend to."

"By your word," Talmon replied.

Talmon bowed to his master and then turned to leave. He and Jerrard exchanged looks for a moment, the reasoning of which puzzled Basille, but what hadn't in the past days. After the brief exchange, Talmon hurried out of the room, and when the doors closed, Basille was alone in the throne room with his family. Basille turned his attention back to Jerrard after watching the doors close. He had no idea how to start the explanation. The word awkward wasn't strong enough to describe the silence in the room. It was Mystic that gained the courage to break the silence first.

"Father? What are you doing here in Scalla? Aren't you supposed to be dead?"

Basille smiled and felt his defenses lower.

"It's not the warmest hello that I could have received Jerrard, but it will do. For the record though, I could ask the same of you. The last thing I knew, you were killed in the fire that claimed our little village as well as the life of your mother. However, it is apparent that we are both very much alive. I'm sorry that I chose now instead of a few years earlier to reveal myself, but there were other matters that demanded more attention."

"What matters could have been more important than your son?" Jerrard asked, searching for some sense in the situation.

"A war for one my dear boy. I was trying to keep my kingdom in one piece while the whole bloody world was trying to send itself straight to hell."

"I could have helped, father," Jerrard interjected, "I'm a good soldier and a good leader. I would have been able to help you."

"From what I have heard from Lord Cedric himself, you did your part for the war effort best at the Lion's side. I couldn't have asked you to abandon your post. In fact, I have heard of many times when you personally saved Lord Cedric's life. What would have become of him if you weren't there?"

"Someone else would have taken my place and saved him. It was duty, not choice, father. The Lion took me in and gave me something to believe in when my life had seemingly shattered. All I had was Lord Cedric and…"

"Erika. Yes, I'm glad to see that the two of you have remained together."

Jerrard looked at the woman who stood beside him, and then back at Basille.

"How do you know about Erika?"

Basille stood and approached his two captives.

"My dear boy, if it weren't for me, you never would have met this sweet little girl."

Jerrard was stunned. His mouth dropped open as if he would speak, and then thinking better of the words he had planned, he croaked out a question.

"How is that so?"

"Twenty years ago when I was traveling through the countryside, I found a poor girl lying in the bushes. Her arm was broken, but she was not bleeding too badly. After I brought her back here and spoke to her for a while, I learned who she was and that she had been out riding and had a little accident. After she regained her health, I promised I would take her back home. However, I received some disturbing news about her family, and after she learned that they had died, she opted to stay here with me. At the time, I still thought you were dead, and there was a void inside of me that had to be filled. So, I took Erika into my home and raised her as my own. About five years ago though, I found out that you were still alive."

"And how did you manage to come across that information?" Jerrard asked, his voice becoming quite hostile.

"As I said earlier, your exploits with the Lion's Mane made you very popular with several of the kingdoms and rulers that I deal with. However, your name was brought to my attention by an old friend. After you left the military, I lost track of you for a few months, but once I found you again, I sent Erika to keep tabs on you for me."

Jerrard shook his head and looked at Erika again. He wanted to say something, but he could not find the words to respond with. His mouth opened but no sound escaped. He felt drained of all reason. His whole world had exploded, and it was all because of his father.

"Erika," he stammered, trying to force out the question, "why didn't you tell me?"

"I couldn't Jerrard," she replied, her voice soft and full of love, "I promised your father."

"Do you remember all those times when she said she was visiting her father?" Basille interjected quickly. "The truth was that she was really visiting me. There was no other way that she could report back as to how you were doing, so she made up the excuse about her poor sick father who couldn't do without her."

"So, I suppose that there is a reason that you have brought me here now. You certainly have not developed a conscience about your spying and lying, so there has to be some other reason."

The truth twisted in the pit of Basille's stomach like a dull blade. He couldn't really tell his son that he wanted him dead. How do you tell you only child that his father is supposed to be his mortal enemy, or that he had killed his own father not five years earlier? There was no real way to say anything about the current situation. There was so much that Jerrard didn't know, but Basille was in no position to tell him anything. He was finding himself in that position more and more. While there was still hate inside him for the man that murdered him all those years ago, Basille could no put aside the face that the man standing before him was his one and only son. The cross was almost too much to bear.

"I brought you here because you are in danger, Jerrard. A few of my old adversaries may have found out that you are my son. I don't have to remind you that the last time these enemies of mine found out that you lived, they burned down our village and killed your mother. I couldn't live with myself if I lost you again when I had the power to stop it. I just wanted you to be safe. That's why I brought you here."

"I thank you for your concern, father," Jerrard responded in a cold hard voice, "but I have managed for this long without your help, and I am fairly sure that I can continue to do so. I have proven that I am very capable of taking care of myself and anyone else who came along."

"And what about my dear, sweet Erika?" Basille questioned. "Do you really think that my enemies would hesitate for one second to harm her in order to get to you?"

That stopped Jerrard cold for a moment. He knew that he loved Erika with all his heart and all his soul. He could never live with himself if he knew something happened to her because of him.

"All right," Jerrard said a few instants later, "where can the two of us be safe? Surely it is not safe here with you."

"No," Basille replied, "not here."

"Then where?"

"I want you to help out a friend. He is in more danger at the present time than he knows how to handle, and I thought he could use an experienced warrior like you at his side. The man I wish you to help is this generation's *Coromor*. Having served in the Lion's Mane, I thought it would come natural to you."

"That's where you're wrong father. I don't like war, never have. I did what I did in that was to help out a friend. Do you actually believe that I would walk into the same danger you apparently want to protect me from? Do you take me for a fool?"

"No, Jerrard, I do not. I thought your sense of duty would be stronger than that though."

"My sense of duty is fine, father," Jerrard contended, his voice filling with more anger.

"Then show me," Basille challenged.

"Where do I find him?" Jerrard answered, drawing closer to the edge of hatred.

"I have heard that his travels will eventually take him to the city of Brea. It would be safe for you to wait there. The man's name is Logan Ranthall. Your best bet to find him will come if you stick close to the man named Arin Domae."

"Very well, father," Jerrard answered in the same cold tone he had used earlier. "I will find this man Logan, and I will do all I can to help him."

"Thank you, son."

"Jerrard," the young man said as he turned and walked away. "I haven't been your son for eight years."

* * * * * * * * * * *

The open saddlebags lay half-full on Jerrard's bed. He was still very angry with his father, but he was more confused than he was angry. Deep down part of him wanted Basille for his father, but another part could not forgive him for what he had done. He would never understand the reasons for his father's private little war that he had fought ever since Jerrard was young. For many years after his father's supposed death, Jerrard tried to find the men who had murdered his mother and father, but to no avail. No one knew anything, or if they did, they weren't saying. But part of him still hated his father. He did not understand why he hated Basille, but something in the back of his mind fueled those fires, and it seemed that nothing would put them out. Suddenly his head ached. He felt dizzy for a moment and sat down on the bed. His body reeled from the onslaught in his mind, and when Jerrard opened his eyes, all he saw was blackness. Suddenly there came a knock at the door. In the instant when the silence in the room was broken, the throbbing behind his eyes ceased, and the blackness disappeared. The attacks were coming too frequently now. They had been enough for him to leave the military, but now they were becoming nearly crippling.

"Come in," he said gruffly, "it's open."

The door opened slowly. As it did, it revealed the woman that he loved the most in the world. They had fallen in love with each other the second they laid eyes on one another, and in the summer of the year past, they had been married.

"Are you angry with me, my love?" she asked softly as she entered the room and closed the door behind her.

"No, Erika, I'm not angry. I'm just confused. When we first met, you told me that you were the heir to a great throne once in life, and that you had to give it all up because of deaths in your family. Deep inside I wanted to be a prince so that I could be good enough to deserve your love. Now that I am again, all I can think about is how much I wish I were still a simple orphaned farmer tending to my fields back in Illimar."

"You can't change who and what you are Jerrard, no matter how much you would like to."

Jerrard stood and took his wife into his arms.

"I know you're right Erika. Do you ever miss it?"

"Miss what?" she said snuggling closer to him.

"Don't you miss being the heir to a kingdom? Don't you ever miss walking through the street, knowing that all anyone can think about is how much they would like to be you? Don't you ever miss being the great and powerful Lady Erika Belnosian?" he asked holding her tightly in his arms.

"I was never the 'great and powerful Lady Erika Belnosian', and I don't think my ego was ever that large. But to tell you the truth, right now I'm very satisfied to be the happy and content Erika Mystic."

All Jerrard could do was smile.

* * * * * * * * * * * *

Basille did not allow himself to react as he watched the huge double doors close behind his son. Jerrard's words hurt him far more than he could ever let on. Moments after the doors closed behind Jerrard, they opened again, and the servant girls who had waited on him earlier reappeared and knelt at his feet.

"The man named Saurn has arrived, and he and three others await you in the study as you commanded."

"Very well," Basille commented trying not to dwell long on the fact that Saurn was not alone. "I will go to meet with him. No one will be granted an audience until I say otherwise, and requests will not be honored. Is that clear young ones?"

"By your word."

The two women left, and a moment later, Basille rose and started toward the study. He stopped just after he stepped through the throne room doors. He looked back into the throne room for a moment and then returned to his private chambers. He took the sword and scabbard off of his bed and fastened the sword belt around his waist as he made his way down the hall. He didn't like not knowing what to expect, so he wanted to be ready for anything, even if it meant going toe to toe with his older brother.

A minute later, he stood in front of the single door to the study. He hesitated for a moment, took a deep breath, and then opened the door. As he entered the study and looked around, he half-expected to see the faces of Warron and Zarsi staring back at him, but the faces he saw contained the eyes of strangers.

Two women and one man were seated in various places around the study. A second man stood by the window looking out over the beautiful town of Scalla. The first woman had long white-blond hair that spilled over her shoulder as well as down her back. Her skin was very white in color, and if not for the little bit of pink in her cheeks, her face would have been as white as the dress she wore. Her blue eyes gleamed impossibly bright, and her lips were as thin and colorless as the rest of her face. The dress she wore had little decoration and it was cut so high that the fabric came to an end just at the top of her neck. Little silver buttons ran from the top of her chest all the way up to the top of her neck. She appeared to be a very proud yet reserved woman. She had a pale beauty that fascinated Basille, but her eyes chilled him to the bone.

While the first woman appeared reserved, the second appeared forceful and strong. She stood beside a tall shelf filled with books. One of her deeply tanned arms rested on one of those shelves. She was about the same height as Basille, and easily as slim. Her long brown hair was pulled back tight on her head, and held back with a thin piece of red fabric. The tight bundle of hair then flooded down her left shoulder. It hung there, and as Basille glanced at it, he noticed that her hair was filled with streaks of red that gave her hair the appearance of fire. Her face too was tan, but unlike the other woman, her lips were full and red. Her eyes glowed green like the finest emeralds in the world, and they peered out at Basille as if she were looking through him directly into his soul. The skin-tight dress that she wore was also red, and its cut was so low that it revealed almost as much as it concealed. He glanced down and noticed that the dress stopped about the middle of her exquisite thighs. Her immaculate legs looked smooth and strong. Basille shifted his gaze up and down her body many times in the seconds that he looked at her, and he turned his eyes quickly away the minute he realized he was gawking.

The man who sat before Basille was the perfect picture of evil. His eyes were set back into his long narrow face. The eyes were a cold, emotionless gray. His lips seemed to be curled into a permanent frown, and his hair was cut short and was starting to fill with streaks of gray. His build was not huge, like Taron's, but he was broader through the chest than Basille. He wore a black tunic that had a stripe of gray down its left side, and he also wore a pair of gray pants.

The other man was very familiar. The violet robe that he wore would have been easy to spot even without the huge viper that had been sewn into the back of it.

"Saurn," Basille said quickly, "this is a truly unexpected pleasure. I never would have expected to see you here in my kingdom."

"That is most likely an accurate expectation, or a lack there of as the case may be," Saurn replied, never turning his attention away from the window before him. "There have been developments in the plan that I thought it imperative that we discuss."

"Do these developments have anything to do with the company that you have brought with you?"

"As a matter of fact, they do, brother Raven," Saurn said as he turned back toward Basille. "My dear brother, I would like you to meet my esteemed associates. The man before you is the merciless Lord Grawn, the Shark. The woman in white there is the genius Lady Ellis, the Leopard. The woman in red is the voracious Lady Bryn, the Fox."

"Three phasia!" Basille said in shock. "How is that possible?"

"It is very possible by dear *younger* brother," the woman in white said in a light, wispy voice. "Many centuries ago, long before you were even born, Grawn, Bryn, and myself were members of the Brotherhood of Phasia. The three of us were especially learned, even for phasia. Searching for more information, we uncovered some shocking things about the powers of the phasia, and even the powers of Shau-ling himself. It was the three of us, not Aralias Imstra, who predicted the coming of the *Coromor*."

"That is true," Grawn added, "but we were also careful to hide the fact of the *Chosen One's* existence. We were very meticulous about tying up loose ends, and…"

"And to make a long story short," Bryn interjected, "when Shau-ling found out what we had discovered and that we had leaked the information out of the palace, and that other phasia were ready to take up arms and fight against their master, he banished us from the Council and from the palace for the rest of eternity. After our departure, you, Zarsi, and Taron were born, and the Council continued as if nothing happened."

"Why have I never heard of this?" Basille asked.

"We were forbidden to speak of it," Saurn replied.

"So, the Brotherhood is thirteen instead of ten?" Basille asked.

"No," Grawn replied in a cold, hard voice. "We have been banished from the Council, so we derive our powers from each other. Saurn has joined us in our fight, and he has said that you will join us as well."

Basille looked at the four of them and nodded.

"Good," Saurn replied triumphantly, "now all of the phasia will be involved in this little war."

"Should we go along as planned?" Basille asked.

"Yes, of course," Saurn replied. "You must meet with brother Warron and continue the assault on Nevi. I will handle Zarsi and Farax in the fields of Vesi Grath. These three know what they must do. Time now is of the essence."

With that, Basille's four visitors disappeared. Basille was again alone with his thoughts. Five of the phasia had been banded together. The *Chosen One* dangled from Saurn's fingers. That was six. If Warron added his strength to their numbers, they would have enough to vanquish Shauling without the *Coromor*. Logan Ranthall was still three short of the critical number, but with Arin Domae and Jerrard, the lines became hazier than ever. Inwardly, Basille wondered which side of the line the coin would fall on, and who would still be standing to claim the prize.

Reality's Price

The swirling blue mass grew larger as the moments passed and pulsed with demonic light. Lightning seemed to flare out from the portal in every direction, threatening and dangerous. In those few seconds, it seemed that the whole of the world had come to a screeching halt. The Jeresei stopped their advance. Then, after what seemed like a great exhale in time, the Jeresei began to move, not to continue their deadly advance, but to look skyward, obviously waiting for something to emerge from the swirling doorway. From deep inside the whirling void a shadow appeared, massive and foreboding, and as the seconds passed, the shadow began to emerge from the mass of blue, its own color coming to light. The form was that of a very large man, certainly taller, if not broader through the shoulders than a Shadowwalker. His shoulders and arms were massive, and they seemed as solid as the trunk of a tree. Once the monstrous individual had fully emerged from the portal, he hovered in mid-air for what seemed like an eternity, a look of malice and hate beaming down on all that was below him. He levitated down from the doorway and landed not five feet in front of boundary the Jeresei had formed to keep Logan and his companions from escaping. The laughter that erupted from the Jeresei the moment that the man's feet touched the ground was almost deafening, and it was obvious to Logan that this man was a phase, and apparently Shau-ling had found them in Taren.

"I take it that you're supposed to be leading these pathetic Jeresei?" Logan asked as the man touched down in front of them. "Shau-ling must not think much of your abilities if he sent you here to die."

He laughed and turned to his cohorts who also began laughing. When he turned back to face Logan and the others, the smile was gone from his face and the angry fire burned in his eyes.

"Who are you to insult the most powerful son of the all-mighty Shau-ling? You must be the pitiful boy who calls himself the *Coromor*. Would you do me the honor by giving me your name?"

Logan laughed softly to himself and felt the sly smile creep onto his face. It took only a second for Logan to know the plan of the phase, most likely before he knew it himself. The *Coromor* was alive inside of Logan, and it was beginning to take over his actions, and all that he had to do was to follow its direction and not try to fight its influence. The power growing inside of him was so sweet and powerful that Logan thought that it would engulf him. Logan imagined himself lost in a sea of power, being buffeted by the tides, letting them roll over him, consuming him. The *Coromor* had looked into the phase's mind and found the plans, the orders, the aspirations, even the very inner pleasures that held a secret meaning for the maniacal monstrosity. Logan was sure that he didn't like the man even before he saw his death in phase's mind.

"Come now Taron, we really must not try to deceive each other. The only way that I would ever reveal my true identity to you is if you were the last phase on the planet and I was about to run you through. You know as well as I do that the second I would tell you my name, you would run back to Shau-ling like the little errand boy and coward that you've always been."

Taron turned and walked toward Elwyne. He touched her cheek lightly and ran his finger down to her chin.

"So *Coromor*, this is the young lady that holds your fancy in this time. You always did have a weakness for the brunettes with blue eyes. I'm surprised that Caris never did catch your fancy; she is far lovelier than this one. Oh, but I forget myself don't I? You have had some trysts in the past with my dear sister. I remember, just a few years ago, you and my sister were very close. But there is no accounting for taste is there. After all, what sane man would invite the Wolf into his bed?"

"You do forget yourself Taron," the *Coromor* replied. "Your words do nothing but strengthen my resolve. Unless you are truly the coward I know you to be, you could challenge me right now. We could see who is the greater of the two, and who does speak the truth."

Taron's face reddened with anger and he balled his fists. Taron had always taken a comment about his honor at more than face value, and his honor was more important than the blood that flowed through his veins. He ripped off the red shirt that he had been his sole wardrobe through every lifetime, at least so far as the *Coromor's* memory was concerned, and took one long step backward.

"You dare to insult my honor! Stand and face me, or will you run away from me as you have in every other lifetime?"

"Every other lifetime?" the *Coromor* scoffed. "The first time we met, I slew you in the palace of Traderes Hoffese, then in the Tower of Credtid. In the last lifetime, I watched you die in the fabled crystal palace in the Mithacarthian Woods. I have never run from you, and I would be glad to watch you die again."

He roared in anger and brought up his fists as if he were ready to fight. A red aura appeared around his body, and his muscles flexed. He seemed to grow in size. The aura shrank away from his shoulders and seemed to intensify as it moved down his arms until the aura concentrated around his fists. Elwyne grabbed Logan's shoulder and spun him away from Taron to look directly into his eyes. It was then that Logan realized that he was truly no longer in control. Whatever Elwyne saw in his eyes, she was frightened and she shrank away as if something had bitten her. Logan didn't return the look, nor did he even pay much attention to the reaction that she gave. Pike was close enough to see the reaction from Elwyne, and as he approached, Logan couldn't help but hear his thoughts.

"No Pike, I'm not alright."

"Logan," he responded undaunted, "I want to help you, but if you won't let me, I guess you can go this alone."

"This is not something that I can be helped with Pike," Logan said coldly. "The only thing I can ask you for is your strength."

Pike laid his hand on Logan's shoulder, and Logan felt their powers link. The power that pulsed through his veins doubled, and it felt as if his heart would burst as the power flooded over him. When Gideon and Talon added their strengths to the link, Logan wasn't sure whether he would be able to remain on his feet. A moment later Logan broke the link, and he could still the power coursing through him, but it was only an echo of the unbridled torrent. However, it would still be more than enough to topple the arrogant phase. Logan knew from the memories of the being that inhabited his body that though the chain was broken, he was still drawing upon the powers of the *Erieal* even though they were no longer in physical contact. This way though, they would all still be able to fight, though the *Erieal* would be at a considerable deficit. That was the trade-off for lending their powers. Taron stood waiting, ready to continue the battle that had started so many generations ago. Where before the *Coromor* was a dim entity lurking in the depths of Logan's mind, it was beginning to take more and more control of his actions and motivations, and Logan wasn't sure how much longer it would be before Logan was merely a passenger in his own body.

"Why are you wasting your time with these pathetic companions of yours? They are not powerful or competent enough to actually help you in your quest." Taron mocked, letting his finger point in the direction of Logan's companions. "Besides, this constant attachment you need with these frail women never ceases to amaze and perplex me. You know that we will constantly target these women first in an effort to destroy you from the inside. You must know that. Or is it that you don't care? Perhaps your motives are as base as ours are. You use them and toss them away like broken dolls when you are done. Perhaps we do you a favor by eliminating them before your boredom becomes too much to resist."

Logan let the jibe pass over him without rising to the bait.

"You and your brethren deal with the women because you are too afraid to face those with real power. If your head contained anything other than muscle, you would realize that it doesn't matter whether or not you succeed in killing the women that we love. In fact, it only makes our hate stronger, and it drives us further and faster toward our final goal," Logan responded.

"You haven't the slightest inkling of what real power is. You and the whelps that call themselves the *Erieal* only think they know what it means to be powerful. How Aldridge ever fell to the hands of a boy is beyond me."

"Are you saying that you could fare any better?" Logan asked trying to lead him into another defacement of his honor.

"But of course. I wouldn't even need to use my powers."

"Is that so? Well, in answer to your question, Aldridge was too sure in his own abilities, and that arrogance was what got him killed. And from your own words, it is clear that you are more arrogant than Aldridge ever was. I will enjoy killing you."

If Logan's comments had any effect on Taron, they weren't visible on his face. The sly grin was gone, and the angry smile that was always with him in the *Coromor's* memories replaced it. The aura around his clenched fists began to pulsate, and their light seemed to gain strength by the second. Logan could still feel the power of the *Erieal* pulsing through my veins, but in the dim and fragmented memories of the *Coromor*, the power was somehow incomplete. Logan mentally prepared himself for the battle that was about to come, and he measured his opponent, knowing in an instant that Taron was by far a physically stronger opponent than Logan had ever faced. It was clear that Taron would take any advantage that he could get, and it would only take one mistake to end the battle. Taking a breath to calm is raging nervousness; Logan reassured his fragmented mind that he wasn't going to be the one who made the fatal error in this battle. For some reason, Logan felt his hands fall to the belt that held his sword to my hip. Before he realized what he was doing, the sword and scabbard fell to the ground. Taron smiled and reset his feet, obviously anticipating his quarry's first strike. Logan leapt at the much larger man before he knew what he was doing. Taron's left hand darted forward; his palm toward Logan's advancing form. The red aura extended from his palm and slammed hard into Logan's chest. The blow stuck like being kicked in the chest by a mule. Logan fell back and hit the ground hard, the breath knocked out of him. When he was finally able to roll onto his side, he could feel a burning in my lungs, and when the pain contracted his chest in a single hard spasm, the cough that followed brought blood spurting from his mouth onto the ground. Though the pain still shook his body like a leaf in the wind, anger pushed the pain away from his mind. Logan wiped the blood from his quivering lips and forced his way back to his feet. The pain in his chest was almost unbearable, but surrender and pain were not options. The *Coromor* would not accept defeat, and seemed to be dragging him through every painful moment. There were memories that flooded to the front of Logan's mind. Echoes of real pain. The memory of lost limbs, being impaled by every manner of weapon, broken bones in every part of the body. The burning in his chest faded by comparison.

"Give up now weakling, you are hopelessly overmatched."

"We'll see about that Taron," Logan replied shortly.

Before giving his opponent time to adapt, Logan leapt again, only this time he was ready for Taron's counter. When his hand struck out again, and the brilliant red aura extended, Logan reached forward with both hands and took hold of the tendril of power. After one hard pull and expulsion of power, the piece of the aura snapped away from Taron's fist and clung to Logan's. The phase roared in pain and anger, and Logan saw the aura reappear around Taron's entire body for a mere second. That was the opening that Logan had been waiting for. As soon as he touched down, Logan collected his feet underneath him, and bounded back in Taron's direction. He thrust his aura-covered hand directly into Taron's chest with all of the force that he could muster. The howl of pain that erupted from Taron's throat echoed throughout the town and was answered by the growing thunder of the storm that raged from the black clouds above. Taron's brilliant aura flickered for a moment, tried to reassemble itself, and then finally shattered. The phase fell to the ground in a heap, and the Jeresei rushed to protect their leader.

"You should have known that you could never defeat the *Coromor* in a battle, Taron," Logan's voice called out. This time the words were his thoughts and not those of the *Coromor*. He was in control again, but he didn't know how long that would last.

"This is only a temporary victory Dragon, the final battle is coming, and you will never survive. I doubt you will survive the rest of this battle. Jeresei, strike!"

Logan heard the clang of metal and the sound of weapons being brought to bear. He knew that his friends had been waiting for the duel to devolve into a full-blown conflict with the forces of the Shadows, and they were not going to be caught unaware as they had been other times during the quest.

"Logan!"

The voice pulsed through Logan like rolling thunder, and without turning he knew what was coming. Pike hefted Logan's sword in his direction, and Logan snatched it out of the air just in time to pivot his body toward the sense of danger that was approaching quickly from behind. Reflex took over, and the naked blade passed through what had been empty air only a moment but was now occupied by the throat of a charging Jeresei. The creature went down without a sound and Logan watched as ten more stepped up to take its place. A moment later, the sense of danger flared again, and Logan dropped to his knees and then rolled to his left, just in time to avoid a stream of fire that pulsed through the air and struck the on-coming Jeresei. Lane had started the assault with his magic, and sooner or later Gideon, Pike, and Talon would add their strengths to the battle. Safely out of the way of the magical assault, Logan popped up to a knee and cut down another of the Jeresei. There were too many of them, and before he knew it they were surrounded once again. No matter how skilled the members of the party were in combat, the sheer numbers of Jeresei were enough to overwhelm them. The next moment, the ground around Logan began to shudder and shake violently. With one final heave, a fissure opened beneath several groups of Jeresei. Dozens of them fell into the fissures, screaming as they plummeted to their deaths.

* * * * * * * * * * * *

Pike watched as Gideon's handiwork cut the numbers of the enemy by more than half. Suddenly he heard a scream from somewhere behind him. It was a familiar scream, and when he turned he was more scared than he had ever been in his life. The huge hulk of a man who had called himself

Taron stood behind Pike, just ahead of the remaining ranks of Jeresei, and in his arms he held Eldar. Her face was filled with fear, and Pike knew that this man Taron could snap her in half without even thinking twice. One of his massive hands was clutched around the back of her neck while the other held a huge sword which he had produced out of the nothingness.

"You are Pike Rhuiden I assume," the phase said slowly in a thundering voice. "My brother Zarsi made a lot of fuss over your powers, as well as your obvious connection to this little girl. He seemed to think that you were the most impressive of the new *Erieal*, though I cannot say that I am impressed. You seem as weak and frail as this little morsel."

"Your brother Zarsi is dead Taron," Pike answered quickly. "And if you don't release her right now I'll send you to meet him."

"Do you think that your powers could ever vanquish one of the Brotherhood? You are pathetic. My brother Zarsi is alive and well, but that is more than I can say for you and your little wench."

"Pike."

Eldar managed to say his name before the hand constricted and crushed her spine. The death was quick and painless, and when she slipped from Taron's grasp and slumped to the ground, Pike exploded in fury. He had never thought of channeling his power so mercilessly before, but the only thought on Pike's mind was avenging Eldar's murder.

"You bastard!"

Pike flung his hands forward and closed his eyes. Taron fell to his knees screaming in agony. Suddenly, water began to spew from his pores, and as his screaming gained volume, so did the volume of water that gushed forth. Talon was quick to add his powers, and when he threw his hands forward, Taron grasped his throat, and the screaming stopped. His life was being ripped away from him in two facets. Pike was pulling the water out of his body, and that would eventually dry up his blood, and his heart would explode. Talon on the other hand was pulling the air out of Taron's lungs, slowly killing him. Taron managed to pull his aura up around him, and when he did, he created a flash of white light that blinded the two members of the *Erieal* long enough to break their concentration and free him from their powers. He turned from them and opened a portal and fled back toward Shau-ling's palace, happy to be alive. When Pike regained his sight, he ran over to Eldar's limp body and cradled her in his arms. His tears streamed down his face, and he held her tight, trying to use his powers.

"Live damn you," he said in a low raspy voice, "for all of the powers I have in my body, please live."

Talon walked toward him and placed his hand on Pike's shoulder as he had done in Sador. They exerted all of their powers into the limp body of the woman they both loved above everything else in the world, but nothing could save her. Taron had stolen her life and not even the powers of the *Erieal* could bring her back.

* * * * * * * * * * * *

Gideon watched as the Jeresei fell into the chasms that he created. Elwyne was safe behind him, and not one of those Jeresei bastards had even gotten close to her. Lane was beside him doing his best to take down those who managed to avoid his chasms. Lane turned for a moment, and when he turned back he grabbed Gideon's hand and pointed out into the battle zone.

"Jasmen's in trouble, Gideon. I can't get there in time, and I'm afraid that if we use our powers that we might hit her. You're the only one who can save her Gideon, I'll guard Elwyne."

Gideon nodded and sprinted toward Jasmen. Lane continued to use his streams of flame and fireballs to kill Jeresei after Jeresei. When he turned, he saw that one of the Jeresei had managed to escape his gaze. It sprinted toward Elwyne, and she didn't appear as if she was able to handle the sly Jeresei. Lane had never seen Elwyne fight anything before. He tried to set the thing ablaze, but it dodged the stream of flame and leapt at Elwyne. Lane moved quickly and jumped between the beast and his target. The Jeresei's claws struck true and embedded themselves deep into Lane's heart. Elwyne could do nothing but sever the Jeresei's head from the rest of its body and watch as Lane slowly died.

* * * * * * * * * * * *

The battle had stopped. It was as if the Jeresei were regrouping for another assault. Logan ran back toward Elwyne, and when he saw Lane's body, he didn't need to be told what happened. The rest of the group were making their way towards the pair, using the brief respite as their own opportunity to regroup. Gwydeon was visibly limping, and Midarin was doing her best to help him. Gideon was covered with cuts, as were Talon and Pike. Alexander and Talos appeared to be fine, and when Logan looked around and didn't see Eldar, he feared the worst.

"They killed her, Logan," Pike said in answer to the silent question. "That bastard Taron killed her like she was nothing. Talon and I almost had him, but he got away, ran through one of those blue portals."

"We can't take another engagement with them, Logan," Gwydeon said quickly. "If they rush us again, we'll be joining Eldar and Lane amongst the dead."

"Talon, Pike and I can assure yer escape, Logan," Gideon said. "We'll follow if we can."

"No. I can't afford to lose the three of you," Logan replied. "If we go, we all go together. That's the way it's always been. Talon, you take point, Pike the rear. We're going to fight our way to the docks and board the Monster of the Deep. If any one of us falls, keep going."

The looks that answered Logan's command told the story better than words ever could have. This was the first time that they had really had to cope with death and loss. Pike was dying inside that much was clear to anyone who looked into his eyes. However, no matter what he was feeling, he hefted his axe and was the first to agree to Logan's plan. With Pike's support, the rest nodded in agreement, and it was clear that everyone was ready to do what needed to be done in the next tense and bloody minutes. Before the Jeresei had completed the reformation of their ranks, the group turned toward the docks. Suddenly, blue portals opened all around them, and hundreds of Jeresei poured out. The Jeresei had not simply been taking an opportunity to regroup, but were waiting for reinforcements. The odds had shifted from difficult to impossible in a heartbeat. The party was out of options. As suicidal as it seemed, a forward charge through the ocean of red-skinned Jeresei seemed to be the only choice left to them. Just before he charged forward, Gwydeon grabbed Logan's shoulder and spun him around. Another portal had appeared behind them, but this portal was green instead of blue. When it opened, men not Jeresei streamed from the portal. They ran past and collided with the Jeresei. The carnage in Taren had just begun, and there was no telling how long it would go on. Paying little heed to the battle, the wounded and confused party made their way towards the dock, and ran headlong into another force of soldiers who seemed to be guarding the docks. These men were dressed in full armor, and they all had the symbol of the Lion on their breast plates.

"My lord Dragon," one of the guards said quickly, "we have been instructed to escort you to the Monster of the Deep and make sure that you arrive safely in Marcwell."

"How many of you are there?"

"Almost two hundred my lord Dragon," he answered.

"Twenty will take us to the docks, the rest will assist the brave army that saved us from the Jeresei. After we are on the ship and safe, those men will return and assist the rest of your force. These are my orders and they will not be questioned. Is that understood?"

"Yes my Lord Dragon," he answered gruffly.

He turned and relayed the orders to his men. Within minutes the surviving members of the People of the Dragon were safe on the Monster of the Deep. From the vantage point on deck, they could still see the battle that raged on land. As the ship began to depart the docks, a form appeared on the pier they had just pulled away from. The man's face was very familiar, and Logan had to blink several times to make sure he was truly seeing what his eyes were telling him.

"We have done all we can to help you my old friend," David's voice said as if it were carried by the wind. "Take care of my sister, and know that we will fight for you on the Other Side as if we were all still with you. The Army of the Dragon is strong on the Other Side, and whenever you need us, we will be ready to fight. Eldar and I have been reunited, and already Lane is serving a purpose. Grieve not for them; their battle is not yet over. Make them pay Logan, the circle must be complete."

CHAPTER 13

They all stood dumbfounded and watched as his form disappeared from view. The first person that had been lost had come back to save their lives, and for that they would all be eternally grateful. It was time to make Shau-ling pay for all of the pain that he had caused the world, and his death would justify all of the suffering and the loss endured. But first, there were some questions that needed to be answered. The only person that Logan knew to ask had been pulling the strings from the beginning. He had been sitting in Marcwell quietly orchestrating this entire war, and now it was time for Cedric Binosear to be made accountable.

Chapter XIV

Pain

The waves hit softly against the hull of the ship, and Pike Rhuiden could hear the soothing sound even through the din of angry and sorrowful voices that screamed and echoed inside of his head. Pike had locked himself in his cabin on the Monster of the Deep the second it left the docks of Taren, and the rage had been building ever since. The better part of the bottle of ale he found in the cabin was already gone, and it wasn't nearly enough. He could not get the picture of Eldar's dying form out of his mind; the terror in her voice as she said his name for the final time. The thing that tore at Pike more and more was that her death had no meaning. She wasn't able to fight, and her life was stolen from her like she was nothing. It could just as easily have been anyone else, and for that reason, her death served no purpose. If anyone should have died in battle, it should have been him. Pike had always been the one who took chances in battle, and he could not help but think that one day it would get him killed. He vowed at her side though that he would not die until he saw Taron dead at his feet. Eldar should have died with her sword in her hand, fighting, not broken like a doll, cast away by a petulant child. There were several knocks at his door, and only after the seventh did he bother to answer it. There was only one person that would have continued to knock, and Pike knew she would keep up until he answered.

Persistence had always been a hallmark of the Tamerlane family. While Pike had first experienced it in the form of David Tamerlane, he had learned recently that Elwyne Tamerlane, the younger sibling of the family, was just as persistent, if not more so, than her older brother. Elwyne rarely took no for an answer, a fact that had kept Logan coming back for her attention time after time. Pike rose slowly off the bed and tried his best to hide the tear-soaked pillow underneath a pile of clothes. He walked slowly over to the door, opened it, and then turned back toward the bed, not bothering to acknowledge his visitor. She waited until he had seated himself back on the bed before she decided to enter. When she did, she shut the door and sat beside him on the bed.

"Do you want to talk about it?"

"Do I have a choice?"

The hostility was thick in his voice, but she tried hard to push past it. She had dealt with Logan like this before, and she thought that she could handle Pike in the same way.

"I just want to help you Pike."

He shot up from the bed and walked to the port hole that looked out over the calm sea.

"And what if I don't want your help, Elwyne? How can you expect me to sit here and tell you how I feel, when I don't even know myself?"

"Just tell me what you feel inside."

"What I feel inside?" he roared as he turned back toward her. "I'm angry as hell, Elwyne. I'm not one of the phasia; I can't hide from what I've done or what I am. I have to deal with it just like everything else in my life. Her death is just another thing I have to deal with."

He turned away and moved back to the porthole. When he spoke again, it was more to himself then to Elwyne.

"How could I have taken her for granted? How could I have only thought about myself? How could I have been so blind? After all I've been through on this quest, I don't know if I can be that person again, Elwyne. How can the taverns and the songs and the stories mean anything anymore without her? Is there a way that I could find love again? Is there a way that I can live without her? Maybe this is what Cedric feels like. Maybe this is why he is so intent on protecting us, because he couldn't protect the woman he loved. Now, all I have is this. This fate. This life without her. This hell."

"But Pike . . ."

"For the first time I think I actually understand what Lord Cedric must go through every day of his life. What is tomorrow going to be like when I can't see her smile or her eyes? What about the next day, or the next? If we get through this, if we make it out alive, what's left for me? Aradon is in ruins, David, Lane, Eldar are gone. How many more? How many more will die?"

Pike fell silent for a long time. Finally he looked away from the rolling seas and locked eyes with Elwyne.

"I just miss her."

Elwyne took hold of his hand and watched as tears started to stream from his eyes. He turned away from her and tried hard to hide his momentary lapse of bravado. When he turned back to face her, his eyes were dim, cold and lifeless.

"Pike, I'm . . . I didn't mean to," she stammered trying to find the right words. "Are you all right?"

"Don't Elwyne. Don't say a word, okay? You know, all my life, until just recently, I've been alone. I pretended I liked it that way. To tell you the truth, that's not the way it was. I've been hiding behind a lie all this time. I was looking for someone to love. Just my luck, I found her, but she was taken away from me. Can't be helped, you don't choose who you love. I was just unlucky enough to choose her. There's no denying that it hurts. Maybe it's time for me to be alone again, only this time, it won't be a lie."

Elwyne stood and walked back toward the door after the silence that held between them became too much to bear. When she opened it, she turned back toward Pike for a moment. She wanted so much to go to him and try to help him through what he was feeling, but she knew that he was right. She knew that love couldn't be denied, and it broke her heart.

* * * * * * * * * * * *

When Elwyne returned to her room, Logan knew that something was wrong. Her eyes were sullen, and he could not help but let his mind flash back to Pike's words and Eldar's death. Elwyne was not taking it well at all, and Logan could only imagine how Elwyne was feeling inside. For all of the times that they had conversations about feelings, it was always Logan who did the opening up, and he couldn't remember a time when they talked about the way she felt. The closest he ever really got to hearing about her true feelings was after their traumatic episode in Dreamscape. No matter what they had gone through during the increasingly ill-fated quest, Logan didn't think that any of the members of the group would ever be able to forget what they encountered in Dreamscape, and perhaps that was why they took their mortality and the fragility of life so seriously.

"Are you all right Elwyne?"

"No, Logan, I'm not. I feel like I'm dying inside, and I don't know how to handle it. I thought that maybe by helping Pike, I would somehow find answers for myself, but he is so far gone that I can't help but worry about him. He is so full of rage that I'm not sure if he will act in the proper manner from now on, especially if it comes to the phasia. There is that chance that he will unnecessarily risk his life to get his revenge."

Logan took her into his arms and held her. It felt like the right thing to do, and in some ways it felt like it was the only thing he could do. There were no words inside of him to try to quell her fears, and even if he could find the words, Logan wasn't sure that it would have done any good at all. The tears streamed down onto his shoulder and she did her best to try and regain her composure, but Logan knew that inside she was breaking in two. Since the first time that Logan had felt helpless during the quest, he knew that he never wanted to feel that way ever again. However, it seemed that there was no real way to avoid it. Then as he stood there holding her in his arms, knowing that there was nothing that could be done to stop her crying, the truly helpless feeling overwhelmed him again, and the despair she felt was echoed in his soul. But it echoed somewhere else. It echoed down in the depths of the being that lived deep inside of Logan. The *Coromor* was suffering too, but its suffering seemed to be ten times worse. Logan wished he could understand everything that was happening inside of him, but it was a foolish wish, and part of him hoped that it would never be granted. But no matter what was raging inside of him, he pushed those feelings down, pushed them away, and focused all of the energy he had on the woman he held in his arms, and he vowed silently to himself that he would not let anything happen to the woman that he loved.

* * * * * * * * * * * *

Gwydeon paced the floor of his cabin. Something was eating at him inside, and he couldn't figure out what it was. Perhaps it was the pointlessness of it all. Not just Eldar's death, but the whole fight; maybe even the whole quest. Eldar was the strongest swordsman of them all, and she lay dead without ever being able to bring her blade to bear. Lane was gone too, his magic not enough to save himself, but enough to save Elwyne. It was then that Gwydeon realized that he was clenching his fist. Lane valued life, no matter who's it was. However, Gwydeon knew that Lane sacrificed himself because it was Elwyne, because of who she was, and because of how important she was to Logan. Would they all be called upon to fall the same way? Powers flowed all around them, and now two of the mortals had fallen. What future did Gwydeon still have before him? How could he hope to stand against the monsters that waited for them? The door opened and Midarin walked in and lay down on the bed. When he looked over to her, she smiled and patted the bed.

"Eldar's gone," Gwydeon said, his eyes never leaving hers, "I can't imagine what Pike is going through. And as much as I just want to lay there with you and wrap you in my arms and never let go, I can't."

"I understand Gwydeon," Midarin replied slowly, "do you want to talk about it?"

"I don't know what I can say. Eldar and I knew each other from the time that we were born, and I can't imagine what life will be like without her around. But more than that, how many more of us are going to fall? Pike? Talon? You?"

Midarin smiled and walked over to him. She took him into her arms and held him. They stood there together like that for a few minutes. There came a knock at the door, and Elwyne's voice resounded from the other side of the door.

"Logan wants everyone on deck in five minutes."

"We'll be there," Gwydeon replied.

* * * * * * * * * * * *

Logan stood on the top deck looking out over the water, watching the fires rise from the town that they had departed from so quickly. The lanterns on deck did their best to serve as a source of light in a moonless sky. This night had a dark edge to it, one that Logan had not seen in a long time, and he hoped that he would never see it again. Elwyne walked up beside him and draped her arm over his shoulder.

"Everyone's here, Logan," she whispered into his ear and then kissed his cheek.

When Logan turned to face the remaining members of the group, the looks in their eyes were patchworks of sorrow, confusion, anger, dread, and longing. Logan knew that this was the hardest time for all of them, but once they were able to work past it, they could try their best to get on with their lives. Loss was not new, it was not a new sensation, but this targeted violence, this senseless murder could not be put in any context that would make sense.

"Friends," Logan said in the strongest voice that he could manage, "I know what you all must be feeling right now, and I wish there were words that would lend any meaning to this. But the sad reality that we have to accept is that Eldar and Lane are dead and we betray their memory if we let their deaths stop us from completing the quest that they placed their beliefs in. To tell you all the truth, I don't feel comfortable standing up here and talking about our two fallen friends, and since their bodies are laying in the middle of a battlefield, whatever we say here and now will have to serve as a burial. After tonight, we have to put their deaths behind us and go on with the quest. Who will be the first to speak of our fallen friends?"

Logan stepped aside and waited for someone to step forward. Gwydeon started to pull away from Midarin, but Pike put a hand on his shoulder and pulled him back. He hesitated for only a moment before stepping forward and turning to face the assemblage. There was a heavy weight that sat on his shoulders, and inwardly Logan hoped that if he could say good-bye to Eldar in his own way that it would somehow alleviate some of the pain.

"In case some of you weren't aware of it, Eldar and I were to be married as soon as all of this was over."

While there were some questioning looks around the group, Talon's face betrayed the shock that he was feeling.

"In truth, we were already married according to Aradon customs, and I'm not sure what I want to do about that. Eldar and I truly loved each other, and even though we fought constantly, I think that it made our love even stronger, and it forged a bond that not even death can break. Maybe it's because of the way we loved each other that we fought so much, or maybe it's the other way around. I don't know that there's much else that anyone can say about Eldar other than the fact that she was a very caring person and that she would have given her life to save any one of us without question. She had a kind heart and a free spirit, and I think that was why I fell in love with her in the first place. There was this way that she used to look at me, and somehow, when I looked in her eyes, I knew that nothing could come between us, not even each other, though it seemed like we constantly tried to test that."

He was rambling. The tears began to fill his eyes, and Elwyne did her best to comfort him when the tears started to fall. Talon and Gwydeon joined Elwyne at Pike's side, and it took only a moment for Logan to join as well. The remaining members of the initial group huddled together in that moment, a strange island of normality in a sea of madness. Everyone else knew that the grieving childhood friends needed to be alone that way, and no one would have intruded. There were only five left now, those who came from Aradon. For some reason it seemed that it wouldn't have hurt as much if it would have been someone else, no matter how terrible that was to consider. As they stood there together, holding one another, the others slipped away to their cabins, all except for Midarin and Gideon.

Logan wished that they would have said some words for Lane, but in their own way, the tears were shed for him as well as Eldar. When the crying ended, they did their best to try and think of the good memories. After several moments of quiet, Gwydeon motioned for Midarin and Gideon to join, and though there was hesitation on both parts, they joined willingly.

"I wish the others wouldn't have left," Elwyne remarked as she looked around.

"I think that they understood the seriousness of the situation, and maybe they thought it would be better if we did the grieving our way without them," Talon commented.

"We all thought that maybe you people from Aradon may have just wanted to be together to grieve for your friends. After all, you knew them best," Midarin replied.

Gwydeon looked over and smiled at Midarin. Logan could see the love in their eyes, and when he over to Pike and saw that he was looking at Gwydeon and Midarin as well, Logan could see the pain in his eyes, and Logan knew that he and Eldar had shared that same love.

"So Logan," Pike said trying hard to keep his voice from showing the pain that was inside him, "what do we do now?"

"I was hoping that no one would ask that question. The main concern on my mind right now is what kind of reception that we should expect when we get to Marcwell."

"Why would ye expect anyt'ing other den a nice warm reception when we git ta Marcwell, Logan? Wasn't Lord Cedric da one who wanted ye ta start dis damn fool quest in da first place?" Gideon asked.

"That he was Gideon," Logan responded, "but nothing that we have expected to happen has quite turned out that way yet."

"So you're thinking that there might be an ambush waiting on us in Marcwell."

"That's exactly what I'm thinking Talon, and I'm sorry to say that there's nothing that we can really do about it right at the present time," Logan answered.

"We're behind ye all da way, Logan," Gideon said quickly, "and if at any time ye feel the need fer us *Erieal* ta do da kind of damage dat we were born fer, ye jus' give da word, an' it'll be done."

"Hopefully it won't come to that my friend," Logan said patting him on his shoulder. "Has the Flame been taken care of?"

"It is well hidden Logan," Pike answered. "No one but me could find it."

"Good Pike," Gwydeon said lightly, "just make sure you remember where it is."

Logan saw Pike smile. He didn't think that he would see that again for a long time, but somehow Gwydeon's dry sense of humor always found some way to pry a smile. By the next afternoon they would be in Marcwell, and Logan didn't really know what to expect, and that frightened him.

* * * * * * * * * * *

Logan rolled over in the middle of the night to Elwyne's sobs. He didn't let her know that he was awake and just laid there listening to her cry. There was a reason that she waited until he was asleep before she let herself cry again. Logan didn't know why she felt she needed to hide her tears from him, but there must have been a reason. Maybe she felt that she needed to be strong for everyone else, even him. She was trying so hard to be strong, but he had learned in the past few days that strength is not determined by how well you control your emotions. Real strength is being able to feel sorrow and pain and then be able to deal with it. You don't gain strength by hiding from your feelings, but you do gain strength by feeling. She rolled over and saw that he was awake. Her cheeks were stained with the tracks of her tears, but when she looked into his eyes, she could not contain the small smile, and threw her arms around him and held him tight.

* * * * * * * * * * *

"Logan!"

It was the next day. Logan and Elwyne had slept through the morning, and the rest had let them have their few moments of peace. Pike's voice cut through the room, and when Logan rolled out of bed, the door opened. Jasmen stood beside Pike at the door.

"So, have we reached Marcwell yet?"

"Yes Logan, we have," Jasmen answered.

"We would like to have you on the top deck when the guards from Marcwell arrive. Do you think that you could handle a little demonstration?" Pike asked.

"That all depends on what you have in mind," Logan answered not fully understanding what Pike meant.

"You aren't going to do anything stupid, are you Pike?" Elwyne asked cautiously.

"Don't I always?"

"That's what I was afraid of," Logan said before Elwyne could get it out. "Where's the Flame?"

Pike crossed the room and handed Logan a small parcel. Logan unwrapped it and looked at the Jeweled Dragon's Flame closely for the first time. It looked merely like a chunk of obsidian. However, upon closer inspection, where a finely polished piece of obsidian would reflect light and act like a mirror, this did not. It was as if no light touched the polished exterior of the black stone, but if you looked into the jewels that covered it, sapphire, ruby, quartz, diamond, azure, topaz, emerald, you could see the light shimmering. There was something strange about that black stone. As he held the Flame in his hands, the *Coromor's* elated voice clamored on inside of Logan's mind. It knew what the Flame could do, and it thirsted to feel that power once again.

After Pike and Jasmen returned to the deck, Logan and Elwyne dressed and joined the others topside. The rest of the group with the exception of

Pike, Talon, and Gideon were already on the deck. Whatever they were planning, Logan was sure that it was going to be very interesting. As he looked around, he noticed that Talos was also missing from the group. If Lane still would have been alive, Logan was sure it would have been him wrapped up in this devious plan. As Logan and Elwyne approached they were greeted with warm smiles and looks of accomplishment. They had made it this far, a feat that had seemed impossible mere hours ago. The crew had finished mooring the ship to the dock, and there waited a dozen men who quickly boarded. The leader of the group stopped several feet from Logan and spoke.

"Are you Logan Ranthall?"

"Perhaps, and perhaps not. For some reason I think that you should identify yourself before you ask any more questions," Logan answered.

"I am Kaasi Nived, captain of the royal guard of Marcwell, as well as third in command of the Lion's Mane. My associates are members of the Lion's Mane as well."

"That is all well and good," Gwydeon said stepping forward, "but as far as I remember, a visiting dignitary is always greeted by his equal in rank and authority. In this case, you do not qualify, so you may not deal with the Lord Dragon directly."

Logan was pleasantly surprised by Gwydeon's strength and assertiveness. Ever since Logan had known Gwydeon, he had wanted to be a member of the Lion's Mane. He wanted to be the best, and moreover, he wanted to be the best of the elite. Now, here he was faced with the same men that he had idolized for so many years, and he treated them as if they were beneath them. Perhaps Midarin was rubbing off on him, teaching him how to behave like royalty.

"And who are you?" Nived asked a little perturbed by Gwydeon's arrogance.

"I am Gwydeon Sandar, the captain of the Dragon's personal guard, and the leader of the Army of the Dragon. Since neither Lord Cedric nor Lord Arathorn thought it necessary to come down and greet the Lord Dragon and his companions, we will stay here until such time that they do."

"That is absurd. Lord Cedric expressly . . ."

"Furthermore, any attempt to make us leave the Monster of the Deep will be taken as an act of aggression and we will be forced to retaliate with lethal force."

"You have no right to dictate terms . . ."

"This discussion is over and you will leave this ship now, or we will make you leave."

Gwydeon stood proudly, his shoulders back and his jaw set as he watched Nived squirm. Logan was very impressed with Gwydeon. Thoughts of the future rolled through his mind, and he knew that Gwydeon wouldn't ever believe the scheme that he had conjured up.

"This is not a negotiable situation Sandar," Nived said angrily. "You and the rest of your associates will leave this ship now."

Some of the guards behind Nived had drawn their swords, and Logan had the strangest feeling that this whole situation was about to turn ugly.

"Put down your swords gentlemen," a voice said.

That was Pike's voice, but it came from inside one of the helmets of a member of the Lion's Mane. Nived and his flanking officer turned around, and as Logan looked past them, he saw three of the men take their helmets off, and there stood Gideon, Talon, and Pike. Talos stood nearby, and as he stepped aside, the three soldiers that should have been there were laying on deck, unconscious.

"I don't think that these men will be bothering you very much longer, my lord," Pike said bowing, "they were just leaving."

Nived's face turned bright red. His anger was to the boiling point and it looked like he would explode at any moment.

"I think not," a voice said from behind me. "They are here under my orders, and I would appreciate any assistance you could give them."

CHAPTER 14

Logan spun around and was looking into the face of a man that he only vaguely remembered. When this man had come to Aradon all those years ago, his eyes had been brighter, but now they were gray and dim. His hair was still the light brown that Logan remembered, but it too was streaked with gray. The clean-shaven appearance was not something that Logan had seen from anyone in the last few days. Though his mane had faded a bit in brilliance, he was still the Lion.

"My apologies Lord Cedric," Logan said bowing. "We have been under a lot of stress lately, and my friends and I don't take very well to threats."

"There is nothing for you to apologize for, Logan," he replied. "After the reports that I have heard from Aryx, I thought it best that I come down here myself."

"Aryx is here?" Gideon said a bit shocked.

They were all shocked at the news, but it seemed that Gideon was more concerned than the rest of the group. Logan made a note to ask him why later.

"Yes," Lord Cedric replied easily, "he arrived last night. After I heard what was going on in Taren, I ordered my garrisons from the surrounding area to give aid. Apparently they were able to help."

"Not soon enough," Pike said, the bitterness creeping into his voice, "they weren't able to get there before the Jeresei and that bastard Taron killed two of our friends."

Lord Cedric faltered for a moment and then sighed.

"I am truly sorry that I could not have helped personally, but other considerations held my attention."

"What considerations could have been more important than saving the world, Cedric?" Pike snapped. "You left us all alone, and we were almost killed several times on this damn quest. Your lackey, Aryx, did little else but lie to us, and when he wasn't lying, he was speaking in those damn half-truths and riddles of his. If you gave a damn about what happened to us, you would have come down from your lavish castle and helped us."

Talon had to hold Pike back. When Logan looked back at Lord Cedric, his eyes were filled with not anger, but sorrow. He had no answers for Pike's charges, and all he could do was take the abuse.

"Walk with me, Logan."

Logan nodded and they left the ship and started walking toward the center of Marcwell. The others would rejoin them at the palace, but Lord Cedric had something that he had to say to Logan in private.

"Lord Cedric," Logan said as soon as we were out of earshot of the others, "I must apologize . . ."

"No, Logan," he said softly, "in some ways, your friend was right. He is the one named Pike is he not?"

"He is. I trust that Aryx's stories were not too hard on us."

"They were," he replied, "but I have come to expect such descriptions from Aryx. He is a good man, but sometimes I'd really like to kill him."

Logan couldn't hold back the laugh. It wasn't the uneasy laughter that he had known for the last week, but it was the true laughter that came from an easy heart.

"So you have heard of our adventures thus far?"

"I have. I must say that you have done well to stay alive this long. I would be lying if I were to say that I knew what you had to go through, because I never had to go toe to toe with one of the phasia, at least not until the end. Also, I have heard about the situations in Dreamscape, Trelon, and Sador, and I must say that those disturb me more than any others."

He stopped for a moment and then turned to face Logan.

"I was sorry to hear that you were unable to save my sister."

That had to hurt him to talk about it so soon. He had lost more than any of the new generation of heroes had, even Pike. But more than sorrow, there was resignation in his voice, almost as though he had been expecting the loss. Logan wanted to say something comforting to him, but the older man continued speaking.

"But I suppose that bastard Aldridge had planned it all out too well. Now I think that I understand your reluctance to come here. Aryx was always a little too blinded by obligation to see what was really happening, so I do not hold you responsible for the actions that were taken in response to him."

"Thank you, my lord," Logan replied.

"Cedric."

"Thank you, Cedric."

Cedric turned back in the direction of the palace and continued walking. After a few moments of silence he spoke again.

"I have heard that you and the woman Elwyne Tamerlane are engaged to be married."

"Yes, we are."

"I would be honored if you would have your ceremony here in Marcwell. I know that you Aradonians have your own rituals, but if it is possible, we would be delighted."

Logan did his best to suppress any expression.

"I'll discuss it with Elwyne."

He stopped for another moment, looked at Logan, nodded briefly and then continued walking once again.

"I expect that you and your friends would like to get cleaned up as soon as we reach the palace."

"Yes, we would."

"Well then, after that, I have some gifts for you and your friends, gifts fitting the importance of your visit to Marcwell."

Logan didn't know what Cedric had in mind, but he hoped that the surprises were much nicer than the others they had been subjected too by Shau-ling and his servants. There was something in Cedric's aloof and distracted manner that Logan found disturbing, and Logan couldn't shake the feeling that something was very wrong. Everything that they had been through had made him trust and hate that feeling.

Dreams

Illimar. The once beautiful city filled with towers of glass and wood was now reduced to merely wispy shadow of its former self. Though the battles that raged there were short, the damage and repercussions would be felt by the inhabitants for many years to come. There were other fires that raged outside of the town. The major and decisive battle of the civil war had taken place in the glade just over the great bridge. Some of the grass was burned brown, and there was still smoke that rolled off parts of the forest to the south. Nature had also felt the force of this battle, and the forest and glade could not be rebuilt as easily as the towers of Illimar. It was certainly a costly battle in that sense, but there were also many lives lost. Men and women in Illimar separated the dead with upturned noses and pale expressions. Members of the Army of Illimar, the Army of the Dragon, and even the town commoners were laid out to be given a proper burial. The traitorous army that served the former Queen Saris, whose identity was revealed to have been the phase Caris, and the fallen members of the Jeresei army were collected into massive piles and burned. The attitude in Illimar was morose to say the least, and so it could be said that no one cared to notice the arrival of a stranger.

Out in the middle of the Great River, a swirling blue portal appeared. As if someone had been shoved out of an open doorway, a form shot through the portal and landed in the middle of the river. The man's head broke the surface, and as he swam over to the shore, his curses rose over the sound of the rushing river. He pulled himself over the slightly raised bank and rolled onto the flat, grass-covered ground.

I just have no luck, Korrd thought to himself. *I keep getting knocked out, I almost lose my life to that witch Caris, and now I can't even aim a portal. It could have been worse I guess. At least I aimed high and didn't come out of the portal in the middle of a rock face or something. I hope nobody saw me come out of that portal. If they did, I'm dead.*

Korrd sat up and looked around. He looked back at the river, and he was shocked to see that the portal was still hanging above the raging waters. He put two of his fingers to his temple for a moment and then closed his eyes. Seconds later, the portal began closing, and as Korrd opened his eyes, the portal vanished. He turned away from the river and started walking back towards Rama. Being on foot was not a good way to travel from Illimar to Kandor, but at the present, that was the only option left open to Korrd.

"Ho there, stranger."

The voice was not a familiar one. Korrd spun around, concerned about the fact that his entry was a little more than conspicuous. Three men on horseback, all wearing the symbol of the Army of the Dragon on their chests entered his view. For a moment he started to get worried, so worried in fact that he almost reached for his sword. Thinking better of the rash action, he stood straight and waived at the three men.

"What can I do for you fine gentlemen?" Korrd said in a bright voice.

"We were wondering if you have seen a group of men riding or running this way. They are wanted for crimes against the Lord Dragon, and against the Kingdom of Illimar."

"I have seen no one except the three of you, sir," Korrd answered quickly. "By the by, you wouldn't happen to be headed toward Rama, would you?"

"Do you have business in Rama, sir?" the leader of the men said quickly.

"As a matter of fact, I do. A friend of mine, a man named Antrobus, wrote me not two weeks ago and asked that I come and visit him in Rama. I am from Aradon, and I was hoping to find passage here in Illimar, but with the battle and all, it looks like my prospects are pretty thin."

The man on horseback looked at Korrd strangely for a moment and then sighed softly.

"I'm afraid that I have some bad news for you stranger. Your friend Antrobus, my former commander was laid in the grave not five days ago. I'm sorry that you have to hear it from my mouth, but better to hear it now than when you have traveled all the way to Rama for nothing."

Korrd tried his best to look hurt. If these men had only known who they were actually talking to. He held back a few fake tears only for a moment and then let them fall freely. After a moment or two, he composed himself and choked out a question.

"Do you think that the three of you could take me to Rama so that I could pay my respects?" he said, his voice intentionally wavering.

"Very well stranger, you can ride with me."

* * * * * * * * * * * *

It was nightfall of the first day of the ride to Rama. Korrd and the men had not talked much during the ride, and now Korrd could tell that these soldiers were anxious, and they were not the kind that was quick to trust strangers. The man that he had ridden with for the majority of the day walked over to him and sat down.

"You have not been very talkative stranger," the man said softly, "we thought that perhaps Antrobus' death was hitting you harder than you let on."

Korrd smiled and nodded.

"Antrobus and I were very close. I'm sorry that I haven't been much of a traveling companion; I've had a lot on my mind. My name is David Tamerlane."

"It's nice to meet you David, my name is Sol. Did you say that you are from Aradon?"

Korrd thought back for a moment and realized that he had made a crucial mistake. If there was a way to cover, he had better think of it fast.

"Yes," Korrd responded. "I've lived in Aradon for many years now, with my sister and my friend Logan. They have treated me very well, but they left about a week ago and I heard that they were headed to Illimar. That's why I went there first."

"You are a friend of Logan Ranthall?" Sol asked in disbelief.

"Yes. I've known Logan since he was in diapers," which wasn't entirely untrue.

"I'm sorry that we have treated you so poorly then. A friend of the Lord Dragon should have an escort fit for a knight. Did you say that your name was Tamerlane?"

"Yes. Perhaps my sister was with Logan, Elwyne Tamerlane?"

The shocked look on Sol's face deepened, and then he choked out a response.

"You are the brother of the Lady Dragon?!? I'm so pleased to meet you David. The brother of the Dragon is an honored presence with the Army of the Dragon."

You have no idea, Korrd thought to himself.

"Well, enough of the adulation," Korrd said quickly, "I embarrass easily. I would appreciate it if you keep my identity to yourself however. I am very shy."

"As you wish," Sol answered.

"How much longer until we get to Rama, Sol?" Korrd asked a moment or two later.

"We should reach the twin towns in two days. I would expect that you would like to get some sleep, for we will ride early in the morning."

"Yes Sol, I would. Thank you."

Sol stood, bowed, and then returned to the other two members of the Army of the Dragon. Korrd received some strange looks, but he tuned them out as he closed his eyes and sank into sleep.

* * * * * * * * * * * *

Korrd found himself standing in the middle of the training field back in Aradon. He knew it was a dream the second that he opened his eyes, but this was not one of the nightmares that he remembered, this was something new. He looked all around him and then suddenly saw a familiar man walking toward him.

"Aerith Seth," Korrd said without thinking, "I have seen you in my dreams before, but never like this."

Aerith cocked his head to one side and rested the flat of his blade on his shoulder.

"You may know me, but I've never seen you before," he responded. "Who are you?"

"I am Korrd Ranthall, the *Chosen One*, of this timeline. I am you, albeit a few generations removed."

Seth looked puzzled for a moment and then shook his head.

"Well, Korrd, as flattered as I am that you want to walk in my shoes, you're not the one I was expecting. But, since you're here, I'll give you a word or two of advice before I continue my search. Keep your eye on the *Erieal* in this time, Korrd. They're not what they seem. If you're as wise as you think you are, you would travel your own road, and those who seem most eager to follow are not your allies. Trust me when I say that people who follow you because of who you are, or who you think you are, are the most dangerous to your legacy. Use what you have inside of you, and follow no message but your own heart's words. If you truly fight for what you are meant to fight for, there is no greater advice. Everyone is going to try to control you, but so long as you remain strong and keep to the path of the Light that has been chosen for you, you'll be fine. And one more thing; true power rewards those who use it least. This dream isn't yet over, and if you value your life, and the lives to come in the future, you'll pay attention and not fall into the same trap that others before you have. Farewell and good luck."

With that he vanished, as did the glade of Aradon. Blackness surrounded him, and his eyes closed regardless of his wish to remain at home.

When light returned to Korrd's vision, he was in the middle of a huge circle of people. All of the men and women in the room he recognized from the descriptions given to him by Saurn, but for some reason, everything seemed wrong.

"Korrd Ranthall," the high-pitched voice of Farax called. "You are here to learn what the future holds for you, but you may only ask five questions of the men and women assembled here. Some of these men work for the goals of the Light, some for the aims of Shau-ling, while others have their own agendas that can only be explained by they themselves. Choose wisely. Some of us will speak in riddle and lies, while others will speak in truths. You must determine what the truth is. Go now, ask your questions."

Korrd looked around and then walked over to where his master, Lord Saurn, stood. He thought deeply for a moment and then asked the question that had been burning in his mind since the beginning.

"Are you leading me on the right path?"

"You follow me for your own reasons young one," his voice answered. "You are the only one who knows whether the path is a true one or not."

As soon as the answer was spoken, Saurn disappeared. The answer puzzled him for a moment and then he tried to push it aside as he walked to the next person. The man in front of him was Gwydeon Sandar.

"Gwydeon, you and I have known each other a long time; you will surely tell me the truth. Does Logan still hold me ill-will?"

"The answer is simple," Gwydeon responded. "Do you still hold ill-will for him?"

Gwydeon disappeared leaving Korrd angry and empty all at the same time. Korrd shook his head and then walked over to Caris.

"I killed you far too easily. Why do I feel as if I had been tricked?"

"Perhaps," she said smugly, "because you were."

She disappeared, and Korrd nodded, the anger burning inside of him more and more every moment. He walked over to the image of Shau-ling and then cleared his throat.

"Has Saurn told me the truth about my powers?"

"That is a question that cannot be answered here by the minds that control this world. There are too many factors that determine truth for different people. It all depends on what you believe you are."

Then Shau-ling disappeared along with everyone else in the chamber, except for the image of Aryx.

"Wait a minute; I was supposed to get five questions of anyone that I choose. This is not the person I would choose."

"Fine," Aryx said quickly, "than I shall alter my appearance as I have in every other case in this room. You have talked to me in the guise of Saurn, Shau-ling, Gwydeon Sandar, Farax, and even Caris. Why is it so hard for you to talk to me as White Lightning?"

Korrd walked over to the man who wore the face of Aryx Terian, and looked at him with puzzlement covering his face.

"Who are you?"

"I am most often called Asperon Thorne, but you may call me Guardian."

"Why have you entered my dreams Guardian?"

"A grave mistake has been made, Korrd, and I think that it is partially my fault. I must now do my best to correct my error before other parties become involved."

"What was your mistake?" Korrd asked quickly.

"I cannot tell you Korrd, for it would most certainly seal my fate. I intend to live for at least five more centuries, so you must figure out the riddles that have been given to you. Pay heed to all that you have seen and the choices that you have made in this room of reflections. Things on this plain are merely reflections of the true world, but when a lie looks into the mirror of truth, it sees its own reflection, for a lie in the face of truth is a lie nonetheless. Do you understand me, Korrd?"

"I think that I do, Guardian," Korrd said, his lie not hidden well.

"Then find your answers in the mirror of truth."

The Guardian pointed to something behind Korrd. He turned and saw the huge full-length mirror that stood five feet behind him. When he turned back to say something to the Guardian, Korrd found that he had disappeared. Confused by the Guardian's words, Korrd walked over to the mirror and looked into the glass. When he saw his own reflection peering back at him, he was far more confused than he had been before. Just then, the room faded around him, and suddenly he was alone in blackness again.

* * * * * * * * * * * *

Korrd was in an inn. This was not one that he had been in during his journey, and this new place thickened the confusion in his brain. There was a single door at the end of a long hallway, and when Korrd opened the door, he saw a familiar face in the bed across the room.

"Logan?" Korrd said softly.

Logan sat up in bed and looked into the darkness, barely able to see the form that stood on the other side of the room.

"Elwyne, is that you?"

"No, Logan," he answered. "It's me, your brother."

"My brother is dead, and whoever you are, you better get out of here now before I make you very sorry you stumbled into this inn tonight."

Korrd approached, and when Logan laid his eyes upon him, Logan was more confused than he had ever been.

"Korrd, is that really you?"

"I don't know, Logan," he replied. "I've been in so many places in this dream; I'm not sure if I'm still dreaming, or if I'm awake."

"You are still dreaming," a voice rang out in the silence.

"Is that Asperon Thorne who speaks," Logan asked.

"It is, Logan Ranthall."

"Why are you here, and why has my brother entered my dream?"

"Ask him yourself."

"I take it that you have met the Guardian," Korrd said quickly as he sat down beside Logan on the bed.

"I have."

Logan looked sidelong at his brother, still unsure if he was really seeing him or if it was a very realistic nightmare.

"What are you doing here Korrd? I thought that you've been dead for a long time."

Korrd hung his head and shook it softly.

"It's not easy to explain, Logan. My bet is that you won't remember this discussion when you wake in the morning, but I think that I know the purpose for my visit here."

"What are you talking about?" Logan asked puzzled.

"The mirror that reflects the truth. A lie is still a lie in the face of the truth, and we all mold the truth in our own aspect of reality."

"What are you babbling on about Korrd? Where are you, I want to see you."

"No you don't, Logan. It's not time for us to meet yet, but soon. If there is one thing that you remember about this dream, remember to be careful of who you trust. Those who seem most likely to be your friends are most assuredly your enemies. Those who seek knowledge will want it so that they can destroy you. Remember, my brother. Goodbye. We shall meet soon."

He disappeared, and Logan sank back into bed. The veil of blackness lifted from his eyes and Logan shot up in bed.

"Korrd?"

Elwyne rubbed her hand on his chest and pushed him back down into bed.

"There's no one here, Logan. We are safe here in Taren. Now go back to sleep and we'll talk about this in the morning.

Logan couldn't believe her, but the fragments of dream were fading so quickly that sleep began to reassert itself. Logan lay down and tried hard to piece his dream back together, but all that he could find were bits and phrases about trust. Logan only wished he knew what it meant.

* * * * * * * * * * * *

Korrd woke into yet another phantom room. He was beginning to get frustrated with the whole situation that he had been placed in, but as he was beginning to understand more and more of what he was being shown, the confusion and irritation was lifting.

"Hello Korrd."

Korrd spun around and saw a somewhat familiar face. He had seen this man in the play that turned out to be the history of a man named Aerith Seth. The thin man dressed in black before him was the phase Basille. As Korrd thought back to the previous phases of the dream, he remembered that Basille had not been in the room with the other members of the phasia, and it now puzzled him.

"Basille."

"You are probably wondering why you have been brought to me as opposed to Saurn, your lord and master."

"No one is my master, Basille. I do what I please, when I please."

"You can keep up your pitiful delusions if you wish, and I will leave you alone in your fallacy. However, if you were as open-minded as your brother, perhaps I could teach you something."

Korrd nodded and sighed.

"I am sorry Basille. I have trouble separating what is real and what is the dream. I would have only talked to you that way if you were truly Basille, but I suppose you are going to tell me that you are yet another reflection of Asperon Thorne, and that you are only a reflection of the true Basille in the mirror of truth."

"You assume much," Basille answered, "and I am sorry to say that you are wrong on all counts. I am, in fact, the true Basille."

Korrd stopped dead, and it took several moments for him to realize that he was holding his breath. Unconsciously his fists balled, and once he realized, he wasn't sure why that was his first reflex. Standing toe to toe with a member of the phasia was always a risky proposition, and while he had battle Caris and had been successful, that was in the waking world. However, in this half-dream state, Korrd had no idea what Basille was capable of, or if Korrd's own powers would have any effect.

"If this is still a dream," Korrd managed, "how is it possible for you to be here?"

"I have the ability to travel instantaneously from one place to another, without the use of portals. I simply will it, and I am there. I have found though that I also have the power to travel between the different plains of existence. So, I am able to enter this dream world that Asperon Thorn created for you. It is not unlike Dreamscape, but without the maniacal yellow ball. However, we are not here to talk about me, we are here to talk about you and the quest that my brother Saurn has sent you on."

"Are you here to tell me that Saurn is wrong and that I should follow you so that we can rule the world together? If you are, you can save it. I've heard it from both Caris and Saurn, and I'm sure I'll hear it from all of the other phasia before this is all over."

Basille smile and shook his head.

"We are very arrogant aren't we? I like that. However, I am not here to make those claims, nor am I here to tell you what you should do next. I will however offer you some advice. My brother Saurn is one of the best manipulators in the world. He is cruel, heartless, vain, and arrogant. More to the point, he is also quite insane. Saurn has been away from the Council of the Ten so long that he has begun to draw on his own power more and more to stay alive. He cannot replenish his powers at the Council, so he must cleanse himself with the same powers that he has been drawing on for years. Because of this, he has fallen deeper into madness, and his decisions are becoming reckless."

"So how does that affect me?"

"That all depends, Korrd. It depends on what you believe to be the truth and your true path in this life. I am not as good with riddles as Asperon Thorne is, and I cannot come right out and tell you the absolute truth . . ."

"Why not? Why must there be all these riddles about truth and right and power? There could not be an easy way to the truth could there?"

"The answers are easy if you just look into your heart, Korrd. However, my errand is not to help you to find truth, but to help you find the answers that you seek. They are not one and the same, no matter what you think. What I have for you is the final riddle that will answer the ultimate question that none have yet to answer."

"I'm ready."

"I'm not sure that you are," Basille replied, "but I will tell you anyway. Mark me well because you will never hear this again. In one, the answer is split into the number in the outer circle. Brothers all control the fate of the one who believes he is the supreme, but is truly the pretender. The other will find his fate in the darkness, and when he clutches the black, he will understand the true meaning of destiny."

Korrd thought hard for a minute, and when he looked up, he noticed that Basille had gone and he was alone again with his confusion. He lay down on the floor of this new room and closed his eyes. When he opened them again, he was back in the forest a half day's ride from the twin towns of Rama and Rana. He closed his eyes and tried to sleep without thinking too much about the words and images that rolled around in his mind. All of the words seemed to clash somewhere in the middle of his mind, and he could not help but put more weight on some things than others. The words that bothered him the most still hung clear in his mind.

"When a lie looks into the mirror of truth, it sees a lie, for a lie in the face of the truth is a lie nonetheless."

Those words droned on inside of his head as the night passed by. He was awakened the next morning by the man named Sol. By that afternoon they were in the familiar kingdom of Rama, and after saying his good-byes to both Sol and at the grave of Antrobus, more out of actual sorrow than of acting, he borrowed a horse from the stables and rode toward Kandor. His future still lay somewhere along that path but he knew not where. Someday that path would cross with his brother's again, and then many questions would be answered.

Gifts

Marcwell was always one of the most beautiful cities in the entire world, and that was always how it had been remembered in songs and stories sung by the bards. With the spires of its many churches reaching into the skies, it was easy to see how many could view Marcwell as the perfect picture of beauty. Logan could not help but glimpse around the town as Cedric led him to the palace. The rest of the party was somewhere close by, but Logan knew that Cedric had more to talk with him about privately. Then Logan caught his first glimpse of the huge towers of the Lion's palace. The top of each of the towers were painted blue, and just as with the palace in Trelon, many multicolored tapestries flowed down onto the outer walls of the palace. On the walkway that was suspended to the wall high up into the sky, many guards walked their assigned duty with an arrow nocked onto their bowstrings, and their sword waiting at their hip. On some of the tapestries, Logan could make out a coat of arms, and the closer he looked, the more he could make out. On one of the white banners, Logan saw the crest of Aradon, a hammer and saw crossed over a field of wheat.

"What are those banners, Cedric?"

"Each of those banners holds the crest of one of the cities or towns that are under the protection of the Kingdom of Marcwell. More and more of these cities have added their strength to ours, especially with the threat of a new offensive by the forces of the Shadow. Arathorn says that the kingdom is getting too big and that there is no way for me to keep control of all of them. I have constantly tried to remind him that the legacy of the Lion is a powerful thing, but he insists that it is not enough."

"So what does he suggest?" Logan asked.

"You are learning the ways of diplomacy very well, my young successor. That is good; it will benefit you in the days to come. The first rule of diplomacy is to keep all of your options open. Arathorn says that I should more finely divide the kingdom, and let other lords have more direct control, and allow myself to act as merely an overseer. He says that I am overexerting myself. I believe he thinks that I should invest my closest allies with power in the same way that my sister had direct control of Trelon."

"Rule number two in diplomacy is never trust anyone," that rolled off Logan's tongue, but it came from the *Coromor*. "I suppose that Arathorn and Aryx fancy themselves as more suited to control the lesser kingdoms than you are."

Cedric smiled to himself and then laughed slightly.

"You know more than you let on young one," he said softly. "This talk must move into a more secluded place where there are not so many eager ears. Remember that in this place Arathorn and Aryx are as much legends as I am, and equally revered. And as your name has yet to be forged, there are still perceptions that you will have to fight against."

"For knowledge is power."

"Again you impress me, Logan," he said turning back towards his younger companion. "When we reach the palace, you and I must have a long talk."

"I'd like to have Gwydeon Sandar present as well."

"Sandar," he said sinking into thought. "Yes, I remember that name. An application to the Lion's Mane was received about a youth by the name of Sandar. As I remember, he was from Aradon."

"I sent that application," Logan said softly, "as a favor to a friend. He is the best that I have ever seen with a sword. I thought that he would be a perfect addition to your army. He has dreamed of being the best ever since he first picked up a sword."

"And from what I have heard, he is well on his way. I turned down the application because it was such an unusual request. However, I made it a point to keep my eye out for this Sandar, so I sent someone to keep an eye on him, and it was purely by accident that I learned of you and your father."

"Gwydeon brought you to me and my father?"

"Moreover, you brought me to you and your father. I was very impressed with your father, and he and I became fast friends. I wish I would have known him when he was a soldier in my army during the war. Though I'm afraid that may have greatly altered both of your fates."

Cedric considered for a moment.

"Perhaps it would have changed my fate as well."

He fell silent for a moment and then shook his head as if shaking away a bad thought.

"I don't know if you are aware of it or not, but he and I were in contact with one another almost up to the point that he died. I did not know that he was dead until I received my first report from Aryx. I am truly sorry."

"It been a while now," Logan responded, "but thank you anyway. Now, about Gwydeon?"

"You may have him present, for it must be important for you to make the request."

Then he turned and continued toward the palace.

"After your friends are settled in their rooms, I will have him brought to the study. In the meantime, we can continue our conversation."

* * * * * * * * * * * *

Cedric seemed more and more intent as he schooled his successor on the greater points of diplomacy. He was very knowledgeable, and Logan could not help but be enthralled by his words. Then he stopped and looked at the younger man for a moment.

"How are your powers coming?"

"Strange, Cedric. I don't really understand half of what I do, but I know that there is so much more that I can do."

"What I tell to you now must not be shared with anyone, ever. If you and your friends succeed in vanquishing Shau-ling in this time, you will have to keep this knowledge safe until you can pass it on to your successor."

"I understand."

He closed his eyes for a moment and then rubbed his hands together slowly. A transparent material formed in his hands, and he slowly began to mold it into a ball. The ball grew in size as he molded it, and then when he let it go, it erupted and surrounded both of us and the table between us.

"This is a ward. It will prevent anyone with magic or powers like ours or the phasia from hearing our conversation. In some ways, it will keep the Coromor from influencing your actions as well. I learned early how to form this bubble of peace to find solace during the darkest days of my quest."

Again Cedric fell silent, and Logan could see the weight descend upon him like a shadow.

"Our powers are strange, especially when you learn the source. When the Creator sculpted his world and his creatures, there was a balance of good and evil. That balance shattered because of the advent of man and their disposition toward war and evil. Because of this, Shau-ling was born out of the nightmares of men in a place called the Blight. Shau-ling was not the only thing born in the Blight. The *Coromor* was also formed there, and for a time, Shau-ling and the *Coromor* existed as brothers. The *Coromor* then began to see the world as a place possible of creating good, and he and Shau-ling went to war. The *Coromor* spun out the *Erieal* when Shau-ling created his phasia. A rouge element, the *Chosen One,* was created when there was a rift in the phasia, and some were expelled from the brotherhood."

"There are more than ten phasia?!?"

"Yes Logan, but no one is sure how many more. It has only been through information I have been able to cobble together from the Moridon as well as some close allies that I have learned this much. To be sure, they are as powerful as the other ten, but as to which side they are on, no one knows. This *Chosen One* did not feel a pull to evil, or good, but remained a neutral entity, much like the Jeweled Dragon's Flame. The *Chosen One* would follow the path that presented itself first. I fear that the phasia have already presented that path. However, with two of their order dead, they are slowly losing the ability to overthrow their own master. If it gets to the point where they cannot slay Shau-ling themselves, they become more dangerous."

"How so?"

"They will focus all of their attention and power on you. If they kill you, their brethren will be reborn, and then they can overthrow Shau-ling unopposed. You are more a hindrance than a help. If you kill Shau-ling, they all die and it starts over again in the next lifetime. This way, they could win no matter what happens. In their eyes, you can't succeed."

"Okay," Logan said grimacing from his words, "so what do I do?"

"I'll teach you about your powers, but not now. You must do some work on your own at first. The first step to mastering your powers is to find each individual thread of power. There are four that are easy to find, the fifth and sixth are more difficult. Close your eyes."

It was an uneasy feeling that floated through Logan when he started to close his eyes. There was something wrong with this entire situation, but he had yet to put his finger on it.

"Look through the darkness and find the glowing threads. What can you see?"

Logan pushed his way past the darkness that held his vision, and drifted through the nothingness that was behind it. Suddenly four bright ribbons entered Logan's field of view.

"I see four bands of light. One is green and seems to be attached to the ground. It is brighter than the rest. The yellow and blue ribbons are pulsating, but the red band is dim."

"Those are the bands of elemental power that you draw from the *Erieal*; the green is strongest because your friend Gideon seems to have the best command over his powers. The blue and yellow are pulsating because Pike and the man you call Talon are able to channel their powers only when they are truly angry. They have some control, but not as much as Gideon. The red is dim because . . ."

"Because we haven't found the Fire Brother yet," Logan finished.

"What else do you see?"

At Cedric's prompting, Logan pushed past the four bands of energy and searched deeper into the bleak landscape. Suddenly a beam of brilliant green fire pierced the darkness and it flooded Logan's vision and caused him to open my eyes.

"That my young companion," Cedric said as he too opened his eyes, "is called the Blaze. That is the focal point of all of Shau-ling's powers. If you were to ever gain enough control to touch and focus the Blaze, you could conceivably use Shau-ling's own powers against him. But you should resist the temptation. The Blaze is corruption in its purest form. It will sing to you of all the power it can bestow, and the moment you touch it, you will relinquish control of your soul to Shau-ling. Now, we have some things that we must attend to. I have asked your friends Pike, Talon, and Gideon to join us for a short ceremony. The gifts that I promised must be delivered."

"What about Gwydeon?"

"We can finish this talk later, Logan. Don't worry, you are safe here."

Despite Cedric's assurances, Logan wasn't too sure about their safety. Cedric rose and started out of the room. The bands of light were still fresh in Logan's vision, but the bar of green fire shocked him more than anything he had ever seen in his life. However, there was something inside of the green fire that Lord Cedric hadn't seen, and that confused Logan. Inside the raging flames of green, Logan had seen thirteen smaller bars, each a slightly different color. There were two shades of red, black, and white, but only one of the others. The smaller bars puzzled Logan, but what puzzled him more was why Cedric hadn't said anything about them. That was another question whose answer was still waiting to be found.

* * * * * * * * * * * *

Gideon sat in his room in the palace of Marcwell uneasiness filling him. There were so many emotions inside of him that he had to deal with; he didn't know where to begin. A half-composed letter lay on the desk with a quill and ink. He knew what he had to do, and what needed to be said, but those two matters conflicted so powerfully that he didn't know what he should do. He shifted his weight on the bed, and then popped to his feet. The knock at the door was expected, but when he opened the door, the face was not.

"What the hell did you think you were doing when you came back to the bar in Taren?" Aryx demanded as he barged into the room.

"I was finding out what was going on behind my back, Aryx," Gideon said, the accent completely gone from his voice. "I don't know how long I can keep up this lackey charade for the pleasure of our boss. If these pitiful whelps find out what is going on behind their backs, we're all dead."

"Don't worry about that Gideon," Aryx returned strongly, "after tonight, we won't have to worry about anybody finding out anything."

"What if they fail?"

"Then we keep doing what we've been doing," Aryx replied. "Master didn't put us here for our winning personalities; he put us here because we get results. How close are you to gaining our target's trust?"

"Farther than I expected, but there have been a few new developments that have made the mission more difficult. The deaths of their friends have made them slow to trust, and I think that one of them remembers me."

"Nonsense," Aryx scoffed. "That is truly impossible, and you know it. You just keep you mind on the job ahead of you and I'll take care of the rest."

"As you wish, my lord Aryx," Gideon said as he bowed.

"Now, get yourself up to the armory and meet the rest of the *Erieal*. I wouldn't want you to be late for Lord Cedric's big ceremony."

They both laughed as Aryx left the room. Gideon looked back at the table and sighed. He knew what needed to be done, but he didn't know how he was going to get out of the situation he had placed himself into. The best he could hope for was to be discovered and killed, but that wasn't very likely. He sighed again and made his way to the armory.

* * * * * * * * * * * *

As Logan followed Lord Cedric, he couldn't help but wonder what it was that the secretive man had on his mind. Logan knew that Cedric had gifts for them, and from Aryx's words earlier in the quest, Logan couldn't help but think that the gifts were going to be *Debuisa* for the members of the *Erieal*. There was still that feeling that there was something else though. Cedric's intentions in bringing them to Marcwell had been honorable, at least in theory, but there was more to it than that. He had a hidden agenda that he was going to keep hidden until the very last possible moment.

Pike, Talon, and Gideon were already waiting in front of a huge set of doors. There were fiery letters that were inscribed on the door in a language that Logan didn't pretend to understand. Cedric nodded to the two men who stood guard outside the doors, and they stepped aside quickly.

"No one who does not have a *Debuisa* can open this door, but I keep the guards here just as a precaution," he said turning to Logan.

Logan nodded and waited as Cedric opened the door. The interior of the new room was much larger than Logan ever could have imagined. It seemed as if the entire palace could have fit in this single room. Weapons and armor lined the walls, and in the very center of the room were huge vats filled with molten metal. The light from the fiery vats filled the room and left no corner dim. It was a truly surprising sight. Cedric led them over to one of the vats and he drew his blade and tapped it against the side of the vat. The next instant, a worm-like creature rose out of the cauldron of fire and looked the assemblage over. Its skin was a deep red color, and Logan couldn't see any eyes as he studied the entity. It did have a circular shaped mouth that seemed to cover most of its face. Cedric smiled at the creature and then turned.

"Friends, I'd like you to meet the Elder. He and his brethren have lived in this chamber for centuries, and they have amassed all of the knowledge that they could in the time that they have lived."

"That is very true Lord Lion", a voice said inside of everyone's head.

There were confused looks all around at the voice, and while it did cause some concern to show in the faces of Pike and the others, Logan did not feel any malice from the creature.

"The Elder and his kind do not communicate as we do because of the way that they live. Because they feed and survive almost totally on the heat and sustenance of molten metal, they have learned to communicate through thoughts rather than with their mouths, as we do," Cedric explained.

"Again, your account is true. I would like to say that it is nice to see that with you Lord Dragon, the world still has a chance at life and the tyranny that is Shau-ling may not live much longer. I only wish that you and your companions could find some way to vanquish him here and now and not allow these superfluous prophecies to ruin any more lives. Now, before I command my brethren to bring the Debuisa to you, is there anything that you would like to ask me?"

"Yes there is," Pike responded quickly. "We've heard from many different people that the phasia have a sort of power that is compatible with ours, but it can only be harnessed by the *Chosen One*. I've also heard that when the phasia die, they are sent to a plain called the Other Side. What I want to know is if you can tell me anything more about this, and if there is any way to truly kill a phase, other than killing Shau-ling."

"Those are very good questions Water Brother, and I commend you on how well you and your associates know your enemies. First, the powers of the phasia are compatible with those of the Coromor, but I am afraid that you are right when you say that the only one who can truly harness those powers is the Chosen One. Now, the Other Side is a plain of existence that was created when the first Chosen One, Aerith Seth, was killed by the forces of the Shadow. When that happened, his life force was transferred into a new plain of existence, and he became the framework on which the Other Side was formed. From that time on, any who were intimately connected with either the Coromor or Shau-ling would go to the Other Side when they were killed. Your friends David Tamerlane, Eldar Merin, and Lane Toridon have gone there to assist those who fight for the Coromor on that side of reality. They do not do so of their own free will, they fight because they have dedicated their lives to your cause.

"As to your other question Water Brother, there is a way to kill a phase and not have it appear on the Other Side. In a time long past, a sorcerer by the name of Aralias Imstra, the original prophesier of the Coromor received information from a source inside of Shau-ling's palace and devised a way to destroy a member of Shau-ling's inner circle and by-pass the Other Side. This ability was known as banishment only because it condemned anyone it was used on to the fires of hell."

"So," Pike said quickly, "how does this banishment work?"

"Just like everything in this world, banishment is a combination of the primal forces that the Erieal are masters of. Banishment combines all four of the primal forces, and one of the mysterious 'forgotten strings'. It is because of these 'forgotten strings' that the talent was lost. If you or one of your friends could see a pure black band of power inside that place where the others dwell, that is where the Coromor derives all of his powers, and that is one of the 'forgotten strings'. There is another, but none of us have ever heard of it being found. The green column of fire must be avoided at all costs. If any ever touch it, they become Shau-ling's slaves, because they have tried to use his evil power. If you value your lives, you will try to learn the combinations that hold the most power in this world. The primal forces are strong on their own, but the right combinations are powerful enough to destroy mountains, islands, stars, and most certainly Shau-ling."

"So the trick is finding the lost strings," Logan replied.

"Very true. Now, I will command my brethren to bring you the items that you have sought, and then Lord Cedric can make the announcement that will set the world in motion once again."

The Elder disappeared again, and Cedric turned and spoke.

"My friends, what you are about to receive is one of the most powerful possessions that you will ever receive in your lives. Once you are in possession of these gauntlets of power, you will be able to control your powers as none could ever believe. You will notice that there are some limitations as to your level of power now, but you will soon learn that power is no substitute for control. If you focus your powers on Logan, you should be able to add more power. If you focus on one another, you will stumble on the combinations that the Elder alluded to. Now Pike, you will stand here. Talon, the cauldron to my left is yours, and the cauldron to my right is Gideon's."

The trio moved to their positions and waited. The light in the center of the cauldrons intensified and then a gauntlet began to appear out of each. Each of the gauntlets had a color that corresponded to the primal force that it would control. The gauntlets finally rose out of the fiery metal, and each of trio took their new weapon and put it on slowly. The individual color of the metal faded, and each took on the glowing golden hue that had seemingly always been present at Aryx's side. The *Erieal* of the second generation of the prophecies were now far more powerful, and that power frightened Logan somehow. Though, no matter what, these were still his friends, and without their powers, they would still be the same men that he knew. However, Logan thought he saw a sneer come to Pike's lips for just a moment.

"Shall we have a little demonstration gentlemen," Cedric said quickly. "I am anxious to see if Aryx's account of your powers is true."

Pike looked over to Talon and winked. Gideon looked over to Logan, and when he nodded, the ground shook beneath their feet. A huge pillar of stone rose out of the ground. Pike raised his gauntlet toward the pillar and streams of ice flew toward the stone, chipping away the rock into a coherent figure. Pike had picked this demonstration to vent his anger. After a minute or two, the figure of the massive phase Taron had been carved out of the pillar of stone. Pike looked over to Talon again, and when Talon raised his gauntlet, the stone statue shattered into thousands of tiny pieces. The ground shook again, and a fissure opened beneath the remains of the statue. The pieces fell into the ground from which they were formed, and then the fissure sealed itself.

"Very impressive. Elder?"

"Yes, their powers are impressive. The fourth will surely be found soon, and then the circle will be complete. The other Debuisa *will be given to you before you leave Marcwell, but first there is something that must be done. Lord Dragon, you must focus your mind on the red band of power that lives inside of you, the dim one that you can hardly feel."*

"I have it."

"Direct a pure beam of that primal energy into this cauldron. Each one of the Erieal *must do the same with their powers. Only a pure beam will suffice."*

They nodded and the four directed their energies as the Elder had requested. The cauldron glowed white, and the Elder dove into the center of the mixed energy. A few seconds later, the streams of power broke, and the Elder emerged with a ring floating above it.

"This is a ring of power. This will help you better control all of the primal forces as the Debuisa *helps the* Erieal *control the one power that they have a grasp on. This ring will not help you find the 'forgotten strings' but it will not hinder such a search. Go now in peace and rid the world of the scourge that is Shau-ling."*

Logan took the ring and placed it onto his ring finger on his right hand. For some reason the *Coromor* that was inside of Logan did not like the feel of the ring, nor of the new power that coursed through his veins. As soon as they left the armory, Logan took the ring off his finger and put it in his pocket. Cedric gave Logan a sidelong look and then turned his attention back toward the hallway in front of him.

"Pike, Talon, Gideon," he said softly, "you will return to your quarters and prepare yourselves as you have been instructed. You will be summoned once the deed is done. Thank you for your cooperation with the Elder. I hope that you find the gift as useful in your time as the *Erieal* did in my time. Shau-ling will never know what to expect."

The three bowed shallowly, none as shallow as Pike, and then went back toward their quarters. Whatever Cedric had in mind was only supposed to be for Logan, and whatever it was, he still got the strangest feeling that it wasn't going to be pleasant. Cedric led Logan down another passage and then up a towering flight of stairs. Within a few moments, the pair was standing on the top level of the palace, on an open-air balcony that overlooked the rest of Marcwell. Cedric led Logan to the edge, and as he looked over, he could see that the courtyard of the battlement that surrounded the palace was filled with people. Cedric looked back to Logan for a moment and then spoke in a voice that could only be compared with the sound of rolling thunder.

"Friends, allies, and men and women of Marcwell. What I am about to say will echo throughout the world as a shout of jubilation and rejoicing. The tyranny that is Shau-ling will end soon, and my successor, a man who will brave the terrors of hell itself, will deliver us from this darkness. This man, the Dragon, is the one man who can travel into the depths of Shau-ling's palace and plunge his sword into Shau-ling's black heart. I introduce him to you now my friends, the man who will save us all from a bleak and horrible fate. All of you take heed and welcome this brave man with all of your might. The Dragon, our protector and savior, Lord Logan Ranthall!"

Burden of Destiny

From the lofty position on the top of the palace of Marcwell, Logan overlooked the group of men and women that had gathered below to hear Lord Cedric's proclamation. He looked back out over the horizon and could see the Mithacarthian Woods stretching out over the countryside below. Beyond the wood were the docks where the Monster of the Deep was anchored. The last words of Lord Cedric's proclamation still rang loudly in the ears of everyone who had gathered to hear them, most strongly however in Logan's. His words were serious and powerful and the crowd below was shocked and elated in the same breath. However, after a short pause the crowd had begun to cheer and they still hadn't stopped applauding and shouting. Cheers bounded back and forth for the Lion and then the Dragon and back again. It was surreal to Logan to hear people chanting his name. Logan stared down at the crowd for a long time and then realized that the sun was beginning its slow descent in the late evening sky. It had not seemed that they had been in Marcwell all that time, but the next morning would bring a new adventure, and the ripples of the proclamation would spread through the world. The rise of the new day would signal the beginning of the reign of the Dragon.

Logan felt Lord Cedric's hand on his shoulder, and Logan quickly turned to face his predecessor. The serious expression that the Lord of Marcwell had worn earlier in the day as well as during his proclamation had faded into a warm and inviting smile. His eyes were brighter now, and it seemed as if a great weight had been lifted from his shoulders. After looking at Logan for a moment, Cedric pointed to the flag pole where four of his finest soldiers were standing. Logan followed where he was pointing to and turned to look at the members of his royal guard and saw the large banner that they were holding in their white gloved hands. The size of the flag was almost indescribable, and part of Logan thought that it had once been the main sail of a massive ship. The background of the flag was a brilliant blue that almost countered by the magnificence of the sky. On the huge field of blue was the regal and intimidating form of dragon. The dragon was sprawled out over almost the entire field, and its wings were extended which gave the appearance that the dragon was soaring through a bright trouble-free sky. The four soldiers carried the banner over to the massive standard and hoisted it into place. It stopped near the top of the pole and flew alongside the Banner of the Lion, Lord Cedric's symbol. As soon as Logan realized he was holding his breath, he exhaled slowly and then took a long deep breath. The crowd below had been transfixed into awe-struck silence, and Logan felt the reverence flow through him like a fog of intoxication. Was this what true power felt like?

"That's your symbol, Logan," Cedric said proudly. "People for miles around will see that flag and make their way to the palace. Then, they will honor you later tonight at the feast that has been prepared for you and your brave companions. After the banquet, your quest will truly begin. Now that the Flame has been recovered, we can make our way to the Hall of Terrors, and you can bury the Dragon Sword into Shau-ling's black heart."

"I still don't understand why you picked now to proclaim me as the *Coromor*. True, it will gain great support, but it will also bring the phasia down on our heads," Logan said looking back out to the crowd.

"And that's what I'm hoping for Logan. You see, we have no idea where Shau-ling is. However, if we find one of the phasia, or if one of the phasia finds you, we can capture it and force it to tell us where Shau-ling is. In effect, Shau-ling's most loyal servants will seal his fate. And I wouldn't be expecting too much popular support from the people around the world. What you receive here in Marcwell will probably be the most you ever have."

"What?"

Cedric leaned against the top of the wall and looked out over the people.

"The *Coromor* may be an important figure that will determine whether the people of the world live or die, but most people don't realize that truth. They take the literal translation of *Coromor* as the true one. 'He who brings destruction' is more real and frightening to them than the story of Shau-ling that parents use to frighten their children into obeying."

"What about your followers outside of the city?" Logan asked.

"There are not enough of them to sway the opinion of the public. In reality, they do not spread any of their beliefs for fear of what the people in those towns might do to them. No matter how much good I have done, there are those elements that insist that my reign has been filled with more ill and peril."

With a mild amount of disgust for the ignorance that Lord Cedric had just described, Logan turned away from the crowd and looked up again at the massive Banner of the Dragon. Despite Cedric's misgivings, all of those people, and all those who would eventually learn of Logan's existence, knew what he was and they at least partially believed that no matter the cost or trial that he was there to fulfill the prophecies. It was the first time that Logan truly felt the weight of what he was and what he had to do fall upon his shoulders. His heart ached, and he was beginning to dwell on Cedric's words, as well as those spoken by Aldridge when he felt the familiar light touch of a hand upon his shoulder. When he turned, he found Elwyne's beautiful soft blue eyes waiting for him. They were soft and full of love, and whatever doubts and trepidations that had filled his mind only heartbeats before were instantly erased. She wrapped her arms around him and laid her head on his chest. Logan rested his chin lightly on the top of her head and looked over to Lord Cedric. He lingered for only a moment looking at the two of them before he turned away made his way over to the staircase that led below. Logan's eyes followed him until he was out of sight, and then found Talon, Pike, and Gideon coming up the stairs. Elwyne broke the embrace and looked in Logan's eyes again. For the first time he noticed that she was wearing what appeared to be a very expensive blue gown.

"Incredible isn't it Logan," she said cheerfully, "Lord Cedric picked it out for me himself. I asked him where he got it, but he said it wasn't important and that there were a lot more like this one."

"What do you think Logan?" Pike called as they reached the top of the tower.

Logan looked up and saw the newly arrived trio wearing perhaps the finest clothes they had ever worn in their lives. Talon and Gideon each wore swords on their hips, while Pike apparently had chosen to keep his axe as his weapon of choice. There were white gloves in their belt loops, and each wore a fine set of black pants that could have easily been custom-fitted. Pike was wearing a blue shirt, Talon was wearing gray, and Gideon was in green. The three of them standing there was one of the funniest sights that Logan had ever seen. He could remember many times when Pike and Talon's parents had tried to get them to wear clothes with some level of finery with no success. They were common men with common tastes, and comfort was more important than style. And of course, Gideon's history as a thief and a mercenary certainly created the perception that finery was alien to him as well. Elwyne led Logan over to their companions and Logan could not but laugh when Talon puffed out his chest and let a self-satisfied smile come to his lips.

"I better go back downstairs and change. Here I look like a country boy just out of Aradon, and you look like fine upstanding lords and lady," Logan said with a smile.

"I feel like a flintin' fairy," Gideon mumbled.

"If you think that we look good, Logan," Talon remarked quickly, "you should see Midarin and Jasmen. Gwydeon has been with Midarin all morning, and I barely had time to see either of them before we had to go to the armory. They haven't been apart for more than two minutes since Sador."

"Yes," Logan said smiling, "I've been meaning to ask what happened between the two of them in Sador. Usually you two are quick with gossip."

"I wouldn't ask if I were you Logan," Pike replied, "you know the way that Gwydeon is about secrets."

"That never stopped the two of you from beating information out of him in the past now did it?" Logan replied.

Talon and Pike both tried to stifle a laugh, and even Gideon cracked a smile. After a mock disapproving frown from Elwyne, Logan chuckled and then started down the stairs. Elwyne followed a step after, and he could hear the light melodic laughter escape her lips. Together they made their way down the towering staircase and walked down the hallway lined with royal suites. Elwyne then took the lead and showed Logan to their chambers that were at the end of the hall. Before Logan could open the door, Elwyne wrapped her arms around him once more and leaned in for a long love-filled kiss. When she pulled back, the intoxicating smile was still on her lips.

"I'm going to go and see Gwydeon and Midarin for a moment, but I'll be back shortly."

"You aren't going to try to beat the information out of them are you, Elwyne?"

"You know me better than that," she said smiling.

She kissed him again and walked lightly back down the long hallway. Logan watched her until he was out of sight before entering the room and shutting the door behind him. There was a large wardrobe in the corner of the room that Lord Cedric had prepared with clothes befitting the station that Logan found himself occupying. It took only a moment of perusing the clothes to realize that while they were all fine and lordly, few if any were truly to his taste. It was then that he realized a suit of clothes had been laid out on the bed for him. No doubt Elwyne realized the trepidation he would have at the daunting wardrobe and made a selection she felt best suited him. Again he could not help but laugh at himself as he began to change clothes. Before he was able to put on the new shirt that complimented the new pants he had just finished pulling on, there was a blood-curdling scream that resonated down the hallway.

* * * * * * * * * * * *

Elwyne walked slowly down the hallway and could not get the smile off of her face. Being in Marcwell had turned into a dream. She was wearing a dress fit for a queen, her childhood friends were dressed in fine clothes, and they were going to attend a feast in her fiancé's honor in a matter of minutes. Every girl who dreamed of being a princess would have wished to be in her shoes in that moment. She felt like she was walking on air. The palace of Marcwell was grander than her imagination could have crafted in her wildest dreams, and she only wished that Eldar would have been there to share the experience with her. Thoughts of her lost friend grounded her slightly from her reverie. Since Eldar's death, Elwyne had felt lost in a way that she didn't have the words to describe. All around her she saw the suffering that the loss of both Lane and Eldar had caused. In Aradon, Eldar had been the glue that had held them all together. She was equal parts mother, big sister, and conscience. Now that role fell to Elwyne. Her path however would be harder, because she had to keep Logan on his path, and keep the raging and disparate personalities together no matter the trial. But no matter how strong she thought she was, no matter how prepared she felt to take up the mantle, the realist in her knew that she would not be able to do it alone. That was why she so desperately wanted to talk to Gwydeon and Midarin.

Gwydeon had always been the most level-headed member of the group, and in times of turmoil, for better or for worse, he always found himself in the middle trying to keep the peace. Though he didn't necessarily have the talent to diffuse the situations, he certainly was able to keep them from escalating to a breaking point. By that time, either Eldar or Elwyne would have intervened and dealt with the problem. But there was another more disturbing thought that entered Gwydeon's mind when she thought about Gwydeon. Pike, Talon, and Logan all had powers of some type or another, and in some ways they were different men then they were when they left Aradon. Would Gwydeon, even with his force of will be able to stand up to them now that they were more than mortal men? However, something had happened in the town of Sador, something that made Pike and Talon look at Gwydeon in a very different way. Whenever Logan spoke now, or gave orders, Pike and Talon looked at Gwydeon first, almost as if they respected his opinion more than their own. Of course, after Eldar's death, Pike was singular of purpose and needed no one's approval but his own rage. If they were going to get through this alive, Elwyne needed to know what had happened in Sador, and she needed Gwydeon's support to keep Logan from spinning wildly out of control.

Midarin Rice was a different matter altogether. When Elwyne had first encountered the woman, Elwyne instantly felt repulsion. Not because of anything the woman had said or done, but simply because of her existence. Perhaps it was nothing more than petty jealousy. Perhaps it was because in some ways Midarin had already had everything that Elwyne wanted and had thrown it away over nothing. As she had come to learn more about the former princess however, Elwyne felt the shame of her judgment weighing on her. In some way, Elwyne felt that she needed to make up for the phantom slight, and the only way she knew how to make amends was to in effect welcome Midarin to the family properly and bring the woman into her confidence. Elwyne had been able to forgive Cairyn Binosear for her slights, and strange as it was to think about, she counted the new Queen of Trelon among her friends. Between the three of them, hopefully they would be enough to hold everything together.

As Elwyne rounded the corner into the hallway where Gwydeon and Midarin's suite was, Elwyne was surprised to find Jasmen walking toward her. Despite Talon's childishness, he had been correct when describing to Logan that Jasmen indeed looked like a completely different woman than she had in her travelling attire. The ebony dress that clung to her body easily could have been a size too small, and to Elwyne's sensibilities it was far too short and was far too revealing. But Elwyne countered her own thoughts by remembering that Jasmen was a performer, and part of her responsibility was to keep all eyes focused on her at all times. To her credit, she had been able to hold her own thus far, and didn't run scared when the army of Jeresei descended upon them. As soon as Jasmen saw Elwyne she smiled and waved.

"You look positively gorgeous, Elwyne," Jasmen said running her fingers through her long blond hair. "Logan's going to faint when he sees you."

Elwyne felt the blush, but it didn't color her cheeks.

"I think he's still too shocked with Lord Cedric's proclamation to see anything properly. But he better keep his eyes in his head when he sees you."

She wasn't sure if the joke had the impact that she wanted for a moment because if felt flat coming off of her tongue. Perhaps it had sounded too much like jealousy because Jasmen didn't react for a moment, but then her smile widened, and for her part she blushed slightly.

"I must admit, I don't think I would ever have to sing on key ever again if I wore this on stage. But Logan is too devoted to you to give anyone a second look. Besides, how could a simple little minstrel girl like me ever be a match for the Lady Dragon."

Now Elwyne felt the color come to her cheeks. However, in that moment Elwyne felt an undercurrent to the woman's words, a hint of venom in the flowery compliment. Before Elwyne could comment or even properly react, Jasmen continued speaking.

"I've been meaning to ask you, Elwyne," the slightly taller woman said sweetly, "aren't you worried with all of the craziness going on that something might happen to you? I mean, after Lane and Eldar? What do you think Logan would do?"

The frown came to Elwyne's face instantly. There was definite malice in the woman's voice.

"Is that a threat?"

Jasmen put up both of her hands innocently.

"Why would I ever threaten you, Elwyne?" Jasmen said with a sly smile. "I mean, it could have just as easily been you that Taron appeared behind. It could have just as easily been your pretty little neck that he snapped like so much kindling. What would Logan have done then? Maybe he wouldn't have even made it to the safety of Marcwell. He could have just gone crazy and kept fighting until he was overwhelmed."

Jasmen leaned in, all pretense gone.

"You are nothing but a distraction to him; a liability that someone will exploit. Your very existence weakens him, and should anything unfortunate happen to you, how would he ever go on? How would he ever forgive himself?"

Before Elwyne knew what was happening, the woman was on her. Jasmen moved quickly, her hands finding both of Elwyne's shoulders and slamming her hard against the wall. Unable to brace herself for the attack, Elwyne's head slammed against the wall and for a moment all she could see was blackness and bright exploding spot of light in her field of vision. There was something hot that was slowly sliding down the right side of her face and neck, but she didn't have time to consider it before she felt cold steel pressed against her throat. Elwyne felt Jasmen's hot breath on the side of her face as the viscous woman leaned in to whisper in her ear.

"I'm going to slit your pretty little throat," Jasmen whispered, hate and malicious glee seeping into her voice, "and then I'm going to leave you here for someone to find. Logan will be so distraught that he may just leave Marcwell immediately, or better yet he may pull this whole palace down around Cedric's ears. Either way, I'll be right there beside him, consoling him, taking him into my bed, and just when he falls asleep in my arms, I'll bury this same dagger in his heart. My master will be pleased, and I will be rewarded. In the new world to come, I'll be a queen."

Elwyne didn't need to see to know the woman was smiling, she could feel it crawl across her skin like slime. Knowing that she was only moment from death, Elwyne held her breath and acted. She slowly brought her hands together in front of her as Jasmen slowly drew the blade from one side of her throat to the other.

"Savor these last moments, Elwyne," Jasmen hissed, the pleasure clear in her voice. "And think about Logan in my bed as you take your last breath."

The pressure of the blade against Elwyne's throat increased and there was a sharp pain like being stung by a bee. Trying to ignore the pain, Elwyne drew the thin-blade dagger that Gideon had given her from the concealed sheath that was strapped to her wrist under the long sleeve of the dress and in a single hard motion plunged it into the center of Jasmen's chest. The woman's scream deafened Elwyne and the blade in the assassin's hand sliced deeply into the left side of Elwyne's neck as Jasmen fell backwards. Her vision cleared slightly, Elwyne lunged forward, her hand finding Jasmen's dagger that was held loosely. It took little effort to wrestle the weapon away, and the Lady Dragon wasted no time in burying the assassin's own blade in her throat. Blood poured from the twin wounds as the blond woman fell to the floor, all light quickly draining from her eyes. For a long moment Elwyne simply stood in the center of the hall, looking down at Jasmen's fallen form. She wasn't aware of the blood that trickled from her ear or from the wound on her neck. She had even forgotten for that moment that her ears were ringing and her head throbbed. Elwyne didn't even consciously recognize the growing commotion around her. All she saw was the look of shock and horror in Jasmen's eyes, and all she knew was that the woman was dead by her hand; and she wouldn't regret it for a moment.

* * * * * * * * * * * *

Logan ran down the hall as fast as his feet would carry him, sword in hand. He wasn't sure who the scream had come from, but the fear in his heart would not release the through that it had been Elwyne. By the time Logan rounded the corner and saw the scene laid out on the floor of the hallway, Gwydeon and Midarin had already arrived along with Pike. Palace guards flooded into hallway from both directions, but Midarin did her best to keep them from interfering.

"What in the hell happened here?" Pike asked in shock.

Gwydeon knelt down and examined Jasmen's body. With one look up at Logan and a shake of his head, Logan knew that their companion was dead.

"Jasmen attacked me Pike," Elwyne replied after a moment or two, her voice slightly wavering but free of remorse. "She all but said that she was under the orders of Shau-ling, and she was supposed to kill me so that she could get close enough to Logan to kill him. She was an assassin lying in wait all tis time."

"She was well suited for the job," Gwydeon commented. "With Elwyne out of the way, she could have plied her charms on Logan without any interference. It would have been impossible to try to seduce you while Elwyne was still alive. No wonder she was always asking about the two of you."

There was something about the matter-of-fact tone of Gwydeon's voice that disturbed Logan. They had been jumping at shadows for so long; it was only a matter of time before one of them jumped back. Maybe they were all becoming too jaded, or perhaps the reality of their situation had finally set in.

"That's true Logan," Midarin commented. "She did ask a lot of questions, but I thought it was because of the stories she said she was going to write. I never thought anything of it."

Logan grimaced and pulled Elwyne to him. She resisted for a moment, her eyes never leaving Jasmen, but finally she relented and buried her face in his bare chest. The wound on her neck was not deep, but it would require attention, and there was no telling what damage had caused the trail of blood that had flowed from her ear. He could feel her hot tears against his skin, and his heart broke a little with every tiny almost inaudible sob. Midarin was at their side a moment later and she put her arms around Elwyne and started to pull her away.

"I'll get her cleaned up. She'll be alright."

As the two women walked in the direction of Midarin's room, Logan could hear Elwyne's voice.

"I killed her, Midarin. She tried to kill me, and I killed her."

Midarin's hand rubbed Elwyne's back gently.

"You did well," the former princess's voice said soothingly.

Logan watched them go, and then turned his attention back to Jasmen's dead form. With a single motion of his hand, the guards moved in and recovered the body.

"It's over now, and there's nothing that can be done, other than keeping our eyes open and watch each other's backs," Logan said finally.

Gwydeon moved to Logan and put his hand on his friend's shoulder.

"She's alright, Logan. She handled herself very well, and we'll all be a little wiser for next time. Why don't you go finish getting ready and we can get to this feast that Lord Cedric promised. Maybe a little light-hearted merry-making will wash this away."

Pike laughed.

"I'll drink to that."

The Feast

Though Logan tried to take heart in his friends' reverie, his mind was focused on Elwyne and the horror that she had just experienced. They had all experienced horrors on this journey; all been forced to do things they never thought they would do. He had hoped, probably foolishly, to spare the woman that he loved the worst of it. Perhaps that is why he had always been so intent on her returning to Aradon. As long as she was close to him she would be a target. But perhaps now, now that his name was public and every creature that served the Shadow knew who he was, the safest place for her was by his side. Without another word, Logan turned away from Pike and Gwydeon and walked back down the hall toward his suite. He was still only half dressed, and now blood was smeared across his chest. It was certainly no way for him to appear at a royal feast in his honor. Upon returning to his room, he picked up the discarded white shirt off the floor that Elwyne had laid out for him and placed it back on the bed in an attempt to smooth out any wrinkles. He then moved to the small basin of water on the far side of the room and did his best to clean the blood off. It wasn't a substitute for a bath, but it would have to do. A moment later he pulled the shirt quickly over his head and then returned to the hall to find Pike and Gwydeon waiting for him. There were no words shared between the three men, though Pike gave a mocking nod of approval to Logan's attire. That brought a half smile to Logan's lips, and the three made their way toward the banquet hall. At the end of the hall that led to the wing of suites, Gideon, Talon and Talos waited. As soon as the Gideon and Talon saw the approaching trio, they moved quickly down the hall to meet Logan and the others. Talos walked behind them, as usual not in a hurry to get anywhere.

"Is it true, Logan?" Talon asked.

Logan nodded in response.

"Jasmen tried to kill Elwyne," Gwydeon said flatly. "She has been an agent for the phasia all this time, lying in wait trying to get close to Logan."

"She thought she would have a better chance with Elwyne out of the way."

Gideon walked quickly up to Logan and bowed his head.

"I'm sorry, lord. I shoulda been dere ta protect her. She shouldn't a had ta soil her hands wit' dat woman's blood."

Logan hesitated for a moment and then put his hand on Gideon's shoulder.

"It's not your fault, Gideon. If there was anywhere we should have been safe, it should have been here. Who would have expected that an assassin would have been able to get to us in the palace of the Lord Lion?"

Gideon nodded, but Logan could tell that his words didn't ease his mind.

"Now that I have been proclaimed as the *Coromor*, we are pretty ripe targets for the forces of the Shadow no matter where we are. We have to be vigilant."

Gideon nodded again and stepped back.

"Lord Cedric has sent word that we are to join him in the throne room prior to attending the feast, Lord Dragon," Talos said finally. "He said that he has more gifts that he wishes to bestow, and these things should not be put off."

Pike mumbled something under his breath and then clapped Logan on the back. Following Talos' lead, the group made their way in the direction of the throne room. Once they had left the comforting confines of the suite area, Logan began to notice that the halls seemed darker, and the faint glow cast by the torches that lined the hall didn't provide much in the way of light. With the huge windows on one side of the hallway, it was obvious that during the day, the hall was flooded with the suns brightness, but in keeping with the themes of the stories that Aryx had told during the journey, the palace of Marcwell was a much gloomier place when night fell. It took only a matter of minutes to traverse the distance to the receiving hall of the throne room. Much to everyone's surprise, the receiving hall was not empty, but was in fact lined with guards in full dress armor. At second glance, Logan noticed that the men were not simply palace guards, but they were in fact members of the elite, the Lion's Mane. At the center of the back wall of the massive receiving hall were two large wooden doors that had been stained black with the symbol of the Lion carved into it and in-laid with gold. Steel bands reinforced the doors at the top and the bottom and were designed to withstand significant assault. Standing beside these large wooden doors that led to the throne room stood Lord Arathorn Geoffry and Aryx. Midarin also waited amongst the soldiers.

This was the first time that Logan had ever really seen Lord Arathorn, but he recognized the powerful and revered man immediately from well-circulated descriptions. He was a tall man, even taller than Cedric. He was clean shaven, and his hair was short and graying. His build was not huge, but it seemed adequate for his height. But there was more to the man than physical size. There was a palpable presence that he exuded, a quiet confidence and power that loomed over all of them making him feel like he towered over them all. The sword that Arathorn wore on his hip was so large that it looked like only a god should have been able to wield it. Each of the two legendary men was in ceremonial armor, and as always, Aryx wore the long cloak with the striking bolt of white lightning on his back. Aryx was not carrying his sword or his *Debuisa*. Arathorn was not wearing his *Debuisa* either. The group approached them slowly and Arathorn greeted them with a thick grave voice.

"Good evening to you, Lord Logan. I apologize that I have not been able to welcome you to Marcwell until now. There are always matters that need attending to in a kingdom as vast as Marcwell, especially now that the war with the Shadows has been rejoined. Lord Cedric is awaiting you and your companions inside."

"Very well," Logan replied.

Arathorn nodded and he and Aryx took up position on either side of the massive wooden doors. Together the two pulled the doors open, and as soon as the first crack appeared between the doors, bright light flooded into the receiving hall. The spacious throne room had been almost completely filled with candles, and only a single wide path to the throne remained open. Arathorn bid Logan and the others to remain where they were, then he led the armed guards into the throne room. They lined the path to the throne, and then Arathorn returned.

"Before you may be allowed to enter the exalted presence of the Lord Lion, you must leave your weapons here."

Logan drew his father's sword from its scabbard and laid it gently on the floor beside the door. Gideon took all of the concealed knives out of his shirt and pants and piled them. Gwydeon took the sword and scabbard from his side and laid them with the rest of the weapons. Talon stood his sword up in the corner and looked back at Logan uneasily. Logan understood how he felt, and with the situation that had arisen with Jasmen, Logan also felt uneasy without his blade. Pike was slow to relinquish his prized axe, but after a few moments he laid it with the rest. Talos was not armed, at least not in the sense of tangible weapons. As Logan watched the others relinquish their weapons, Midarin whispered in his ear.

"Elwyne is fine. Alexander is looking after her, and they will meet us at the feast. I gather they weren't invited to this little presentation anyway."

Logan nodded, but his gaze never left Lord Arathorn. After everyone had disarmed, Arathorn looked the group over for a quick moment before nodding and turning back toward the throne room. He led them down the long soldier-lined path and stopped at the foot of the raised floor that held Lord Cedric's throne. As Logan expected, Lord Cedric was seated atop the golden throne. Each in turn bowed to Lord Cedric, and then he stood and addressed all in the room.

"Friends, this is one of the greatest days in the history of Marcwell. The fate of the world rests on the shoulders of those standing before me. The gifts of the *Debuisa* that were bestowed before were not mine to give, so much as they were entrusted to me as the first of the prophecies. However, now I do have gifts from my own kingdom and my own heart that I wish to bestow. Titles do not bring greatness to a person, greatness of deed brings titles. You and your companions have more bravery in them than anyone could ever imagine, Lord Dragon, and I hope that you all survive the ordeal ahead of them. Lord Logan, come forward."

Logan walked up the small flight of steps that led to the throne and stood before Lord Cedric.

"Logan, my friend, you are no longer the common man that you once thought you were. Behind me, on the throne, is a sword forged by a long forgotten weapon smith. He is the man who first envisioned the true evil that Shau-ling was, and he knew that there would be a powerful force that would rise out of the desolation to counter Shau-ling's evil power. He forged seven great swords, and he somehow knew what the prophecies would say before they were ever written. This sword, the Dragon Sword, has been in my possession for several years now, and it is your birthright as the second coming of the *Coromor*. It is my duty as the first *Coromor* to present it to you. Kneel, Lord Dragon."

There was a flutter of hesitation in Logan's heart before he fell to one knee and bowed his head. Lord Cedric turned and picked the ancient blade up off the golden throne and held it in his hands for a long moment before placing it in Logan's outstretched hands. Once the polished steel touch Logan's flesh, he felt the jolt of power. He looked at the marvelous weapon and saw that the hilt of the sword consisted of two dragons intertwined and their wings extended to form the cross from which the blade emerged. On the blade was yet another symbol of Logan's lineage; a dragon in flight, much like the one on the Dragon Banner, was etched in gold on the blade of the sword. Logan held the blade in his hands for a moment and then rose back to his feet.

"Lord Dragon," Lord Cedric said proudly, "these companions of yours have served you well in the past days. With your permission, I wish to make them knights of the kingdom of Marcwell. Of course they will still be in your service, but my time grows short and soon you will sit on my throne and call my kingdom yours. What is your decision Lord?"

"Very well."

"Gwydeon Sandar, please kneel."

Gwydeon went to one knee and bowed his head low. Lord Cedric turned again and took a sword from the group of weapons that lay on a low table beside the throne. He descended from the platform and stood in front of Gwydeon. He drew the new sword and laid the flat of the blade on Gwydeon's left shoulder. The sword was much like those wielded by members of the Lion's Mane, but instead of a Lion etched on the flat of the blade, it was a dragon.

"Arise, Sir Gwydeon Sandar, Protector of Marcwell."

Gwydeon rose and took a step back. Cedric sheathed the sword that was designed much like the Lion Sword that my father had entrusted to me, and then Cedric presented it to Gwydeon. Gwydeon received the sword and then bowed again.

"Pike Rhuiden, please kneel."

Pike knelt and waited. Lord Cedric looked down at him for a moment and then drew the Lion Sword that hung on his hip. He laid the flat of the blade on Pike's left shoulder and commanded him to rise.

"You are somewhat of a difficult one, Rhuiden," Cedric said quickly. "I know that you will not use one of these Dragon Swords in battle, so I had the Elder devise a special weapon for you."

He signaled for Aryx to approach, and then the candle light caught the object that he held in his hands. Aryx carried a large, double-bladed war axe. Across both blades of the axe was etched a golden dragon similar to the one that was etched on all of the swords. Pike was taken aback by the axe, so much so that he bowed again and then went back to one knee. Cedric received the axe and then laid it in Pike's hands.

"Arise, Sir Pike Rhuiden of Marcwell. You have earned all of the accolades that you will receive."

One by one each member of the company became knights in the service of Marcwell and protectors of the Lord Dragon. All that remained was Midarin.

"Princess Midarin Rice of the Kingdom of Brea," Cedric intoned, "as you know, your position as a member of the royal court of Brea makes it impossible for me to give you title in Marcwell without causing significant diplomatic tension. However, I cannot let your actions on this quest go without recognition. So, I had one of my master fletchers prepare this."

Cedric recovered the only parcel that remained on the low table and held it carefully in his hand before pulling free the twine and wrapping that held it. What lay beneath was a fine longbow made of what appeared to be a dark wood with filigree of gold etched through it. Even the bowstring seemed to shine.

"I'm told it is the finest bow in my kingdom," Cedric said as he placed it in Midarin's hands. "May it serve you well in the days ahead."

Midarin seemed at a loss for words for just a moment, and then as if old training took over, she bowed slightly but respectfully.

"Thank you, Lord Cedric, I shall treasure this gift and put it to good use against our enemies."

Cedric smiled and then lifted his voice again.

"To the heroes of the second generation, and to the Lord Dragon!"

Cheers went up from the members of the Lion's Mane that were assembled in the room. As the cacophony continued, Cedric spoke in a more subdued tone.

"We shouldn't want to keep out guests waiting forever. Let us make our way to the banquet hall for a fine meal."

After a round of cheers from those gathered in the throne room, the soldiers led the way to the banquet hall. The banquet hall was on the far side of the palace, but was easily accessible from a hallway that exited the receiving hall. Along this hallway were tapestries that depicted the great victories during the War of the Lion, and were obviously intended to awe any guests lucky enough to garner an invitation. The hall itself was massive and filled with light, though the source was not readily apparent. One of the walls of the hall was made completely of glass, and had a door which led out into part of the Mithacarthian Woods. There were three large feasting tables that were placed together to accommodate the lords, ladies, and knights. A great many people were already gathered, with many more still finding their seat when Cedric entered. As soon as Cedric and Logan appeared, all who were seat immediately stood and began to applaud. Two of Lord Cedric's servants showed the members of the company to their seats at the table of honor. Lord Cedric had the center seat with Arathorn, Aryx, Lady Diana Terian, and Mailock on his left, with Logan and his party on his right. There were other knights and soldiers sitting at the other tables in the hall, but none that Logan recognized. A few minutes after they had all been seated, the outer doors to the banquet hall were opened and people from the town moved in an orderly fashion into the hall. They stood in the room, all trying to catch a glimpse of those sitting at the head table. There was a great amount of excitement in the crowd, but they remained in perfect control of themselves. The other set of doors opened from the kitchen, and dozens of servants brought covered platters of food to the tables and the crowd of people. A servant uncovered one of the platters of food and sat it in front of Logan. There were ripe pieces of green Seluiyn fruit that surrounded a cut of meat.

Lord Cedric nudged Logan and said, "that is Arteran boar, lad, it is very sweet."

Logan smiled and nodded, but in the pit of his stomach he was having a great difficulty with the amount of attention he was receiving. Elwyne was seated at his side, and her proximity was making it better. If she felt any after-effects from her ordeal, it didn't show on her face, which was constantly graced with a smile. She seemed to be dealing with the surreal nature of the situation far better than Logan was. After the last of the platters of food had been brought to the table, Lord Cedric stood and began a toast.

"Friends and citizens of Marcwell, I am here to thank you for the wonderful turnout in the name of the Dragon. I do not intend to speak long, for this is to be his time. I would however like to propose a toast to the Dragon. May you outlive Shau-ling, and bring order out of this chaos."

"Long live the *Coromor*!" the multitude shouted.

"Yes," a voice shouted seemingly from the center of the crowd, "long live the bloody *Coromor*! Ha! Ha! Ha!"

"Find that man and arrest him!" Lord Cedric shouted to one of his guards.

"No need, Lion," the voice shot back.

The doors that led to the Mithacarthian Woods flew open and a black clad figure burst into the room. Several of the guards rushed to capture him, but they stopped short when he pointed in their direction. It appeared as if he had frozen them with a thought. Arathorn and Aryx both made a move to draw their weapons and attack, but Lord Cedric's extended hand restrained them. After the intruder was sure that no one else would make an attempt to hinder him, he strode across the room and stood in front of the table of honor. He pulled back the hood and revealed his face. Logan had seen that man before, but he could not remember where. Out of the corner of his eye, Logan was sure he saw Cedric grimace. Within another few seconds, another black robed figure burst through the front doors of the banquet hall. He approached the table and stopped beside the first figure. He pulled back his hood and Cedric shot to a standing position.

"Erdric, I should have known."

Erdric Belnosian, the son of the mayor and brother of the woman that Lord Cedric was to marry. The man who was supposed to be Cedric's ally was standing there in front of them with what Logan could only guess was a servant of Shau-ling.

"Greetings Dragon, or should I say Logan Ranthall of Aradon. Tis a pleasure to finally meet the man we are going to kill," the mystery man said shortly, "it is such a pity that our game has to end now."

"Game," Logan replied in disgust, "what game?"

"Why the game whose stakes are your life and the lives of six generations to come of course. I didn't think your successor would be so dim, Cedric. However, I suppose you would like to know exactly who has beaten you, wouldn't you? Well, I'll tell you. Your predecessor there knows me well; he was the one who sealed my fate in the last generation. My dagger would surely have ended the second battle of Lakestone had it not been for a cruel twist of the Creator's fate."

"Jeroch," Lord Cedric said the hate clear in his voice, "I was wondering when you would crawl out of the grave. I watched you die in Exeter Lake, and I'll be happy to watch you die again."

"Yes Lion, you did watch me die. But now, I intend to avenge that death upon you. But I have a personal score to settle with the men who call themselves the People of the Dragon. They have robbed me of my youngest son. Do you gentlemen remember a man named Hawk?"

"That was your son?" Pike responded angrily, "After the way we destroyed that weakling and his army, I'm surprised that you would claim him at all. You had better pray that you are stronger than her was."

"I should kill you for that, Rhuiden. However, revenge is not the chore that I have been sent on this time."

"Then what is your chore, Jeroch?" Lord Cedric asked.

"Simply to deliver a message from my lord and master. However, before I deliver my message, I wanted to ask the Lord Dragon's consort if she enjoyed her gift."

Logan saw Elwyne tense.

"It was a pity to waste such a pretty little thing like Jasmen, but ultimately all humans are disposable."

Jeroch opened his cloak and pulled out a long parchment. It was sealed with a large black wax seal, with the symbol of a dragon pressed into it. Jeroch opened the letter and showed it to us. The words were written in blood red ink, and was signed in large print, 'Shau-ling, master of this world.' Jeroch turned the letter back towards him and began to read.

'Hello Dragon. By the time this letter is being read, I already know who you are. This means that I can find you at any time, and in any place. My servants are very dedicated to their work, Dragon, and now that you have revealed yourself to me, it will make their job that much easier. As you have probably guessed, I knew all along that you and the Lion would eventually find each other, with White Lightning's help of course. This is why Erdric has been keeping an eye on the Lion for me. Believe me, Dragon, he has been one of my phasia for a long time, ever since the poor boy prince died in an unfortunate accident that I planned thirteen years ago. As much as I would like to see your broken body brought to me by my servants, Dragon, I hope that you make it to my palace so I can have the pleasure of crushing every breath of life out of you with my own hands. Long live the Shadow!'

As soon as Jeroch read the last phrase of the letter, Erdric leapt up onto the table with dagger drawn. He lunged at Logan, but Lord Cedric was quicker. He shoved his younger counterpart out of the way and blocked the deadly blade with his outstretched hand. Lord Cedric's powers must have been protecting him because the blade stopped two inches from his flesh. Logan drew the Dragon Sword from the scabbard on his side and leapt at Erdric. The phase jumped back off the table and drew a strangely shaped black sword. The blade of the sword had a large curve in it near the hilt which made it a longer sleeker weapon. He lunged again, and the two powerful blades crossed. Logan could hear shouts behind him as he and Erdric fought for a leverage advantage. Suddenly, the glass wall exploded in a burst of light and sent them sprawling to the ground covered with glass. Into the room rushed an army of Jeresei and a group of monsters that Logan had never seen before.

The creatures were huge. They towered over the Jeresei, and their heads nearly brushed the ceiling. They looked as though they were made of granite because of the texture of their skin, and the mottled gray color. Regardless of what they were, they were advancing very quickly. Before Logan could move, the army of Marcwell as well as the heroes of the first and second generations of the prophecies stormed past and cut off the army of the Shadow. There were flashes of light everywhere, and Logan knew that Talos, Arathorn, Aryx, Cedric, and the *Erieal* were doing all that they could.

It took several attempts, but Logan managed to get to his feet, but was quickly dropped to my knees by a stinging pain running through his back. When he turned, he saw Erdric's black blade thrusting toward his head. Logan rolled to one side to dodge the blow and jumped to his feet, holding the Dragon sword out in front of him in a practiced defensive position. The pain in his back was almost too intense to bear, but Logan knew that if he let his concentration lapse for even a moment, he was finished. Their swords crossed again, and in Logan's weakened state, Erdric was easily able to push him to the ground. The tip of his sword came quickly down, and again Logan rolled out of the way and got to one knee. A hard slash of the Dragon Sword did little to halt the advancing phase as his reflexes were much better than a normal human's. He parried the blow and buried the tip of the curved blade into Logan's sword shoulder. A feeling of weakness passed over Logan almost instantly, and it felt as if the wound had begun to drain all of his energy. Logan dropped to both knees and started to lose my grip on the Dragon Sword. Erdric stood in front of Logan with his sword raised high and a wicked smile on his lips. He was going to end the battle there and then. Shau-ling had really won. Suddenly, Erdric fell and his sword skidded across the floor. The last sight that Logan saw before he collapsed was Lord Cedric's face staring down at him just before the darkness fell.

* * * * * * * * * * * *

Logan felt a slap across his face, and he opened his eyes. Elwyne and Pike were hovering over him with worried expressions on their faces. Elwyne smiled as soon as she saw that his eyes were open, and Pike pulled him into a sitting position and handed him the Dragon Sword.

"Glad to see you are still alive old friend," he said, "I hope that you can walk. We are all getting out of here."

"Why?" Logan asked sluggishly.

Though he was conscious, Logan still had very little energy, and simply talking required a great effort.

"Marcwell is under siege. The one Lord Cedric called Jeroch is leading a huge force. The soldiers are holding them outside the palace gates for the time being, but that won't last long. Our only way out of here is through the Mithacarthian Woods. Lord Cedric says we could make for a town called Barer."

"Where's Erdric?"

"Lord Cedric took care of that piece of trash. That was before all hell broke loose. Come on, we haven't got much time."

"Then let's get out of here," Logan muttered.

Pike helped Logan to his feet, and together the trio picked their way through the dead and the dying to the gaping hole in the glass wall of the banquet hall. Lord Cedric and the rest of the company, including his companions from the first war were waiting with horses in a small glade outside of the palace. They had managed to cut an island of sanity in the eye of a storm of shadow. Dozens of dead Jeresei and even some of the massive stone creatures lay scattered around them. As Logan mounted his horse with support from Pike, he heard shouts coming from the banquet hall.

"Hurry friends," Lord Cedric shouted, "the army of the Shadow is upon us."

As soon as they were all in their saddles, Lord Cedric and his horse bolted toward a hidden gate. One by one the company went through the gate and quickly followed Lord Cedric down a concealed path. Before they knew it, they stood atop a hill that overlooked Marcwell. The battle still raged below, but it was a losing one at best. Hundreds of Jeresei assailed the walls, cutting down the brave royal guard of Marcwell as though they were common men. The massive stone creatures ripped through the walls like paper and toppled the shining towers with a single slam of a fist. Just before the group turned away from the carnage, Logan saw the tower that flew the Dragon Banner fall.

Chapter XV

Revelations

There was an unusual air in the Pen. Warron knew that something incredible had happened. He walked slowly back toward the Hall of Terrors, and he was quickly joined by Zarsi.

"Do you know what is going on?" Zarsi asked.

"No," Warron replied, "but whatever it is, it's very big. The Pen is almost empty, and there's not a Jeresei to be found anywhere. I have even heard rumors that master has redesigned the Shadowwalkers and Kalbraks."

Zarsi was a shocked by Warron's description of the massive flux of creatures out of the palace. The only time that the Pen had been empty in the past was during the War for Power. Then again, the war raged once more, and the phasia were massing armies to launch attacks on unsuspecting cities, not to mention one another. One such attack had already been launched on an under-manned Illimar, and Shau-ling had demanded that Jeroch take a huge force to Marcwell. Apparently, Shau-ling's concern for the *Coromor* and the *Chosen One* had seriously diminished, and it would not be long before this tremendous offensive would conquer the world.

The only thing that continued to bother Zarsi was the fact that Shau-ling had redesigned the Shadowwalkers and Kalbraks. They had been tremendous soldiers in the past, and if Shau-ling had thought it imperative to reintroduce them to the fold, he had probably made some improvements upon their design. The Shadowwalkers were eight foot tall menaces. They were endowed with a direct line into Shau-ling's Blaze. They could call on it at any time, and Shau-ling would never say a word. Granted that they could not draw on it with as much efficiency as the phasia, but it was still an intrusion on the master's own life-force. Even when Shau-ling had robbed them of the daytime sight, they were still too powerful for their own good. In one of Zarsi's most chilling memories, he could remember seven Shadowwalkers killing Taron without the interference of any other phase. The Shadowwalkers were very powerful, powerful enough to destroy a phase on their own, and if master had made them even more powerful, they were too much of a threat to be ignored.

The Kalbraks were another story. These foot soldiers had always been the lowest of the beasts. They had no true powers other than the four foot talons that extended from each of their ten fingers. When Shau-ling created them, he took a lizard and inflated it to the size of a Jeresei. They were supposed to be the lackeys of all other beasts. However, because of their long striking distance, they became more valuable as fighters than as servants. Because they were descended from a lowly lizard, they had a strange sense of survival and battle that no one could ever quite figure out. This just heightened their prowess in battle, and thus made them a much more dangerous adversary.

"What are these redesigns?" Zarsi asked almost fearfully.

"No one is truly sure. Some say that it is just a myth, but I'm sure that it's been done. Without the Shadowwalkers, one of our best tactics to harass larger kingdoms was lacking, and I'm sure Master took that into account. The Kalbraks are another story. I think Master is still trying to do better than what Jeroch stumbled upon by accident with the Jeresei. I was just on my way to the throne room, and I would appreciate the company."

"Still intimidated being alone in Master's presence?"

"Aren't we all?" Warron answered with a question.

Zarsi could only nod in response. They both knew that Shau-ling had a tendency to deal with his traitors one on one, and while two of the phasia weren't a match for Shau-ling's awesome power, it seemed that he was a bit more reluctant to try and finish off two at once. Maybe that was his Achilles' heel. Or perhaps it was yet another in a long line of tactics meant to fill the phasia with a sense of security. There were times that Zarsi felt as though Shau-ling was just toying with them, allowing them their petty jealousies and dreams of ruling in his stead. No member of the phasia had risen as high or had fallen as far as Zarsi had, and it gave him a different perspective than the others.

Within a few moments, they were standing in the center of the Hall of Terrors. Something was different about the room now. The light was much dimmer, and there were no sounds of breathing or cursing coming from any of the cells that lined the walls.

"Master has ordered that the Hall of Terrors be cleared, and that the creatures be moved to the Holding Pens in the lower level until master calls for them. He believes that some of the traitorous phasia might be able to gain control of them and use them against his armies," the Flame said from the far end of the chamber.

The two phasia walked over to their brother and waited. The Flame was rumored to be older even that Jeroch, but not quite as old as Shau-ling. It was believed that the Flame was the first of Shau-ling's creatures and the template for the phasia. However, Shau-ling saw that he had made his creation too powerful, so he condemned it to hold his door and be at his beck and call at every minute of eternity. But despite his power, the Flame was not considered a true threat by any of the phasia, even if they chose to show him deference. Every member of the phasia knew that if they were going to successfully assault Shau-ling, they would have to either go through the Flame, or make their assault with his help. Because the depths of his power had never been tested, most members of the phasia chose deference over antagonism when dealing with the monstrous creature.

"What is going on, Flame?" Zarsi asked.

"I do not know, Cobra," he replied. "There has been some development with the *Coromor* but no one knows what. Master has been in his chambers all morning working on the Kalbraks and the Shadowwalkers."

"So it is true," Warron said angrily, "Master has gone on and redesigned the beasts. What has he done to them?"

"I do not know, Boar," the Flame replied softly, "Master has not allowed anyone into the throne room all morning. If you would like, I could announce you and ask if he will see you now."

"I would," Warron replied.

The Flame disappeared and the two phasia were left alone in the empty Hall of Terrors. For some reason the dim and mysterious light made Zarsi tremble even more. He had always been afraid of what might happen to him in the Hall if Shau-ling ever truly wished to eliminate him. How Cedric Binosear and his followers had managed to survive their ordeal in the Hall was anyone's best guess, but it was certainly an impressive feat. Only the most arrogant or short-sighted of the phasia would have dismissed something that few of the phasia themselves would be hard-pressed to duplicate. A few seconds later, the Flame reappeared and the doors to the throne room opened.

"Master said that he will receive you know, but only briefly. He said that he has much to attend to, so you will have to make your visit brief."

The two phasia nodded and walked into the throne room. The light in the room was dim as always, but now there was a strange green glow cast on the walls. They both walked forward and bowed as they reached the foot of the throne.

"My Lord Shau-ling," they said in unison, "we seek the wisdom of the master of the Shadows."

"Arise, my loyal subjects," Shau-ling said in a strangely jubilant voice. "What is it that you require of me?"

"We were wondering what has happened. The Pen is empty, and none of the phasia are here in the palace," Warron replied. "We've also heard that there has been a development regarding the *Coromor*."

"The prophecies have come full circle, my children. The Lion has given me the identity of the Dragon, and now that I know that Logan Ranthall is this generation's *Coromor*, I have mobilized all of my forces in an attempt to kill him before he finds out where I am. I have also ordered the remaining phasia to launch crippling attacks on several of the largest cities. This will keep the traitors far from my palace where they are easily controlled. More than that, it will keep the Lion and his meddlesome sycophants from flocking to the Dragon's banner. I want Ranthall and his followers to be isolated from those that might follow him blindly because of who he is. An unfocused weapon is not a weapon at all."

"What about Saurn?" Zarsi asked.

"At the present," Shau-ling replied, "Saurn is not a factor. I do not believe that he has enough power to launch an offensive against this palace, even with the Pen almost empty. However, I am taking precautions that will keep Saurn from trying anything. As you have probably heard through many sources in the palace, I have decided to redesign the Shadowwalkers. I was going to try to revamp the Kalbraks as well, but I found that it was a useless attempt, so I remade them as they were."

"You have already begun the rebirth of the Kalbraks?" Warron asked a bit more than shocked.

"Yes, Boar," he replied. "They have been modified slightly to be more vicious and merciless in battle, but I think that they will serve their purpose without much more direct intervention. Perhaps I was too hasty in their destruction to begin with. If the phasia continue to misuse the tools at their disposal, perhaps it is the phasia that should be held responsible. After all, it is hard to blame the hammer, if the person wielding it has not the strength to carry it."

Shau-ling fell silent for a moment to let his jibe sink in before continuing.

"As for the Shadowwalkers, they required much more of my attention. Now I believe they will fulfill their purpose with a renewed vigor and lethality."

Shau-ling rose and walked over to a covered cage that stood in the corner of the room. Warron and Zarsi followed quickly behind him.

"However, these changes are not without cost. This version of the Shadowwalkers is more of a blunt instrument than the original. They are not as free to think as their earlier incarnations were, so they must have a leader. For that purpose, I have created something very special. Observe."

Shau-ling turned back toward the cage and pulled off the tarp. From inside the cage, bright white eyes opened, beaming out with what the two phasia quickly recognized as Blaze energy. Shau-ling opened the cage door, and a creature stepped out. The appearance of the beast was like that of a Shadowwalker, but while there were many similarities, there were striking differences. The skin of the beast looked nothing at all like skin, but more like black steel. The talons on the beast's hands were also black, and the glow from them made them look impossibly sharp. Its wings were held close to its back, and when Shau-ling nodded, they sprung out away from its body. The wings looked more like a collection of sword blades than the normal wings of a Shadowwalker, and the tips of the wings glowed as brightly as the talons. On top of the thing's head were two long horns and it appeared that Shau-ling had taken the horns of a bull and stuck them on this beast's head. While some would have seen these as merely for decoration, the trained eye realized that with the power and speed that this creature could manage in flight, the horns represented a fearsome weapon. As Zarsi looked at the thing's face, the eyes of the beast changed suddenly from white to bright red. Zarsi looked down and saw a shadow moving around this new monster's feet. When he looked closer, he realized that the shadow was not a shadow at all, but was really a very thin tail. The tail ended in an arrowhead shaped projection, and it too glowed with lethal sharpness. To Zarsi, this weapon was reminiscent of the tails of the thrice-damned hopping balls of fur that Farax had called Snags. The wings folded back again, and Shau-ling turned back to face the awe-stricken phasia.

"You see, these new Shadowwalkers do not suffer from the delay when they fold back their wings. That makes them much faster, and much more dangerous."

"You mean," Zarsi managed to choke out, "all of the new Shadowwalkers are like this?"

"No, Zarsi," Shau-ling replied. "You might call this one a bit of an experiment. This is my prototype for a new kind of soldier. The other

Shadowwalkers are similar, but they do not have the horns or the tail, though I have considered adding at least the horns. Their eyes are also natural, and are not armored as they are in this incarnation. However, they do have this new steel forged skin, and the bladed wings. I think that its adds something to the appearance."

Warron nodded and then spoke.

"What then, if I may ask, is this?"

"This, my faithful children, is the one creature that will strike fear into the hearts of all men. He is all that I have ever wished that I could create. I had to destroy many of my other one-of-a-kind creations in order to salvage enough parts for this little pet of mine, and I assure you, it was well worth the trouble that I went through. He will be the perfect general for my armies, and the perfect hunter to track down and destroy the traitors in our midst. However, I must say that I have out done myself in one little area of this beast's construction. Wouldn't you say my newest servant?"

"I WOULD MY MASTER," the thing answered in a deep tone. It was almost as if Shau-ling had taken the power of the Voice and melded it into this new creature.

"What are you?" Shau-ling asked the creature.

"I AM TO BE CALLED NIGHTWING. I AM ALL THAT THE SHADOWWALKERS WERE, WHAT THE JERESEI ASPIRE TO BE, AND WHAT THE PHASIA TAKE FOR GRANTED. I WAS FORGED IN THE FIRES OF THE BLAZE, AND I WAS ENDOWED WITH THE POWERS OF ALL OF THE PHASIA."

"That can't be possible," Zarsi interjected. "How could it have the same powers as we do?"

"Three of our order are dead, my child," Shau-ling answered. "Erdric lost his life at the hands of Cedric Binosear, Aldridge was killed by my hand on the Other Side, and for all I know, and Caris was banished by the *Chosen One.* I severed their strings from the Council and merged them into this one creature. Because I have allowed it to be so, Nightwing does not suffer from the limitations of combining powers as you phasia do. He has the one ability that you do not, and I doubt that you can guess why."

Zarsi thought hard for a moment but shook his head. When he looked over to Warron, he saw that his brother too was lost in the words of their illustrious master.

"Would you care to show them my pet?" Shau-ling said as he turned to Nightwing.

Suddenly all of Nightwing's 'skin' turned bright red. It seemed as if it generated a glowing red aura from somewhere inside itself, and the two phasia could only remember seeing that glow one other place in their lives.

"You captured a *Debuisa* from one of the *Erieal*," Warron said shocked.

"No, Warron," Shau-ling replied, "I have done much more than that. I learned through various sources in this palace that one of my phasia was in league with White Lightning. However, this alliance on its face did not concern me. Then, I learned that the phase was using his influence over White Lightning to plan strikes on the *Coromor*. In case you haven't figured it out yet, some members of my phasia have known the identity of the *Coromor* for some time now, and I think that they were hoping to use him against me. Taron will surely pay for his insolence as well as his treachery, but that time will come sooner or later. However, manipulation was never Taron's strength; he was too dim to function that highly. In time though, I shall uncover the other members of your brethren who aided in this scheme. After I learned of this deception, I seized White Lightning when he was supposed to meet with Taron to discuss their next move. Would you care to tell them what happened next, Aryx?"

The phasia spun around several times looking for their mortal enemy, after a moment they realized what had truly come to pass, and they looked at Nightwing.

"I WAS BROUGHT BACK HERE TO THE PALACE AND GIVEN MORE POWER THAN I COULD EVER IMAGINE. MY POWERS HAVE BEEN JOINED WITH THOSE OF THE PHASIA IN A WAY THAT HAS NEVER BEEN KNOWN IN ANY OTHER LIFETIME, AND FROM THIS POINT ON, MY POWERS WILL BE USED IN AN

EFFORT TO FURTHER THE CAUSE OF THE SHADOWS. THE *DEBUISA* THAT I ONCE WORE WAS MELTED IN THE FLAMES OF THE BLAZE, AND IT WAS THE MADE INTO WHAT IS NOW MY SKIN. I CAN DRAW UPON IT WHEN EVER I WISH, AND I NEVER HAVE TO FEAR BEING CUT OFF FROM THE POWERS AGAIN. I AM NOW POWER PERSONIFIED."

The ear shattering laugh that the beast let loose was something that the phasia would never forget. It was the way that the power seemed to echo through Nightwing's words that the phasia found uncomfortable. Nightwing walked past the fearful phasia and made his way through the Hall of Terrors toward somewhere.

"I hope that you and the rest of the phasia will accept Nightwing into the Council when the time comes."

"Surely master, you can't be serious," Warron objected. "He is not a member of the phasia, no matter what powers you give him. I will not ever call that half-breed my brother."

"I can accept a little resistance Warron," Shau-ling responded as he moved back toward the throne, "but I will not accept much more of your pompous, arrogant drivel. I have warned you before about questioning my decisions and belittling your brother creatures, and I shall not do it again. The next time that you make a statement about Nightwing, or any of my other creations, I suggest that you be ready to defend yourself. I can just as easily add you to the list of traitors that Nightwing will destroy. As you have seen, I have rendered the phasia obsolete, and soon I will have the ability to make as many of these Nightwings as I wish. Jeroch was commanded to discover how these *Debuisa* were made and to bring that knowledge and all those materials back to me here. Soon I will have an army of Nightwings, all loyal only to me."

"Is that wise master?" Zarsi asked trying to cover for a very scared Warron. "Surely this use of the forces of the Light as your servants can not be a wise decision. The Creator maintained the balance of a reason, and I cannot see this tipping the scales as a good thing master."

Shau-ling rose and screamed in the Voice much louder than any had ever heard in their long lives.

"NOW HEAR ME ALL OF THE PHASIA THAT STILL LIVE NO MATTER WHERE YOU ARE. YOU ARE NO LONGER THE HOLDERS OF MY FAVOR OR OF MY POWERS. YOU WILL BE LUCKY IF I DECIDE NOT TO CUT OFF ALL OF YOUR POWERS COMPLETELY. REMEMBER THAT YOU WERE MADE BY ME, NOT THE CREATOR. FROM THIS POINT ON, NONE OF THE PHASIA, SAVE JEROCH ARE TO BE ALLOWED INTO MY PALACE WITHOUT BEING SUMMONED. IF ANY OF YOU SET FOOT IN MY PALACE FROM THIS POINT ON, I WILL INTRODUCE YOU TO THE POWER THAT HAS TAKEN YOUR PLACE. I HOPE THAT YOU STAY ALIVE LONG ENOUGH TO SEE ME VANQUISH THE *COROMOR*, BUT IF YOU ARE NOT, CONSIDER YOURSELF LUCKY. ALL PHASIA WHO SURVIVE LONG ENOUGH TO SEE THE DAWN OF THE NEW ORDER WILL BE MY FIRST TARGETS FOR DESTRUCTION. THAT IS ALL THAT I WILL SAY TO YOU. FAREWELL."

It took the phasia a few moments to recover from the incredible use of the Voice. It was a horrible feeling that echoed through their heads, and they could neither defend themselves nor leave Shau-ling's presence.

"Nightwing!"

Shau-ling's voice echoed past them, and a moment later, the newest member of the Council returned. This time, he was holding a huge double-bladed black sword.

"YES, MY MASTER?" Nightwing responded.

"Take these pitiful creatures out of here and make sure that they leave through their portals. You should be able to track them. After that you can make a sweep of the palace. Kill any creature that should not be here, and then report back to me. I have a little job for you."

"AS YOU WISH."

The Frontier

Lord Cedric's proclamation had served to bring the phasia down on top of them, and now they had lost anything that could have been considered a safe refuge from the ravages of the war. A member of the phasia was dead, but there was still no information about the location of Shau-ling's palace. If anything, Lord Cedric's idea had nearly gotten everyone killed. Jeroch. That name kept ringing in Logan's head as they sat watching Marcwell be slowly torn apart. He wanted to fight, he wanted to ride down into the maelstrom and use the powers at his disposal to save the people of Marcwell. With all of the power at Cedric's disposal and with Pike, Talon, Gideon, Arathorn, Aryx, Diana, and Talos' abilities they could have done severe damage to the army of the Shadow, and perhaps even take Jeroch's head to go along with Erdric's. But Logan knew that they should not take the risk, that they shouldn't fight a battle they couldn't win. If Cedric had thought they could prevail, they would still be knee deep in blood. Perhaps it had been Logan's wound, and how quickly he had come to death that precipitated the retreat, or perhaps it had been something else. No matter the cause, something had been watching over them that evening, and Logan felt in his heart that David's spirit had served to save their lives again. It seemed that other than a few scratches, most of the company had made it out of Marcwell intact. The worst wounds were to Logan's back and a nasty looking gash on the side of Talon's head. While the fires still raged below, it was with a heavy heart that Cedric turned toward a path that led deeper into the Mithacarthian Woods. About two hours after riding through the dense forest, complete with twisted dark forms of trees and bushes, Cedric called for the company to halt in a crescent shaped valley for the night. The entire time camp was being set up, it was clear that the situation was weighing heavily on Lord Cedric. However, once the fire had been lit and the majority of the group settled in, he seemed to calm. Talon, Arathorn, and Aryx chose to take the watch, and everyone else tried their best to make some sense out of the events of the last few hours. Cedric broke the silence first.

"I have been here before," Lord Cedric said softly, "and I must tell you that I like it no more now than I did then."

"Would it be too much of an intrusion to ask why?" Elwyne asked in an equally soft voice.

"Not at all," he said sitting back and relaxing. "It all goes back to when the quest first started. I had been volunteered by the mayor, then Arthur Belnosian, and the city council to go to Askronilka. I was supposed to gather a striking party to try and free Lakestone from an army of monsters that had overrun. I had no idea at the time what I was stepping into, so I begrudgingly agreed. As I was getting ready to make my way through this very forest, which, at the time, was the quickest way to Askronilka, I found my first ally. The mayor's daughter, Erika Belnosian, offered to come along. I thought that it was a bad idea, but she insisted. After a bit of an argument, we agreed that she should come along."

"As the story is told in Brea, she didn't give you much of a choice," Midarin added.

"Exactly. We left secretly that night, as was the wish of the council, and we made our way to the crossroads. A few years ago I had the crossroads dismantled, but they used to stand just outside the city entrance to the woods. The crossroads were a prison of sorts. It was set aside for those people who were too dangerous to society and to themselves. When a person was tried and found guilty of a crime so heinous that it disgusts the entire population, the person is placed in one of the four cages at the crossroads. After the cage was locked, the key was broken in two and laid just under the cage, well within the view of the prisoner. Then, the prisoner is left there until he dies, or someone frees him. That's how Erika and I met a man by the name of Khisanth."

There was a cold undertone in Cedric's voice. It was obviously not a pleasant memory.

"He was sitting there in one of the cages, yelling and screaming for someone to help him. After hearing his long sad story, Erika and I decided to free him from captivity, despite the possible danger. Later that day we camped here for the night. Just after we had fallen asleep, a group of Shau-ling's monsters crept up on us. We had little warning before they struck, but the fact that we had discovered their presence did little to weaken their resolve. We killed most of their ranks, and they all began to flee back into the forest. One of the monsters ran back further into this inlet. All of us knew that it was a dead end, so Khisanth ran after the beast. From deep in the inlet, we heard a scream, before we were able to catch up with Khisanth's reckless pursuit. To our horror, Khisanth lay on the ground; face down, with a crossbow dart sticking out of his back. Shau-ling's forces had robbed Khisanth of his life, and if they would have had a chance, I would have been the next target. That is the situation that you are in now, Logan. And that more than anything is the reason that we are here, and not fighting for the people of Marcwell, no matter how unpalatable the decision is."

Everyone sat there silently for a few moments, and then Gwydeon tried to lighten the atmosphere of the conversation.

"What is this town that we are heading toward?" Gwydeon asked.

"Barer has been on the fringes of my kingdom ever since I took the throne. It is a town in an area called the Frontier. The Frontier is a collection of independent kingdoms that have survived on their own for hundreds of years. I am sure that we will be safe there until we can get a few leads as to the location of Shau-ling's palace."

"Do you expect for us to find anything of value in Barer?" Pike asked the doubt heavy in his voice.

"There is always hope, Pike," Logan answered. "We've made it through a lot of things during this quest with little more than hope and faith to guide us. It's always gotten us through in the past."

"Tell that to Eldar," he said as he stood and walked away.

The pain was still deep in his voice, and Logan knew that walking away from the fight in Marcwell was not sitting well with him. Pike wanted any chance he could get to exact his revenge, and if there was any chance that he could have been the one to end Erdric's life, he would have taken it. Until he had a chance to make things right in his heart and in his mind, every creature that served the Shadows would be wearing Taron's face. Elwyne started to go to him, but Logan held her back.

"It's best if he is left alone for a while, Elwyne," Logan said softly. "He has to work this out for himself."

Cedric looked toward Pike for a moment and then followed him. Gwydeon started to say something to him, but thought better of what seemed like a useless gesture. Whatever Cedric had on his mind, it was best to let him say what he wished. None of them had known the great man long enough to make judgments about his actions, but inwardly Logan hoped that Cedric wasn't about to make matter worse.

* * * * * * * * * * * *

Cedric walked slowly after Pike, trying not to seem more judgmental than usual. He knew that this was difficult for Pike, having been through a similar situation himself. He thought that perhaps his insights could be a help to his new ally.

"I don't want to hear your advice right now, Cedric," Pike said roughly as he turned to face the older man. "I would appreciate it if you would turn around and go back to camp with the others."

"The Mithacarthian Woods is not a place to be alone in Pike, especially if you don't have your wits about you."

"Are you telling me that I can't take care of myself? Surely you didn't come out here to warn me about the wildlife. What do take me for? You must think that I am so monumentally naive that I don't see anything that happens around me."

The anger rushed through Pike's voice like breakers crashing up against the sands of a coastal beach. Cedric could have reacted to this anger and resentment in much more constructive ways, but he felt that a response of equal vigor served the purpose well enough.

"You are naïve, Pike, and if I were not in a generous mood, I would be inclined to call you stupid. All of those people sitting back at that fire care about you, and they would give their lives if they could do anything to help you. But no, you are the mighty Pike Rhuiden. No one needs to help you because you can handle everything that comes your way. You've always protected yourself and anyone else who came along."

"You don't know me, Cedric."

"I know you Pike. I was you for a long time before I realized that there was more to living than being brave and strong. You can still be strong and show your feelings and your pain, Pike."

"You're going to lecture me about pain?" Pike said, his face full of barely restrained rage. "I have to live without her every day of my life from now on. I close my eyes every night, and I can't help but see her face and here her calling my name. I see her there in that same frozen moment and I can't do anything to save her. I relive that minute in time over and over again, each time it just hurts more and more. How can you expect me to live through that every single day for the rest of my life?"

Cedric shook his head and sat down on the stump of a tree that was nearby.

"Let me tell you something, Pike. Before you ever accuse anyone of being insensitive to your problems, you better know a hell of a lot more about that person than you knew about me when you made that accusation. You don't think I know what it means to live with pain every day of my life? I started my quest as a boy not much older than you are now. I was a king, but I knew nothing about what it took to be a true leader of men. I went on my damn fool quest full of pride and righteous indignation. I thought that it took bravery to be a king. I thought that warriors didn't fear death, and that's why they were strong. I was gravely mistaken."

He stared Pike in the eye, his words cutting the younger man to the core.

"Warriors are brave because they know that if they take one wrong step, they could be dead. It's the fear, not the lack there of, that makes them brave. I learned that the hard way. When the first of my true friends died on my quest, I hurt, but it could never match the pain that I felt when Erika was killed right there in front of me. I know the helpless feeling that you described so well, and I can assure that every member of your party does too. You are sadly mistaken to feel alone in this, Pike. I know that it's hard to talk about, but eventually, there comes a time when you can't hold it inside any longer. Hopefully, you'll realize when that time comes. When it does, your friends will be waiting to help you."

Cedric turned and left Pike alone with his thoughts.

* * * * * * * * * * * *

Logan saw Cedric come back from deeper in the forest alone. He wasn't truly worried about Pike, because Logan knew that his hot-headed friend would eventually work out his problems for himself. That had always been Pike's strongest feature. It seemed like no matter what happened, Pike just brushed it off and went on with his life like nothing had ever happened. This was the first time that Logan had ever seen Pike's emotions get the better of him. He wasn't really that distraught when David died, but he and David had problems, most because of Eldar.

"He'll be fine," Cedric said coldly. "We had better get some rest. I want to be in Barer by mid-day."

He walked away and stood beside where Arathorn and Aryx kept watch. Diana moved to join them, followed by Mailock. It took only a matter of moments before the heroes of the first generation were gathered in discussions. Logan's stomach turned. Something about Cedric taking control and acting as though he was the lord and master frayed Logan's nerves.

"Logan," Gwydeon said as he put his hand on his friend's shoulder, "we need to have a talk. Talon, Midarin, and I have something that we really need to talk to you about."

"Alright. We'll go deeper into the forest. I'm sure that you want Pike to hear this."

"Very true," Midarin replied.

The four moved away from the rest of the group with Logan giving Elwyne a reassuring squeeze on her shoulder before he walked away. Logan nodded in Gideon's direction and then looked back at Elwyne which brought a curt nod of understanding from the thief. It didn't take long for them to come to where Pike sat on a small stump, turning the haft of his axe in the dirt.

"I don't need another lecture guys," he said in a much lighter tone than he had used earlier, "our patron saint Lord Cedric already took a few notches out of my belt. I think that my ego is back in check."

"I'm sure that Elwyne will be happy to hear that," Logan commented. "She has been ready to slap you around for a long time now. I even heard her compare you to Antrobus. She has said on several occasions that you are worse than he ever was."

"I wasn't that bad," he replied.

Midarin and Gwydeon nodded.

"Okay, so maybe I was pretty bad. You have to give me a little slack after what happened."

"We forgive you Pike," Talon said softly.

"Now," Pike said rounding on me, "what are the four of you doing out here on a night like this."

"It's not me, Pike," Logan said raising my hands, "this time it's all Talon."

Pike turned and looked at his longtime friend and trouble-making companion. There was a look of surprise mixed with disbelief that Logan had seen so many times on Pike's face since the beginning of the quest, but for some reason, this was not a serious look, but more of a bright and comic one.

"Okay Talon, what is this all about?"

Talon walked over to one of the many stumps and sat down. He motioned for the others to join him. After everyone was seated, Logan saw Pike's smile fade as Talon looked them over. This was not going to be a pleasant conversation.

"I've been keeping an eye on Aryx and Gideon ever since what happened in Taren. Remember when we had to leave the *Inn of Good Faith* rather quickly that night?"

"The night the guards crashed our party?" Pike asked.

"The same. I was the last one through the tunnel, and I didn't remember passing Gideon on my way through. When I got to the glade where the rest of us waited, I didn't see him. I thought that maybe he hadn't gone through the passage and he was still in the inn. I ducked back into the passage and waited. I couldn't see anything from that side of the bar, but I could hear a conversation that was going on. A man, whose voice I didn't recognize was talking to Aryx. He told Aryx that he was disappointed that their plan had failed, and that he expected better. Aryx apologized and said that there were just too many things about Logan and the rest of us that he couldn't control. The other man said that he was worried that we may actually make it to Shau-ling's palace, and that Aryx was to make sure that we went to Marcwell and that we would be taken care of there."

"Are you saying that Aryx is in league with Shau-ling?" Pike asked.

"I don't think it sounds like that at all, Pike," Gwydeon interjected. "It sounds to me like the person that Aryx is taking orders from is not totally aligned with Shau-ling, but has his own personal agenda for us. Maybe he wants to gain control of Logan."

"By killing him in Marcwell?" Midarin asked.

"Maybe that wasn't the intention. It could be that the attack was meant to eliminate us but leave Logan under the control of the phasia," Gwydeon responded.

"That makes sense," Logan said. "When Erdric attacked, he could have inflicted far more damage than he did, and I think that the blade of his sword was poisoned."

"That means that they might have wanted to take you alive," Pike commented.

"Possible," Talon said, "but there's more. After Aryx left the room, the strange man had a conversation with Gideon. The man made some accusations as to where Gideon's loyalties lay, and that he should look at himself before he judged Aryx."

"Are you saying that Gideon could be a traitor?" Logan asked.

"Even if he's not," Talon responded. "There's a lot more to him than he's letting us know about. I mean, how much do we really know about him, about his past?"

"Logan," Pike said quickly, "face it. Gideon sold us out in Rama, and he sold us out again in Taren. I say we kill him now, and cut our losses before another of us gets killed."

"There has to be more to it than that," Logan replied shaking his head. "Do you really expect me to kill one of the *Erieal* based on one half-heard conversation? I'm sorry. I just can't do that. As far as Rama, it was the man from Illimar who informed about us, not Gideon. If he had been part of that, Elouix would have known much more than he did."

Logan stood a frown turning his lips.

"We have to all remember that we are now responsible for the lives of six generations, and I'm not going to jeopardize that one a matter of one man's word against that of another. I know that you and I have been friends for a long time Talon, but you're just going to have to give me more than that to go on."

"There was another conversation, Logan," Talon replied a little downhearted. "I knew that this wouldn't be easy for you, so I wanted to wait until I was sure. I saw Aryx walking down towards Gideon's room, so Pike and I followed him. He looked around for a moment before he knocked, so we hid in a small side passage. He went in, and I used my powers over the wind to allow us to hear their conversation better. By the way, it's a wonderful trick. I should teach you sometime."

"Anyway," Pike said bringing the conversation back to the point, "Aryx and Gideon were talking about how the plan had to go on, but Gideon was having problems getting close to one of us. He didn't say which, but I assume that it's one of the five of us. We're the ones who are the hardest to manipulate, and the most stubborn. No offense, Midarin."

"Oh, none taken. And thank you for the compliment."

"So," Talon continued, "that may not seem like much, but there were two other things that stood out. Aryx and Gideon both alluded to something that was going to happen that night, and I can only assume that he meant the attack by the phasia."

Pike grimaced at the mention

"And the second?" Logan asked.

"Gideon spoke without an accent, and he wasn't using his powers," Pike said, "I checked. Gideon is not what he appears to be."

"You're right Pike," a strange voice said from the direction of camp.

All heads turned to see Gideon walking towards them.

"Gideon," Midarin said quickly, "what is the meaning of all this deception?"

"It's a very long story, but I suppose that I owe you that much. My name is Gideon Viruci, but I am far from an Alimidarian thief. I may have been born there, and started on the streets doing what I needed to survive, but most of my life was spent in the kingdom of Scalla. It's a kingdom under the control and protection of a phase by the name of Basille. He identified what I was early on and has been training me for years. He and Cedric have been allies for many years, but the Lion still does not realize that Basille is a phase."

"How is that possible?" Pike asked.

"Basille is not like the other members of the phasia. He isn't cruel or evil and I think that he is actually sympathetic to the cause of the *Coromor*. I can never be too sure about Basille though. He is a master of diplomacy."

"The third rule of diplomacy is to straddle the fence and keep both ears to the ground. Basille must play both sides until he figures out which has the upper hand and then he sides there," Logan commented, sure that the voice wasn't completely his own.

"Or he waits until one is weak enough that he can conquer it," Pike chimed in angrily.

"I don't think that Basille meant any ill will toward any of you, and I am certain that he has split from the rest of the phasia and is acting on his own now," Gideon said.

"So he was not complicit in the attack on Marcwell?" Gwydeon asked.

"He certainly wouldn't have been in league with Jeroch. They hate each other."

"So what was the attack that you were talking about with Aryx?"

"Basille had agents in the palace that were supposed to launch a token attack. It was supposed to make you uneasy about staying in Marcwell and more determined to follow your own path. Basille thought that if you became disenchanted with Lord Cedric, than you would be more receptive to his advice."

"You mean his control," Pike interjected.

"No," Gideon replied, "I mean advice. Basille does not want to lead you; he wants to help you vanquish Shau-ling. However, he can't do it directly because he is afraid of what might happen to him if Shau-ling were to find out. Shau-ling doesn't trust the phasia as it is, but he still does not believe that the phasia would betray him like this."

"So what are the chances of us getting some help from this Basille?" Gwydeon asked.

"He will not involve himself until the time is right, if at all," Gideon replied. "Especially as long as we are following Lord Cedric. It would not be in his best interest to reveal his identity to his old ally."

"Great," Talon said. "This is just the help that we've been looking for. Someone who wants to help but won't. How long did you intend to keep us in the dark, Gideon?"

"As long as possible," he replied. "Basille wanted you to think that you were doing well on your own, that way when the time came, you would accept his help freely."

"What about Aryx?" Logan asked. "Is he in this with you?"

"No. Aryx is working for a phase, but I'm not sure which one. He knows a lot about me, but I haven't been able to find anything out about him. In fact, I had a talk with the phase that controls him, but I couldn't recognize the voice."

"I'll tell you who it was," Pike said angrily as he stood. "Aryx was working for Erdric and Jeroch. I'm willing to bet that he had something to do with the attack on us in Taren too."

Pike's *Debuisa* was a brilliant blue. Logan didn't realize what his hot-headed friend was planning until he sprinted toward camp. Everyone followed, fearing the worst. When Logan heard the shouts rising from the camp, he knew that all hell had broken loose. When they broke through the barrier of trees and shrubs, Pike was sending a barrage of ice daggers towards an unsuspecting Aryx. The veteran warrior whirled around in time to put up the familiar barrier of lightning before the shards struck. He then dropped to a knee and channeled a bar of pure flame toward Pike. A shell of ice appeared around Pike long before the flame got there. Diana Terian, Aryx's wife and member of the previous generation's *Erieal*, rose and a net of wind flew toward Pike. Talon was quick to enter the battle and turn Diana's own weapon against her. She found herself trapped by her own powers, and there was no way for her to escape. Suddenly, a hand of pure rock erupted from the ground and grabbed Pike. Gideon jumped into the fray and shattered the hand with his powers. By this time, Lord Cedric was up. He thrust his hands towards the second generation's *Erieal*, and they rose into the air, rendered powerless by the unbridled powers of the *Coromor*. Suddenly, a force inside of Logan exploded. His eyes closed of their own accord and when he looked into that place where the bands of power dwelled, Logan found that around each of the bands was a thin outline of blackness. Something about these new lines of force called to him. He had never seen the lines before, and when Logan touched the slimy black coating on the bands of power, he felt them pull away. It felt natural, as though it was something he should have been doing all along. Within a matter of seconds, Logan had fashioned the lost black string that the Elder had spoken about. When he opened my eyes, he could still see the black string, even though my eyes were open. In Logan's mind's eye, he broke the black string in half and held the two halves so that they could not touch. The string writhed and pulsated in his hands, trying to break free of his grip to make itself whole once more. Suddenly, Pike and the others dropped from where they had been suspended, and Lord Cedric fell to the ground. Arathorn ran over to defend his lord, his sword held ready to counterattack at a moment's notice.

"Cedric, are you all right?"

"I'm fine old friend, but something has robbed me of my powers."

"Not something Cedric," Logan said with an echo of power and pride in his voice, "someone. I have found the source of our powers, and with a thought I can turn them off. It does not take a use of my powers to do this; I draw on the *Erieal* for my strength. Don't bother trying to undo what I have done, it won't work."

"What are you doing, Logan?" Cedric asked in shock.

"I am dispensing justice Cedric. I have been told of a plot to destroy us and everything that we stand for. I have also found out that the very man who is at the heart of this plot is none other than Aryx Terian."

"So what would you have me do, Logan?" Cedric asked. "Do you want us to stand by as you act as judge and executioner? I have not heard these charges that you have levied, and I want to know from what sources you have obtained this evidence."

"I am the source of this evidence," Gideon said in his natural clear voice. "I have been conspiring with Aryx for many weeks now, and I know for a fact that he is in league with the same phasia that attacked us in Marcwell."

"And who are you in league with, traitor?" Arathorn said as he stood.

"Gideon has told us everything that he has done since he has been with my company, and I have placed my faith in him," Logan replied.

"I have not heard his defense, Logan," Cedric said as he fought to stand. "If I am to value your justice, I will hear them from Gideon's mouth now."

"We are not in your court, Cedric," Pike challenged. "Logan is the Coromor of this generation and he is the law here. What he values to be just is what will be done."

"Then you're a fool to follow such a tyrant," Diana replied. "My husband is not a traitor. He could not possibly have been involved with the attack on Marcwell. He is one of the greatest heroes to take up arms against the Shadows, and he has done more in his lifetime than the group of you could do in yours."

"Ask him," Midarin said as she raised her bow. "Let him answer these charges with his own mouth."

Aryx stood and drew his sword.

"I will only answer these charges only with my steel and my powers. There is no other way that I will receive justice."

"He incriminates himself with his actions," Gideon interjected. "Any word that is not a denial is surely an acceptance of fact."

"Are you afraid to duel, traitor?" Aryx goaded.

"Never," Gideon growled.

The situation was tense. Logan could feel Cedric's powers growing, no matter how he tried to keep them contained. All of the *Debuisa* were the colors of the primal forces, and it was clear that all-out war could start at any moment.

"You seem to be the one in control here, Logan," Cedric said, "but at what cost? You have become the very thing that you are fighting. Power has made you a tyrant, interested in dispensing your own brand of justice without thinking of the consequences. You attack without provocation. You speak in half-truths and hear-say."

"You dare talk to me about manipulating and dispensing justice without a thought?" the being inside of Logan thundered. "What have you done since the beginning of this quest? You have pulled my strings and done whatever you pleased without even thinking to ask my opinion or how I felt."

"I did what I thought was best. I have been through this before and..."

"And what?" Logan interrupted, his voice harder than steel. "You may have been through this before, but this is my life, and you should have respect for that. You are not putting your life on the line every day. You don't have thousands of blood-thirsty monsters chasing after you. You don't have to deal with the death of your friends every single day, but I do. Even when you were the Coromor you didn't face the kind of single-minded destruction that we have seen every step of the way. Your friend there cost me the lives of two of my friends, maybe more. Maybe he is to blame for all of your subjects who are lying dead in the ruins of your capitol."

Cedric paled; the sheer loss of life a raw nerve.

"You've said yourself that you had your suspicions about this man when he was first brought to you, and from what I've seen and heard, those fears have never been quelled. Don't speak to me about what you think is best. I believe that my course of action is best, and I say that the duel will be fought."

Gideon looked over at Logan for a moment and then nodded. He and Aryx both stepped forward and raised their swords.

"If either of you even thinks about using your powers, I'll know. The second that one of you reaches for that band of power, I will strike you down without a word."

There was not another word that escaped anyone's lips as the two men rounded each other. Aryx struck out first, but Gideon parried the lazy and uncharacteristically weak blow and quickly buried his sword deep into Aryx's gut. Aryx fell and lay on the ground dying. The blood oozing from his stomach was not red. A yellow pasty substance leaked from the wound, and the form that was Aryx dissolved into nothing. Not even his *Debuisa* remained.

"What the hell was that!" Diana screamed.

"A changeling," Talos answered gravely. "Shau-ling must have molded the changeling to look and act like Aryx, and then merged it with the powers of a phase in order to duplicate Aryx's powers. There's no telling when the switch took place, but it has happened."

"How long have you been dealing with Aryx, Gideon?" Cedric asked.

"I had correspondence with him for about a month before the quest started, but Aryx didn't say anything to me about his darker plans until that night in Falke."

"After the meeting with Asperon Thorne," Pike said quickly. "He would have been ripe for the picking then."

"That's probably when the switch was made," Cedric said softly. "There is one way that we can know for sure, but I think it's safe to assume that Aryx is dead. He would have been too dangerous to try to take captive."

Diana's tears fell from her eyes, and she tried to hold the sobs of sorrow back. Elwyne went to her and held her as she mourned the loss of her long-time husband. Arathorn was also quickly at his sister's side, but she seemed too far gone to hear any comforting words. Feeling shame fill him, Logan released the black string of power and sank down onto the ground.

He had been right, but wrong all in the same breath. He felt terrible and still the feelings of hate and resentment churned in his gut.

"We will make our way to Pramine," Cedric said slowly, "there are men there who are in communication with the Other Side. If he has not arrived there, then there is still hope. I would ask you to please continue to Barer, but I would understand if you do not wish to. I am sorry that I did not believe the charges that you levied, but you must understand my feelings."

"I do, Cedric," Logan replied. "We will go on to Barer, and I hope that we can meet again soon. There are too many questions that need answering, and too many things that went wrong that didn't need to if we had been honest with one another from the start. Secrets are killing us, and so are the half-truths that have been flying. It's probably better that we're going our separate ways. You can fight the war your way, and we can fight it ours."

Cedric started to say something, but Logan turned away from the rest of them and walked back toward the camp. Elwyne left Diana's side and hurried quickly to Logan's side and too his hand. Cedric and Diana's words had shaken Logan. He was beginning to worry about what he was becoming and the more the being inside of him showed itself, it seemed more and more unpredictable and volatile. Was he becoming the power hungry tyrant that Cedric said he was, or was it something far worse? Was this the way that the phasia were? Was Shau-ling beginning to win control of Logan's mind? As they rode on toward Barer, Logan's thoughts swirled even more, and he could not help but entertain the darkest and disturbing possibilities.

Dark Battles

It was never an envied position to be in the doghouse of an angry Shau-ling, but Warron and Zarsi had never been in this deep, and pain would soon take on a new meaning. Because of them, all of the phasia, except of course for Jeroch, had been banned from entering the palace, except by invitation. Moreover, there was the overgrown lap dog that had been assigned to escort them out of their own home. First Shau-ling had insulted the phasia by redesigning both the Shadowwalkers and the Kalbraks, but then he had to make this Nightwing thing their leader. The man that the phasia had fought so hard against in two lifetimes was at the core of this new creature, and now suddenly was in the good graces of their lord and master. White Lightning was now supposed to be accepted as their ally and their brother. It was an almost impossible cross to bear. White Lightning had sealed the fate of so many creatures that had served the Shadows over the years, and he had even committed the murder of several powerful phasia. Now though, the entire Brotherhood was to forgive all past sins and transgressions, accepting the fact that he had been forged anew in the cleansing fires of the Blaze.

Nightwing escorted the two phasia out of the Hall of Terrors and into a receiving area that lay just beyond it.

"NOW," Nightwing said in a clearly metallic voice, "MASTER HAS DECREED TWO THINGS FOR YOU PITIFUL PHASIA. IT HAS

BEEN DECIDED THAT YOU ARE MORE VALUABLE TO SHAU-LING THAN HE FIRST REALIZED AND HE ACTED MORE IN ANGER THAN IN RATIONAL THOUGHT. WARRON, YOU ARE TO RETURN TO YOUR KINGDOM AND AWAIT YOUR BROTHER BASILLE. MASTER SEEMS TO THINK THAT HE WILL COME TO YOU IN AN ATTEMPT TO SECURE YOUR ASSISTANCE IN SAURN'S SCHEMES. MASTER HAS DECREED THAT YOU ARE TO KILL BASILLE AND BRING HIS BROKEN BODY BACK HERE. YOU APPARENTLY HAVE THE ABILITY TO BLOCK THE POWER ABSORPTION FOR A LIMITED TIME, AND MASTER HAS A USE FOR BASILLE'S STRING OR POWER. A PLAYTHING HE WOULD LIKE TO TEST, BUT WITHOUT THE POWERS OF A FULL MEMBER OF THE PHASIA, THERE IS NO LIFE IN HIS CREATION. HE GLADLY WOULD HAVE SACRIFICED ONE OF YOU, BUT APPARENTLY YOU TWO HAVE NOT MADE YOURSELVES EXPENDABLE YET. DO YOU UNDERSTAND MASTER'S ORDERS WARRON?"

"I do understand them, Nightwing. But I would have liked it far more if Master would have allowed me to correct the mistake he made by introducing an abomination like you into our ranks. I am warning you here and now that if you ever set your metallic, Lion-loving feet inside the Council, I will personally show master the gravity of his error in making you."

"AN IDLE THREAT, WARRON. EVEN YOU ARE NOT POWERFUL ENOUGH TO DEFEAT THREE PHASIA AT ONCE, AND I HAVE THEIR POWER PLUS THOSE OF A MEMBER OF THE *ERIEAL*. YOU WOULDN'T STAND A CHANCE, BUT I DO INVITE YOU TO TRY. PERHAPS SHAU-LING WOULD WELCOME BEING RID OF THE PIG. NOW, GO."

Warron stared into the red slits that served as Nightwing's eyes. His fists were balled so tightly that his knuckles were white and even the dulled nails on his fingers had dug deeply into the flesh of his palm and drew blood. Keeping his temper barely in check, he channeled a simple flow of power, created a portal, and then stepped through. Zarsi now turned his attention toward the monstrosity that stood before him. Fear had wound its way into the silent heart of the scarred phase, and Zarsi inwardly wondered if the sacrifice that Nightwing described to Warron needed the lives of two phasia rather than one. Zarsi was a powerful member of the phasia, and probably had the best command of the gifts granted to him by the Blaze. However, even he would not be a match for the combined powers that Nightwing boasted. If the winged beast had intended to kill Zarsi, it would not be much of a battle, and Nightwing could crush the life out of him with merely a thought.

"What does master have in store for me, Nightwing?"

"YOU HAVE EVERY RIGHT TO BE AFRAID, ZARSI," Nightwing said in that eerie Voice-like tone, "BUT YOU NEED NOT WORRY THAT I WILL BE THE CAUSE OF YOUR DEATH. MASTER HAS YET TO ORDER YOUR TERMINATION. HE HAS HOWEVER SEEN FIT TO APPOINT YOU TO LEAD ON OF HIS ARMIES. YOU AND FARAX WILL COMMAND A GROUP OF JERESEI, STONE, AND SOME OF THE NEWLY REDESIGNED SHADOWWALKERS AND KALBRAKS. YOU WILL LEAD THIS ARMY AGAINST SAURN'S PHANTOM ARMY IN THE FIELDS OF VESI GRATH. WHEN SAURN MADE HIS CHALLENGE, HE SPECIFICALLY REQUESTED YOU AND FARAX. AN OLD GRUDGE IS FUELING THE CHALLENGE I ASSUME. YOUR ORDERS ARE TO PROCEED TO KANDOR AND TO RELAY THESE ORDERS TO FARAX. THEN, THE TWO OF YOU WILL PROCEED TO THE FIELDS OF VESI GRATH WHERE YOU WILL MEET YOUR ARMY. DO EVERYTHING IN YOUR POWER TO ENSURE THAT SAURN AND HIS ARMY ARE VANQUISHED. DO YOU UNDERSTAND THE ORDERS THAT HAVE BEEN GIVEN TO YOU ZARSI?"

"Yes I do, Nightwing," he responded fearfully, "I hope that we are never on the opposite sides of Master's favor."

"IT'S MUCH TOO LATE FOR THAT SENTIMENT MY DEAR BROTHER. THE PHASIA HAVE BECOME OBSOLETE. YOU AND I BOTH KNOW THAT IF MASTER ORDERED ME TO EXTERMINATE ANY ONE OF YOU, I COULD DO IT WITHOUT HESITATION OR DIFFICULTY. I KNOW WHAT EACH AND

EVERY ONE OF YOU ARE CAPABLE OF, AND THERE IS NO WAY THAT YOU CAN HARM ME WITH YOUR PATHETIC POWERS. IF IT WERE EVER TO COME DOWN BETWEEN THE PHASIA AND THE BEING THAT I HAVE BECOME, I WOULD WIN WITHOUT QUESTION. SHAU-LING HAS SEEN THE MISTAKE THAT HE MADE WITH THE PHASIA, AND HE HAS LEARNED THAT HIS ORIGINAL MOULD WAS SUPERIOR. THE FLAME AND I ARE MORE KINDRED THAN I AM TO YOU PHASIA. SOON ENOUGH, HE AND I WILL HOLD ALL OF SHAU-LING'S FAVOR AND THE PHASIA WILL BE EXTINCT. PERSONALLY, I WOULD TAKE GREAT JOY IF MASTER WOULD ORDER ME TO DESTROY JEROCH FOR HIS AMUSEMENT, AND I WOULD DO SO WITHOUT REGRET. IT WOULD BE ENJOYABLE."

"We've all thought that way Nightwing, and even though times have changed, at least for now, Jeroch still holds most of Shau-ling's favor. You would be a fool to think that Shau-ling would ever order the death of the first-born of the phasia."

Zarsi did not wait for a response before he created and stepped through a portal. He was happy to get out of the situation alive, and the last thing he wanted to do was to pick a fight with his much larger and more powerful sibling. Nightwing looked on for a moment as the swirling blue portal closed behind Zarsi. The words stung him for some odd reason. With a thought the wings extended away from his back and he began to fly through the palace, looking for anyone who did not belong. As he glided upon the still air, turbulent thoughts ran through his head, damning all that he had become.

Lord Cedric stood in the middle of that inn looking more like a regular soldier than a king. When Lady Erika finally introduced him to me, I thought I was going to die. He made me a knight on the spot, and that was because Lady Erika trusted me with her life. They had both placed their faith in me, but I failed. I was unable to protect her during the wedding, and for that I should never be forgiven. Now, I have betrayed their trust even more than I had in the past. The foe that I once fought with all of my power has now become the master that I embrace with all my heart. What must have changed in my heart to allow this heinous act to have occurred? Was I ever truly the hero that I was made out to be, or had I just been hiding from my true nature?

Nightwing flew fast and hard down the winding passages, trying to outrun the memories and the thoughts of betrayal and hatred. When he caught a hint of motion out of the corner of his eye, he stopped quickly and hovered in the middle of a large chamber.

"WHO IS THERE?"

Nothing answered for a long moment. Moments later, several Jeresei emerged from the shadows and leapt at Nightwing all at once. Hundreds of claws reached out for him, some tearing at the metallic skin while others stabbed toward the more vital organs, like his heart and brain. Nightwing collapsed under the weight of all the Jeresei that swarmed him, and he reflexively covered his eyes as more and more of the long sharp talons stabbed down at him, ripping at the hard metallic shell that protected the soft flesh beneath. Suddenly, the echo of a familiar feeling wrenched through his body as one of the Jeresei's talons penetrated the armor and sunk into the vulnerable skin. Nightwing could feel the thick blue blood spurting out from around the talon that skewered him. The blood squeezed through the hole in the armor and fell to the cold stone floor in globs. Suddenly, the pain hit. Nightwing screamed in agony and then forced his arms out from his body with all of his might. Jeresei scattered everywhere, slightly surprised by the strength of their adversary. Though shocked, the Jeresei recovered quickly, a credit to their design, and leapt at Nightwing again. He rose and batted his wings in the air, pushing the Jeresei away from him. One of the red skinned beasts had managed to get behind him, but as it leaped, the whisper-thin tail darted up and wrapped itself around the throat of the beast. Nightwing spun, and as the tail constricted around the neck of its victim, the head dropped to the ground, and the body flew toward its brethren. Another Jeresei leapt at Nightwing, but it was caught by the face in one of the massive clawed hands. Nightwing sank his black claws into the sides of the Jeresei's face and then crushed its skull like it was nothing. The sickening sound of the Jeresei's skull breaking resounded through the chamber, and some of the Jeresei appeared to lose some of their ferocity.

CHAPTER 15

"YOU ARE FOOLS TO BELIEVE THAT YOU CAN HARM ME. SUCH AN ATTACK WILL ONLY RESULT IN YOUR DEATHS. DID YOU THINK YOU WOULD FIND ME EASY PREY?"

None of the Jeresei responded for a moment and then suddenly, they all leapt at him again. Nightwing was more prepared for this assault however, and when his wings extended in a fraction of a second, he was able to elevate over the diving Jeresei. He hovered near the ceiling of the chamber for a moment and then opened his mouth and let the fires of the Blaze rain down on his adversaries. Many of them burned in the white flames that spewed from Nightwing's open mouth, but many of them were able to take shelter in the shadows again, as they had seen similar tactics employed by Nightwing's predecessors. One of the Jeresei climbed up the wall in the shadows behind Nightwing, and then leapt onto his back. The Jeresei punched all five of his long talons into Nightwing's side, and began to rip away pieces of the metallic skin. Nightwing spun to the side, more out of reflex to the pain than anything, and the Jeresei dangled from his side, the talons still buried deeply in Nightwing's side. Suddenly, the talons gave way, and the Jeresei fell. Nightwing swooped underneath him and the bladed wings caught the body of the Jeresei in their rapid movements, filling the room with sounds of tearing muscle and cartilage. As Nightwing flew lower through the room, more of the Jeresei emerged from the Shadows and attempted to strike. The feint had worked, and Nightwing sped through the chamber, quickly snapping necks and ripping off heads where it was convenient. Finally, as he looked around the room, he noticed that none were left standing, but many crawled on the ground, bleeding profusely from gaping wounds left by severed appendages. Nightwing hovered again just above the ground and looked on for a moment before continuing his sweep of the palace. He would leave the unfortunate few alive, and those that did not bleed to death would take word of their failure back to the one who put them on their suicidal path.

Many thoughts still swirled through his mind as he flew faster and faster down the darkened corridors. He thought that if he flew fast enough, he wouldn't have to remember. Suddenly one thought entered his mind that caused him to come to a dead halt in mid-air.

Diana.

The thought of his wife swirled in his mind. He could remember pieces of conversations, whispered words of love, and talks about the future as they lay together in the middle of the night. He could remember his last words to her, and he could see the scene of their wedding inside his mind. Then he realized the one sensation that he would lack for the rest of his existence, the one thing that would haunt him for the rest of his days. Shau-ling had dedicated his life to remorseless cruelty, and so in designing his creatures it was possible that the need for tear ducts was not at all necessary. As Nightwing hovered above the ground, lost in the torrents of memory and sorrow, he vaguely remembered what it felt like to cry, and when he tried, nothing. He then realized the totality of his prison, and that he would never again know the feeling of a tear falling down his cheek, and he would never know the relief of the pain that his tears used to bring. He was trapped; trapped by pain and sorrow, forever.

I remember the nights with her, the man that used to be Aryx Terian thought as he hovered there in the dark passage, *when we would just lay there in bed together taking about how much we loved each other. I can still see the look in her eyes and feel her up against me. When Cedric talked to me before the wedding, he said something that never made sense until now. He said 'I am happy that you are in love Aryx, I hope that it guides you for the rest of your days. I am both too old and too young to be in love again my friend. Too old to know that my fears are just the phantoms of reality and merely imagined by a weak doleful mind, but also too young to not be terrified by them. I hope that you never find yourself in that situation my friend, and that Diana will keep you happy and content in her love for the rest of your days. It is a horrible thing to have to live without a woman that you love Aryx, especially when you know you could have done something to keep her with you.' I understand those words now Cedric, and now that I realize that I will never be able to be with her again, I hurt all the more. But my sorrow was not the same as yours my old friend. Your love was stolen away from you and you can never see her again. Mine though still lives, but to her, I suppose that I am to be considered dead. I only wish that I could see her one more time to tell her that I am sorry and that I still love her even after all that has happened. But in the end, I am doing this for her. I am doing this so that she has a future.*

"Nightwing."

Master calls. I must go to him.

Nightwing shook the thoughts out of his head and then flew back toward the Hall of Terrors. It seemed so empty without the lights and the creatures, but only the Aryx of the past had been there and somewhere in the memories of the phasia that had been melded into his genetic makeup, he remembered the Hall as it was. The door at the end of the Hall was standing wide open, and as Nightwing flew through he was face to face with Shau-ling and hundreds of Kalbraks.

"I am pleased with your abilities Nightwing," Shau-ling said coldly, "and your first test has been passed well enough. However, I was disappointed when you were damaged by the Jeresei. I would have thought that you would have been more prepared for that. Your mind must have been wandering."

"I AM SORRY IF I HAVE DISPLEASED YOU MY LORD SHAU-LING, BUT I WAS NOT EXPECTING THE JERESEI TO ATTACK. I UNDERESTIMATED THEIR POWER AND THEIR FIGHTING PROWESS, AND I ALLOWED MYSELF TO BE HURT."

"While ordinarily I would have no time for such weakness, I will accept your apology my humble servant. But I must know how vulnerable you are and how much more work needs to be done to your armor. You are not to return this attack Nightwing, and if you begin to die, pray that I recognize it. Kalbraks, attack."

The lizard-skinned Kalbraks approached slowly, their three foot long talons nearly scraping the ground as they walked. Suddenly, the first one struck out and put a long scratch into Nightwing's armor. More and more clawed and sliced at him before huge pieces of the armor began to flake away, revealing the human skin underneath. Nightwing screamed out in pain and then fell to the ground, still more of the mindless Kalbraks advancing and drawing red human blood with their talons.

"Stop my servants," Shau-ling ordered.

The Kalbraks moved away as slowly as they had attacked, and Shau-ling approached the broken form of his creation. Nightwing looked up at him through a huge rip that ran from the top of his head, through his right eye, and down to his chin. Shau-ling looked through the wound and saw the human eye peering through it.

"I thought that would be the case my servant."

Shau-ling raised his hands toward Nightwing, and the metal that had once served for his skin disappeared, leaving the naked body of Aryx Terian lying on the floor of the royal chamber. Seconds later, clothing appeared around Aryx, and one of the Kalbraks helped him to his feet.

"When the Elder and his kind made the *Debuisa* that I used for your skin, there was apparently not enough to be stretched to that extreme and remain its original strength. I must endeavor to do better this time. Follow me, my child."

Aryx stood straight and followed his new master to the foot of the throne and then through the swirling portal that led to the Council. Deep in the back of his mind, new thoughts were forming, and Aryx could not help but smile.

So, the process can be reversed. If Shau-ling can do it, that must mean that some of the phasia also have the power but on a limited scale. If a phase were to bond with the powers of the Coromor *then there could be a chance that they could change me back if it came down to it. But do I really want out? If the world does fall to Shau-ling, would I be better off under his control than I would be out on my own? How is it possible that I can think of escape now and not earlier? Perhaps it is the metal and the pieces of me that were Shadowwalker that were Bonded under Shau-ling's control.*

His thoughts trailed off for another moment or two before they arrived in the Council. From the instant they arrived, Aryx knew that he was not alone. He looked around and found that Jeroch was also in the Council, and near him laid a pile of strangely colored metal.

"The deed has been done my lord," Jeroch said proudly. "Marcwell fell to our forces after a limited battle, and the armory that held the Elder and the metal for the *Debuisa* has been taken."

"And what of the Elder?" Shau-ling asked.

"They have been disposed of my lord."

"Good. However, there does not appear to be as much metal here as I had anticipated. With the test that I have just witnessed, I do believe that there will only be enough metal to recreate Nightwing. I was hoping that I would be able to create an army of Nightwings, but it appears that I was mistaken this once."

"Is there no way that we can recreate this metal my lord?" Jeroch asked.

"No," Shau-ling replied. "This metal only occurred in the caves where the Elder were born. It was a strange after-birth that sustained them before they were cast into the molten metal. After that, the metal was no longer needed, so it was usually cast out. It was by accident that they eventually discovered the properties that made this metal so valuable. Now that all of the Elder are dead, there will be no more metal ever produced, and for that I am both thankful and disappointed. It is very true to say that this metal lives, and by forming it, the life energy is transferred from the metal to the wearer, and for that reason it can harness the power of the *Erieal*. I am afraid that if I used it on anything but an *Erieal* or a phase, that it would be nothing more that exquisite yet expensive decoration. I applaud your efforts Jeroch, and you are free to roam the palace as you wish. You are the only member of the phasia that still holds my favor, and I would advise you to be wary of your brethren. They would like to see you dead long before me, and I believe that it would make their lives a bit easier. Come Nightwing."

Aryx followed quickly as Shau-ling made his way to the inner circle of the Council, but felt Jeroch's resentful gaze burning hole in him. Shau-ling raised his hands toward the metal, and it floated toward him and came to a rest right at the edge of the center circle. Shau-ling stood well back from the center, near the edge of the perimeter that contained it.

"Step into the Circle of Power my young friend," Shau-ling commanded.

Aryx looked at him for a moment before he obeyed, but he walked quickly to the center and waited. When his recreation had taken place earlier, he was not conscious, but now he knew that he would feel the full force of the Blaze. Shau-ling closed his eyes and the outer and inner circles that they stood on began to lower. Seconds later they reached a lower level with clear walls that created a barrier around them. In Aryx's mind, he knew that going down should have brought them to the floor of the ocean, and that he should have been able to see water outside of the glass-like walls. However, instead of the waters crashing softly against the walls, all Aryx could see the white-hot fires licking up against the clear walls. Shau-ling was mumbling something under his breath, and Aryx began to slowly rise off the circular platform. He looked down almost reflexively, and saw the circular platform below him retract. In that instant, green flames erupted from the floor, and Aryx was engulfed by the column of heat-less green.

It was like being immersed in pure joy and rapture. It was as if all the worldly pleasures had been concentrated into this single beam of light and fire stored here, wherever here was. Aryx looked around and saw that the sheets of metal had also risen into the fires, and they had begun to surround him. The metal started to mold to his legs first, and he could feel his skin searing and burning as the metal touched flesh, but the pain was immediately doused by this feeling of overall joy. The metal bonded slowly, and as it passed his waist, he notice the tail begin to grow slowly out from behind him, and it whipped around in the flame, reflecting the green light in all its glory. His arms were soon coated, and then he saw the black metal talons extending from the tips of his fingers. Another sheet of metal had risen toward him, and it approached his face slowly. This burning sensation was the worst of all that Aryx had felt, but unlike the others, this burning was not extinguished. He could feel the metal bend and pull at his skin, but the searing heat never lessened. Pain racked his body as the metal horns extended from his head, and his eyes were covered with the thin red film. Aryx could not help but cry out in pain as the process continued, but suddenly all the pain stopped, and he felt nothing, not even the joy of the Blaze.

He felt himself being lowered. When Aryx opened his eyes again, his vision had returned and he saw his master looking at him with a gleeful face.

"Marvelous my dear Nightwing," Shau-ling said proudly. "You are now going to be my most powerful creation. I have made improvements on your design, and I must say that I am truly impressed with myself. You are still able to draw on the Blaze and the powers of the phasia, but now you can direct all of your powers as a member of the *Erieal* through your skin and release it as a single burst. Because you have been melded with the powers of the phasia, you also have a limited ability to draw on the other primal forces. While you will always be able to draw on Fire with the most power, you can now touch Water, Wind, and Earth. You now have powers that my phasia will only dream of, and they will envy you for it. However, you do have one limitation this time around. Because of the depth that you must draw on the powers of the Blaze, you must return to the Council every seven days in order to replenish your powers. If you do not, you will become as vulnerable as the rest of my phasia."

"I UNDERSTAND MY LORD," Nightwing responded without hesitation. "YOU SAID THAT YOU HAVE A MISSION FOR ME TO ACCOMPLISH?"

"Yes my young apprentice. You are to travel to a town by the name of Barer and then find the Castle of Nevi. There you will find one of my traitorous phasia, Lord Grawn. I fear that you will not be in time to prevent him from helping the *Coromor*, but it appears that he had found a way to shadow himself from my foresight. When you find him, kill him."

"I UNDERSTAND COMPLETELY MY LORD SHAU-LING. CONSIDER GRAWN DEAD."

Chapter XVI

A Tangled Web

Barer. From Cedric's descriptions, Logan thought that Barer was a small, if not insignificant town in the middle of nowhere. He couldn't have been much more wrong when he first got a glimpse of it from atop a large hill. There was a lot of activity in the town, and there were many forces of men that went in and out of town in the minutes that the group stood looking down upon the town. In the distance, Logan could see what looked like a castle, but there was no way that he could be sure. Gideon dismounted and walked up to where Logan stood.

"Do ye think that we'll find da help dat Lord Cedric was talkin' bout? I would think dat dere would be more trouble down dere den we could usually expect."

"You're using your accent again, Gideon. Why?"

"I got rather used ta it, me lord. If ye don't mind too much, I'd like ta continue usin' it."

Logan looked back at him for a moment and sighed.

"Why did you do it, Gideon? I thought that there was a trust between all of us, and that if there was anything, you could tell me."

"Logan," he responded, the accent still thick in his voice, "when I joined yer force, I joined because ye and yer friends saved me life. For dat I will be forever grateful. But I made a promise ta da man who helped me to find the true path."

Gideon swallowed hard.

"I was a thief in Alimidar, and I did me best ta make me living on da streets. Lord Basille caught me one day when I was tryin' ta pick one of his guard's pockets. He took me in when I was barely ten and taught me everyt'ing dat I could ever want ta know."

Gideon spread his hands and his voice changed to something much softer and pleading.

"He is truly a wise man. He once had a child of his own, Logan, but one of da other phasia killed both da child and Basille's wife. So, since dat day, Basille has been taking in orphan children. He either gives dem to families dat can't have children of dere own, or he keeps dem in his own palace, like he did wit' me. He cares fer his people, and dey love him fer his kindness."

"So," Logan said trying to understand, "you're telling me that he's like a father to you."

"He's more of a father dan I've ever had, Logan. My father threw me out into da streets when I was five, and I learned the art of thievery den. I barely stayed alive for da first few years, but eventually I was making a pretty good living. Basille took me in and taught me how to be a member of da court. He even taught me how ta speak without da accent. I've kinda sunk back into it since I've been with ye and yer friends."

"That's a nice story, Gideon," Elwyne said as she approached them. "Logan and I have been talking since we left Marcwell, and he and I are both glad that I chose you for my protector. It makes things on Logan a bit easier and he doesn't have to worry about me too much."

"And if you still feel you're up to it," Logan continued, "I would really appreciate it if you would stay on as her protector. The attack on Marcwell shows us that nowhere is safe, and if you were trained by a member of the phasia, then you have better control over your powers and are in a better position to protect her."

He looked shocked. Logan didn't think that Gideon ever really expected to be trusted again, given the history the group had with betrayal. But the difference with Gideon's betrayal was the fact that its motivations were never to hurt anyone, even when his hand was forced into something unsavory. What Gideon had done was contemptible at best, and even though his ultimate intention was to help, what he had done should have been inexcusable. Logan knew that they needed Gideon to succeed in the quest, but it was something more than that. Logan knew that he personally needed Gideon. His value was clear, even if he wasn't a member of the *Erieal.*

"I would be glad ta serve as da Lady Dragon's protector me lord. Would ye like me ta keep da accent, or would ye rather me talk in a civilized voice?"

"Elwyne?" Logan asked turning toward her. "He's your protector, you make the decision."

"I like the accent," she said quickly, "there are far too many of us that seem civilized."

"By yer word," came his curt response with a deep bow.

"Now," Logan said as he straightened, "let's get down to Barer and see what help we can find."

There were smiles all around for the first time in a long time as they rode into the town of Barer. It was so strange to see a town wholly unaffected by the war with Shau-ling. Logan would not have been too surprised if these people had never even heard of Shau-ling. The stables were nearly full with the horses of other travelers, and apparently Barer had become a sort of safe haven from the tyranny of the Shadows. Logan couldn't think of a more welcome place than such a haven. He could only hope that his presence did not bring an abrupt end to the happiness that reigned in Barer.

"Gideon, Midarin, Talos, have any of you been here before?"

"I've been here before, me lord," Gideon answered. "Dere is a nice bar at the end of dat street. I suspect dat we'll find somewhere dere who's willing ta help us."

"I remember the last time that you selected a bar for us, Gideon," Pike interjected, more as a commentary than as an actual objection, "you set us down in the middle of a bar fight that eventually pitted us against the entire Army of Illimar."

"Hey," Gideon responded, "we won didn't we? Now quit yer grippin' and follow me."

The witty repartee was back, and Logan was happy that some of the levity had returned, at least for the moment. One of the things that Talon, Pike, and Logan had always shared was the slight cuts and personal comedy in words and actions. They kept each other on their toes, mentally speaking, and it also helped to solidify their friendship. For a time, Elwyne and Eldar had engaged themselves in this game, but their involvement came and went as did the relationships inside the circle. Gwydeon was the best at the game though. It seemed that he always had the right words about him. He was a master of words where the rest of us were just amateurs. Women should have been falling all over him with just a word, but for some reason, Gwydeon always clamed up around girls, at least until Midarin had come into his life.

Gideon led the group down a long winding street, one dotted by many common-looking shops and taverns. Gwydeon, Midarin, and Elwyne were wrapped in some sort of conversation, apparently the one they had tried to start in Marcwell. Logan walked slightly ahead of them, trying not to make it obvious that he didn't want to be privy to their words. Pike and Talon traded jokes back and forth, with a wide-eyed Alexander laughing along. Logan sure that the boy didn't understand most of the punch-lines, but Alexander was surprisingly knowledgeable for his age.

"How are you faring, my Lord Dragon?" Talos said as he walked up beside Logan.

Logan found himself shocked to hear words from Talos. He had been one of the anomalies of this quest. His people, the Moridon, had been all but exterminated by Shau-ling in the last generation, and regardless of the tragedy, he was ready to give his life for the same cause. Before the quest, Logan had never heard of the Moridon, even though one of the heroes of the War of the Lion was among the remaining members of the tribe. Still, Talos had remained a mystery.

"I'm fine Talos. I was however just thinking that you have never really talked much to anyone here. I'm wondering perhaps . . ."

"That I might be a spy trying to win your confidence?"

"Or trying to destroy us from within. I don't mean to make wild accusations about people who are supposed to be my friends but . . ."

"I understand, Logan," he interjected. "Do not worry about hurting my feelings; I am far too old for that. When I was just barely eighty, my people gave their lives to a cause that they believed in. The mighty Lord Arathorn that you only met in passing started us on this path. One day, he returned from a mighty adventure, and with him, he brought a boy not much older than you. At the time, there was hundreds of our kind living in small groups around the town of Trelon. The lord of Trelon was a nice man who let us live there so long as we served to protect the town. At the time, the only recognized ruler was Lord Cedric in Marcwell, but no one had ever seen him. You can imagine our shock when the boy who came to us was this same Lord Cedric. At the time, there were only rumors about the powers of Shau-ling, but we only had the prophecies to go on. The leaders of the tribe decided that they would assist Lord Cedric. I however was still in training, so I was left behind with a handful of others to keep an eye on the city of Trelon."

"You say that you were eighty then? How could you still be in training at that age?"

"We of the Moridon are on a different calendar than the rest of the world. Now, seven years later, I am one hundred years old. To become a master mage, or a Herlae, you must be at least ninety. When the rest of the Moridon were killed in the raid on Shau-ling's palace, I became the last of the Herlae, and along with Mailock, the last of the Moridon. I am just glad that I have a chance to earn the same honorable end as my brethren."

"You actually want to die?" Logan asked.

"I am not afraid of it, Logan. The Moridon are a warrior people. We believe it is better to live fast, fight hard, and have an honorable ending, much like everything else in nature. We begin the fight of life in this way, almost defenseless. If we do not learn to adapt and survive, then nature has ordained that we were not supposed to survive. The Moridon had lived for years on that system of beliefs, and so we believed that we were ordained to succeed because of the way that we had always lived. If I have the opportunity to give my life to save yours or to save the life of one of the other members of this party, than I will for the greater good of the world. Make no mistake, even though I am your friend, I will do what I wish. My errand is one of the spirit and not of the flesh, and in battle I will act of my own accord. It is the way the Moridon have lived since the time of the Hand of the Light, and it is how they will live until the last of our number draws our last breath."

"I appreciate your honesty, Talos," Logan said, more out of kindness than out of truth. "I wish that you felt differently about your role in this quest, but you have your own beliefs, and I have no right to try and change them."

He nodded and continued forward. Logan stopped for a moment to wait for Elwyne, Gwydeon, and Midarin. Elwyne could tell that something was bothering Logan, and it was usually her first prerogative to ask him about it instead of waiting on him to open up in his own time. This time though, it was as if she already knew what had been said.

"Do you think he'll fight, Logan?" she asked quietly.

"Yes," Logan said still watching him, "he'll fight. But if you're asking me what will come first, the quest or his beliefs, I can't be sure."

"That's something that we all have to deal with Logan," Midarin replied. "All of us fight for our own reasons, and revenge is a powerful motivation, even if ultimately it's self-defeating."

Her comments struck a chord in Logan's heart, and he couldn't help but shift his glance not to Talon, but to Pike. Her words were meant to be encouraging, but it forced Logan into much more introspective thoughts.

He knew that she had a lot of reasons for remaining with the party, but part of him wondered if love for a man she had known for so little time was enough. It was strange to find that he was now questioning everyone's loyalty, but in light of what had happened with Aryx, Jasmen, and Gideon, Logan found it hard not to be a bit skeptical. Inwardly he hoped that the real Aryx was still alive, but something poked at Logan in the pit of his stomach that said that Aryx was. Perhaps it was the uncertainty that was truly eating at Logan's confidence.

Minutes later they were all seated in the center of *The Shy Maiden*. This was the little out-of-the-way bar that Gideon had been so insistent upon. They had only been seated a few minutes before Pike and Talon were making advances on the bar maids. Apparently, Pike had thought it best to drown his sorrows in beautiful company instead of alone. Logan knew that he would never be the same old Pike, but at least he was making the attempt. The door to the bar opened and closed several times a minute as they sat and talked, and before long, it became an ignorable background occurrence. However, one of the times that the door opened, Logan didn't hear it close. Elwyne tapped him on the shoulder and when he turned, he was greatly surprised at the person standing in the doorway.

The woman was very beautiful, but also very familiar, and intimidating in her full armor whose breastplate was emblazoned with the symbol of the Dragon. When Elwyne whispered the name Leane in Gwydeon's direction, Logan saw him stiffen. When that happened, it was obvious what was going on. There was a two-fold problem that Logan now hard to deal with. Gwydeon's fling from Rama had now shown up in Barer. The first part of the problem was that Gwydeon and Midarin had become lovers, and Gwydeon had moved passed his flirtation with Leane. The second part of the problem was that Leane was now the leader of the Army of the Dragon, and if she was there, then something was very wrong.

Gwydeon sighed hard and then waived at the new arrival. Her face changed back to the hard face of a soldier and she approached without returning the greeting. She saluted Logan with a raised arm across her chest and then bowed slightly.

"My lord," she said in a strong military tone, "I'm glad that I have found you here in Barer. The Army of the Dragon has been deployed in Kandor, however, I had to detach a garrison to Marcwell when we saw the size of the battle that raged there."

"That's very good Commander Torne," Logan replied trying to sound regal. "But you could have sent this news to me in a letter. Why did you decide to leave your army to come here to deliver this news?"

Gwydeon stiffened a little more, and then stood. Leane looked in his direction and then her gaze fell back to Logan.

"I must say that I did have certain personal reasons for leaving my charge, and for that I must apologize. Deserting my post in the time of war is not an easily forgivable offense, but I thought that I was needed here far more than I was needed in Kandor."

"I see," Logan replied. "I must admit that I admire your convictions. I'm sure that Gwydeon will be happy to have you with us."

"And why would that be sir?" her military voice never softening. "Mister Sandar is a very caring person sir, I have heard that about him, but I do not see why he would be so happy to see a woman that he has no real ties to."

Gwydeon's expression was filled with disbelief, but when he started to speak, Midarin squeezed his hand and shook her head. Leane's face was impassive, her look one of steel control. Elwyne had told Logan that Gwydeon and Leane had shared something special in Rama, but apparently, that had either been forgotten, or something else was at play.

"I have heard of the matters concerning the girl named Jasmen and also of the traitor Aryx Terian, and so I am here to offer my services as your personal guard. It is not to say that you are not capable of protecting yourself, but it appears as if you are too close to this whole undertaking to realize what is going on around you. I would like to think that I would be a capable guard. Therefore, with your permission, I have delegated my authority to another member of the Army of the Dragon, and I will travel with you full time."

She put her hand on Logan's shoulder, more as a reassuring gesture than anything else. Her words sounded soft and comforting to Logan's ears, even in the harsh military voice that she had been using. Looking up into her eyes, Logan began to experience feeling of warmth toward her. All he could do was nod and look up into her brilliant eyes. When she removed her hand from his shoulder and saluted again, it was as if the world started moving again. Logan's head spun, but he couldn't understand why. Elwyne just looked at Logan as if to ask 'what are you doing?', but he shook off the question and asked Leane to sit down. She sat across from Elwyne, and Logan could have sworn that he saw Elwyne shoot a look of death in Leane's direction. The temperature and attitude in the group had dropped to well below zero, but some reason, all he could think about was Leane.

"My Lord Dragon," she said in a voice that sounded like a choir of angels, "I have heard several rumors that a phase has taken control of the faction that rules the Frontier. It is said that this man, Lord Aplee, controls several of the smaller kingdoms in the area, and he is prepared to launch an assault on Barer. Don't you think that this is a lead that is worth investigating?"

"By all means," Logan said without hesitation, "we should leave right away. If this man Aplee is a phase, than we could perhaps find out the location of Shau-ling's palace and put an end to this quest in no time."

Gwydeon shook his head and beamed at Leane.

"That's being rash and unreasonable, Logan. We have no idea where this information comes from. This could be just another rumor started by a member of the phasia to get us on another wild goose chase like what happened to you in Castleer. Don't you think that you should check out this information before you act on it?"

"It comes from the leader of the Army of the Dragon, Gwydeon," Logan replied in a harsh tone. "Don't you think that she is an accurate enough source? Or perhaps it's because you are becoming a bit jealous."

Everyone at the table looked at Logan, shocked at the venom in his tone. Elwyne tapped Logan on the shoulder but he ignored her.

"Now," Logan continued, "unless there is a good reason that we should not follow this lead, we shall depart in the morning toward the palace."

Logan rose from the table, anger filling him. Without another word he moved away from the table in the direction of the rooms that had been arranged for by Gideon. Leane followed a step behind, he gaze turning back to Elwyne for just a moment before the pair disappeared upstairs. Once he was inside the room, Leane shut the door and stood guard outside of the room. As soon as he was in the room, Logan felt as though all of the strength had been drained from his body and he practically collapsed on the bed. As soon as his head hit the pillow, it seemed that he drifted into sleep. The next time that Logan woke, he couldn't even remember if he had been dreaming.

* * * * * * * * * * * *

"Do you believe that?" Midarin said as soon as Logan was out of earshot, "I mean, he took her word like it was the doctrine of the Creator. Then he just ignores Elwyne like she didn't even exist."

"There is definitely something wrong with this whole situation all right," Pike replied, "but as to what, I have no clue. After what Gwydeon told Talon and I about what happened in Rama between he and Leane, I would have thought that she would have been a little happier to see him. It was as if Rama never even happened for her. He isn't that bad is he, Midarin?"

"This is no time for jokes, Pike," Elwyne scolded. "There is something wrong, and I intend to find out what."

"I'll go with ye," Gideon added.

Elwyne nodded and the two of them walked up the flight of stairs and were stopped short of the door by Leane.

"The Lord Dragon is sleeping and he has requested that he not be disturbed by anyone."

"He will be disturbed by me," Elwyne replied. "I am his fiancé, and I can disturb Logan anytime that I please."

"I don't want to harm you, Miss Tamerlane," Leane responded strongly, "but if you keep insisting on disobeying a direct order from the Lord Dragon, than I will be forced to remove you."

"Do ye know who ye are talkin' to lass? Dis is da Lady Dragon, the soon ta be wife o' da Lord Dragon dat ye are forbidding her ta see."

"That matters not, thief," she replied in the same cold tone. "She is not the Lady Dragon yet, and until she is, she does not have the power to countermand the orders of the *Coromor*. Now will you leave quietly, or will I have to draw my sword and make you leave?"

Gideon reached for one of his daggers, but Elwyne stopped him. She pushed him back down the stairs, and when they sat back down at the table, Elwyne was far more concerned for Logan's safety than she had ever been in her life.

"No luck?" Talon asked.

"No," Elwyne responded. "She would keep Shau-ling outside of that door if he came down here looking for Logan."

"So what are we going to do?" Alexander asked.

"I don't know Alexander, but what I do know is that something is very wrong and it is all because of Leane."

"Perhaps it would be wise to have some kind of strategy in case Logan does something that is so far out of his character that it endangers both us and the quest," Talos suggested.

"I concur," Pike responded. "Someone should take command in Logan's absence."

"All right," Elwyne responded. "Who is the lucky person?"

"I say that Pike takes the lead," Talon chimed in quickly, "he pulled us through in Sarmeel, and he did a great job in Sador."

"I second that," Gwydeon added.

"What do you say, Pike?" Elwyne asked.

"I don't know, Elwyne. However, if you all believe that I can do it, I promise that I will do my best. So, as your new leader, I'm going to place a few orders on all of you now, because I think it's needed. Gideon."

"Yes, Pike?"

"I want you to stick with Elwyne like glue. If that woman is going to make a play for Logan to gain control of the party, it would be a lot easier for her with Elwyne out of the way."

"As ye wish."

"Talon."

"Yeah Pike?"

"You are going to be my right arm while we have to go through this. If there is anything that you can hear or feel through the wind, I want you to tell me right away. I don't think that Logan will be much good in a fight if he acts like he did a minute ago, so we're going to have to be his sword and armor."

"You got it," Talon replied proudly.

"Gwydeon."

"What do you want me to do?"

"You and Leane had something in Rama, and I'm really sure that she hasn't forgotten all of it. She would really like us to believe that, but I know that it isn't true. You need to try and find some way to break through to her. There is something more to here than meets the eye, and right now, you're the only ticket that we have."

"I'll do what I can," he replied a little less than optimistically.

"Elwyne, your job is one of the hardest. You need to try and get close to Logan and bring him out of whatever is holding him. I know that you can get through to him. You always had a way with the most pig-headed of us all, and right now, I think that Logan is at the top of the list."

"Whatever you say, Pike," she responded.

"Talos?"

"Yes, Pike?"

"Is there any way that you can use your powers to scan Logan's mind to see what happening to him?"

"I can try, but I don't know how much influence his being the *Coromor* will have on my results."

"Try anyway," Pike replied, "we have to know everything we can about what's going on in his head."

"What about me, Pike?" Alexander said eagerly.

"I need you to stick by Talos and do whatever you can to help him. You've been a big help to us so far by helping him, so I need you to continue doing that."

"Okay," he responded a bit disappointed.

"And me?" Midarin asked.

"You have the hardest job of all Midarin. You are my last resort. If at any time I believe that Leane is in fact in control of Logan, I am going to have to act in a split second. I don't know who or what Leane is, but if she is a phase, then I don't think our powers will do much good against her. But, maybe an arrow in the back of the head could serve to end our problem very quickly."

"You just give me the word Pike, and I'll be happy to oblige you," Midarin responded as she clutched Gwydeon's hand. Pike knew that the undertaking would be harder than she was letting on, but he tried to push it away.

"All right. For now we go on a planned. Logan says that we're going to leave at first light for this palace, and so that's what we are going to do. Don't let on that anything is amiss. Just handle yourselves as you normally would and try not to seem too distracted by Leane. You all know what you're supposed to do, and I expect that you will do your best for me as you would for Logan. Let's just hope that all our fears turn out to be just imagined."

Were they all right? Pike didn't know for sure, but if something were going to happen, he wanted to be ready, even if that meant that he had to take his own friend down.

Decisions

The knock at Logan's door the next morning was the first sound that he had heard all night. His mind had been quiet, and the dreams and nightmares that had plagued him for the last week were finally gone from his mind. The door opened before Logan had said a word, and he still lay in the bed as if he had been on his feet for a week and the last night had been the first sleep that he had managed. Leane was standing in the doorway when he finally sat up and looked.

"What is it, Leane?"

"My Lord Dragon," she said, her voice a resounding chorus of lovely and perfect notes, "it is just about time to depart for the Castle of Nevi."

"Thank you Leane, I'll be down in a moment."

She stayed in the doorway for a moment and then closed the door. Logan was alone again. For the first time he realized that Elwyne had not slept with him that night, and for some reason, he found himself strangely thankful for the quiet and privacy. After dressing, he opened the door and found Leane there waiting. Her sword was drawn, and she appeared to be ready for a fight.

"What's wrong Leane?"

"Nothing my lord," she replied kindly, "I just thought it best to be prepared."

"Sheath your sword commander, there is no place for that here."

She took hold of Logan's arm and looked deeply into his eyes for a split second.

"You really don't want me to do that do you, Logan? It would be a shame if something bad were to happen to you because I wasn't prepared to defend you."

"I suppose that you're right Leane," Logan replied docilely. "Is there anything else that you think I should consider?"

"No Logan," she replied with a smile, "that's all for now, but you might want to consider a change of wardrobe. I think you might look good in a green tunic."

She let go of Logan's arm, and took a step back. He stood there for a minute just looking at her.

"You know, this shirt doesn't feel right. Maybe I ought to change. Could you wait on me for just another moment?"

"As you wish my lord," came her curt military response.

Logan went back into his room and picked up the saddle bags that he had neglected the first time he left the room. It took only a moment to dig into one side and pull out one of the fresh green tunics that had been the only allowed wardrobe during his time in Rama. Though there was a dim memory of distaste for the color, it seemed that it no longer bothered him. The black shirt went into the pile of clothes in his bag, and the green tunic went over his head and as the soft cloth rubbed up against his sore flesh, Logan felt content.

"That looks much better, my lord," Leane said as she walked into the room, "and don't let anyone tell you otherwise. Now, when we reach the Castle of Nevi, you will deal with a man named Lord Grawn Aplee. You will find that he is very disagreeable at first, but that will pass. The instant he tries to get you to trust him, you must attack before he has a chance. If he has an opportunity to prepare for the attack, your powers and those of the *Erieal* will be useless against him. Grawn is a very powerful phase. When we get downstairs, you will relay those orders to your friends. They will seem very agitated as to the content of your commands to be sure, but you will stand fast to your convictions because what you believe is right. If it comes down to your friends or the good of the quest, you must know what path is the true one. Do you understand me, Logan?"

"Yes Leane," Logan replied quickly, without hesitation. "You are most certainly right about the tactics. I'm glad that you were able to see it almost as quickly as I did. I just wish my friends could have as much vision as you do."

"That is precisely why the time will come when you must strike out on your own and do what is right. These people are holding you back from your true potential, and because of them, you are not able to put all of your energies into fighting Shau-ling. Remember that I will fight beside you and follow your orders no matter what."

"By your word."

She smiled meekly and then followed Logan down the flight of stairs that led to the common room below. As he had expected, the other members of the party were waiting at a table near the center of the room, and they instantly stopped their conversations as soon as Logan came into view. Something was very wrong, and Logan truly started to believe that his friends were plotting against him. Though he wanted to put more faith in them than that, the betrayals that he had seen from Jasmen and Gideon made it nearly impossible to overlook the possibility of further betrayal. Pike was sitting very close to Elwyne; perhaps too close.

"What are you doing, Pike?" Logan demanded, his hand going to the hilt of his sword.

He stood quickly and backed away from Elwyne. She did not look shocked as Logan had suspected, but the look in her eyes could only make him see the guilt that was written all over her face.

"So," Logan said without waiting for an answer or an excuse, "the rumors are true. I didn't want to believe that my own friends were plotting against me behind my back, but now I have no choice."

"Logan," Pike started.

"Don't bother trying to explain, Pike," he responded angrily. "You thought that you had hidden that little conversation from me last night, but you were gravely mistaken. I know of the secret orders that seek to undermine my authority, and I hold none of you responsible save Pike Rhuiden. If you will swear that you will follow none but me, all will be forgiven, and I will take care of Pike personally."

"Logan," Elwyne said as she stood, "you don't know what you're saying. That woman has poisoned your mind, and I think that she is trying to turn you against us and use you for her own twisted schemes."

"You would dare make accusations when you do not turn the mirror on yourself as well," Logan scoffed. "You were not with me last night my dear devoted Elwyne. Could it be that this plot against me has driven you from my bed and into the bed of the ringleader of this whole perverse game? Are you now Pike's lover?"

She slapped Logan hard and then turned to face Pike. Logan could hear her crying, but he didn't care. His anger boiled in his blood, and all Logan could think of was how much he wanted Pike dead.

"Tell me Pike," Logan said coldly, "does she keep the place beside you warm now that Eldar is gone?"

The ax was out of the loop in his belt in an instant. Logan didn't wait but a fraction of a second to draw his sword. It was in that next second that Gideon stepped in between them. The battle lines had been drawn and Logan didn't know or truly care what side the rest of his so-called friends would take. It didn't matter much in the end. They were no match for his power.

"That's enough Logan," Pike said angrily, "I will not let you throw away everything that we have built together. You're willing to throw away love and friendship for the words of a woman you don't even know. Think about what you're doing, Logan. Do you realize what you're about to force me to do?"

"He is very aware Pike," Leane started.

"Shut your mouth, bitch," Midarin snapped. "You have no place in this discussion or in this party."

"And I'm sure the motives of a whore are much more highly regarded, especially if that whore just happens to be a princess," Leane retaliated.

"That's enough!" Logan thundered. "Who will stand with me and who will stand against me with Rhuiden and my former lover?"

Pike lowered his ax and took two steps back. Elwyne stood strongly with him, and Leane stood to Logan's right. Gideon looked back and forth for only a moment and then stepped to Logan's side. Talon didn't hesitate to fall in beside Pike. Talos and Alexander sided with Logan after a moment, and Midarin fell in behind Pike. Gwydeon was the only one who was left in the middle.

"What will it be Gwydeon?" Logan asked softly. "I don't want to have to see you on the other side of the battlefield wondering which of us is going to die first."

"I have no intention of dying to the sword of one of my friends. You are being totally unreasonable, and I will not let you destroy the world and your friends because of Leane or whatever is going on in your head right now. I don't know why this change came about Logan, but it's got us all scared to death."

"I haven't changed Gwydeon," Logan replied, "all of you have. There are things in this world that we do not have an understanding of, and I believe that we have to be as wary of these unknowns as possible. If there is a chance that this Aplee is a phase, we have to exploit this chance before it is taken away from us."

"Then let us find out for you," Pike interjected. "The five of us will go to the Castle of Nevi and find out for you."

"That is unwise my lord," Leane said stepping forward. "These traitors could be in league with the phase, and perhaps this is part of their trap."

"You do not make the decisions here Leane," Logan growled. "I am still the *Coromor* and I am capable of telling what is or what is not. When I want your input, I will ask you for it. Until then, you can keep your opinions to yourself."

She was angry. She started to step forward, but something held her back. When Logan saw the flash of motion out of the corner of his eye, he knew that Gideon was about to move to intercept her.

"I will accept your plan on two conditions. Leane will accompany you and she will make sure that you are not planning a trap. Is this acceptable?"

"It is not," Pike responded. "I don't trust Leane, but I will make you a counter proposal. Talon, Gwydeon, and I will go to the Castle of Nevi, and we will only accept Gideon as your liaison. We both know that he can be trusted at this point, and he is most certainly at your side. Gwydeon is neutral, so can we be sure that he will not act unjustly. Talon and I will give you our vow that we will not do anything to act against the best interests of the quest. You've never had a problem with accepting our word in the past, so I don't see why you should now."

"I accept your counter proposal, Pike, and I swear to you that I will not take any actions until you return," Logan said as he shook Pike's hand.

As Logan stepped back, Leane rounded on him angrily.

"Are you sure that is a wise decision my lord? You have already seen that Pike and Talon cannot be trusted in any way. I have even heard rumors that Talon betrayed his own friend while they were in Taren. Isn't that right Talon?"

"I don't know what you're talking about," he said defensively.

"Don't you now. One night in Taren, you were surprised to find a woman at your door in the middle of the night, do you deny it?"

"I deny nothing."

"Who was the woman, Talon?" Leane prodded.

Pike turned and looked at his friend. He could not believe what he was hearing, and he could only imagine the worst.

"It was Eldar, Pike. She and I became intimate after the two of you broke it off in Aradon. I had no idea that the two of you had taken the vows, or I would have never done it."

Pike shook his head violently and slumped into a chair.

"How could you do that to me Talon?" he said in a weak voice. His heart was breaking inside of him, and it was all he could do to speak.

"I swear that I didn't know until after she was already dead, Pike. She never wanted to talk about you, and she only wanted someone to comfort her. That's not really important though Pike, I'm not the enemy here."

Talon turned away from his pained friend and faced Leane.

"For a person who has just joined our ranks, you see to know a lot about what went on after we left Rama. I want to know just how you found out about Eldar and I."

"Friends are a wonderful thing to have, Talon," Leane responded, "you should have remembered that before you betrayed yours."

Talon reached for his sword and stepped toward Leane. Pike reached up and grabbed his friend's arm, restraining him. Talon turned back to face his friend, and Pike stood and clutched Talon's shoulder.

"I forgive you Talon," Pike said as strongly as he could manage. "I just wish you would have come to me and told me what was going on. We can talk about this in length later however. We have a job to do."

Pike took two steps past Talon and stood right in front of Logan looking dead into his eyes.

"Talon, Gideon, Gwydeon, and I are going to go to the Castle of Nevi. If we don't return within two days, you should assume that we're dead and go on with the quest. I would ask that you please try to talk to Elwyne and get your life back in order, Logan; none of us like to see you like this. I hope for your sake that Leane is right, because if she's not, I'll personally come back here and gut her."

"You'll have to go through me Pike," Logan responded coldly.

"Then you better pray that we find the *Chosen One* and that he is strong enough to kill Shau-ling, because if I have to kill you Logan, I will."

His words hung heavy in the air as he turned to leave. Talon and Gwydeon both looked on for a fraction of a second before they followed. Gideon put his hand on Logan's shoulder to reassure him, but Logan shrugged it off as he watched his former friends leave the inn. Gideon walked past and followed them quickly. Just inside the doorway, Gwydeon turned and blew a kiss to Midarin, and she started to walk toward him. Leane was quick to cut off her path.

"And just where do you think you're going bitch?" Leane growled.

"I'm going to say good-bye to my future husband. It's a terrible thing to have to be without your lover because of another woman, I'm just happy that Gwydeon had the good taste not to venture into that frigid place that you offer so many other men. How is it that you can keep men in your bed when they feel that icy chill rubbing against them?"

Leane snarled and then drew a dagger and thrust it at Midarin. She was quick enough to elude the blade, and then Midarin struck Leane in the nose with her clenched fist. Leane toppled to the ground, and blood flowed freely from her newly broken nose. Midarin looked at her handiwork for a moment and then stood over Leane menacingly.

"Don't test me, or I'll make sure you never draw another breath."

Elwyne pulled Midarin away from Leane.

"Nice punch," she said quietly to her new favorite companion.

Logan helped Leane get to her feet and then he escorted her upstairs to help her get cleaned up. Logan didn't even notice Pike and the others leave.

* * * * * * * * * * * *

Pike and Talon walked slowly up to the gates of the Castle of Nevi with Gwydeon and Gideon on their heels. The ride from Barer had been a quiet one, and no one had wanted to discuss the situation that would await them when they returned. It was an awkward place that they found themselves in. On one hand they were torn between loyalty to their friend and doing what they felt was right, and on the other they found themselves debating the differences between fears and imagined realities. None of them really wanted to accept the fact that Leane was controlling Logan, but there was too much evidence to debate the other side of the argument. It was possible that Logan was beginning to lose his mind as they had been fearing throughout the entire quest, but after seeing Lord Cedric, they couldn't help but think that those fears were imagined.

The Castle of Nevi was a little smaller in the aspect of height compared to the rest of the palaces that they had seen over the duration of the quest, but what it lacked in height, it made up for in sheer size. It seemed that the castle stretched on for miles in all directions, and that a person could walk around inside of it for a year and never be in the same room twice. The front gates of the palace were massive, and the wooden doors that served as the entrance were almost big enough to push a house through. Ten guards held the gate, and as Pike approached them, the men all tensed and looked as if they were ready to attack at the slightest provocation.

"Stay where you are," one of the guards said and then took a step toward Pike. "State your business or leave at once."

"We are envoys from the *Coromor*," Pike responded stepping closer to the man. "We were sent to find Lord Aplee. I carry a message for him from the Lord Dragon."

The guard looked puzzled for a moment and then he turned back to his comrades. Pike motioned for the others to approach. Talon, Gideon, and Gwydeon dismounted and fell in to the right and left of their friend.

"Give me this message, and I will see that it is delivered to my lord," the soldier responded.

"That is not acceptable," Pike said shaking his head. "This message was given to me and I cannot repeat it unless I am in Lord Aplee's presence."

"Then I cannot allow you to pass . . ."

"It's alright, Kras," a cold hard voice said from somewhere above them, "you may let them pass."

Pike looked up into the windows that were above the gate, but he could see no one because the sun was in his eyes. The guards scrutinized the four adventurers for a moment and then opened the gates and let them pass. One of the guards took hold of the horses, while another led Pike and the others through a huge courtyard into a central building inside the walls of the castle. The inside of the building was very dim, and it was hard to make out any of the decorations that adorned the walls. The guard stopped short of a door in the far wall of the building, and he motioned for Pike and the others to step through. As they did so, they were greeted by a very interesting looking man.

He sat in an ancient wooden chair, his elbows resting lightly on the arm rests. His fingers were laced together about the level of his chin, and his cold gray eyes stared out through recessed eye sockets. His gray hair was cut short, and it was neatly trimmed behind the ears. He wore a black tunic with a single bar of gray down his left side that complimented the gray breeches he wore. If he was the Lord Aplee that they had been sent to find, he was the most reserved in the manner of appearance that they had ever met.

"Gentlemen," he said in a hard voice, "I trust that you have not come here under false pretenses, and I would thank you for coming in the Lord Dragon's name. I was wondering how long it would take him and his forces to seek me out. I am Lord Grawn Aplee."

"You seem very confident in the fact that we would find you, Lord Aplee," Pike replied.

"I was. The reason you are here is because there have been rumors that I am a member of the phasia."

"That's true," Gwydeon replied. "How could you have known that?"

"Because the information you received came from a woman by the name of Leane Torne," a woman's voice said from the shadows of a staircase.

Pike and the others turned their attention to the small stairway that lay recessed in the far wall. The first thing they all saw was exquisite tanned legs emerge from the shadows. The more they saw of the woman as she made her way slowly and gracefully down the stairs spoke more and more of her elegance and beauty. She wore a short red dress that ended about mid-thigh, and it clung to her body like wet paper. Her face was a beautiful as the rest of her, tan and lovely. Her eyes shone green, and sparkled like emeralds set in a backdrop of coal. Auburn hair with streaks of red fire hung down her right shoulder, pulled back and held by a single piece of red cloth.

"This is my wife," Aplee said quickly, "Lady Bryn."

"'Tis a pleasure to meet you," she said curtly.

"The pleasure is ours," Gwydeon replied with equal majesty. "How do you know Leane Torne?"

"We don't," Bryn responded. "However, the woman that you are dealing with is not the Leane Torne that you remember. Leane has been taken over by a member of the phasia known as Caris. All of the phasia have the ability to meld with a person and take over their features and voice, as well as their memories. Caris has obviously done this to get close to Logan Ranthall so that she can control him."

"How do you know who Logan is?" Talon said reaching for his sword.

"Please, Sir Talon," Grawn said softly, "there is no need for that here. We are all friends. As you have obviously been told, I am a member of the phasia, as is my wife here."

Talon and the others all tensed, but they did not draw their weapons.

"Why are you telling us all of this?" Gwydeon asked.

"Thousands of years ago," Bryn started, "we were banished from the Council of Ten, which is the ruling body of the phasia, and also where we derive our powers. Shau-ling believed that we were plotting against him, so he banished us and created other phasia to take our place. Just recently we were brought out of hiding by our brother Saurn. He is now in control of the *Coromor's* counterpart, the *Chosen One*. He has been using this man to exterminate members of the phasia, and it would only be a matter of time before he turns on us."

"So," Grawn continued, "for this reason we have made ourselves known to Caris, and through her, we made ourselves known to you. However, there is now a danger to Lord Logan that we have to make you all aware of. Shau-ling has cut off the strand of power that Caris draws from. That means that her control over her powers and of Leane is slowly weakening. Eventually she will go insane as Saurn has, and she will be more content to kill Logan than to use him for her own purposes. That is why you must kill her before that happens."

"Is there any way that we can save Leane?" Gwydeon asked the concern filling his voice.

"Not now," Bryn answered. "If you could have separated them before the string of power was cut, there might have been a chance, but it is too late for that now."

"I don't know if I can trust you," Pike said coldly.

"What are ye talkin' 'bout Pike? Dese people may be phasia, but I t'ink dat we can trust dem," Gideon responded.

"That's easy for you to say, Gideon," Talon snapped, "you've been in league with them from the beginning."

There were sparks of recognition at the name from both Grawn and Bryn. Though Pike thought he saw more annoyance on Grawn's face than anything else.

"Is this the boy that serves my brother Basille?" Grawn asked.

"I am," Gideon answered.

Bryn could not hide the smile that tugged at the corners of her mouth.

"It is good to see that Basille is finally following his true path and helping the *Coromor*. I'm sorry to say that it took me longer to do so, but I would like to do all that I can to help," Grawn commented.

"I still don't trust you Grawn," Pike said, "but I will accept your help on two conditions."

"These conditions are?"

"Tell me how you know who Logan is, and then tell me how I can get rid of Caris."

"Very well," Grawn replied. "When Saurn approached us with his plan to exterminate Shau-ling and the other phasia, he gave us his proof with the *Chosen One*. This man, Korrd, has some tie to the *Coromor* and has known his identity from day one. Somehow, Saurn was able to draw the *Coromor's* identity out of Korrd's mind and use it as a motivation to direct his strikes. As for the second question, I will send my wife Bryn to help you dispatch our sister and also to help you during your travels."

"I accept all the help that you have given us Grawn, and I hope that after this is all over we won't have to hunt you and your wife down," Pike said coldly. "We will be leaving as soon as you can be ready my lady."

"I shall meet you at the palace gates," she responded.

The four friends left the study and walked slowly back toward the palace gates. Pike had an uneasy feeling in the pit of his stomach, and he walked softly over to Gwydeon and paced beside him for a few steps before he could say anything.

"The man by the name of . . ."

"Korrd," Gwydeon responded, "yes, I know. He was supposed to have died. If Korrd is the *Chosen One*, we had better prepare Logan now."

"Do you really think that's wise?" Pike asked more afraid than concerned. "In the state of mind that Logan's in now, I don't think he could take it."

"Then we'll just have to play it by ear and hope that someone else kills Korrd before Logan has to face him."

There is a place inside the human heart where all of the fears of the flesh are stored. It was in this place that Gwydeon knew Korrd Ranthall. He hoped inwardly that his fate would never be realized, but that ache in his heart would not subside, and he felt the pains of sorrow and expectation all the way back to Barer.

Bite of the Cobra

Farax sat on the throne of the royal palace of Kandor and sat uneasily. He had not heard from any of the other phasia since they had agreed to the uneasy alliance in the Council chambers before Basille's and Saurn's return. It was an uneasy peace that held between the phasia, and Farax couldn't help but wonder how long it would be before one of the phasia, or the *Chosen One* decided to make him their next target. These thoughts of death at the hands of his own kind made him a bit frightened, but he had always been the most flighty of all of the phasia. Perhaps it was because he had taken Zarsi's challenge of Shau-ling all those years ago more to heart than the other members of the phasia. Farax had always been afraid of what Shau-ling could have done if he had truly put his mind to it, and so he tried to never give Shau-ling a reason to look at him as a traitor or a competitor. It was a hard cross to bear considering the fact that Shau-ling saw everyone and everything as a threat to his utter dominance. If Shau-ling were to ever conquer the world as he had envisioned, the phasia would surely become extinct rather quickly.

The phasia had never been a tight nit group, but at least they were always consistent in the enemies that they had kept. Farax had been able to play all sides of the coin in most lifetimes, and the only enemies that he had really made had been Warron and Basille. However, while it was hard to call any member of the phasia an ally, Farax found himself lichening himself to the likes of Jeroch, Zarsi, and Erdric. As Farax sat, he felt a rift of power entering his palace. He knew that a portal would be forming in a moment, so he backed away from the area of the rift and prepared himself for a fight. The portal opened, and his old ally Zarsi stepped though. Farax almost relaxed, but he scolded himself for being stupid and kept hold on his line of power.

"What do you want Zarsi?" Farax said in his high-pitched whiny voice.

"You needn't fear me old friend, I have not come here to kill you. If I did, you know that I wouldn't have created a portal this close to your kingdom. I am not as foolish as some of the other phasia believe me to be."

"If you are not here to rob me of life and kingdom Zarsi, why have you come?"

Zarsi rounded his friend cautiously, still very aware that Farax had not released his string of power.

"I am under orders from Shau-ling to find you and take you to the fields of Vesi Grath in the Domani Wasteland. We are to take command of Shau-ling's army that awaits us there, and we are to accept the challenge of our brother Saurn. Other than those facts, I have no information. All I know is that Saurn made a challenge and requested that we lead the opposing army. I think that he must have a personal vendetta to settle with us after what we did to him in the plains of Marcwell all those years ago."

"That deception was one of our best my brother. He believed that we were on his side completely, but after we had vanquished the army of Jeroch and Erdric, we turned on him and buried our blades deep into his heart."

"And he has yet to forgive us," Zarsi added. "Saurn is one of the few phasia that holds grudges, and he has held this one for eight lifetimes. I don't believe that he will let it go until he pays us back personally."

"I do not doubt that one bit Zarsi," Farax commented, "and I hope that he does not get the chance in the fields of Vesi Grath."

A silence held between the two brothers for a moment, and then Farax spoke again uneasily.

"Were you in the palace at the time of the hail?"

"Yes," Zarsi answered. "Master has banned us from the palace because of some comments that Warron and I made about his decision to redesign the Shadowwalkers and the Kalbraks. He has also created a monstrosity that he has dubbed Nightwing. I don't want to go into it now, but it is not a good development for the Brotherhood."

"So," Farax said softly, "Shau-ling has decided that he will step up his extermination agenda a few lifetimes. I can't say that is good news, but it may be beneficial to our cause. If we separate ourselves from him now, we may be able to survive long after the *Coromor* succeeds in destroying him."

"You are hoping for master's destruction?" Zarsi said in disbelief.

"Think on it Zarsi. I believe in my heart of hearts that it is much better to be alive than dead. If Shau-ling conquers all, he will hunt down every last one of us in order to ensure that he will never be challenged again. If the *Coromor* wins and we find some way to survive the transition, there might be a way to convince him that we did not survive the transition and that all of the phasia are dead. If that happens, we could rule as we saw fit and we wouldn't have to answer to anyone but ourselves."

Zarsi thought hard for a moment and then shook his head.

"This is a pointless discussion right now Farax and you know it. We have a job to do, and I intend to do it. If we both survive the battle with Saurn, then I will be glad to debate this point with you some more. Come, we must leave now and meet our army."

Farax nodded and then opened a portal to the fields of Vesi Grath. These fields did not exist in the real world, but they were the only part of the Blight, the legendary birthplace of Shau-ling and the phasia, that existed in a plane of reality. They could not be found by any human that did not possess the ability to utilize portals, and beasts of the Shau could not dwell there without the permission of Shau-ling. Farax knew why Saurn had chosen this place to do battle. He knew that Shau-ling could not interfere in a battle that took place in the Blight because Shau-ling could not reach the Blight. His power could not enter or exist there.

When Zarsi and Farax set foot onto the mythical fields, Zarsi took a deep breath and spoke in a joyful tone.

"It is good to be home isn't it Farax?"

"Yes it is my brother," Farax responded, "so long as we do not die here in the fields that spawned us."

The lack of sentiment disturbed Zarsi for a moment, and then the two phasia walked over to their army. Stone dominated the front line of the army, while members of Kalbraks, the Shadow's shock troops, looked prepared to lead the charge. Jeresei abounded everywhere, and huge Shadowwalkers dotted the sky.

"Creatures of the Shadow, the battle you will fight today will ensure your place in the history of the ancients. We have been sent on a mission by the master himself, and you all know what it would mean for you if you were to fail. You would be better off to die in the attempt than to live to face the wrath of your master. I will order the charge after the war council. I will not give you any orders save one. You will be victorious."

Where any army of humans would have cheered at the speech, the creatures who served the Shadows knew that if they did not do as their leaders had requested, they would surely die. There was also the chance that by failing, they would also be responsible for the death of their entire breed. The burden was heavy, and it might also have been considered too much for any normal being to take.

Farax and Zarsi turned away from their army and looked across the wide expanse that would soon serve as the battle ground. About the same time, they noticed that a single figure was walking out from the opposing army waving a white flag.

"Do you think that Saurn has decided to give up before the battle has even begun?" Farax asked.

"Not a chance dear brother," Zarsi chided. "It is more likely that Saurn would like to discuss terms of our surrender. If it's a war council that he desires, than I suppose that we should give him one."

Farax nodded and the two phasia walked out slowly to meet their older brother. The look in Saurn's eyes disturbed Farax as soon as he saw them. All of the phasia knew that Saurn was falling further into the madness that claimed his mind, but no one knew exactly how crazy he had become. No one had been away from the Council of the Ten as long as Saurn had, so there was no accurate way to measure the effects. It was probably true that Saurn still had a great command of his powers, but there was no way to tell how deeply he had to draw on them to stay alive.

Each of the phasia drew on their string of power to stay alive. Each of these strings extended from the Council, but it seemed that each string had a limited duration. A phase could feel his powers weakening, and if he was not able to return to the Council at that time, he would have to draw harder on the powers that flowed to him. However, the more power a phase drew from the Council, the more power he would crave. After a time, the power that phase craved would be far in excess of the power that he could draw at one time from his line of power. When that happened, the phase would have no choice but to return to the Council and totally revitalize himself. If that phase chose not to return, as Saurn had, the madness that the power craving would cause would be unrivaled in evil and in sheer lunacy. Saurn had never totally lost control of his faculties; however, it appeared that the madness had directed them in other arenas. This need for power had probably made him crave the full power of the Blaze, which only Shau-ling dominated, and made him contemplate patricide.

"Are you planning to surrender my dear brother?" Zarsi asked in his sly voice.

"Quite the contrary my dear brother," Saurn answered, "I have come to offer you a chance for life. If you in your infinite wisdom here and now renounce all of your ties to Shau-ling, than I will grant you a place in my new order. I will allow you to live on the single condition that you will swear your allegiance to me and all that I stand for. Together we can crush Shau-ling with the help of my other allies and the *Chosen One*. I must however warn you. Even if you win this battle, the *Chosen One* will hunt every last one of the remaining phasia down and pick you off one by one. My death will not ensure your victory, and it may even seal your own fate. The only way that you can possibly survive would be by your surrender."

Farax drew his sword and smiled.

"You are a fool Saurn, and you are far crazier than I ever imagined you to be. If we kill you, your alliance will fall apart, and those who you value as allies will crawl back to the palace on their hands and knees begging for Shau-ling's forgiveness. Go back to your army and order the attack. If you have any honor left in that body of yours, you will stay until the battle is over and then die on the blade on my sword."

"The battle may not last as long as you believe it will my dear younger brother. While I may have some honor left in my body, I believe Zarsi does not."

Farax looked at Saurn very puzzled for a moment and then realized what had happened. Before he could even reach for his powers, the blade of Zarsi's sword plunged into Farax's heart and forced him to the ground. The last sight that Farax saw was Zarsi's face looking down at him with that maniacal grin. He felt the blade twisting and turning deeper into his skin before the final throws of death took him.

"Quick Saurn," Zarsi said concentrating his powers on Farax, "banish him before I lose grip on him."

"I'll do no such thing," Saurn laughed, "I'm concentrating too much of my energy on killing you instead."

Zarsi didn't even have time to react before the stream of the Blaze hit him full in the chest. Farax's body disappeared as Zarsi was thrown clear, his concentration broken. Saurn laughed louder as he pummeled Zarsi with rocks and boulders from the surrounding plains. The assault stopped for a moment, and Zarsi managed to force himself up on the one arm that wasn't broken in the assault.

"Did you really think that you could win by treachery Zarsi?" Saurn scoffed. "I cannot allow any of the phasia to live who would oppose me, and so you are at the top of my death list. Be happy that you are not going to be around to see my new order Zarsi, it will be less painful for you in the end."

Zarsi tried to speak to his brother. He tried to plead his case, but the time for pleas was long past. He had sealed his own fate when he agreed to the destruction of Farax, and while he never put treachery past Saurn, he had apparently overlooked how much the madness had affected him. The Blaze struck true, and Zarsi felt every part of himself burst into flames instantaneously. The pain only lasted for a few moments before he disappeared from that plane of existence. The last sound he ever heard was the crazed laugh of his former brother and the sound of his own flesh burning.

* * * * * * * * * * * *

Nightwing flew through the skies above Barer and sighed deeply as he flew toward the Castle of Nevi. His errand was not one that he had expected, but the assassination of a phase was what he was born to do. Shau-ling had informed him of his plan for the future, and Nightwing felt an inner pride that he would be at Shau-ling's right hand when the final battle was won. All of the doubts were long gone from his mind, and it seemed that the rebirth had strengthened his resolve and dedication. Within a matter of seconds, the Castle of Nevi was in view, and he swooped down to finish his job.

Nightwing let his feet touch the ground just at the foot of the palace, and he saw the ten guards that held the front gate approaching him cautiously. Nightwing extended his wings long enough to draw out two of the sword 'feathers' and he prepared himself for battle. Suddenly the guards realized that they were facing a hostile adversary, and they charged. The quickest member of the guard to reach Nightwing was armed with a long spear. Nightwing stood his ground as the spear took him full in the chest. The shaft of the spear shattered, and the guard sprawled toward Nightwing, unable to stop his forward momentum. Nightwing sidestepped the guard, but let the claws of his hand rip at the soldier's throat as he stumbled past. Blood flew everywhere, and as the other soldiers recovered from the death of their comrade, Nightwing licked his claws and raised his swords for battle. The guards hesitated for a moment, and Nightwing launched his own attack. The wings sprung out from his body in a second, and the bladed 'feathers' dislodged themselves from his wings and sped toward the soldiers. None were able to react quickly enough, and they fell to the piercing blades. The soldiers didn't even have time to scream.

Nightwing surveyed the carnage for a moment and then attended to himself. He extended his left wing and wrapped it around his side. With his claws, he scratched at the channel that had held the bladed 'feathers'. He felt the mild sting of opened flesh, and then the pasty blue blood began to flow freely from the channel. As it dripped, the blood began to solidify, and soon the left wing had been refilled with sharp blades. It only took another minute or two to refill the right wing. Then he concentrated his powers on the two swords that he still held in his hands. First, he focused the powers of fire onto one of the blades, and it burst into flames leaving on the metal hilt in its previous form. The other blade was changed with the powers of earth. Nightwing was cautious to keep the two swords apart from each other, and he stuck the blade of the earth sword into the huge wooden castle gate. Nightwing hovered above the ground and backed away from the gate. He then hefted the fire blade toward the door, and when it struck the blade of earth, a huge explosion rocked the countryside. Rather than the door being blown down by the explosion, it appeared that it had been obliterated. Nightwing smiled to himself and flew into the castle.

Hundreds of soldiers awaited him on the other side of the gate, but they appeared more frightened than the first set that he had faced. The Blaze ripped from Nightwing's open jaws and decimated the first few ranks of soldiers. Those that didn't break ranks and scatter were burned in the second assault. No matter how fast the soldiers ran, Nightwing was always a little faster. More and more fell to either claws or tail, but they always fell in pools of their own blood. Minutes after the fray started it was over. The courtyard of the castle was filled with dead and dying members of the army, and Nightwing stood at the doors of the palace's central building.

"I must say that I am very impressed with you whoever you are," a voice said from behind Nightwing.

Nightwing spun around and was faced with the man that he had been sent to kill. Lord Grawn, a member of the banished and disgraced phasia stood not three feet away from him, the cold hard look glowing in his eyes.

CHAPTER 16

"I HAVE BEEN SENT TO KILL YOU. YOU'RE DEATH WAS ORDERED BY SHAU-LING HIMSELF, AND I AM NOT TO RETURN UNTIL BOTH YOU AND YOUR TRAITOROUS WIFE LADY BRYN HAVE BEEN TERMINATED."

"Then you will only have to deal with me. Lady Bryn was cut down some years ago when another member of the phasia tried to take over my kingdom. I was away at the time, and Bryn managed to push back the invaders, but not before the fatal blow was struck."

"YOU WOULD MAKE THINGS EASIER ON YOURSELF IF YOU WOULD KNEEL AT MY FEET AND TAKE YOUR DEATH EASILY. YOU MUST KNOW THAT YOU CANNOT CHALLENGE ME WITH YOUR DIMINISHED POWERS, AND THERE IS NO WAY THAT YOU CAN PENETRATE MY ARMOR."

"We'll see."

Grawn's hand shot up from his side, and from his open hand, and line of the green Blaze slammed into Nightwing's chest. While Nightwing may have been fast, Grawn was more accurate. Nightwing looked down at his chest and saw that some of his armor had melted in the heat of the Blaze, but as he concentrated his powers on the molten metal, it reformed into his armor.

"A PITIFUL MANEUVER, GRAWN, BUT I MUST CONGRATULATE FOR LANDING A BLOW AT ALL. I MUST SAY THAT I HAVE UNDERESTIMATED YOUR ABILITIES. THAT SHALL NOT HAPPEN AGAIN."

The whisper thin tail darted up into Nightwing's hand and detached from his body. Before Grawn had a chance to react, the tail-whip lashed out at him and wrapped around his neck. Nightwing jerked back on the whip, and Grawn's head rolled to the ground. The decapitated body stood for a moment before it fell backwards spilling red blood into the courtyard, adding to the sea of blood from his followers. Nightwing released the tail, and it reattached itself just before he sped off toward the palace of Shau-ling.

* * * * * * * * * * * *

Warron sat in the palace of Barer and watched as the mysterious shadow flew away from the castle far on the horizon. As Warron looked closer, he could see the flames coming from the palace. No one had the knowledge that Warron had set Grawn and his sister Bryn up in that palace, but if Shau-ling were to find out, it was a safe bet that he would soon be the next target for this new phantom assassin. Suddenly a familiar feeling hit Warron.

"A portal."

Just as the words escaped his lips, three portals appeared around him. Warron reached for his powers, but he knew that it was much too late for that. His brothers had caught him by surprise in his own kingdom, and there was no way that he was going to get out of the situation alive. He sat on his throne looking fearfully at the portals, and then he felt a hand touch his shoulder. He reflexively grabbed the hand and tossed his assailant toward one of the open portals. The portal closed before the phase reached it, and the thin black clad figure sprawled across the floor, the wind knocked out of him.

"It's nice to see you too Warron," Basille said softly getting back to his feet.

"I would not advise that you do that to any of the other phasia my old friend. I don't think that any of them would take it as well as I have."

Warron stepped away from his throne and help Basille to his feet.

"You call that taking it well?" Basille asked. "I could think of better ways that you could have taken it, but I guess the things the way they are, I should have expected as much."

"Why have you come here Basille? What has happened that has made you seek me out?"

Basille brushed himself and sat down in a chair. Warron sighed and sat back on his throne, his eyes never leaving Basille.

"Saurn sent me to find you and convince you to join his new regime, but that is not the reason that I came. There is some news about the fates of the phasia and the *Coromor* that you must be informed about if you are to live through this. Saurn is far crazier than we ever believed possible, and he has even enlisted the help of Grawn, Bryn, and Ellis in this fight."

"Grawn is dead my friend, and I can only imagine that Bryn is too. That winged assassin that I've been hearing about from my palace recon reports is the one responsible. Ellis is probably on her way back to Shau-ling's palace right now to tell master what is going on behind his back. My bet is that he will kill her after he gets all the information."

"The winged assassin?"

"Yes," Warron said fearfully. "Shau-ling has redesigned the Shadowwalkers, and he created a thing called Nightwing to lead them. He has the power of three of the phasia, and he also has the powers of one of the *Erieal*. Before you ask, I will tell you that master has captured White Lightning and made him into this Nightwing creature."

"I'm afraid that soon Nightwing may have the power of five phasia instead of three."

"What has happened?" Warron asked shocked.

"Saurn challenged Farax and Zarsi to a duel of armies in the fields of Vesi Grath. There were two betrayals, and both Farax and Zarsi are now dead. I can only guess who Saurn will target next."

"So you came here to warn me that Saurn might decide that I am expendable after all. Thank you for your concern Basille, but I believe that I can take care of myself."

"Then you are a fool. Saurn could get inside this palace without you even feeling a string of power. He can teleport instantly from place to place without portals, and he could slit your throat in your sleep if you weren't ready. Set up wards, set up anything. There is also another danger that you must be aware of. The *Coromor* is here in Barer, and it is only a matter of time before he finds out that you are a member of the phasia."

"I will take that when it comes, Basille," Warron reassured his friend. "You and I have dealt with many adversities over the years, and we will get through this one whether the *Coromor* succeeds or not."

Basille nodded, but he was still very worried about the life of his friend. However, he could not but be worried about himself as well.

* * * * * * * * * * * *

Nightwing flew back into the long tunnel that served as an airborne entry to the palace of Shau-ling. The speed of his flight put him outside the door to the throne room mere seconds later. As he touched down on the Hall of Terrors, the Flame appeared before him.

"The master did not expect you back so soon Nightwing, I will announce you."

The Flame disappeared, and an instant later the door to the throne room opened. Nightwing stepped in slowly, and stood before the large golden throne waiting for his master to appear.

"What do you have to report my faithful servant?" Shau-ling's voice rang out from the walls of the chamber.

"THE TRAITOR GRAWN IS DEAD AND I HAVE COME HERE TO REQUEST A NEW ASSIGNMENT SO THAT I MAY BETTER SERVE MY LORD AND MASTER."

"What of Bryn?"

"ACCORDING TO GRAWN, SHE WAS KILLED IN A RAID BY ANOTHER MEMBER OF THE PHASIA."

"I thought so," Shau-ling commented.

"WHAT DO YOU WISH FOR ME TO DO NOW MY MASTER?"

"Find Warron and kill him."

CHAPTER 16

With that the lights in the chamber dimmed to nothing and Nightwing walked slowly out of the throne room wondering how much longer he would be this valuable to his master.

Seduction

Despite how many times they had been betrayed to that point, Logan had put treachery past all of his childhood friends that had been with him since Aradon. Never in his worst nightmares did he for a moment think that they would turn on him and sacrifice all that they had fought for. How could Pike and Talon forsaken friendship and turned their loyalty to the very devils that caused the death of the woman they both loved? How could Elwyne leave his side when all of their hopes and dreams were just beginning to look plausible? Midarin must have been more wounded by Gwydeon's dalliances with Leane than she let on, but even that was no reason for her to betray Logan's trust. If there was anyone that he thought he would be able to count on as a supporter, he felt that it would be Gwydeon and Midarin. They both seemed that they understood the gravity of the situation. But perhaps Logan's judgment was significantly more flawed that he ever expected. Elwyne was at Pike's side now, and she should have been the first in line to try and comfort Logan, but she wasn't. Midarin seemed more contemptuous now than she ever had. Leane had certainly found a way to expose the traitors in their midst. She wanted to make sure that nothing harmed Logan, and he respected her zeal. Those were the easy ones to figure out. Gwydeon was a little harder. Leane and Gwydeon had a tryst while in Rama, but now she regarded him as nothing but a fellow warrior for the light. In some ways, she saw him in a position of servitude, a soldier serving his lord and master. Gwydeon would never bow a knee to a man who ruled with an iron fist. In fact, the tip of Gwydeon's blade would be the first of many swords to enter Logan's heart if he were to ever become a power hungry tyrant. Hadn't Cedric predicted that for Logan though? Cedric saw the raw power that Logan had at his command, and Cedric was willing to kill Logan rather than let him become the very evil that they were all fighting against. Logan could not help but admit to himself that he would not blame Cedric for that under any circumstances, but then all of their fates would be sealed.

No, Logan thought, *it shouldn't be that simple to destroy all of mankind's hopes. There must be another way. In fact, I know there is. The only thing is, Korrd is involved in this somehow, and I can't shake the feeling that I'm doing something wrong.*

"You are, Logan," a voice said from behind him.

Logan spun on his heels quickly and turned to face Leane. She was no longer in her warrior garb. She wore a long flowing emerald colored dress that was cut very low in the neckline. Her eyes were different somehow, and from all Logan could tell she was a different person than he had helped a few moments earlier.

"What is the meaning of this, Leane? You have not been summoned, and I specifically remember ordering you to stay in bed until my friends returned from Lord Aplee's palace."

"You did give those orders my dear, sweet, Logan, but I have chosen to ignore them. As for your friends, they will be returning within the hour, and I must prepare you for the fight ahead."

"What fight?" Logan asked impatiently.

There was something about this woman that unnerved Logan, especially with the new more conciliatory tone she had adopted. She brought out all of the darkest and malevolent qualities inside of him. The deepest parts of him screamed in rebellion, something inside compelled him to follow her directives.

"The fight that is inevitable when your friends return and it is revealed that they are in league with the phase Grawn and his equally hideous wife, Bryn. In fact, they are bringing that witch back with them as we speak. If she were to corner you with three of the *Erieal* at her back, you would not stand a chance. You have a natural talent when it comes to using your powers, but luck will not be enough to defend yourself from such an assault. However, if you were to allow me to teach you the real meaning of power, they would not stand a chance."

It was a tempting proposal. Not even Lord Cedric had made such an offer to teach Logan about the powers that accompanied being the *Coromor*. He had discovered a lot by accident already, but parlor tricks would not be effective enough against a force with the kind of power that a full member of the phasia and three of the *Erieal* represented. When Logan had defeated Aldridge, he had the help of Aryx. Even though the veteran warrior had not truly intervened, the bolt of lightning he channeled in Logan's direction had provided the edge that eventually won the battle. Logan knew he would need a lot more than that to battle the other phasia as well as Shau-ling.

"What do you want in return for your instruction, Leane?"

"Please, Logan," she said softly as she approached. "Call me Caris. It is a name that I am far more comfortable with."

"Well then, Caris," Logan replied, confusion not even entering his mind, "what is it that you require in return?"

"Merely that you give me a child, my dear boy. Your former lover can no longer give you the very thing that the future requires to survive. If I were to give birth to your heir, his power would rival that of the Creator. Our places in history would be confirmed for the rest of eternity, and not even Shau-ling could stand against our son."

She reached out and gripped Logan's shoulder lightly. All of his reservations were gone, and there was nothing he could do but nod in agreement. Caris released his shoulder and some of his will returned, but that same feeling of peace and devotion to her remained.

"Teach me."

"As you wish, my lord."

A sly and disarming smile came to Caris' lips for just a moment before all of the inner pleasure that she felt disappeared from her face, and the stern cold gaze of a taskmaster returned.

"The first lesson is to harness the elemental powers that lie within you. As I understand, Lord Cedric has already taught you to feel the strings; that will speed this part of the lesson up considerably. Each time you take hold of a string, you are able to channel its power in whatever form you wish. The first and easiest to use is the string of fire. Take hold of the string, and focus it on the fire place before you."

Logan closed his eyes and found the strings waiting there in the blackness of his mind. The red string was dim as before, but he could hold it as easily as he could the other three, it simply felt empty, incomplete. In Logan's mind he took hold of the string with both hands and felt the power course through him as the flames enveloped his soul. Per Caris' command, Logan channeled the power towards the fireplace in the far wall of the room.

"Do not be merely content to create a flame on the logs, Logan. Be more inventive and then tell me what you did."

Logan's first impulse had been to have a stream of fire erupt from his fingers, but Caris' prompting required that he respect her wishes; there had to be other ways to ignite the logs. Then it came to him. Inside each of the logs, Logan could see the small pieces of matter that composed the logs, and that they moved very slowly. Using the fire that burned inside of him, Logan accelerated those small pieces of matter and created a fire inside the logs. When he opened his eyes, the logs were gone, and a red flame roared from the ashes.

"Very impressive, my dear," Caris said quickly. "That is the most destruction I have ever seen caused when starting a fire. Now, imagine that you were to start a fire of that magnitude inside a man's heart. You could dispatch almost anyone in mere seconds like that. Not one man in the entire world could stand up to such an assault. Only a member of the phasia could divert such an assault, but only if they were to witness the threads of power that cause the attack."

"What do you mean 'witness the threads of power'?"

An intoxicating smile spread across Caris' face.

"You may not be aware of this, Logan, but members of the phasia have the ability to see any threads of power that are used. We know the combinations involved and the results of the combination the instant they are used against someone within our field of view. Once we see how the attack is made, we can figure out how to defend it."

"How would you defend an attack such as that?" Logan asked.

"Come come, my darling boy, think about it. You used the powers of Fire to accelerate the particles of matter that made up the logs. The only way that a person could slow down the particles of matter would be if a person were to channel the powers of Water to negate the acceleration. All of the primal forces would negate each other in a similar way, but sometimes a combination is necessary. To find out how, you must think of how to undo what is being done. Only then will you be safe."

Logan thought hard and said the first thing that came to his mind. He could not censor himself in front of the woman.

"Is there any way to hide the threads so that the phasia cannot see what I'm doing?"

"Not that I am aware of. The only man who was ever able to shield his weavings from the eyes of the phasia was a man by the name of Aerith Seth."

"Who is Aerith Seth?"

"Aerith Seth was the first *Chosen One*," Caris responded as she sat down beside him. "He was a monstrous little troublemaker, but he was as inventive as he was irreverent. He learned that because there is a black film around all of the primal strings, he could wrap all of his weavings in this blackness. There was no way that any member of the phasia could discern what was involved in some of his more complex weavings. It was a trick that only he could accomplish, and he used it to distance himself from the members of the phasia that sought to control him."

"Couldn't you learn what he was using simply be seeing the result?" Logan asked softly edging toward her mesmerized by her soft, sensual voice.

There was this power that she exuded, and the closer he got to her, he could feel the peace and contentment growing.

"No, but the thought was logical, my dear. You are learning quickly what it takes to be powerful. And now, for the next step. I will enter your mind and teach you to control the thoughts of others, and how to shield yourself from their influence. Of course, I will never teach you to how to block me out, but your defenses will be enough to hold off the paltry abilities of the other phasia."

She kissed Logan gently on the lips, and his body relaxed completely. Her power over him was absolute, but he did not care. To him, she was the whole world, and he would do anything to please her. Logan didn't care who she was or what she was. All that really mattered was that he served her well and that she never left his side. If Logan had to forsake everything to please her, he would. Logan was even prepared to bend his knee to Shau-ling if she asked, and the proposition did not frighten him as much as part of his mind knew it should. She laid him down fully on the bed and held his head in her lap. The last thing Logan remembered seeing was her brilliant green eyes flicker in the lamplight before his eyelids brought him into the realm of unconsciousness.

The void held Logan when he opened his eyes. There was nothing but the familiar and comforting darkness, and he felt nothing but peace. There were sounds outside of the darkness, but none of them were loud enough to be recognized. Then Caris' voice broke through the blackness like a warm soft ray of sunlight.

"Relax, my darling, I am probing your mind. You will see things, and from those you will form a shield of thoughts. I do not know how powerful this shield will be, but when it is adequate, I will tell you and bring you back. Then we can speak about more important things."

Logan could feel her smile. Suddenly images floated through the void like scraps of paper blown on the wind. One of these images landed at his feet, so he picked it up and looked at it. On the thin, paper-like substance was a picture of Gwydeon. He was holding his sword out in his hands like he did in the royal hall in Marcwell. Then Logan saw himself enter the picture and knight him as one of the *Coromor's* protectors. The pride on his face made Logan feel proud that he was a friend. Suddenly the paper tore from Logan's hand and lanced skyward. He looked up and saw a brilliant white light directly above. While he hadn't noticed it before, there was the sensation that it had been there all along. As he looked into the whiteness, he could see the room in which his physical body lay. The whiteness must have been a hole in the void. That was why his mind was vulnerable. The piece of memory floated toward the whiteness, and then clung to it, sealing the hole just a little. More and more memories floated by, and each one that Logan looked at was of one of his friends. Almost all of the memories were happy, but there were those that shocked and brought tears to his eyes. The ones of David always rattled him. Before Logan realized it, the huge patch of whiteness was nothing more than a sliver of light.

"That is enough Logan," Caris' voice said, only this time her voice was much fainter.

It felt to Logan as if the haze had been wiped away from his eyes, and he was beginning to see the woman that he had been so devoted to for the devil that she was. The woman's power was weakening, and inside the void her power had no real effect. Another memory leapt into his hands. Logan saw Elwyne's face and her seductive eyes just as he had that night in Rama. The love inside his heart swelled until Logan thought he was going to burst. That last powerful memory sealed the crack, and the void was whole. Logan felt a power that had never been there before, and Caris' scream rang clearly through the walls of the void. When he opened my eyes again, she had retreated to the door, and she was again in warrior's clothes.

"What's wrong Caris?" Logan teased. "Didn't you believe that I had enough power to turn away your charms?" You forget that we have tangled before in several previous lifetimes."

Logan was no longer speaking. The *Coromor* had control, and it was doing what he had been powerless to do. If Logan had consciously known what it was that Caris had been doing, he might have been able to turn her away, but that was an uncertain venture at best.

"I don't know you, shadow," she hissed. "You are merely an aberration of what the *Coromor* is. By listening to me, Logan Ranthall has become his own worst enemy. He will no more know what he is than will his friends. That is, if he has any friends left after tonight."

She spat at Logan and threw the door open. It took him a minute to regain his wits, but Logan had soon righted himself and was running after her. Members of the party had cut off Caris' escape, and she was standing in the middle of the staircase looking back, her eyes filled with barely restrained hate.

"You see, Logan," she said softly, renewing the seductive tone, "I told you they would bring the witch Bryn back with them. She has come here to destroy you. Use what you have learned and kill her before she can erect a defense. If you kill me first, you will never stand a chance against her and your traitorous friends. Kill her!"

Logan looked up and saw Pike and Talon for the first time. They were both brandishing their weapons, but so were the others. After realizing that he was unarmed, Logan closed his eyes for the briefest of moments and when his eyes opened again, a blade of lightning extended from his clenched fist.

"Where is the one called Bryn? If she is among you, I would know now. She will answer these accusations, or I will strike her down where she stands."

No one moved, but a strikingly beautiful woman walked over to the staircase. The *Coromor* inside of Logan recognized her immediately. He caught fragmented memories of the red dress and the fiery hair, but the identity was clear.

"Hello Bryn," Logan said shortly. "It's been a long time."

"Much too long, my old and dear friend. You should have sought me out yourself. Not that I minded dealing with the impetuous yet delightful *Erieal*, but I would have much rather dealt with you."

"Do you not remember the last time dearest? Grawn's jealousy nearly killed us all. Had it not been for Ellis . . ."

Logan's mind was blank. Those memories were not his, nor were they in the voice of the *Coromor* that he recognized. Those thoughts came from somewhere else.

"I thought it was you, my love," Bryn said nodding. "This must be hard for you. However, the truth had to come out sometime."

Suddenly the thoughts fled from Logan's mind and he was back in control.

"Answer the charges, Bryn," Logan commanded.

"You are strong Logan, it is a pity that you have no idea what's happening. I answer the charge that I am a member of the phasia. I am. But I point out that Caris is also a phase. She has taken Leane Torne's body in order to seduce and manipulate you. Had she been successful, you would have given her your heir, and therefore the lives of five generations. Logan's first-born would be gifted with the mantle of the third generation, and she would have killed it to insure her place in Shau-ling's court. He might not be able to vanquish you, but he would be able to rule if the next generation were to never give birth to a *Coromor*."

"It is too late as it is, Bryn," Caris spat. "I could not have had Logan's child had I been able to seduce him. His heir lies in the womb of the peasant girl Elwyne."

"So you have failed in your seduction Caris," Bryn laughed, "so much the better. Shau-ling always knew that you would never be able to turn the *Coromor* from the path of light. Yet, he still let you try in order to keep you from joining in the plot against him. Now that your failure is complete, the *Coromor's* victory is ensured. Your overconfidence in your own abilities was your undoing."

"And your tongue is yours!"

Caris acted before anyone could intervene. The thread of raw Fire entered Bryn's heart and flames erupted from her chest like a volcano. Her scream echoed through the room as Logan ran toward Caris. There was only one impulse left in his mind, and that was her death. Nothing could ever atone for all of the horrors she had caused, but watching her die would be a blow for the forces of the light. Before Logan could strike, a great wind picked him up and threw him down the stairs toward where the rest of the party was beginning to move in Caris' direction. Before he collided with Talos another gust stopped his momentum moments before impact, and Logan fell to the floor in a heap. Talon, Gwydeon, and Pike circled around quickly and helped Logan to his feet.

"I didn't think she could turn her attention back to me that quickly," Logan said, mostly to himself as he turned his attention back in Caris' direction.

"She didn't you pitiful fool," a high pitched voice said.

The space in front of Bryn's burning body shimmered for a moment, and then a person stood there a second later. The man's features were sharp, much like those of a Jeresei. His eyebrows were shaped like the top of a pyramid turned upside down, and they met in the center at the top of the bridge of his nose. His body was slim, and his back was bowed.

"I have come to protect my dear sister," the man continued.

"Farax!" Caris exclaimed. "I thought you were as good as dead."

"I was, dear sister, until an informant warned me of the plot of Vesi Grath. Zarsi was a fool to believe I would go into that battle without suspecting him."

"Excuse me," Talon said stepping forward. "I hate to break up such a touching reunion of filth, but we have to kill you now."

The back and side wall of the inn collapsed in upon the two phasia a second later. Gwydeon picked up Elwyne and carried her out of the inn as the rest of the party scattered. Midarin took up a position on the second story, near the collapsed wall. Her bow was poised and she was waiting for either of the phasia to make an appearance. An explosion rocked the ground and sent pieces of debris flying everywhere. Farax flew from the pile of rock and dove toward Pike. Pike's breath was visible in the air, but the heat was almost stifling. Ice was forming around Pike's fists, and he was waiting for the opportunity to show off a new trick. Farax didn't see the blow until it was far too late for him to do anything about it. Pike's right first landed square in Farax's chest, and his whole body froze on impact. Logan seized the opportunity and strengthened Pike's attack by focusing the power of water on Farax's body to slow him down even further. By the time Logan was done, all of the small particles of matter in the phase's body had stopped moving completely.

"Logan! Watch out!"

Logan spun around just in time to see a beam of fire seconds from exploding through his chest. He didn't have the time to channel his powers and become intangible or do anything else. It was not a ball of flame, but more a beam of pure force, focused to shatter his chest. At the last second, a form leapt in front of Logan and took the full force of the impact. The beam was so powerful that it nearly ripped its way through Alexander's diminutive form. The brave boy lay there on the ground, bleeding profusely from the gaping hole in his chest. All of the bones had been broken, and they stuck out from his chest like daggers. Without thinking, Logan became intangible. Anger flared inside of Logan at the senseless death of the boy who only wanted to do his part to help ensure that the world was protected from darkness.

"Caris," Logan said stepping toward her, still intangible, "you will pay for that with your life."

"You first, Logan Ranthall!"

Her second beam of force passed through harmlessly. But Logan had seen the threads she used to weave the beam. For the first time, he understood what Caris had tried to teach him. It would be fitting to kill her with her own teachings. The beam had merely been Fire bound together with Wind to make it compact and forceful.

"Aldridge's power is handier than I first thought, witch. When I send you to meet your brother, you can give him my regards!"

The beam of force was out of his hands the next moment. When she saw it speed toward her, a knowing smile crossed her lips. A second later the smile was gone and her face showed morbid surprise and horror. The blast ripped through her frail body, and she crashed against one of the ruined walls of the inn, dead on impact. She didn't expect that Logan had placed a thin layer of Earth between the Wind and the Fire, and she hadn't had enough time to dodge or unravel the attack properly before it was on her. It may not have had the full impact that Logan had intended, but it was certainly enough to be fatal. There was a massive hole in the woman's chest where her heart should have been, and the impact with the wall had snapped her neck. Victory had been secured once again, but the cost had been one of their own as well as a possible ally. When Logan stumbled back over to the rest of the group, they were huddled around the frozen figure of Farax.

"What should we do with him?" Midarin asked.

"I'm not sure it matters," Logan said softly, the energy long since gone from his body. "He won't be able to thaw himself out without assistance. Pike's initial freeze was strong, and I was able to make sure he won't be able to move ever again."

"Glad to know that old friend," Pike commented. "And, it's good to see your back among the sane. We've all missed you."

The looks were the same all around, and the unwavering support even in the face of his own selfishness and blindness had robbed Logan of any logical response.

"Regardless of that," Midarin continued, "we can't just leave him here like this."

"Oh but we can lass," Gideon said. "Observe."

A circle of smooth grey stones grew out of the ground a second later. In the center of the circle a pedestal grew up to meet the foot of the frozen Farax.

"Pike," Gideon said softly, "if ye will."

Water filled the fountain a second later, and a small geyser of water erupted from Farax's open mouth and spurted out into the pool. It was a fitting end.

"We'll dedicate this to all of the friends that we have lost along the way. This will be an eternal tribute and monument for all of them. In the years to come, they can look back at this fountain and see that we truly did triumph in the face of adversity. Nothing will prevent us from destroying Shau-ling. Of this, I am sure."

In the following minutes, members of the party engraved the names of all of their fallen comrades into the stones around the pool. David Tamerlane, Elwyne's brother and Logan's best friend growing up. Eldar Merin, the love of Pike's life and the only woman he would ever pledge to marry. Lane Toridon, a childhood companion whose wisdom was far beyond his age, and whose selflessness saved Logan from losing the love of his life. Anne Binosear, the sister of a legend, and a woman who was a shining example of the necessity and burden of leadership and whose place in history could not be denied. Leane Torne, a woman who was sacrificed without need to the vicious schemes of the power mad phase, Caris. Alexander Mealon, though he was only a boy, he had the strength and courage to make the ultimate sacrifice for the future of his world, a world he should have lived to know. And finally, they dedicated a stone to the memory of Aryx Terian. No matter his end or the questions of his motives, he had been a staunch protector and showed them all what it was to be a true hero.

CHAPTER 16

Epilogue

Shadows of Angels

Elwyne was still angry, and justifiably so. Logan knew he had said terrible things, and made accusations that could not simply be forgotten because he wished they would be. Truth be told, in his mind most of the events were still jumbled, and he was unclear what words were his and what words had been fed into his head by Caris' machinations and manipulations. What was clear was that Caris was dedicated to doing everything in her power to destroy Logan and the rest of the party from the inside out. Of course Elwyne had every right to give Logan the silent treatment, and when they finally returned to Aradon, Logan would not be surprised if she broke off their engagement. However, deep down, he knew that was not the kind of person she was, no matter the severity of her temper. She was a good person, and she loved Logan with all of her heart, and she had forgiven him his trespasses thus far. In a span of a few weeks he had gone from a simple farm boy trying to make his mark to a savior, a killer, and a man lost in a destiny that he was both chasing and being chased by. No matter what Logan held true in his heart, Elwyne was the bright spot in his life, and without her, he would never be able to succeed in the daunting task that still lay ahead.

They had just finished the burial of Alexander and Bryn, and not one member of the party was up for continuing their travels so soon after the senseless tragedies and losses that had been heaped upon them once again. In some ways it was like Aradon all over again, and in even worse ways like

Taren. How many more would they lose before the quest was over? The group camped for the night in the forest outside of Barer. The next course of action would depend greatly on how the group accepted Logan again, if they did at all. Pike and Talon seemed to be the most accepting of all, but they had never believed that Logan was capable of such terrible things of his own free will. But Logan distinctly remembered the feeling of rage and the desire to see both of them dead at his feet for countermanding Logan's orders. The more Logan thought about it, the harder it was to take the brunt of the blame for his actions, but at the same time, the rational argument didn't always win out. His mind kept circling back to the central question. Could he have said the things that he said, could he have felt what he felt if it wasn't already somewhere deep inside him?

To his credit, Talon was trying to make the best of the situation and keep the conversation going around the small camp fire, but it was clear that no one else felt like talking. At some point Talon gave up, letting his story trail off into nothing. Before long, everyone was finding their way into what would most likely be troubled sleep, and Logan was left alone with his thoughts once again, thoughts he could not escape. When he could lie there no longer listening to the fire, he sat up and walked slowly away, not paying attention to the direction that his feet were carrying him.

Though his mind was still troubled, Logan found himself strangely comforted by the evening air. There was a veil of calm that seemed to wash over him, and a great deal of the tension in his body was erased in a matter of minutes. Perhaps it was that fact that had always compelled him to walk late at night when his mind was filled with thoughts he didn't know what to do with. More often than not it felt as though the darkness matched the darkness inside of him. Before the madness of the quest, Logan thought he was so troubled. His childhood was one marked by loneliness and restlessness, trying to adapt to a world without a mother and with a father who seemed to blame himself for that loss. After that the darkness latched to his feelings for Elwyne and the confrontation with her father. This far away from those days, he had a new context. Maybe things had not been as difficult as he had believed at the time, and Logan found himself longing for that life again. Before he knew it, Logan had walked to the edge of a clearing and he leaned against a tree, looking up at the clear starry sky. The stars were very bright and beautiful that night. It had been a long time since he took the time to watch the stars, but that night he wanted nothing else but to feel that inner peace one more time. As he stood there looking up, he could not help but feel small; dwarfed by their beauty and magnificence.

"Cosmic thoughts, Logan?"

Logan turned his head slowly, wondering which of his friends had seen him leave camp and followed him. The face he saw was not one that he recognized, but somehow Logan knew the man's features.

"Just taking a walk, friend. Do I know you?"

"No, Logan, you don't. My name is Emries."

"Emries," Logan said thinking to himself. "Does Emries have a last name so that I might try to place is identity?"

"No," he replied as he sat with a tree at his back, "it's just Emries. However, I would be glad to tell you anything you want to know. After all, I was just wandering through the same forest where the *Coromor* and his band of adventurers were staying. I wouldn't be too surprised if you were to accuse me of being a member of the phasia. Though I must say that I would be very curious to hear which phase you would take me to be."

Despite himself, Logan smiled and sat across from the stranger. He should have been concern about the man's knowledge, or at the very least have been on guard for some kind of attack, but Emries' frank manner and matter-of-factness with grave issues was disarming and somehow comforting. He felt like the eye in a hurricane of trouble. At the very least, he was intriguing.

"Well Emries, you seem to know a lot about myself and my friends. You also seem to know some about the enemies we fight against. As for which phase I would accuse you of being, I would have no way to tell. The only phasia I have ever met are either dead or are so unique that I could never be fooled by them. However, if I were to hazard a guess, I would say that you were actually Basille in disguise."

"That is a very good guess, my dear friend Logan," Emries responded. "I once met Lord Basille to tell truth. He was a very fine gentleman in all senses of the word. His ward was a very beautiful woman if I remember correctly, and your friend Gideon was also under his care."

Logan tensed when he heard Emries refer to Basille as Lord Basille. The only times that Logan had heard a phase given a title was by each other or one of Shau-ling's servants. Emries seemed to sense Logan's hesitation and smiled. His eyes were a dark brown, but they had a softness to them that was astounding. He reminded Logan of Lord Cedric in many ways. Emries was a man of about twenty with thick brown hair that was neatly trimmed and parted to one side. There was nothing about his face that was remarkable, save his eyes, and he seemed to be just another average person. He did not look strong of build, in the aspect of muscular size, but was not overly thin. His eyes however were so expressive and remarkable, that the rest of his features didn't seem to matter. He had a power that permeated his entire being, but his appearance was so common that one would not know it until he began to speak. His voice was also remarkable. His deep baritone voice rivaled that of Aryx in possible speaking power, but there was an emotional message conveyed with his words, and that was why Logan felt no hesitation when Emries spoke to him.

"Do not worry, Logan. I am not a member of Shau-ling's sworn, nor am I conspiring with a member of the phasia. I come here merely as a friend of your cause who would help you to understand much of what is happening around you. Though I cannot formally join you, I can tell you what is to come, and what you must do to survive. Ask me what you will, but do not ask where I come from nor who I really am. If I were to tell you now, you would never believe me. Perhaps in time you will figure it out yourself from my words."

"I appreciate your candor in the situation, friend, and I will most certainly follow your advice. However, I don't know what I should ask."

Emries kept his eyes trained at Logan, an unrelenting gaze that should have been intimidating, but Logan just blindly accepted. There was something familiar about him that Logan could not place, like a memory that was in the corner of his eye that he just barely would catch a glimmer of before it was gone.

"Elwyne," Logan said without thinking.

Emries smiled brightly and nodded.

"Walk with me Logan."

Emries stood and made his way back toward the small camp. All of Logan's companions slept soundly around the fire, except for Elwyne who was huddled near Midarin and Gwydeon.

"There is your lady love my friend," Emries said in a strong clear voice.

For a moment Logan thought that Emries meant to wake them all, but then he realized what was happening.

"What are you Emries? Are you an angel come to give me the divine words of the gods, or do you come from the Great Dark One to lead me astray?"

"I told you my friend that I cannot answer such questions as of yet. Have patience Logan, and all will be answered. As for the gods, you will be hearing from them soon enough as it is. Oh, and do not fear the Great Dark One. Believe it or not, he would like to see you succeed just as much as the rest of us would. He will rejoice when he can dispense justice on Shau-ling's perverse soul."

He looked up into the stars for a moment and then turned back to face Logan.

"Ah, but I do forget myself don't I? Matters such as these should not concern you as of yet, and there are other matters that cloud your heart. The first being one Elwyne Tamerlane."

"Does she carry my child, Emries?" Logan asked bluntly.

"She does indeed. Congratulations. She is not yet finished with you my dearest friend. She worries for you more now than ever. She has seen what you could become and it has frightened her. The accusations that you made against her do not cloud her judgment, but she is waiting for you to speak."

Logan could not help but feel elated; firstly to know that she was going to have his child, and secondly that she might still have him for her husband. Emries had given Logan the greatest gift that anyone could ever give him. But one question still burned in his soul, one which he did not know the source of, and one he wasn't sure he wanted to know the answer to.

"What am I Emries?"

"Having doubts are we my friend? Do not fear. All will be revealed to you in time, but unfortunately it is not my place to do so. Even I am made to bend to the will of the Creator. He has not abandoned this world, at least not yet. He has to see to a few matters first."

Though the question still nagged at Logan's soul, he let his mind slide to his next fear.

"Will I survive?"

"That is a question that I also cannot answer, Logan," Emries answered gripping Logan's shoulder. "However, I can say this. The future is not written, except for two small factors. No matter what happens to you on this quest, no matter what deeds you will accomplish, and no matter what hardships you all endure, Elwyne Tamerlane will survive, as will her unborn child. This child will become the greatest ruler in the history of the world. His might and power will dwarf that of the legendary Cedric Binosear, and he will unite the entire world under his wise and steady reign."

"If that is a small factor," Logan replied shocked. "I would hate to hear what a large factor will be."

"As well you should. What you are about to hear will be for your ears only Logan, and you may not repeat this for the rest of your days. If you were to let slip any of what I am about to tell you, the future will be undone, and the world as you know it will die. Can you be trusted to hear what I am about to say?"

Logan thought long and hard. His decision was not an easy one, but he knew that since he was the *Coromor* and the fate of the future was already on his shoulders, adding one more rock to the mountain would not make it weigh more. Logan nodded his assent and Emries pulled Logan close to him.

"I am from another place, Logan, a place you could only imagine to exist in your wildest dreams. You have sparked my interest more than any other person on this world, but you and your friends and your enemies are in my prime view now. I am what you term to be the Creator, and yet I am not. I do not influence your lives as much as my Creator, but I affect your lives more than you can ever imagine. But your legends, your religion, your very essence is credited to my will."

"So there is someone who created us all, even you?"

"Yes Logan. I know that it is hard to accept, but the Creator is controlling every facet of this world from what we say to all of the actions that happen all over the world at every single moment. On his whim a person could die or live depending on how he feels that day. His power is absolute, and no one has the power to change his decisions. All of us are at his complete mercy, and because of this, I can tell you the second little detail about the future. One day our Creator will grow bored with his world and he will stop making decisions, and he will stop influencing this world."

"So what happens then?" Logan asked trying hard to follow the logic.

"Nothing happens, Logan. When the Creator stops making the decisions and stops dictating what happens, our world ends. Everything will cease to exist, and only the past will remain. One day this will happen, and only our history will be left. Our legacies will be the entertainment for other cultures and then we will fade away completely, only to exist in the memories of other. But I intend to change all that. With your help."

He turned from Logan sharply and began to walk back toward the edge of the forest. Logan started to follow him, but he held up his hand and Logan stopped in my tracks. A veil of mist began to rise from the ground as he walked away. Before he disappeared into the mist, Logan heard his last words ring out in the crisp evening air.

"Remember my words, young Logan. This is not the last time that you will see me my friend. You may speak to anyone you like of me, but remember that of which you are not to speak. Your future lies along a different path from the others Logan, and path that you cannot begin to imagine. The gods will call on you soon, and you will be forced to make a difficult decision that will haunt you for the rest of your days. Good luck my friend and do not lose hope in the dreams and aspirations of the common man."

With those last seemingly empty words he vanished into the mist like a dream. Before Logan realized it, he was also enveloped in the mist. Logan didn't remember losing consciousness, but when he opened my eyes, he was standing at the edge of the forest, leaning against the same tree. Nothing had changed around him, and suddenly he felt the chill in the air. If there was a time to talk to Elwyne and try to make things right again, he couldn't think of a better one. But the nagging thoughts had not gone away, and the mystery of the man named Emries complicated everything.

* * * * * * * * * * * *

Aryx Terian, the hero of the battle of Lakestone, second in command of the Lion's Mane, first among Lord Cedric's personal guard. Adorations abounded everywhere, and there was nothing that had ever been denied to him. He had a loving wife who would do anything to make him happy. When he wanted it, he could have a kingdom of his own to rule with his wife, and then perhaps he could have found time for a family. There were friends all around him that would have given their lives for him without a second thought. But Aryx desired something more deep in his heart. There was a fascination with the power that churned inside of him. This same power that gave him control over the realm of fire, and more specifically, lightning was his to command. For years before he was found in the badlands by Erika Belnosian, Aryx had fancied himself the descendant of a god. Past of him never did part with that belief. It was not natural for a man to have the sort of power that he possessed and deny that he was not a part of the divine. How could a man that control the very essence of nature that most other men feared be merely a fluke. That was why the story of the *Erieal* never did set well in the heart of Aryx Terian. How could a man with his power be a mistake of nature? And yet, with all of the power at his disposal Shau-ling still lived. Four *Erieal* and the

Coromor had not been enough to vanquish that foul beast. That more than anything drove Aryx over the edge.

Arrogant pride got me into this mess, and now all I can do is hope that someone figures out how to kill me before Shau-ling sends me up against Logan and the others.

Aryx Terian died the instant he turned his body over to the maniacal clutch of the beast named Shau-ling. Aryx died, and the abomination known only as Nightwing was born. He was a prototype for a new breed of Shadowwalkers, and so far, the master had been impressed with Nightwing's prowess in killing. He was nothing more than an assassin, and that's all he would ever be in the eyes of Shau-ling. Nightwing flew low over the plains of Barer, and found himself bogged down in a thick fog. He touched down near the gates of the palace of Barer and looked around anxiously.

"You're early assassin," a husky voice said.

Nightwing focused his red lensed eyes on the mist before him and saw a short, heavily muscled man emerge from the fog.

"LORD WARRON. IT IS GOOD TO SEE THAT YOU WILL NOT LET GOOD MEN DIE FOR NO REASON. YOU OBVIOUSLY KNOW WHY I AM HERE, AND I HOPE THAT YOU WILL NOT THINK THAT YOU CAN RESIST ME."

"As a matter of fact Nightwing, I do intend to resist you, but first I want to talk."

"I HOWEVER, DO NOT SHARE THAT WISH. EITHER YOU WILL KNEEL BEFORE ME AND TAKE YOUR DEATH EASILY, OR I WILL BE FORCE TO DESTROY YOU USING ANY MEANS POSSIBLE."

"You are under orders to assassinate me?" Warron asked slyly.

"I AM. THE LORD OF ALL EVILS SHAU-LING DECREED THAT YOUR LIFE WAS TO BE TERMINATED."

"How unfortunate for you."

Three streams of green fire erupted from out of the mist and slammed into Nightwing. While he was unprepared for the assault, there was no damage done to his armor. Nightwing's wings were extended in a second, and he lifted himself into the air, sensing the type of danger he was in. A second later, five of the newly redesigned Shadowwalkers vaulted into the air and surrounded him. Nightwing laughed softly to himself as the Shadowwalkers took up positions to attack. The first hurtled toward him seconds after it lifted off. Nightwing dove underneath the speeding Shadowwalker and let the sharp point of his tail slice through the stomach of the beast. It screeched in pain and tumbled to the ground mortally wounded. Another of the beasts fell as Nightwing plunged one of its bladed feathers into the Shadowwalker's head as he flew by. The three remaining Shadowwalkers decided to take the battle to a new level. Simultaneously, they opened their mouths and belched out streams of the Blaze at Nightwing. There was no time to react for the larger beast, and he was caught in the center of the three way assault. Instead of screeching in pain, Nightwing laughed.

"FOOLS. I WAS BORN AND FORGED IN THE FIRES OF THE BLAZE. DO YOU REALLY THINK THAT YOU CAN HARM ME WITH THE VERY FLAMES THAT SIRED ME? NOW SEE HOW YOU CAN STAND UP TO THE FORCE OF THE BLAZE."

A huge stream of green flame erupted from Nightwing's metallic jaws a second later. One of the Shadowwalkers was caught in the path of the Blaze, and only a cinder remained after the fatal contact. The other two Shadowwalkers fled the battle seeing that they were hopelessly overmatched by their adversary. Looking down, Nightwing noticed that Warron had not moved from where he stood, and so the real battle was about to begin. Nightwing touched down again and noted that the fog had cleared.

"Very impressive Nightwing. You are much stronger than I initially believed. It is unfortunate that you do not serve the phasia rather than Shau-ling."

"THE BROTHERHOOD OF PHASIA IS WEAK AND CORRUPT. JEROCH, BASILLE, SAURN, TARON AND ELLIS ARE ALL THAT REMAIN AFTER YOUR DEMISE. IT WILL NOT BE LONG

BEFORE ALL OF THE DEAD BARK IS CUT AWAY FROM THE TREE."

"Then who will be the next to fall? Surely master will soon see that you are of no more use to him. What will stop him from destroying you and the Flame as well?"

"IF THAT IS THE MASTER'S WISH, THAT IS WHAT SHALL BE. I CANNOT CONTROL MY OWN DESTINY NOW. I HAVE BECOME SHAU-LING'S SERVANT, AND I AM TO DO HIS BIDDING."

"Ah," Warron said approaching is towering opponent, "that's the trick now isn't it. You were once so good and pure, and now you have succumbed to the powers of darkness. How would you like to have the choice?"

Nightwing said nothing.

"So, you are interested. That is good. You were forged in the fires of the Blaze, as were all of the members of the phasia. We each retain the will to choose our own destiny, but we are all evil in nature. You however are not. The metal that surrounds you is also not evil in nature. The only evil about you my dear Aryx lies in your mind. You believe that you are evil, and so you are evil. If I am going to die this day, I wish to die at the hands of the infamous Aryx Terian and not some demon's spawn."

The man that was Aryx Terian screamed in defiance. The armor casing around him shattered and sank deep into his human skin. He was a man again, but in the same token he was more than a man and more than a Shadowwalker. His hatred had made him strong, but the inner fires that had burned within him since his birth made him unstoppable.

"Alright Warron," Aryx said in his natural human voice, "you got your wish. Shall we?"

A sword was in Warron's hand a second later. Aryx laughed and extended his hand toward Warron. The flesh in the center of his palm split, and one of the blade-like feathers that made up Nightwing's wings slid out.

A moment later the blade was in Aryx's left hand, and the flesh had re-sealed itself.

"Impressive Aryx. Do you want some applause, or perhaps a look of amazement will suffice."

Warron smiled mockingly and approached his adversary. Aryx laughed and lashed out with his blade. Warron parried the slash and circled Aryx. The smaller man edged forward quickly and thrust his blade at Aryx's ribs. Dodging out of the way, Aryx had a clean look at Warron's throat, but the smaller man proved to be quicker than he had anticipated, and the blow was never landed. The sound of crashing metal resounded through the plains as the two combatants tested each other. Warron's sword slash finally struck true, and red blood flowed quickly from a diagonal cut on Aryx's chest. All Aryx could do was smile as he attacked his opponent with more tenacity and vigor. Still, no matter what ploys he implied, Aryx could not land a single blow on Warron, but had taken two more slashes across the chest. Warron backed away from his bloody opponent and lowered his sword.

"I thought it would be a delightful experience to fight you one on one Aryx, but I must say that I find the whole duel completely disappointing. I heard that you were the best, and now I see that you are nothing more than a pretender. But I must be inclined to give you the benefit of the doubt because of your current condition. What say we up the stakes? You choose my weapon, and I'll choose yours."

"Fine. Bare hands."

"You do want to die, don't you Aryx? Bare hands for both of us then."

Warron laughed as they both dropped their blades and rounded each other once again. Aryx was the first to attack. His fist landed square on Warron's chin, but Warron was able to bury his fist into Aryx's gut, winding him. Warron's next punch caught Aryx in the temple, and he tumbled to the ground. While Warron gloated over his fallen opponent, Aryx had another plot. The skin on the palm of his right hand parted slighted, and the tip of the whisper thin tail emerged ever so slightly. Aryx rose and the two combatants rounded each other again. Warron punched at Aryx, who dodged the blow and landed a palm strike with his right hand to Warron's side. The tip of Nightwing's tail ripped the soft flesh, and blood poured freely. Before Warron could pull back, Aryx thrust his palm into Warron's chest, creating another larger puncture wound. The strength fled from the smaller man's body quickly and he sank to his knees. Aryx gloated for a moment and then grabbed Warron by the throat.

"Thank you for the wonderful advice and the exercise, Warron. I had been feeling that my skills were diminishing slightly, but now I see that doesn't really matter with all of the new skills and tricks that I have at my disposal. Give my best to the phasia on the Other Side."

The razor sharp tail sprang from Aryx's palm and shot completely though Warron's throat. Aryx released him and stood there as the phase suffocated. It was a slow and painful death for Warron, but it meant nothing but pleasure for Aryx. The battle over, he closed his eyes and let the power of Shau-ling overrun him again. The metal skin erupted from inside his skin and slowly, painfully retook its position of dominance. Red blood flowed everywhere, and when Nightwing was again in control, the normally black armor was stained in places with the red human blood of it alter ego. Warron's body still writhed on the ground, the final death spasms taking him. Nightwing looked down and marked the expression on Warron's face. He had expected to see a look of shock, or perhaps even betrayal, but that was not even close to the look that sat there, forever etched on that dead canvas. Warron was smiling.

The mists had begun to roll in again, and Nightwing extended his bladed wings and flew toward its home and its master. Warron's warnings were fresh in his mind, and that final look of defiance that never came still puzzled the man that had been Aryx. How long would it be before he was wishing for death as Warron apparently had? Was he already?

Down below a form shrouded in the evening mist watched as the armored beast flew away from its kill. The look on the man's face could only be described as resignation. But there was a hope in the man's eyes. The future may not yet have been written, but there was one thing for certain. The words etched in a stone outside of Barer held more meaning than their carvers could have ever imagined.

"Aryx Terian," Emries said into the night, "you will yet again show us what it means to be a true hero."

EPILOGUE

Appendicies

Dramatis Personae

Cedric Binosear
The Lord Lion
First *Coromor* of the Prophecies
Lord of the Kingdom of Marcwell
Twin Brother of Anabel Binosear

Erika Belnosian
Daughter of Arthur Belnosian
Sister of Erdric Belnosian
Betrothed of Cedric Binosear

Aryx Terian
White Lightning
General in the Lion's Mane
Fire *Erieal* of the Prophecies
Knight of the Kingdom of Marcwell
Husband of Diana Geoffry Terian

Logan Ranthall
The Lord Dragon
Second *Coromor* of the Prophecies
Son of Arin Ranthall and Victoria Rhuiden
Brother of Korrd Ranthall
First Cousin of Pike Rhuiden
Relationship with Elwyne Tamerlane

Korrd Ranthall
Second *Chosen One* of the Prophecies
Son of Arin Ranthall and Victoria Rhuiden
Brother of Logan Ranthall
First Cousin of Pike Rhuiden

David Tamerlane
Blacksmith's Apprentice
Son of the Mayor of Aradon
Brother of Elwyne Tamerlane

Pike Rhuiden
Water *Erieal* of the Prophecies
Former Blacksmith's Apprentice
Apprentice Carpenter
Son of Tam Rhuiden
Best Friend of Talon Aielin
First Cousin of Logan Ranthall
Elder Merin's Former Lover

Talon Aielin
Wind *Erieal* of the Prophecies
Apprentice Carpenter
Best Friend of Pike Rhuiden
Professional Carouser

Lane Toridon
Apprentice Magician
Orphan
Adopted by the Town of Aradon

Gwydeon Sandar
Apprentice Blacksmith
Sword Master
Son of Torris Sandar
Brother of Bella Sandar

Eldar Merin

Daughter of Noble Family of Trelon
Sword Master
Champion Duelist
Best Friend of Elwyne Tamerlane
Pike Rhuiden's Former Lover

Elwyne Tamerlane

Daughter of the Mayor of Aradon
Sister of David Tamerlane
Relationship with Logan Ranthall

Arin Ranthall

Member of the Lion's Mane
First *Chosen One* of the Prophecies
Husband of Victoria Rhuiden
Father of Logan Ranthall
Father of Korrd Ranthall

Victoria Rhuiden

Member of the Lion's Mane
Sister of Tam Rhuiden
Wife of Arin Ranthall
Mother of Logan Ranthall
Mother of Korrd Ranthall

Tam Rhuiden

Master Carpenter
Aradon City Council Member
Brother of Victoria Rhuiden
Father of Pike Rhuiden

Torris Sandar

Master Blacksmith
Aradon City Council Member
Father of Gwydeon Sandar
Father of Bella Sandar

Arathorn Geoffry

Leader of the Lion's Mane
Earth *Erieal* of the Prophecies
Brother of Diana Geoffry Terian

Mailock

Member of the Moridon Tribe
Water *Erieal* of the Prophecies

Diana Terian Geoffry

Member of the Lion's Mane
Wind *Erieal* of the Prophecies
Sister of Arathorn Geoffry
Wife of Aryx Terian

Gideon Viruci

Earth *Erieal* of the Prophecies
Professional Thief
Member of Alimidar Thief's Guild

Ren Manderis

Former Member of the Lion's Mane
Former Pirate
Dock Master of Illimar
Alias: Seelious Monk

Midarin Rice

Former Princess of the Kingdom of Brea
Banished for High Treason
Master Archer

Zar Elouix

Lord of Rama

Captain Antrobus
General of the Army of Rama
Murdered by Korrd Ranthall

Alexander Mealon
Standard Bearer
Squire in the Army of Rama

Talos Berder
Member of the Moridon Tribe
Advisor to the Kingdom of Rana

Anabel Binosear
Sister of Cedric Binosear
Queen of the Kingdom of Trelon
Mother of Cairyn Binosear
Mother of Allan Binosear
Alias: Camille Talaat
Murdered by Allan Binosear

Cairyn Binosear
Daughter of Anabel Binosear
Niece of Cedric Binosear
Queen of the Kingdom of Trelon

Allan Binosear
Son of Anabel Binosear
Nephew of Cedric Binosear
Crown Prince of Trelon
Second in Line of Succession

Leane Torne
General in the Army of Rama
Former Member of the Army of Brea

Aerith Seth
General of the Hand of the Light
The *Chosen One*

Hawk Yetre
General of the Army of Sador

Asperon Thorne
Guardian of the Jeweled Dragon's
Flame

Jerrard Mystic
Soldier in the Army of Illimar
Former Member of the Lion's Mane
Son of Basille Mystic

Jasmen Hiedra
Traveling Minstrel
Part-Time Adventurer

Christine Goldenlake
Former Member of the Lion's Mane
Master Archer
Murdered by Jeroch Yetre

Allahanna
Member of the Moridon Tribe
Former Member of the Lion's Mane
Sister of Corin
Murdered by Warron Ysamaran

Corin
Member of the Moridon Tribe
Former Member of the Lion's Mane
Sister of Allahanna
Murdered by Warron Ysamaran

Galanax Pryde

Master Blacksmith
Former Member of the Lion's Mane
Murdered by Basille Mystic

William Hathaway

Former Pirate
Former Member of the Lion's Mane
Murdered by Taron Steen

Khisanth Alghri

Member of the Moridon Tribe
Former Member of the Lion's Mane
Murdered by Basille Mystic

Shau-ling
Master of the Shadows
Father of the Phasia

Jeroch Yetre
The Lord Shadow
First Born of the Phasia

Warron Ysamaran
The Lord Boar
Member of the Brotherhood of Phasia

Basille Mystic
The Lord Raven
Lord of Scalla
Member of the Brotherhood of Phasia
Father of Jerrard Mystic

Farax Soar
The Lord Vulture
Member of the Brotherhood of Phasia

The Flame
Personal Guardian of Shau-ling
Keeper of the Hall of Terrors

Zarsi Aeron
The Lord Cobra
Lord of Sador
Member of the Brotherhood of Phasia

Aldridge Farran
The Lord Hawk
Member of the Brotherhood of Phasia

Saurn Macco
The Lord Viper
Member of the Brotherhood of Phasia

Caris Vale
The Lady Wolf
Queen of Illimar
Alias: Queen Saris
Member of the Brotherhood of Phasia

Erdric Yarrow
The Lord Scorpion
Member of the Brotherhood of Phasia

Taron Steen
The Lord Jackal
Member of the Brotherhood of Phasia

About the Author

Brian Kershner is a life-long dreamer, writer, and problem-solver. He grew up absorbing anything and everything he could get his hands on, and as a child of the Star Wars era he constantly wanted to see the worlds beyond the little Indiana town he grew up in. There was no adventure too far, and no problem too big.

Emboldened by parents who always supported his curiosity and his thoughtfulness, Brian found himself bounding from Space Camp to Laser Summer Camp to Athletic Training Camp to Piano Lessons to Football Practice to Basketball Practice to Choir Practice and back again. Despite all of the roaming and traveling, his family remained close-knit and supportive.

Though he flirted with the idea of becoming a doctor, Brian's attentions always fell back to the computer world. He got his first computer when he was six, and not long after found his way into a word processing program and began crafting his own fantastic worlds and even more fantastic characters.

As he has grown and changed and experienced life, so too have his characters. He continues to write, craft, and create; whether it is websites for his customers, or characters and worlds for his audience.